The Devil's Workshop

THE DEVIL'S WORKSHOP

by

JOHN SCHERBER

SAN MIGUEL ALLENDE BOOKS

San Miguel Allende Books
San Miguel de Allende, Gto, Mx.

ACKNOWLEDGMENTS

Any book starts as an idea, and by its completion becomes a joint effort.

Thanks to my wife, Kristine, for her extensive editorial and critical comments.

Thanks to my readers: Jan Baross, Patti Beaudry, Donna Challancin, Bob Fredricks, Donna Krueger, Marcia Loy, Susan Page, Phyllis Pitluga, Lynda Schor, Jocelyn Scoggins, Gail Tobey.

Cover Design by Lander Rodriguez
Cover Painting *Le Chein Messager* by Georges Mazilu
Author Photo by Gail Yates Tobey
Web Page Design by Julio Mendez

ISBN 978-0-9832582-2-3

San Miguel Allende Books
San Miguel de Allende, Gto, Mx.
www.SanMiguelAllendeBooks.com

ALSO BY JOHN SCHERBER

NONFICTION
San Miguel de Allende: A Place in the Heart
A Writer's Notebook
Into the Heart of Mexico
Living in San Miguel

FICTION
(The Murder in Mexico Series)
Twenty Centavos
The Fifth Codex
Brushwork
Daddy's Girl
Strike Zone
Vanishing Act
Jack and Jill
Identity Crisis
The Theft of the Virgin
The Book Doctor
The Predator
The Girl From Veracruz
Angel Face
Uneasy Rider
Lost in Chiapas

(The Townshend Vampire Trilogy)
And Dark My Desire
And Darker My Wrath

To Kristine

PROLOGUE

The only question remaining now, in the entire life of Mark Sands, was how long it would take him to hit the sidewalk twenty-seven floors below. Funny how your life could be reduced at the end to a single point, with no dimension but speed. After his first startled shout he almost seemed to be slightly removed from his own plummeting body—perhaps it was a way of not feeling the terror.

That Sands, at fifty-four, was a realist, partly accounted for his success as a money manager, not that it would save him in this situation. As his body accelerated, he felt his mouth twist into a grimace. The wind clawed his navy pinstriped suit jacket back over his arms, but he didn't cry out again. As he passed the Jacobsens on the twenty-fourth floor, neither of them looked up from their sofa. Sands' neatly trimmed silver hair stood up like a halo behind his head, every strand rigid.

Sands had come back from a long business lunch at 3:30. His wife, Megan, was not at home. After a couple of martinis, he didn't feel like going back to work, and the stock exchange was already closed. When he paused in the vestibule of his condo, he checked the phone messages and found nothing of interest. Walking into the dining room, he was about to set the mail on the table when he noticed the children, eight of them at least. Shocked, he stopped when he saw another one still emerging from the painting on the wall, one foot reaching outward over his antique buffet. But they weren't children, they were only small, and it seemed to Mark Sands, rather dirty. It was only a first impression, but he would never have another.

There was a moment of shocked silence. One tapped the shoulder of another who had not noticed Sands come into the room. Soon they were all watching him in silence, their eyes narrowed, waiting for his next move. Mark Sands felt a sense of horror and insanity rush over him. His hair stood up on the back of his neck. This did not correspond to any reality he knew. Not sure how to react, with the mail still gripped in his hand, he took a step back. The nearest of the small people dipped his hand into his pocket and withdrew it palm upward. He blew across it with a knowing grin. Mark Sands was engulfed in a powdery cloud that glittered in the afternoon sun. What an odd effect, he thought. How could this be a weapon? He lost consciousness and fell face first to the parquet floor.

He regained consciousness after only two or three minutes, filled with terror and helplessness, but unable to move his limbs. Many tiny grubby hands lifted him over the parapet at the edge of his broad veranda, thrusting against his back, his arms, his buttocks. The fingers on his calves were sticky, lifting his skin as they moved. He knew exactly what they were doing, and he tried to struggle, but his eyes were just clearing and his limbs were still heavy and unresponsive. Then came the sudden shift of his weight on the parapet, and he went over the edge. His sense of horror was not muted by the fading effect of the drug in the powdery cloud he'd breathed.

Painters were working on ladders on nineteen, and Mark Sands was still accelerating. People on the sidewalk were growing larger, almost like real people now. A man stopped and pointed upward at him. His mouth was open as if he was shouting, but Sands heard no sound but the rushing wind.

A woman at her desk on the eleventh floor looked up and screamed silently as he passed. Mark Sands' jacket came free of his arms and drifted away above him at a gentler pace, moving out over the traffic on Fifth Street.

How had the little people emerged from the painting over his buffet? It was his Cantú masterpiece, *The Last Supper*, the prize of his collection. And they were the characters from the painting. He recognized the odd, ragged leather outfits. Had he been murdered by these nightmare versions of Christ and the Apostles? Mark Sands' fingers clutched wildly at the rushing air as he approached the sidewalk. It flew toward him like something that had been waiting there his entire life.

His final thought was that he would feel nothing when he hit the pavement. As usual, Mark Sands was right.

CHAPTER 1

The same Friday, at just after six o'clock, a client of Mark Sands named Rebecca Stuart found herself in Santa Fe, approaching the Born & Born Gallery on Canyon Road. It was mid-March, and the sky had deepened overhead into the violet blue of a New Mexico evening. Once a dusty burro track winding among unpretentious adobe houses, Canyon Road is now the art center of Santa Fe, a town that lives on the art business, and any given Friday is opening night for half a dozen galleries.

As she scrambled up the graveled street, Rebecca was cursing herself for her choice of shoes, having paid less attention to getting from her rental car to the gallery than how she would look after she arrived. Her publicist had made her image-conscious, and Rebecca's life seemed at times to be moving so fast she found herself in unfamiliar terrain. She thought of it as getting ahead of the map, and it wasn't always comfortable. Pausing to listen to the people around her was a way of keeping her balance, but it wasn't what she always did.

At the age of twenty-seven she'd gotten lucky when her first published detective novel turned into a surprise bestseller, and her agent had quickly cut a deal on the film rights. Her life had become a round of book-signings, public readings, and media appearances. Everything had worked out perfectly, for a while. But then there was book two. Rebecca had heard horror stories about book two.

Confident of repeating her success, she'd written it quickly even before the first one appeared in print. It was rewritten, edited, and emailed to her agent within eight months of starting it. Rebecca was on a roll. But her agent had reacted with a series of objections. The characters were flat this time, she said, and the ending was a letdown. The book was too long and occasionally self-indulgent. Six more months of revisions followed and a year later the book was published to indifferent reviews. In spite of heavy promotion by the publisher, portraying it as the logical successor to her first, the book sold only a disappointing 31,000 copies. It went out of print just as her first book was being promoted again ahead of the movie release. It wasn't long before she'd seen remainder copies priced at $1.95. She stopped going to bookstores except for signings.

Rebecca discovered she did not know how to stumble gracefully, and it wasn't about her shoes. It was a skill she didn't think successful writers like her needed. After a few months, the rapid success of her first book had begun to seem inevitable. Now, it looked like no more than the face of a coin whose reverse was failure. Flipping it the first time had come up heads, the second time, not. One reviewer said hers was not a lasting talent, only luck, after all. She had imagined her career extending to the horizon with a string of bestsellers. Now each move was more tentative.

She aimed for redemption with her third book, wrote a hopeful synopsis, and emailed it with a few sample chapters it to her agent, who responded after a week.

"They don't want to see a synopsis anymore, just a finished book. They're not happy with the chapters you sent, either, Rebecca. Since the second book didn't earn back its advance, if the third manuscript isn't spectacular, they'll show you the door. That wasn't their phrase, but I know this business. I've been at it since before you were born. There isn't a year that passes anymore without the bottom line getting thinner."

Rebecca was speechless for a moment. Taking them at their word, she had regarded her editor and others at the publishing house as her friends, people she called by their first names. She'd been told that her first book had placed her as a key member of their team, and now this? Where was the loyalty? Where was the idea of nurturing a young author's talent? Was that gone too? Was the publishing industry run by accountants now, people whose reading ability was confined to numbers?

"So what can I do?" she managed to say in a small voice. As soon as she hung up she planned to check the fan mail on her website for reassurance.

Her agent had tried to reassure her.

"Start by not thinking like it's still 1940. These days, no matter what they tell you, publishers only want to be friends with big winners. They don't bring people along anymore. It's all on your shoulders. Think how you did it the first time, and you'll see how to do it again."

But what was the process that had worked so well? Had she even understood it? Rebecca had never analyzed it, but she knew it hadn't changed between the two books. After the success of the first one, she was almost afraid to look at it too closely, for fear her magical, but mysterious approach might disappear. She was never blocked; she wrote the first thing that came into her mind. Once it was down, she revised it several times, always working rapidly, as if her electricity were about to go off and make her screen go blank. So how could one book work so well and the next hardly at all? It came to her one night at the edge of sleep—thinking she knew the look of success, she had repeated herself, and what was fresh and original the first time was now somehow stale and tired-looking to a public always waiting for the next new thing.

The conclusion was unavoidable: she had to create a new look for it every time.

Although her publicist had portrayed her as a first time writer who'd never put pen to paper before and somehow come up with a blockbuster, the truth was she had been writing since the age of seven, when she concocted a cookbook for her mother. By the time she was twenty she had written three wretched romance novels that she burned in the fireplace of her parents' home one night when they were out. It had taken some courage to see just how wretched they were. What especially hurt was that she'd always been interested in art, and each of these books was filled with detailed illustrations, often of scenes with erotic content she didn't want her parents to see.

Shopping for a different subject, she settled on mysteries. Looking back on it now, it seemed like fate.

At twenty-four, she was working as a paralegal in a firm specializing in criminal law. The atmosphere was filled with raw material. She could hardly wait to start writing when she came home from the office. In nine months, she finished the novel she called *Grunge*. It embodied everything she had learned about the craft of writing in seventeen years of cookbooks and romances. Her quirky detective hero, Lester Grunge, was a lifelong outcast because of his strange appearance and habits. Bathing only when he changed his clothes, he believed nothing of what people said about themselves, instead only observing what they did. In compensation, he developed a cynical view of people and events, and used it to observe things in crime scenes that the police missed. It taxed Rebecca's imagination to come up with examples of this, but she ultimately did, finding many of them in her dreams. As she worked, the dreams seemed to increase in frequency to meet her writing needs.

On finishing the book, she was rewarded with rejection slips from twenty-six publishers. It had been a long apprenticeship, but, if rejection was the measure, Rebecca was finally a professional writer.

At this point she changed her strategy and found an agent. Within four months, the agent had sold the book, gotten Rebecca an advance that was surprising for a new author, and she was on her way. A year later, when Grunge came out and hit its fourth printing within six weeks, she quit her job at the St. Paul law firm of Malwick & Finch, stopped dressing like a lawyer wannabe, and found a publicist who put her on tour in the national chain bookstores. He dressed her in cropped jackets and fluted skirts, dropped waistlines and strappy heels.

When she realized how much attention she was getting from 50-year-old men who liked to linger after the signings were over, she fired the publicist, saying to him, "I'm not a Hollywood celebrity. I want to be taken seriously as a writer."

Rebecca stopped wearing her blond hair long,

and had it cut into a spiky mop that punctuated her new image. She rejected the Hollywood tabloid look and replaced the openwork heels with spike-heeled knee-high boots. Her instinct told her to keep the short skirts, and she finished out her book tour with astounding sales, already searching for her next subject. In the back of her mind she could sense the impatience of Lester Grunge as he awaited his third case, although she didn't know yet what her third book would be, after the skeptical response of her publisher to those first excerpts.

It had been a giddy ride, and at times it taxed Rebecca's young maturity. She had quickly found she needed a lawyer, then a financial manager. There was now too much business to do and there were times when she needed to escape. What pleased her most was gallery hopping. It reconnected her to a lifelong love of art.

Her new prosperity had made her interest in the painting of others more affordable, and Rebecca was in Santa Fe to buy a painting. The opening night at Born & Born featured a new show by the Méxican artist Rafael Cantú. His work was, like that of Rebecca herself, too quirky for some. Several critics had called it "mannered," a word others had also applied to Lester Grunge.

On the Internet, Rebecca had watched Cantú's work develop for several years, long before she'd had enough money to consider owning one, and she'd stopped in Santa Fe twice before to see his work in person. Cantú made her feel vaguely uneasy in a way that she remembered from her teen years. It was like the way she'd tried to make her parents feel when she was thirteen and fourteen, as if their view of reality were inadequate, lacking essential facts that only she knew. She told them things from her dreams as if they were real, to observe their reaction. It had worked well then; they were often off balance, unsure whether what she told them was true or not. Rebecca tried to create the same sense in her work.

But after the failure of her second book, she planned to filter her dreams with more care before using them, sorting through their sketchy corridors for the plausibly twisted, but rejecting the ridiculous and extreme. Some critics had said *Grunge II* was over the top, and Rebecca had decided that the next book would still be uncomfortable, but more firmly grounded in reality.

Uneasy can be good if you're a mystery writer, trading in your own and other people's nightmares. The paintings of Rafael Cantú represented the most complete and coherent set of dreams she had ever seen outside of her own, although she wasn't sure this was where he got them. By the time she left this evening she would add one to her collection, and the world of Rafael Cantú would intersect with her own.

She knew that Edward Born had represented Cantú in his gallery longer than any of his other painters. Edward was the only Born there. There had never been another. Rebecca always thought that Edward had titled it Born & Born to convey the sense of a family enterprise, going back to the previous generation, or possibly two, respected for its long history of expertise. But more likely, it was that Edward had ego enough for two.

The gallery girl looked up from the front desk as Rebecca walked in, giving her a friendly smile and immediately glancing at her shoes. "Christian Louboutin?" the girl said, grinning and nodding approval.

Rebecca lifted her foot to show the distinctive red

sole. They added four inches to her five-foot-two height. Rebecca had indulged herself in only a few luxuries when the money started flooding in. Another one was the entry-level supercharged Mercedes coupe she'd left behind in St. Paul. A girl had to have a little red car, didn't she? Now that she spent half her time being scared to death of what came next, it was reassuring. Maybe she'd be driving it to job interviews at Burger King if she had to go to work again. This was a joke she made to herself; she had plenty of money on hand, it was only the future that looked chancy.

The Louboutins also enhanced the shape of her legs, already so perfectly proportioned that, if it weren't for her height, you wouldn't realize she was short. Besides the shoes, she wore a brief black skirt and a tailored white shirt under a black fitted-leather scuba jacket. A wide smile and slightly upturned nose, green eyes and, of course, the sassy spiked blond hair completed her look.

Born & Born Gallery consisted of two public rooms, backed by a storage area and an office. Across the manicured courtyard behind the building, anchored by a fountain with naked stone putti flying around the inner rim, Edward Born had his own residence. In the gallery, the adobe walls were painted a pale putty color, which boosted the warm tones of every picture. From the ancient beamed ceiling, pin-spots on spidery wires illuminated each of them without going beyond the frame. Rebecca picked up a glass of champagne at the rear table, ignoring the platters of snacks, and moved toward the other room. Over the doorway, on a vellum scroll in calligraphy the color of midnight, were the words,

GIVE ME TWENTY MINUTES AND I'LL

SHOW YOU HOW THE WORLD ENDS

Rebecca paused a moment to study this, then dismissed it as an artist's statement, something notoriously flaky, even when the artist could paint as well as Cantú. She had made statements like this herself during interviews, and forgotten them ten minutes later. Coming into a gallery, she always started at the right edge nearest the door. Just inside the room was a small painting entitled Joker with Red Beret. A slope-shouldered young male looked downward to the lower right corner of the frame, cocking an enormous ear toward the viewer. The "beret" was a rusty reddish triangle of cloth, stiff in texture, perhaps dyed leather, but old and faded, fastened to the side of his hairless skull with a rivet. The rivet was a nice touch, she thought, a fashion statement for Cantú's world, like a body piercing. That's what I like, Rebecca thought, but I want one bigger. Right now anyway, I can afford it.

She moved out of earshot of another couple looking at the same painting, wanting her reaction to remain undiluted. When it came to art, she didn't much care what other people thought.

The magisterial bulk of Edward Born appeared beside her like a barge that had slipped its moorings. "Why do I feel you're prepared to commit this time, Rebecca? I couldn't help noticing that *Grunge* is on the New York Times bestseller list again because of the movie. It's got legs. Still not as good as yours, by the way." He was too tactful to mention the quick disappearance of *Grunge II*.

"Hello, Edward. You knew I wouldn't miss this opening." Interesting that you'd notice my legs, she thought as she glanced at his jowls, rolling comfortably over his collar like a muffin top on a pleated paper cup.

"You're up there with Patterson and Connelly now."

If only, she thought. I'll never be able to catch them. She made a mental note to look at their work again. How did they repeat their success so easily?

Born turned to face the pictures. "We were lucky to get this many Cantús for tonight. He's got an opening in Geneva this week as well, but I can't help but feel he'll do better with us. Just my impression, of course." His tone suggested there could be little room for doubt, and his opinion would outweigh the informed views of most others.

Knowing him even as little as she did, Rebecca thought it had probably been years since Edward Born had ideas or thoughts about anything. The external world filtered through his consciousness more as feelings or sensations. His intuition had jettisoned his intellect in a brief and uneven scuffle a generation before. None of this had damaged his credibility in the art world, where a refined instinct is often seen as the mantle of connoisseurship. Edward Born wore it like an expensive cologne, hanging majestically in the air even after he swept grandly from the room. If there was ever a biopic about Edward, Rebecca had once thought he could be played by Orson Welles in a cape. Too bad Orson was gone.

"Cantú's work almost makes me shiver," she said. "Does he owe something to Hieronymus Bosch? Look at this one." Although this reflected her opinion accurately, Rebecca had rehearsed this statement as she walked up Canyon Road. The authoritative Born always made her nervous when she tried to talk about art.

They stopped before a larger picture with four

figures, titled *Girl with Three Players*. The girl, nude, was moving toward the viewer and starting to pull a cloth around her hips from behind. She was flanked by three males. They all wore archaic clothing that looked pieced together from ancient castoffs. None of them regarded the viewer or each other. One sat on a low table with a single playing card near him: the ace of diamonds.

Beneath the card player, a tattered and pieced-together table cloth stretched nearly to the floor, and protruding from beneath the edge, Rebecca saw a single paw, clearly that of a small dog, probably more shy and unwilling to look back at the viewer than the other figures were.

All of them had the elongated nose characteristic of Cantú's work, but the girl's was less pronounced. She was pretty in a mostly human sort of way, and not entirely nude. She wore dark opaque stockings that reached just over her knees and had the effect of her making her nakedness more striking. The three males all had the enormous ear; the girl might have, but it was concealed in her thick black hair. Rebecca thought she almost looked Méxican.

Rebecca was about to ask Born a question, then stopped. His answers were usually more than she wanted to know, and she often found them intimidating. After her bestseller, people expected her to be more sophisticated than she really was. Every time she talked to Edward, he was full of arcane nonsense, not all of it art related, but nonetheless impeccably accurate, and it sometimes left her unable to respond. You can't argue with expertise, she thought, I should be doing more research. She hated doing research herself, it only slowed her down, so she couldn't get by without an independent researcher,

Jeremy Wyman. She had long ago come to depend on him. Born was waiting for her to say something, and she suddenly had the crazy thought that Cantú himself might look like the people who populated his work. It was improbable, yet that would account for the intimacy of the look, as if he lived among them and drew from among his neighbors as models. "Does Rafael Cantú ever come to these openings?" she said. "I'm curious what kind of painter would do these pictures."

"Never here in Santa Fe," said Born, putting his hands on his wide hips, "even when he was at Mentor Gallery, before I had him. It is odd. Most artists like to work the crowd, and the gallery owners always want them to. There's no doubt the buyers like to meet the painter. It's like meeting a best-selling author." Born gave her a coy smile that she disregarded.

"Have you got a photo of him?"

"No, and that's funny too. I've got nothing but his biography and exhibition list, but I'll see if I can get you one. It shouldn't be a problem." His eyebrows went up in a promising look.

"I'd like that." At the same moment her cell phone went off and she reached to silence it—the ring tone was "*We're in the Money*," which didn't always work well with the setting when it went off. It was becoming increasingly ironic as well. Several people glanced at her pointedly as she walked out of the room to take the call. Their looks made her feel like she was too young to be there. Everyone else seemed to be at least fifty anyway. Born moved on to another prospect, swaying slightly and rubbing his hands.

Outside, Rebecca checked the surface for grime with her fingertip before sat on one of the two wooden slab benches in the brief front yard before Born & Born Gallery. The weathered wood was chilly on her bare legs.

"Rebecca, it's Jeremy." The researcher was panting, as if he'd had to run a long way uphill to call her. It was so like him to reach her in Santa Fe; he'd become almost like her personal assistant. She willingly put up with his eccentricities because he'd been devoted to her ever since she started with him halfway through Grunge.

"I hope you're sitting down," he continued, after he caught his breath. "Mark Sands went off his penthouse veranda this afternoon. Twenty-seven floors. It was on the six o'clock news." (Pauses to breathe between.) "Nothing else has been released. Nobody knows why."

Rebecca stood up abruptly in shock. Her stomach clenched at the sudden image of Mark Sands falling helplessly through the air, knowing he had only seconds to live. For a moment she couldn't speak, and her eyes took in nothing of the street in front of her. The thought of Sands dying in this way only alarmed and confused her. Her image of him was that of mastery, control. She couldn't make any sense of it. Why would he kill himself? Mark Sands always looked like he was at the top of his game. Had that only been his appearance?

"I can't believe Mark would do that! Imagine how his wife is feeling!" For a moment, Rebecca couldn't recall her name. She'd met her only once.

"No comments on the news about that. That's all I've got so far. There was nothing in the market to provoke it. The Dow was up thirty-six points. Not great, but OK. It's not like there was any crisis."

"All right, thanks. Keep me posted if you hear anything more."

Mark Sands had managed Rebecca's money since the initial royalty check came in. He had waived his normal account minimum of $1 million for her because *Grunge* was then already in its eighth printing and it looked like the royalties would be coming in for years. Everything she knew about money had come from him. His firm, Outremer, Inc., specialized in offshore investments, often tax sheltered, and recently he'd been focusing on commodities as well. In his suite of luxury offices on a high floor of a newer St. Paul office tower, he received occasional visits from only a few more than a hundred clients, a limit he imposed, he said, to assure the maximum in personal attention. Why would he kill himself?

As she came to her senses, Rebecca surveyed the steady stream of cars moving up Canyon Road. The scene was absurdly normal. The sky had darkened further but stayed clear, and was now peppered with stars. A calm rested on the air that her life no longer reflected. As she went back inside, Rebecca didn't notice she'd left the half-full champagne flute on the bench. Beyond the fact that most of her investments were in foreign countries, she knew little about how she was positioned or why. She had always looked at her monthly statements the moment they came in, but her inspection was mainly focused on the bottom line. When the first huge royalty check came in, the future had lengthened out before her like an endless gilded corridor. Now, for the first time since then, she was truly worried. When *Grunge II* failed, it was some consolation that money was still coming in large amounts from *Grunge*. Now she had lost her financial advisor. It was time to get serious.

As Rebecca walked back into the gallery, she felt

anger well up inside her. She wanted to spit in the face of everything that was coming at her. She knew she was better than all of this, she was a survivor.

Once inside, she returned to the painting of the three players and found herself looking directly into the eyes of the sassy naked girl. She almost felt like a link formed in the empty space between them. Suddenly Edward Born appeared at her elbow again, seeing the steely look in her face and sensing a sale.

"I'll take this one," she said, ready to wrap things up. The ticket on the wall gave the price as $24,000. Maybe the disastrous news about Mark Sands had made her more decisive, even to the point of spending the money to affirm the safety of her assets, even if that didn't make much sense on the surface. Life now seemed shorter and more unreliable than before.

"Can you ship it to St. Paul for me?" she finished.

"Of course, then you won't have to pay the sales tax, which otherwise would be . . ." He took out a calculator from his jacket pocket and punched in a few numbers, "$1770. The crating and shipping will cost you only about $150. A wise choice." He removed a paper of red dots from his jacket pocket and pressed one to the corner of the label with a flourish.

"By the way," he went on, "just so you know— while you were outside, I emailed Rafael Cantú and asked him to fax me a photo of himself. I said it might guarantee a sale. I'm sure we'll have something in a day or two and I'll forward it to you."

Back at her bed and breakfast, Hacienda Nicholas, Rebecca changed into jeans and a suede jacket and sat in the chilly courtyard for a while. After Jeremy's news, she didn't feel like mixing with the others in the great room for cocktail hour. Sipping a glass of white wine, she puffed on a cigarette she'd borrowed from one of the other guests, even though she hadn't smoked in two years. She pulled her jacket more closely about her and thought about Mark Sands. The financial advisor she knew could carry the market fluctuations on more than five hundred million dollars of his clients' money without stumbling. How did suicide fit with that?

If it hadn't been so important in her own life, it was almost crazy enough to be the kind of question that could fuel the plot of a book.

Back home on Sunday afternoon, Rebecca unpacked, sorting out a few things for the dry cleaners, then contemplated the walls of her loft condo. When the rambling two-story railroad warehouse in St. Paul was restored to the elegance of polished brass and seasoned limestone, and brought to market just as *Grunge* was taking off, she'd opted to divide the space into rooms, rather than leave it open and echoing. This strategy was as much about providing more walls for art space as anything else. As her career blossomed, she had seen herself as a collector on a grand scale. That looked more chancy now.

On the outer wall, constructed of pale yellow limestone from the river bluffs nearby, her attention was caught by a five-foot space next to the tall window facing her workstation. She had avoided hanging anything there until now, waiting for the perfect painting that could stimulate her imagination during pauses in her writing.

Now it was on the way.

Holding the photo image Edward Born had provided of *Girl with Three Players* against the wall, she could see how the smoky mottled olive background on the painting would be perfect with the seasoned naked stone, and the mysterious feeling of the image would enhance the twisted reality of her books.

When the doorbell rang, she pressed the intercom button, knowing who it would be.

"It's Jeremy, Rebecca. I've got more on Mark Sands." She buzzed him in. She'd asked him to follow the story for her, because she hated watching the news. Too much reality was a distraction in her work.

Once inside he slumped into a chair, his reddish-orange hair too long as usual, and sweat gathered on his upper lip. He could perspire even in winter. Occasionally she had the sense that he was looking at her appraisingly, but his eyes always went elsewhere when she looked back at him. He was not someone she would ever consider hooking up with. Jeremy was too needy at times; his loneliness could be seen written in capital letters across his face. She was sure he didn't know this about himself, and she would never mention it, valuing his help as a professional.

"There was nothing; no note, I mean, according to the newspaper." He was shaking his head. The frayed hems of his khakis were damp from the snow. He was wearing brown high-top tennis shoes. Where had he found them? Rebecca wondered if there was a special nerd store in St. Paul; more probably they were from somewhere on the Internet.

"I don't know how to read that," she said. "If it

was a sudden impulse that came over him, then he might not have felt he could explain it to Megan. Was there anything on the news last night?" She came over to the sofa opposite him and sat with her legs curled under her.

"No, but there were some items on the web. His wife came home to find a crowd gathered on the sidewalk. It was awful. They were just taking him away in an ambulance. The odd thing was a sprinkling of some kind of sparkly dust on the dining room floor mixed with a powdery chemical. They found the same thing on his shirt and on his jacket, which he wasn't wearing anymore when he landed. It had pulled off during his fall and landed on a bus. Imagine."

"What are the police saying about the powder?"

"Only that it was there. They're not saying anything more until the chemical analysis is finished. They interviewed Bill Stokes, his investment analyst, and he said there's nothing wrong at Outremer that would cause Sands to kill himself. He had no explanation. Stokes said Sands had gone to lunch with two guys who were taking a medical device company public and he didn't come back to the office afterward. Mark was going to fly out to Vail on Saturday morning. Not unusual, I guess."

"Well, he did fly out, I guess." It was the glib kind of retort Rebecca would have cheerfully put in the mouth of Lester Grunge, but it didn't reflect her own feelings about Mark. While they were not yet friends, he had been something short of a mentor to her. She'd developed a frank admiration for his self-confidence and his nimble reactions to the changing investment climate in the half-dozen meetings they'd had. There's something here I'm not seeing, she thought. A confident guy like Mark Sands does not go flying off a building.

"I hope my money's all right," she went on, not sure whether she'd said this aloud. Her next thought was that she wished she were less dependent on other people for investment insight.

"If there's a developing problem," Jeremy said, "it's probably too soon to show up on the Internet. You should probably call Bill Stokes. He's running Outremer now while this gets sorted out. He has to be reassuring the other clients already."

"So the police aren't saying anything yet." She said this to herself, looking out over the river. A thread of something was starting to take shape in her head, a ripped-from-the-headlines kind of story idea that seemed inappropriate this soon, but she couldn't help it. It was the way she processed reality, mining it for ideas, sometimes nothing more than threads that would lead to larger things. If she thought about them enough in daylight, the threads often reappeared on their own in the small hours of the night.

"As you say, nothing yet," Jeremy said, jolting her back to the St. Paul riverfront. "Anything else?"

"Jeremy," Rebecca paused and touched her index finger to her lips, "see what else you can find on Mark Sands. Do the family search, business records, the works."

"You're onto something?"

"I wish I knew. I need to find out exactly what's going on here."

CHAPTER 2

It was because of his neck that St. Paul Police Detective Ken Abrams walked the four blocks from his office to Outremer Investment Management on the following Monday morning. He'd been bothered by a pair of kinks there and in his lower back off and on for the past year, well, ten months. They weren't always there, but tended to come to life when he got up suddenly from his desk. To avoid them, he'd been moving more slowly, which he didn't think was right. Some days walking helped, other times it was stretching. His Workman's Comp doctor hadn't been much use. Waiting for red lights to change, Abrams would lift his shoulders and roll his head around on his neck, like a bowling ball searching for the pocket. People often looked at him oddly. He usually ignored them, but at other times he looked right back at them with an icy stare he usually reserved for interrogations.

This day had a steely gray cast, much like a metaphor for a new homicide investigation; cold, unwelcoming, and unyielding. At his office he scanned the morning paper for information beyond what he had told the reporters himself, details they would have padded the story with to make it seem to their editors that they had different sources. Mostly they didn't, but it might still be true. Today they had taken the usual easy way, speculating on financial mismanagement, even fraud leading to suicide. The paper enjoyed playing to the blue-collar need to believe that all people with money must be criminals. While this was occasionally right, Abrams' job allowed no such stereotypes.

He owed his drive and steady judgment to his mother, a weathered fireplug of a woman barely five feet tall in stout shoes (her feet were nearly square). He was an only child who'd come after she'd given up on having children, possibly with some degree of relief because of the problems it would avoid. In each of the three early pictures he had of the two of them, she still looked surprised that she'd become a parent after all.

She'd made a point of not indulging him, because she herself had never been indulged, and that had worked for her. Knowing that her place in the scheme of things was not prominent, she nonetheless defended it with tenacity, looking out at life from under dense black hair shaped like a winter cap with earmuffs and a visor. It effectively kept the sun out of her life. Short as she had been back then, she was even shorter now, yet she still seemed to be looking over his shoulder most of the time, only occasionally with approval.

"Don't ever get a job where you have to wear a suit," she'd told him more than once, starting in high school, always wagging a finger. "The dry cleaning bills will eat up your paycheck." This was her idea of motherly wisdom. Her middle initial was F. She had never told him what it stood for, but he'd always suspected it was for Frugal. The truth was that it stood for Fannie, something she didn't wish to call attention to, and therefore never brought it up.

Ken Abrams loved her for what she had taught him, and for her terse good sense, but when dating, he now preferred tall women with a lighter hair color. He liked words like *lithe, graceful, long of limb.* He had never analyzed this tendency; it had never required an explanation. Although he'd survived a couple of near misses with women who wanted to marry him, he usually thought of himself as married to his work. In dating he went back and forth between authoritative, talented women who often ended by irritating him, and submissive, nurturing women who easily bored him, who he ultimately found he didn't much respect. He thought if he ever had a child of his own, it would be later in life, and not as a surprise.

In the aggressively modern lobby of Mark Sands' office building, he encountered Bill Ruppert waiting for him, a police accountant who worked white-collar crime, and they took the elevator up to the twentieth floor. Abrams didn't mind Ruppert, whom he had worked with seven or eight times before, but he considered that the accountant operated on the safe side of things. Well, someone had to do it. Abrams himself had never fired his gun on the job, nor had he been fired at, but that didn't necessarily make him feel safe. He suspected there'd be a bullet looking for him one of these days, and he didn't expect to see it coming.

"The papers are all over this one," said Ruppert, looking straight ahead, as if conveying bad news.

"Does that make you nervous?" Abrams himself liked playing with reporters because he didn't respect the papers much.

Ruppert shook his head. "They never mention me."

Abram's name came up in the papers whenever he had a high profile case. Usually the stories were favorable, but he couldn't help wondering if they'd continue that way much longer. Changes had begun for Abrams near the time of his fortieth birthday. He was certain it had nothing to do with turning forty, but he developed a problem with insomnia. About seven months earlier, on a night when he was sleeping well, he had a dream in which he'd arrested a fugitive dentist wanted for the murder of his wife and teenage daughter. The man was handcuffed, and as they walked toward the police car, Abrams had pulled out his service revolver and shot the man in the back of the head, execution style. The detective felt nothing. At that instant he awakened, yet the dream continued for a few more seconds as the body dropped vertically to the street, not pitching left or right or even forward, but straight down like a bundle of rags dropped from above.

It was only when he fully awakened that Abrams found himself appalled at what he'd done. As the scene faded he was sweating heavily, sitting upright and staring at the pale glow from the street lamp beyond his bedroom window. How seriously did you take a dream? This one went against everything he practiced in his job, but it was still just a single dream; there was no pattern; not yet anyway. He often dreamed things he'd never do in real life, but this time the fact that he felt nothing at the moment he killed the man was the most disturbing part of it. He had always thought that fatally shooting someone would bring on a fire storm of emotion. That he hadn't reacted made him wonder about himself.

The dentist was real, and now out on bail, awaiting trial. Initially, it didn't seem like the dreams would recur, until the next one came two months later.

There had been other, unrelated, dreams between, of course, and Abrams often remembered them, but the second disturbing one opened with an arrest, a handcuffing, and another walk toward the car, this time with a black teenager wanted in a gang shooting. They were just coming through the door of the gymnasium and out to the school grounds—the school grounds!—when Abrams pulled out his gun once again. He fired calmly into the back of the boy's neck, but the calm he felt was only a mental calm. Even asleep he was aware of the fierce gritting of his teeth and the tension in his neck. A muscle in his calf constricted and doubled it up against the back of his thigh. As before, he awakened with the gunshot and, with open eyes, watched the boy pitch forward on his face onto the gravelly tarmac.

This was more upsetting, and it didn't evaporate within a day or two. The distance to the next dream was only two weeks instead of two months, and for a while that remained the trend. Now as he stood next to Bill Ruppert in the elevator, he was thinking about last night's dream, the second within a week. It was number sixteen. All the victims had been people Abrams himself had arrested over his career. Some were still in prison, some had gotten off, a few awaited trial. He did not see himself as an avenging angel, rectifying the shortcomings of the legal process. There was no moral underpinning beneath the act; it was simple murder.

"You OK?" Ruppert asked, turning to look at him.

"Sure, it's spring, isn't it? What's to not be OK about?" Abrams said in the lighter tone he used when he didn't want to talk about things, wondering what made Ruppert ask.

"A lot of heat on this one. The papers love it." To Abrams this sounded like more of what Ruppert had said before.

"Nothing unusual," said Abrams, thinking there was a singsong quality to his own voice. Lately a portion of himself seemed to be detaching from the rest of him and drawing back from his job. He'd always prided himself on his competence, but he was beginning to wonder whether what he did had any meaning or effectiveness. At the same time he was losing interest in activities that had been his mainstay recreation, like hiking around the chain of lakes in neighboring Minneapolis, even as he felt the need for exercise more than ever. Instead he watched television. He'd been getting leg cramps at night more often, so he started eating bananas regularly. Someone had told him that cops tended to eat poorly.

Yes, he still solved cases, and people went to trial. Some went free and some went to prison, but it seemed that Abrams himself now went nowhere in his job. So far no one had noticed his increasing disengagement, but it wouldn't be long before someone did. In four months he was scheduled for a review and he was dreading that day.

He felt now like a gray man in a gray job, trying not to draw attention, dodging the looks of his superiors, just as he had formerly tried to excel. He didn't know why this had changed, but it did not square with his view of himself. Suddenly he saw the Mark Sands case as having special significance. It could illustrate how well he could do with a high profile death.

Before the doors opened on the twentieth floor,

he glanced at his hair in the bronze mirrored walls of the elevator. It was perfect and unchanging. He got it cut by the same barber every two weeks at the same time on Saturday morning. Some people thought he was blessed with hair that never grew. He didn't contradict them.

On the way out of the elevator Abrams wrapped his spent breath gum in the original wrapper and put it back in his pocket, and the two investigators walked into Outremer at 9 AM.

They weren't there because they thought Mark Sands hadn't committed suicide. But every apparent suicide was investigated with the possibility that it might be a murder. Inside the lobby, Abrams introduced himself and pulled up a chair across from the receptionist's desk. Noting the contents of her desktop and the way it was arranged, he decided she was organized and efficient.

He set a notebook down on her desk and leaned back and crossed his legs, unbuttoning his coat. It was an invitation for her to relax. People had more to say when they weren't tense. She was taking a call and he waited.

Abrams usually felt he had no special reason to be remembered, and he wanted it that way. Since he made his living by studying people, it was better when they didn't notice him enough to realize it. Average height, brown hair with no curl but all still there, he wore well-kept high-quality shoes that were important to him because he was constantly on his feet. At 40-years-old he told himself he was proud to not be feeling it yet, at least physically; he was still denying to himself that his increasingly stressed mental state and creaky neck and back had anything to do with his age. He was able to not find this contradictory. The alternative, that he was burning out, was even less palatable, and he hadn't considered it, although he wouldn't have disagreed that he was often more insightful about others than he was about himself.

His Brooks Brothers suits didn't cost a lot of money and were mostly in fashion, not because he cared much about style, but the more strenuous parts of his job wore them out, and he replaced them fast enough to stay current. Abrams made just over $51,000 a year as a not very senior detective. He could have made more as an assembler at the Ford plant on the southern edge of St. Paul, building the F150 pickup, and had more paid vacation time as well, but he had always liked his work. Besides, the Ford plant had been scheduled for closing, but crime never stopped; it was like job security.

The receptionist's nameplate said Martha Pennock. Apparently in her early thirties, she wore a dark blue pinstriped suit with the jacket closed over a pink button-down oxford shirt, but no tie. Her blond hair was pulled back and fully under control, much like her desktop. Abrams decided the outfit made her look severe, but that could have been the office image, suggesting that Outremer took its clients' money seriously.

"Very sorry about Mr. Sands," he said, as he pulled the chair closer to her desk. His standard opener. "You understand that I'll have to ask you a number of questions because we need to find out if there's any business reason for his death."

"He wouldn't have killed himself," she said matter-of-factly, with her mouth turning downward, "if that's what you mean. Everything has been going very well this year. I feel terrible for Megan."

"That would be Mr. Sands' wife?" Abrams already knew this. He had interviewed Megan Sands briefly on Saturday, but he wanted Martha Pennock to tell him about her. He always tried to appear to know less than he did, except in court. Lately he was beginning to feel that he really did know less than he thought.

"Yes. They've been married only two years." He wrote that down to encourage her, although he'd already gotten it from Megan Sands herself.

"What's she like?" He asked in a gossipy tone, giving her a broad smile.

"I really don't see her much except for company functions. She doesn't stop in here otherwise."

"How is she with the employees?"

"Very nice, really, but not in a personal way, if you know what I mean. She doesn't seem to want to know us individually, although she always makes a point of talking to us. It's mostly polite conversation."

"Did she and Mr. Sands get along?"

"As far as I could tell." She shrugged. "He never talked about his personal life."

Deciding he wasn't going to get much from her on Megan Sands, Abrams gestured to the man still standing near the door and starting to fidget. He usually gave the accountant time to scan the room and get a feel for the business image. "This is my associate, Bill Ruppert." The accountant wore an argyle sweater vest under his suit coat, over a white shirt and blue tie that didn't work with the vest. "While I conduct the interviews I'd like you to set him up at a work station so he can look at the books. That would be client files, personnel, expenditures, so on."

She nodded, rose and beckoned Ruppert into an inner office. Abrams scanned the room. Modern leather furniture, copies of Forbes and Barron's on the coffee table. A stack of *Wall Street Journals*. Old hunting prints on the paneling, with buff-colored paper foxed in places, packs of dogs chasing things. Profits perhaps? It looked like they were running them down OK. He wondered what kind of money you needed to walk into this place.

When Martha Pennock returned, he said, "How long have you been with Outremer?"

"Five years last month. I was with Smith Barney before that. This is much better."

"How is that?"

"Well, the clients, of course. There aren't that many of them and they tend to be a better quality than in the big wire houses. You don't get the people who just want to invest their tax refunds or put down five hundred dollars to fund a college education for their kids. Out-remer's minimum account is one million dollars."

Writing this down, Abrams wondered what kind of quality he himself was, with nothing going but a condo in a second tier suburb and his police pension, still thir-teen long years off. Could he survive another thirteen years? He had seven years of payments behind him on the condo, but he'd started with a low down payment. It didn't seem like his mortgage balance ever went down much, and there was never a bonus for solving a murder.

"Miss Pennock . . ."

"Mrs. My husband's a broker, but not here. He's with Principal." The tone of her voice suggested that her own status was elevated by being married to a broker.

"Mrs., then. Was Mark Sands under any kind of strain? Were there any little things that might suggest that? Perhaps barking at people?" Abrams suddenly thought of himself. "Forgetting things?" He thought of asking if it seemed like Sands was burning out. He'd heard that happened to people in the securities business, but decided not to go there.

"No, never. He was very careful to get everything right, but at the same time, he tried to give the impression of being easygoing. Not that he really was. Anybody who's easygoing in this business isn't paying enough attention to it, in my opinion. But appearing to be that way is mainly to keep the clients relaxed during tough periods."

Abrams was starting to get a feel for Martha Pennock now, noting her insistence on proper titles, her inclination to make sure he understood her statements exactly as she meant them. There also was something behind her facade that was a little iffy, some slight hostility toward him or his process, and she was clearly class conscious. Her move from Smith Barney to Outremer represented a step up. He felt she probably had a tendency to rank people on sight and then sit back and watch as their behavior confirmed her first impression.

"Have there been any clients who didn't seem like they ought to be clients? People who deviated from your normal profile or didn't fit with your clientele, although they had the money to use Mark Sands' services?" Abrams felt she could answer this one better than anyone else in the office.

"None," she said, without hesitation.

"Does anyone ever come in with large amounts of cash, say, $10,000 or more?

"We don't accept cash. I don't know of any brokerage house that does." Her tone suggested he should have already known this, and it reminded him that he'd never been in a brokerage office before.

"How about dissatisfied clients?"

"No, not so far this year. There were one or two last year, but I think they may have had expectations that were too high. It happens in any firm. Sometimes when people come into money for the first time in their lives . . ."

"Could I have their names? I'll also need the names of everyone who works here."

"Of course, but neither of those clients was unhappy enough to move their accounts." He noted that she was already prompting his reaction to the dissatisfied clients. She wrote the information down from her computer and handed it to him.

"Don't be offended if I ask you this," Abrams continued, "because I know you said Mr. Sands had been married only two years. Was he seeing anyone else, an old girlfriend, for example? One who might have stayed in the picture? Or was there a woman calling him, one who might not have been a client, or perhaps one who was, and called a little more often than she would strictly need to for business? You'd be the one routing the calls, right?"

"There was nothing like that." Her hand came across the desk in a horizontal motion, as if slicing the idea in half. "And Mr. Sands certainly had the opportunity. He was a good looking man, and many of his clients were women, sometimes young widows bringing in insurance money."

"Any sign that he might have done drugs?" Thinking of the powder found in the dining room. He hadn't seen the lab report yet, but white powder could mean a number of things.

"Never!" Her tone made Abrams feel she was

signaling him that he'd gone too far, a point he always worked toward, since it often provoked interesting reactions, but he never began there. "Mr. Sands relied on his judgment every day," she finished.

"Did he drink too much?" He was enjoying this now.

She gave him a sour look, as if he were approaching an extreme limit and he ought to be ready to be called on it. "He'd have one or two at lunch sometimes, but not every day, and he was never tipsy, if that's what you mean. I didn't see him in the evenings, but I doubt that it was much different." Abrams knew Sands' blood alcohol level had been .06 at the time of his death, low enough to drive with no problem, but he had walked home. Downtown St. Paul was small enough for Sands to do most of his business on foot if he wished, weather permitting, and his condo was three blocks from his office.

"Did you ever see him outside the office yourself, Mrs. Pennock, socially I mean?"

She glared at him. "I can't believe you'd ask that."

"Thank you. I think that's all, but I may call you again if I come up with more." He knew that his suggestion of impropriety on her part would make her eager to call him if she saw anything in the office that might be of interest. It would put the spotlight on someone else.

Abrams moved into the inner office and stopped next to Ruppert.

"How does it look?"

"Clean so far, Ken." Ruppert shrugged and leaned back in his chair. "I'll run the usual credit and background checks on the employees when we leave but I'm not seeing any flags here. They would've been cleared anyway, just to get hired in this business. I should be done by lunch tomorrow, and then I'll start verifying the firm's deposits at Wells Fargo."

There was one other broker and an analyst to interview. After talking to them and getting nothing more than Martha Pennock had given him, Abrams sat in Sands' office, trying to get a fix on the man himself. The desk that Abrams was about to search sat at the center of three floor-to-ceiling windows overlooking the Mississippi from the twentieth floor.

He turned and looked at the view, realizing that right at his feet was a drop similar to the one that had killed the money manager. Suddenly both his hands gripped the edge of the desk as he imagined the sensation of hurtling earthward, accelerating into pavement. It was not an inviting way to go; there was too much time, as little as there was, to wonder if you'd made an irreversible mistake.

The desk was polished steel up to the top, which was of the same wood as the wall paneling. Design was not his best field, but Abrams felt it would have looked fresh and stylish about ten years back. The chair was steel finished in the same way, with a black leather seat and back. The top of the desk held a phone with eight buttons and a flat computer screen with a keyboard and mouse. Next to the mouse was a note pad with nothing written on the top sheet. He held the pad obliquely to the light and could make out nothing, but rubbing the flat edge of a pencil he carried across the paper brought a brief message into view. It said, "Finn Med. Flanagan's 1:15."

On the left corner were five pink phone messages from Friday afternoon. Abrams stuck these in an envelope and put them in his shirt pocket.

The computer tower was concealed behind a door within the desk. In the drawers on the other side were volumes of charts with multiple trend lines, bar charts, zigzags, breakouts, tools from the arcane investing world that Abrams didn't understand. The pencil drawer held not a single pencil, but a collection of razor-point pens and an assortment of colored paper clips. From among them he pulled out a strip of braided leather, made from five strands of colored rawhide about eight inches long. At one end was a translucent yellowish brown bead of a material he didn't recognize. He pressed it to his nose and discovered a musty scent. An odd thing, but one he couldn't read. Was it possibly a craft project Sands had made as a Boy Scout and kept for sentimental reasons?

In a thick file in the last drawer he found art catalogues, more than a dozen. He flipped through them, recognizing none of the names. Most of the galleries were in Santa Fe, three were in New York, one in Palm Springs. Abrams had counted more than a dozen paintings and prints in Sands' condo. A serious collector, with the funds to support his itch, but where was the despair, the signs that his life was blowing up? For Mark Sands, everything had been pointing up, not earthward at a target on the sidewalk. Abrams knew he must be missing something.

On the office walls were four paintings, more than Sands would need for a properly decorated look. He must have been really interested in art. All were urban scenes, two in cafes, one on a street corner with eight or ten figures waiting for a light to change, one in a barbershop. Together they suggested that Sands appreciated the underlying cadence of city life. That fit; he lived and worked in downtown high rises, and Wall Street itself had its own rhythm, the constant ebb and flow of money in motion.

Subject to Bill Ruppert finding something wrong with the books, Abrams left Outremer with the feeling that, unlike the dogs in the hunting prints, he hadn't found his fox yet. After getting the names of Sands' lunch guests on Friday, he walked back to police headquarters on Tenth Street, near Interstate 94 where it cut through downtown. It was a crisp morning, but the air held a promise of spring. The sun had burned away the gray layer. It might hit forty degrees in the afternoon. His neck was better but his back was still iffy.

His office, which did not provide a view of the burgeoning spring day, or anything more interesting than a row of desks, was overheated, so he pulled off his jacket before he sat down to write reports on the interviews while they were still fresh in his mind. His notes never held all the detail. After an hour and a half he paused for lunch, then flipped through the notes to find the phone numbers of the two dissatisfied clients. He didn't reach the first, but left a message. The second client was Rebecca Stuart, a name he thought he'd heard, but couldn't place. She picked up on the third ring. He introduced himself.

"This is about Mark Sands, isn't it?" she said. "I heard what happened. I called his office this morning and Martha said the police were already there."

He always paid particular attention to the response to his opening line, since people were not always prepared for his call. Her voice was young, the pitch a bit high, and she talked rapidly. Nothing seemed veiled in her tone. He wondered how many people who could meet Sands' account minimum would be less than thirty years old.

"I feel like I've heard your name?" he said.

"Maybe you've read my books, Detective Abrams. I'm a mystery writer." There was pride in her voice.

"That's it." It came back to him. "*Grunge*, isn't it? Interesting title. I haven't had a chance to read it yet."

"You can wait and see the movie. It'll be out in September. I can get you a Grunge T shirt, in the meantime. It has the name on both sides. Black or olive? The lettering is white. I'll bet you're a large." He thought she was speaking too rapidly, as if she were a little nervous.

"That's OK, I can't take gifts from suspects. Anyway, I'm not sure grunge is my best look."

"Suspects? What do you mean, suspects?" Her voice was suddenly shrill.

"Please don't take offense, but until I can narrow this down a bit, everyone who had a relationship with Mark Sands is a suspect. That would include all his clients. It doesn't mean you need a lawyer," he finished, thinking he used to be able to say these things better. Spooking people this early in an investigation often resulted in information drying up.

There was a moment of silence, then, "All right. How can I help you? You must know that Mark managed my money, and how much." With the continued success of her first book she had finally met Sands's account minimum, not that it mattered now.

"One of the things we looked at in his office was whether he'd had any problems recently with his clients. Your name came up, I'm afraid, Miss Stuart."

"Not the first time I've been labeled as a trouble maker." He heard a hint of pride in her voice again.

"Possibly, but I think this was concerning a commodity trade."

"That? It was last year. I was pretty green, I'm afraid, and I didn't understand that you don't always get out at the top. Mark had to explain to me that just because we didn't sell at the very highest level, we still made money."

"So you were satisfied in the end?"

"More or less."

"I see," Abrams said, wondering how much money she had left on the table.

"Your next question is where was I when he died, right?" she asked.

"Why would you ask that?"

"Because I write crime novels, and you always have to look at a suicide as if it could be a murder. Anyway, I was in Santa Fe, buying a painting. You see, Detective Abrams, I know the value of an alibi. I invent them all the time. You're free to check this one out, if you want. I was at an art opening at Born & Born Gallery on Canyon Road and I was staying at Hacienda Nicholas on Faithway."

He wrote this down. "Was anyone with you?"

"Like my boyfriend? No, I sent him on his way a while back." He could hear satisfaction in her voice.

"Ever run into Mark Sands there? You knew he was an art collector, right?"

"I knew it, but I didn't know what he liked, and I never saw him in Santa Fe. Nor was I ever in his apartment."

"But you saw his office?"

"Of course. Several times, but I can't recall what he had hanging there. It wasn't anything I'd own, or I would have remembered. They were colorful, I guess."

"Did you ever see him personally, out of the office I mean?"

"Are you kidding? He was a good looking guy, but he was old enough to be my dad."

"I see. In the times you met with him, did he ever suggest he was depressed?"

"Never. He was—I don't like this term, but I'll use it anyway—a take charge kind of guy. You had the feeling that whatever it was, he was on top of it. Nothing less."

"Well, thank you Ms. Stuart. You've been helpful. Keep on writing."

"Depend on it. And Detective?"

"Yes?"

"Mark Sands didn't . . ."

"What?"

"Nothing. I was only thinking out loud."

Knowing what she was about to say, Ken Abrams put down the receiver. Friends and associates of people who killed themselves never wanted to believe it. He stared at her phone number in his notebook. He'd never interviewed a successful writer before and found himself wondering what she looked like. Was she tall and willowy with light hair? Slender with long legs and a graceful neck like Gwyneth Paltrow? And was it time now for him to get back to work? He had no sense that she was other than blunt and honest, and her tone to him hadn't been condescending, unlike that of Martha Pennock, who seemed eager to amplify whatever small status she had.

As he was about to leave later that afternoon, Bill Ruppert stuck his head into Abram's office.

"Anything?" Abrams leaned back in his chair.

"Nothing, but when I called the bank to set up the client audits I asked them to fax Sands' financial statements over to me at his office. The guy had a net worth of twenty-one million dollars."

Abrams leaned back in his chair and put his palms together. "Now I'm wondering about the wife, Megan. Married two years and suddenly she's the most eligible widow in town. What do you think?"

"I'm just the accountant, I don't get paid to think," Ruppert said with a modest grin that suggested he was happy enough to leave it all behind when he went home at the end of the day.

Abrams felt anger flare up instantly and a flush darkened his face and neck. "Well, maybe you ought to start, goddamn it! I'm sick of hearing shit like that." In his view, everyone in the department was paid to think. Now, as Ruppert took a quick step backward out of the doorway, Abrams regretted not keeping it to himself. He rubbed his hands over his face.

"I'm sorry, Bill. Something's been eating me, I don't know what. Get the name of Sands' lawyer from Martha Pennock, if you would, and have him fax us a copy of his will. I'm wondering if everything goes to the widow." He watched Ruppert leave the room and noted his heart was pounding. There was nothing wrong with the accountant, it had just been a typical flip comment that everyone in the department made now and then. It was another one of Abrams' overreactions. Next Ruppert would show up in handcuffs in one of Abrams' dreams.

When he got back to his office the following morning, the toxicologist's report was waiting on his desk. He read the single page through twice and dialed the crime lab.

"I got your report, Bret," he said, "but what is propofol?"

"It's a common anesthetic. The unusual thing here is that it's supplied to hospitals in liquid form, it's never furnished as a powder the way you found it at the scene."

"Could you reduce it to a powder in a lab?"

"Sure. There are some simple drying processes that would work, but normally you wouldn't want to do that because it's injected at a dosage determined by body weight. What they call a drip. Even though it's fast acting, the effect isn't all that strong, so it has be administered continuously or the patient wakes up after a few minutes."

"What's the advantage of that?"

"Control. In minor surgeries you come out of it right away. It's not so heavy handed. You don't have to go to the recovery room and spend hours coming out of a drug-induced coma."

"And what's this other thing here? The plastic compound."

"It looks like glitter. It's a particle with a mirror surface on one face, similar to what you can get at cosmetic counters and party stores."

"That's crazy. Why would anyone mix glitter with propofol?"

"You're the detective. I just analyze the stuff."

"I mean, would it have any medical effect? Pretend I'm a layman here."

"That's easy. No effect that I can see. It's inert, so it doesn't react with anything else. In a sense it would just pollute the propofol."

"OK, now say you've got the propofol in powder form, forget the glitter for a moment. Could you get high from it?"

"It would just put you to sleep, Ken. It's not an upper. It would turn any party into a slumber party fast." There was a note now in Bret's voice that suggested he might be dealing with a person of diminished mental capacity.

Abrams frowned, looking out to the larger room beyond his office. "How long would you be out?"

"Depends on how much of it you breathed. But you couldn't breathe much because it would put you down within seconds and then you'd stop breathing it, unless someone continued to spray it into your nose. In this powder form, that would be the only way to keep you out."

"So a person could snort it, then?"

"More likely it could be blown into his airways, like in a cloud. It's fast acting. You could put it in one of those puffer things like you would use to blow the dust off electronic parts, say inside a computer or a stereo."

"Could you drop someone to the floor with it?"

"I see where you're going with that. I think you could, but you might want to experiment with it before you took it into court."

Abrams thanked Bret and hung up, his eyes moving back to the scene in Sands' condo, touching his thumbnail to his lips. Sands would have been disabled in the dining room and carried to the edge of the parapet and then lifted over. Possibly he wouldn't have still been conscious during the fall, depending on how long it was. There was a physics professor at the University of Minnesota who worked with the police who could tell him how long it took to fall twenty-seven floors, but in the end, it wouldn't have mattered, except to Mark Sands.

The case had rotated 180 degrees. Ken Abrams knew he was now looking at a murder.

The glitter would have made the compound look like pixie dust, sparkling in direct light, so the victim couldn't miss it. The killer was a joker, but not there for a burglary. Megan Sands had said nothing was missing. Getting into the condo before she got home, Abrams had seen for himself that none of the rooms had been tossed. The police had secured the scene and Megan had not been permitted to enter. If she wanted to make it look like Sands was killed during a break-in, she would have suggested later that something was taken, possibly something she'd removed earlier herself.

A defense lawyer could argue that Sands had launched some of the propofol into the air himself and breathed it to dull his senses for the leap, but what was the point of the glitter? And why take it in the dining room if he was going to jump from the terrace outside? How could he control the dose? If he overdid it he'd simply lose consciousness and not be able to jump. It didn't compute and it still looked like murder. Apparently the killers hadn't gone very far out of their way to conceal it. Maybe it was a message of some kind. This case was starting to look less gray than some of the others on his desk, but Abrams' neck was hurting again. Since no one was passing his office window he rolled his head on his shoulders.

CHAPTER 3

It was after midnight and a few hours into the following Friday. A week had passed after the Rafael Cantú opening and Mark Sands' death. Edward Born lay asleep in his monogrammed mauve silk pajamas, custom-made to his impressive dimensions by a tailor in Beverly Hills whose business had taken a disturbing downturn after the death of Liberace. Born dreamed benignly of movement on the walls of his gallery, housed just thirty feet away on the same plot of expensive Canyon Road real estate. The movement was taking place among the paintings that had sold during the Cantú opening and the following six days. They were now being either carted off to the shipper or picked up by local buyers. In Born's dream they glowed briefly, one by one, and disappeared.

In his dream he stood in the gallery, and as he turned to watch the process evolve on the adjacent wall, a movement caught his eye. He turned more to the left. In a painting titled Sleeping Nude, an approximately human girl who had been lying across a daybed was starting to stir. A small hairless boyish figure at the edge of the canvas, poised with a robe to give her, was now really moving toward her, his right knee thrust forward to expose a reconstructed joint, mostly metal and crudely made.

Edward Born began to squirm, his feet moving

back and forth at the bottom of the king- size mattress, in his dream taking a few steps back from the painting. As he retreated, other Cantú pictures came into view, all now with movement. The most distressing part was that some of these were sold, and Born needed them to stay exactly the way they had been when the red dot went up on the wall next to them. Although his bedroom was cool, he began to sweat. Trying to flee the unpleasant turn his dream had taken, he rolled to his right, buried his face in a pillow, then sat upright, fully awake.

Once conscious, he couldn't shake the sensation of fear that accompanied the dream. He told himself it was only a ridiculous fantasy, fueled by some lingering shred of anxiety that he still sometimes had over business, yet the show had sold well, there was nothing to worry about. Rafael Cantú was prolific and his annual open-ings were among the most predictably successful of any at Born & Born. Not quite reassured, he was beginning to lower himself back to his pillow when he heard a noise. It could have been a human voice calling his name, but that made no sense. He lumbered to his feet and looked out his bedroom window across the dark courtyard toward the back of the gallery.

Through the single grilled office window on the back adobe wall, he saw a dim glow in the lower part of the room. It was not the quality of light that the ceiling fixtures would provide; they were all stronger than what he was seeing. The gallery doors and windows were all wired to the security system, which rang both in his home and at the monitoring station, so he knew nothing had been triggered. He pulled on a green brocade robe and drew a .22 revolver and a set of keys from his bedside table. The absence of any alarm suggested that he had left a light on himself in the office when he closed up, but which one? Something was not right. Besides, he was by nature too meticulous to leave any lights on.

Outside, he crossed the court and paused at the back door of the gallery, his ear to the weathered wood. When he heard nothing, he pulled out the keys and unlocked it. Once inside, he punched in the code to disable the security system and surveyed the office. Of course! He had somehow forgotten to shut down the computer when he left. The screen sent an eerie glow throughout the room, but why hadn't the screen saver, set for ten minutes without activity, cut in and dimmed it? He should have been seeing tiny winged hogs flying smugly across the screen in a tight V formation, each one bearing on its side the monogram, B&BG.

Born switched on the overhead light and sat down at the desk, sliding the safety back on as he set the pistol next to the computer. To his eye, nothing had been disturbed. The screen was open to his email inbox, and he saw that the last incoming message was from Raphael Cantú. Born suddenly remembered his request for a photo for Rebecca Stuart, sent a week before, and opened the message. Oddly, it had been sent at 2:55 AM, only a few minutes earlier, and consisted of a single line, without salutation or closing.

"You have asked the wrong question," it said. "You will not try again." This was not at all like messages he typically got from Cantú, who always had the good manners so integral to the Méxican character, but then, artists can be a goofy lot. Born was accustomed to the mystical, the cryptic, the downright flaky; rarely the businesslike, the career minded, the focused. He was occasionally flaky himself, in his dramatic clothes, his choice of boyfriends, in his sad weakness for antique cars that he was unable to maintain himself. But never when it came to business. What would he tell Rebecca about her request for Cantú's photo? He got to his feet with a puzzled sigh and went out into the second gallery room, leaving the pistol next to the computer.

As he turned on the lights to do a quick check of the paintings, he was shocked to come face to face with one of Cantú's small people seated unsteadily on the shoulders of another. Together they were not as tall as Born. The clothing of both was leathery and ragged, giving off the soft musty smell of things long buried and forgotten. The upper creature gave Born a shy smile, showing irregular teeth, and without a word opened his grubby hand, blowing across the powdery palm with surprising vigor. The look of complete astonishment remained on Edward Born's face as he hit the floor.

Within seconds they were upon him.

Early that Friday afternoon Rebecca again checked her account balances online. They were OK, but she was still agonizing about the succession in Outremer's management. She could start researching other investment managers, or have Jeremy do it. She was now hating the idea that when you had money, you had to deal with money. It was natural that you had to worry about money when you didn't have any, but who knew it went both ways? No one had told her this when she began, but then no one expected her to make any money.

She also checked the UPS site, hitting the tracking link Edward Born had supplied by email on Tuesday. The Cantú painting would be arriving before five.

At that point the phone rang. It was Detective Abrams again.

"Something has turned up and I wonder if you could come in for a few more questions," he said. "It's something about your alibi."

She felt immediately on guard. "Something like what?"

"You know, Ms. Stuart, I found out years ago that it's always better to have these conversations face to face. It's something about eye contact, body language."

"Maybe tomorrow," she said, thinking hard now about the "suspect" exchange the last time they talked.

"I'm sorry, but it can't wait."

"Then you'll have to come over here because I'm expecting a package to be delivered and it's important. Do you need the address?"

"I've already got it."

So Abrams could come over and check her out and check the apartment out and think whatever he wanted to think. There was nothing wrong with her alibi, he probably just wanted to meet her; that wasn't unusual. She went into the bathroom and checked her face, and standing on her toes as she bent forward toward the mirror, added a touch of lip gloss. The rest was OK. She always stood on her toes looking in the mirror, even though it went all the way down to the sink. It gave her a sense of being taller.

Abrams was not her main consideration at the moment, whatever he thought about her alibi. Despite her experience with crime fiction, Rebecca naively believed that if you were innocent you could simply tell the truth and then you'd have no problems with the law. Having an honest face and charming dimples would also help.

She had spoken to Bill Stokes in the Outremer office twice during the week about the direction the firm was now going to take, both times feeling like a newcomer who was uncomfortable about calling. He told her he was in long distance negotiations with Megan Sands to manage the firm. Stokes was the logical candidate, at least on an interim basis, but from what he told Rebecca, they were still some distance apart on "terms," which she took to mean compensation.

Twenty minutes later the doorbell rang and she buzzed the caller in downstairs, expecting she would see Detective Abrams when she opened her door. Instead there was a sharp rap half a minute later and a man in an olive uniform handed her a clipboard to sign, gesturing to a flat carton leaning against the wall. This would give her something other than money and alibis to think about.

When he was gone, she cut the tape with a scissors from her desk. Cushioned inside the thick cardboard cover and foam packing, the Cantú painting was perfect. Taped to the outer face of the foam was a note in Edward Born's florid script beneath the gallery masthead, "Hopefully the first of many, Rebecca. Enjoy. E.B." After she unwrapped it, she set the painting on her desktop and leaned it against the wall behind. At forty inches wide, it was perfect for the space.

Her gaze was first caught by the girl, just as it had been in the gallery. She was not quite normal, but more so than the other figures, the "three players" of the title.

However, having said that, it was not obvious how she differed. Perhaps something in her posture or proportions was not quite right, or in her expression. From the front she was anatomically correct, and what might be missing or different from behind could only be guessed at. Maybe it was the same vacant stare as the smaller males around her, self absorbed, distant, lacking in connection, even evasive. Rebecca took a step closer and leaning over the desk, looked intently at the girl's eyes, realizing with a start that they were violet. She had missed this in the gallery.

This was a good omen—Rebecca didn't want a picture that yielded its secrets all at once, she wanted to continue discovering new things over a period of years. But as she stared into the girl's eyes, there seemed to be a subtle change, almost a shifting of the direction of her gaze from nothing in particular toward Rebecca herself, who began to feel she was hallucinating. The sense of a link between them came back to her, just as she had felt in the gallery a few days before. Or perhaps it was more like that phenomenon in the desert where the heat of the highway causes it to shimmer and undulate, almost to dissolve.

She shook her head and blinked several times. When she looked back at the canvas the girl's gaze was again remote. How could Rebecca have thought the girl was looking back at her? It was the same vacant look as before. Some of the old masters had used a technique in portraits that caused the sitter's eyes to follow the viewer around the room. Cantú had done the opposite. Normally his figures pointedly avoided any contact with the viewer, as if they were in hiding, or afraid.

The bell rang again and she buzzed back, sighing with a mixture of irritation and interest, remembering that she apparently had a problem with her alibi. She threw open the door to the detective, facing him in jeans and a black tee shirt that said BITE ME across her chest. At the last minute she had stepped into a pair of three-inch clogs she kept near the door. No one ever saw her without shoes unless she was naked. Then her height didn't seem to matter as much.

"I did it," she said. "I killed the sucker because I wanted Megan for myself. Anything else?"

"I wasn't that far into the case yet, Ms. Stuart, but thanks for confessing. It makes my job that much easier. Ken Abrams, St. Paul Homicide." He put out his hand, showing his badge with the other.

"Call me Rebecca," she said, shaking his hand. "Come in."

When he gave her his card she looked at his hands, the long fingers, the well groomed nails, noting that there was no ring on his left hand. His face was oval with a firm mouth and blue eyes. She guessed he was in his late thirties. His shoes, another thing she always looked at, appeared to be Eccos. He took his feet seriously, and she made a mental note to put better shoes on Lester Grunge in book three. This was going to be fun. She could tell Abrams was more than pleasantly surprised by what he saw, and she instantly knew she hadn't made a mistake in making him come to see her. He was on her turf now.

"I'm going to ignore your confession because I didn't have a chance to read you your rights first. Give me a little warning next time."

"Have a seat." She gestured toward a pair of identical Southwestern print sofas facing each other, then sat down across from him as he pulled off his coat. "What's the problem with my alibi?" She folded her arms over the BITE ME letters. They tended to call too much attention to her breasts, which she felt were OK, but could have been a bit larger in situations like this.

"I talked to Hacienda Nicholas and they have no record of you staying there the Friday Mark Sands was killed." He shrugged apologetically, but stopped short of suggesting they must have gotten it wrong.

This is going to be good cop with bad news, she thought. "That's silly. I always stay there. I was there Saturday night too. Oh no, I know what it is. I didn't register as myself. I always did that on my book tour too."

"Then who were you?" He pulled out a sheet of paper from his breast pocket and unfolded it.

"Lena Grunge. Sometimes it's Mrs. L. Grunge, but I think I used Lena. I'm sorry, Detective Abrams, to make you come over here just for that. That name is on your list, isn't it?" She was suspecting now that the alibi problem was just a cover for the visit.

He nodded. "I thought it might be you." He was grinning now, looking around the room until his eyes stopped on *Girl with Three Players,* leaning against the wall on her desk. The smile left his face.

"What's that picture?"

Her eyes followed his gaze.

"That's my alibi you're looking at. Great, isn't it? That's what I was doing in Santa Fe."

"You just bought this painting?"

"Yes, and it came about half an hour ago. I was waiting for it. That's why I didn't come to see you at the station. Is something wrong?"

Abrams rose and moved over to the painting, leaning across the desk in front of it. Rebecca came up next to him, not quite touching elbows.

"Isn't it wonderful? Look at the technique, it reads almost like fifteenth century."

"I wouldn't know." He regarded it skeptically.

"Trust me, my degree was in art history." He turned and looked at her face, inches away. She didn't move. Rebecca knew the detail of her features held up well when you got that close. She had spent some time scanning it as well, and thought of herself as almost beautiful. It appeared that he did too. Her green eyes always helped if the guy wasn't color blind.

"You mean you didn't major in English?"

"I never could spell." It was her turn to shrug.

"But this painting is new, right? I mean recent?"

"Sure, the artist is still alive. Look on the back, it's dated last year."

He studied it for a minute but didn't touch it, a look of distaste curling his lips.

"What?" she said.

"I've seen this before, not this exact one, but a painting with the same characters. Mark Sands had one, but larger. I'm sure it's the same artist. I'd never seen these little people until I saw that picture in his dining room."

The information hit her like an electric shock. Abrams was handing her a connection between Mark's death and Rafael Cantú. A serious look came over her face as she pulled back from the desk and put her hand on the detective's shoulder, turning him toward her.

"I have to see it. This is important."

"Why? It's just another one of these same paint-ings. Does it matter?"

"I can't explain it, but I feel like it does, it's got something to do with Mark's murder, I know it." She wished she were the same height as he was, so she could look directly into his eyes instead of at his teeth.

"How could it? No one tried to steal it. Anyway, I haven't said Mark Sands was murdered."

Rebecca shrugged as if what he thought about it didn't matter. "I always thought he was. Suicide never made sense. Let me into his condo, please, I know I can help with this. I know how to find things that cops miss. You probably don't want to hear that, but it's true. Every day, I have to write plots and develop pieces of evidence that cases hang on."

He looked at her doubtfully.

She felt like she was now trying to cross from one kind of detective world to another, without a passport, and without any skills other than what she'd imagined or researched.

"And what makes you think cops miss anything in the real world?" he said bluntly.

"Don't you have any unsolved cases?" she asked, keeping her voice neutral.

Abrams turned away.

"I get your point, but I can't do it, Rebecca, it's a crime scene." He looked away through the window, his eyes following the line of the river as it curved toward the Robert Street Bridge. "Megan Sands is still in France and we haven't released the apartment yet."

It sounded weak to her. "But you *could* release it. What more can you be doing up there? It's been a week.

Your forensics guys must have gone through it on Saturday morning at the latest."

She saw a surprising look of frustration cross his face, knowing at the same time that she was not asking very much. They could release the scene at any time. She took a chance.

"Detective Abrams, Ken, just do it!" She was gripping both his shoulders now, looking up into his face. Immediately she could see it was the wrong thing to say. She'd been too commanding. Maybe something in his background made it hard for him to take orders from short people, even in tall clogs. Probably his Chief of Police was six-foot-three. She watched Abrams wait a moment to let his pulse drop.

"Listen, I've been doing this for twelve years. Do you think because you've written one lousy—OK, I take that back—one very successful detective novel, and one not so successful, that you can shed any light on this at all? Because what this looks like to me is a random crime. I'm sure it isn't, but there's nothing up front that tells me where to go with this, nothing."

"But you're not that far into it yet!"

"Far enough to know that Sands' business is straight, his wife is straight, the guy had no mental problems, and he had a lock on the good life. I'm sorry if I'm yelling, I know you're sincere, but please, please, step aside here. You'd only be in the way."

The ugly, stressed look on his face did not fade as he moved sideways out of her grip, grabbed his coat from the sofa, and without putting it on, went out the door, leaving it standing open. She stood at the window for a moment, staring down at the parking lot. Abrams came into view, crossing the tarmac with an impatient step, and threw his coat in a bundle into the passenger side of an anonymous brown Ford. He drove off with a squeal of tires that she could hear even with the window closed. She sat down on the sofa again with her arms folded and waited for the tears of frustration to stop coming out of her eyes. This was not going to stop her. She turned away from the window and went back to the painting.

Jeremy had put a picture hanger on the wall for her on his last visit. Never helpless about household things, on sheet rock she would have done it herself, but she'd been uncertain how to proceed on the stone. With his usual directness, Jeremy had simply picked a spot in the mortar between two layered yellow stones and hammered in a stout nail.

Now she got up and lifted the picture into place, noting that her guess about height was correct, then backed off about ten feet, checking the level of the painting. Normally an artwork of that size, about two feet by a little more than three feet, is at a good viewing distance that far away, but Rebecca now had a sense that she needed to be closer to it. Maybe it was a matter of watching the detail for subtle changes, and having it at the edge of the desk as she worked was right. If uncomfortable was good, she'd chosen the right painting.

Two hours later she was back taking another look at her current project, about a man who had been murdered with a wastebasket. After her publishers had declined to even look at a synopsis, and frowned on the first three chapters, her heart was no longer in it. With the Sands case unfolding, this idea seemed even more lame, and Rebecca had not yet figured out how someone could be killed with a waste basket. All she could think of now was Lester Grunge standing in his quirky posture, one hip thrust outward, examining Mark Sands' condo in detail.

When the phone interrupted her thoughts, it was Jeremy again.

"Duh," he said. "Now I'm feeling stupid, Rebecca, not my usual condition. Sands translates as Arenas in Spanish. The Arenas family were Spanish nobility, still are. They made their money in royal land grants when the Moors were ejected from Granada in the 1490s. The first Arenas in the records furnished King Ferdinand of Aragon with part of his army. They plowed their profits from plundering Moorish estates into more land and they're still the largest property holders in northwestern Spain."

"How does this connect?" she said. "I don't write historical novels. And how does Mark come in to this?"

"You know what he looked like, Rebecca. When I saw his picture in the paper I thought he might be Hispanic. Didn't you think that too? That's why I plugged in Arenas. Sometimes people change their names to seem more northern European, especially with the kind of business he was in, and in this part of the country, where everybody is Swedish or German."

"I never thought about that. After all, he said his name was Sands. It sounded English. I guess he could have been Hispanic, but his skin was pale. His eyes were brown, though."

"Upper class Hispanics usually have pale skin and they're careful to keep it that way. You never see them on the beach. Anyway, a man named Alejandro Arenas changed his name to Alexander Sands here in Ramsey County court in 1937. The wife's name doesn't appear in the public record, so it's possible she was deceased at the time or they were divorced. He changed the last names of his two sons and a daughter as well. Two months later he opened an investment firm called Sands and Whitelaw. Apparently they specialized in buying up distressed properties at the end of the Depression, sensing better times ahead."

"So? Maybe he saw the war coming." As always, she had to estimate how much weight to give Jeremy's work. It was reliably accurate, but not always relevant. It was a distinction he wasn't able to make himself. He sold information in bulk without filtering it.

"He may have. Here's the clincher; Alexander was also Mark Sands' grandfather."

This was a twist Rebecca couldn't fit in. She knew enough Spanish to get through the line at Chipotle or Taco Bell, but she'd never been to Spain or México.

"So where is this going?" she asked.

"Just about where you might think. Before that part of the family came to St. Paul they settled first in Miami on their way from Santa Elena."

"In México?"

"Right. That very big city in the north-central part, founded by Mark's ancestor, Juan de Arenas, in 1529. He had received the territory from Hernan Cortés as a grant for his services during the conquest."

"Wait, so Mark Sands was Spanish nobility, somewhat removed." Rebecca could feel her pulse picking up now. Maybe she really could walk away from the waste-

basket thing, which hadn't gone very far, anyway, and re-
cast book three based on the Mark Sands case. Even if it
ended as a suicide, that could be an effective twist to a case
that more and more looked like a bizarre murder.

"Exactly."

"So let's say it's a murder, but where's the motive?
This is not a turn I was expecting. Is it Spanish politics?
Méxican politics?"

"I didn't see anything on that in the files."

"What then?"

"Ah, I just do background, Rebecca, remember?
Anything else?"

Here they were again. As good as Jeremy was, he
always reached a point where the trail ended and Rebecca
had to pick it up. She thought for a moment. "No, I don't
think so."

After Jeremy left, Rebecca leaned back in her
chair thinking this was not the first time the research had
taken an odd turn. Staring at her new Cantú painting, she
was not quite seeing it and not quite seeing either what
connection between Mark Sands and his distant relations
during the Conquest would get him murdered nearly 500
years later. He had been born about fifteen years after the
name change. It was possible he had never heard about it.

She tapped her pencil eraser against the desktop
for a moment, then found Edward Born's number in her
card file and dialed it. In the conversation about Mark's
México connection, she realized she hadn't heard back
from Born about Rafael Cantú's photo.

Six rings followed, and Rebecca was just about to
hang up when the gallery girl answered, now blubbering
in place of her usual poise.

"Is Edward Born available?" Rebecca asked after a startled pause.

The girl tried for a moment to compose herself. "Mr. Born is dead. He was killed last night, strangled. I'm sorry."

Rebecca gasped. "What! How did it happen?"

"I don't know, I don't know." Her voice trailed off in a whine. "I found him in the gallery this morning with a leather thing around his neck. It was awful. Maybe the police can tell you more."

Rebecca thanked her and gently replaced the receiver as a slow shiver went through her. Now Edward was gone too, and it appeared there was reason to connect him with Mark because of the Cantú painting he owned, even though Sands had not been strangled. She stared out over the rail yard across the river, then back at *Girl with Three Players*. Even more than before, she felt she had to get into Mark's apartment, if only to see which Cantú painting he had. It was just possible that she now had enough ammunition to make it happen.

Back at his office, Ken Abrams began to regret shutting Rebecca down. It was not that it wasn't appropriate, it was more his manner as he did it. It was too much like a number of other times lately when he'd almost lost it over next to nothing. He'd always been better than that. Rebecca's tone had been urgent, but not threatening. He struggled for a while with the marginal possibility that she might have something to contribute to the case. In his view, crime writers made up anything they needed to push the story forward, but the reality was, that after chasing down every lead you could scrape up, you often waited months or years for a break that never came. Then, no matter how solid, the jury could still do whatever they wanted with it.

Yet Rebecca seemed scrappy and intelligent. In a way, he even liked the way she had confronted him, although it had given him one of those hotheaded reactions he'd been having too many of lately. Surely it counted for something that she'd published a hugely successful detective novel. He made a mental note to pick up a copy of Grunge. Once he'd read it he could decide.

It was not as if he had any great insight himself into the case at this point. It had been no understatement when he told her he saw no direction to take. Everyone connected with Sands looked innocent, and the physical evidence pointed in unclear directions. For example, with all the footprints in the Sands dining room, the security cameras showed no one unusual entering the apartment. Had they come by helicopter and dropped onto the terrace?

So far, the only thing that looked remotely intriguing was that propofol had turned up on the database in two other crimes. Neither of them had occurred in the Midwest. That was his only lead. Abrams was going through his interview notes from Outremer again when his phone rang. He knew the voice on the other end.

"It's Lena Grunge," Rebecca said.

"Good afternoon, Miss Grunge. Nice of you to think of me, but I haven't changed my mind. I do wish, though, that I'd found a better way to deliver the message. Please accept my apologies."

71

He had a smile on his face as he said this, picturing her sitting cross-legged on her desk chair before the Cantú painting in a short silk robe, bare legs glowing in the sun. He already knew how fine her skin was, at least on her arms and neck.

"I think you might change it when you hear what I've got," she said, keeping her voice even and relaxed.

"Go ahead, I'm listening."

"Mark Sands was Hispanic," she began hopefully, "and his grandfather changed the family name. They were originally called Arenas."

"Jesus Christ!" He slammed his fist down hard on the desktop and an ounce of cold coffee slopped out of his cup and onto his cuff.

"What do you mean?" she said. "It sounds like you've got something more."

"Let me take you back a couple of steps." Abrams was speaking rapidly now as he wiped the desk with a paper napkin. "I've been looking at the MO, and I did a search that came up with two other instances involving the use of propofol and glitter. One was a strangulation murder late last year in Houston, the other was a rape in Newark in September."

"Unsolved, I imagine."

"Both."

"What is propofol?" she asked. "And how do they connect to Arenas?"

"Propofol is an anesthetic used in minor surgery, not usually found as a powder. Traces of it were found on Mark Sands' shirt, tie, jacket, and skin, as well as in his airways. It was also found on the floor of his dining room, in each case mixed with glitter."

"Glitter?"

He thought he could sense the blank look on her face, wondering whether she touched one of her eyelids and then looked at her fingertip to see if it sparkled. It couldn't have been something she'd ever thought of for a crime scene. Enjoying this, he rolled his chair back and put his feet up on his desk, forgetting that he'd decided not to let her in.

"Right. Don't ask me why. Interestingly the ligature in the Houston strangulation was a braided set of five strands of leather. Highly unusual, almost ritualistic. No sign of a struggle, the victim's fingernails were free of any skin residue, so the man had been sedated with the propofol before he was strangled."

"Mercifully, and there was glitter present there too?"

"In the same proportion as with Mark Sands."

"Who was this man?"

"This is interesting. He was the auxiliary bishop of the Houston archdiocese."

"Was it a robbery?"

"No sign of it."

"Who was the rape victim?"

"A student teacher from Newark named Ana Maria Arenas, twenty-one years old, unmarried."

"Arenas!"

"Yes, now you understand my reaction."

"I'm getting there. Any DNA traces?"

"None, but signs of forcible entry. She didn't dream it, although she was sedated."

"OK, but now you throw in the Mark Sands case in St. Paul and you're all over the map. How does it fit together?"

"Well, as it turns out, there is a link between these other two, besides the pixie dust. The bishop's name was Alvaro Arenas. I've got a girl about to start work on their family trees now to see if they're related. Does that get your blood moving?"

"It's already boiling. I can't believe this. I guess you're going to let me help now?"

"Exactly. You're in," he said. "I'm willing to consider you an amateur investigator with close ties to the case. That justifies it."

"That's great," she said coolly.

Now that he had taken a step toward her, she seemed to be taking a step back. It was not the first time he'd seen that with women. If he had expected her to be jumping up and down on the other end, he was disappointed. Maybe she wasn't as young as he thought.

"Now you sound reluctant."

"Not at all. In fact I've already got the next piece of this for you."

"OK."

"The art dealer in Santa Fe where both Mark and I bought the Rafael Cantú paintings was murdered last night."

"How do you know it was the same dealer?"

"He's the only one in the States who handles Cantú."

"Now your painting connection idea is looking better. What's the MO?"

"The receptionist said only that he was strangled last night. She saw a leather cord of some kind on his neck when she found the body."

Suddenly Abrams knew they were all part of the same case.

"My God, this is stunning. Give me his name."

"Edward Born. It was at Born and Born Gallery."

He wrote it down rapidly. "OK. It's late in the day, but they're an hour earlier in Santa Fe. I might still be able to get hold of someone who's covering this. Should I let you know?"

"You'd better. It'll get you first place on my acknowledgment page. I always pay my debts. When did Mark Sands' death change from suicide to murder?"

"As soon as I got the lab report on the propofol."

After he hung up, Abrams looked at the phone for a moment. Budget constraints had ended the department policy of having detectives working in pairs except on the organized crime beat. But it looked like he now had a partner, one who could carry her own weight, and even part of his.

CHAPTER 4

By 9:30 on Monday morning Rebecca had walked the three miles to Ken Abrams' office, skipping over runners of ice that crossed the bare sidewalks from yesterday's afternoon melt. He hadn't called her back on Friday, so she assumed he had nothing yet from Santa Fe. She already knew she'd be writing about Mark Sands' murder, but she wasn't ready to say so, even to Jeremy, although her instructions to investigate Mark Sands had probably tipped him to it. It didn't bother her that she knew nothing more about the case than the death of Edward Born and what Abrams had shared with her, she'd written *Grunge* without any idea what it was about until the fifth or sixth chapter. Then things started falling into place. She knew there was a lesson in that: it was to trust her process. *Grunge II* had been a failure of concept.

She thought of this approach as character-driven. Get the people down on the page and they would start acting on their own. She hadn't outlined *Grunge* before starting, trusting serendipity to guide her, and it had worked. For her the process was now the flow. She was not going to second guess it.

Maybe she'd even solve the case before Ken Abrams. Then she'd own it.

It was not a bad morning for late March, the sun

coming at her flat and edgy, and most of her route hugged the Mississippi on the north side, the river still mostly gray and frozen but the ice showing that spongy look of early spring. The southwest-facing embankments were largely free of snow, showing straw-like stubble, but nothing approaching green yet. She wore an old pair of running shoes that she saved for wet, messy weather like this, and a fleece-lined buckskin jacket.

As she got closer to downtown St. Paul, she found herself going faster rather than slower, feeling as if she were approaching the center of the Mark Sands mystery. After she cleared security at police headquarters, Rebecca took the stairs up as she always did if it were four floors or less, stopping at the restroom next to the staircase to check her appearance. Maybe Ken Abrams would find a place in her Mark Sands book, if he measured up.

At the end of a short corridor, she was stopped by a duty officer one the other side of a pair of double doors.

"Detective Abrams," she said. "He's expecting me."

The cop picked up his phone and pressed a button. Nothing happened in response.

"Why don't you have a seat. I know he's in, but he's not at his desk." He gestured to a pair of benches along two walls. Rebecca eased onto the empty one, looking at a black woman with two teenage boys across the corridor. She had a grip on each of them. One of the boys looked back at Rebecca with interest, the other looked at the floor.

She saw the waiting area as boredom in shades of brown. Where the wooden benches and the trim were both the color of mud, the walls were a lighter color, more cinnamon than chocolate, and the ceiling was a pale tan like spoiled buttermilk. I should spend more time in places like this, she thought, I made my police facilities too up-scale in *Grunge*. They even had pictures on the walls. This is a dump. For the next book, maybe Jeremy should go around taking photos.

Abrams emerged from the same doors she'd used coming in, walking swiftly. She knew he had something more, and she jumped up and walked beside him.

"Sorry again about Friday," he said. "I shouldn't have run off like that. My office is this way." He pointed without slowing down.

"You already apologized," she said.

"I know."

When they got inside she pulled a copy of *Grunge* from her oversize Hermes bag and placed it before him.

"How kind of you," he said, opening it to the fly-leaf, where she had written, "For Ken Abrams—Partners in Crime," and signed it.

They looked at each other for a moment and then, feeling like she was supposed to go first, she said, "Did you talk to Santa Fe yet?"

"Just after I got in this morning. Have a seat." He sat down and leaned back in his chair. "The ligature that killed Edward Born, which I guess is what's most inter-esting to us, was a woven loop of five strands of leather, two yellow and three green, with an amber bead at both ends. They're going to fax me a picture of it. I talked to a detective named Ira Shapiro and he didn't think it was an Indian object, at least not from the groups in that area. I guess he would know. There's no amber in the environ-ment out there. I called Houston too and they're faxing a picture of what they found on the bishop. Oddly, I saw a much shorter piece of the same kind of braided leather work in Mark Sands' desk at. I didn't think much of it at the time, and I still can't explain it. Maybe he found it at home?"

"And there was propofol and glitter found with the bishop too?" This was starting to fit together better, but she was also thinking she should have worn some makeup with glitter for this meeting. It was not something she normally used before evening.

"Once again you're ahead of me on this. From the description I got from the Houston police, it sounds like what we had with Mark Sands. It was also found in Born's airways, on his robe, and on the floor around him. It was the same pattern around the body, right down to the soft footprints, as small as in Sands' dining room, but only two pair this time. I told Ira Shapiro what we had done and he'd thought of something else on the propofol angle that we missed. They're looking at veterinarians too."

"That makes sense. I was thinking on the way up here, Mark was a big man, although he wasn't overweight, and so was Edward Born, about six feet tall and maybe 250 pounds. If the killers were small, as the footprints suggest, the propofol would even the odds."

"You're not surprised at the connection?"

"I'm not, but I can't tell you why. It was just something that occurred to me when I talked to the gallery." She was wondering if this sounded thin, like some New Age investigative process that used intuition exclusively. It was hardly the insight she'd suggested she'd be providing to pick up on what the police missed.

"This is the way you'd set up one of your own books, isn't it, maybe even the next one?" he asked.

"Probably. I like to think about the investigation in terms of connections. It takes a good detective to see them." She felt like he'd bailed her out.

"Well, the Born murder is one I wouldn't have come across without your input, and I think I'm good."

She gave him a softer look. "I hope this isn't a sore issue, but I still want to see Mark's condo."

Arbrams paused for a moment.

"You know that we've been all through it."

"Of course, but I haven't, and I especially need to see that painting."

"You're setting a scene in your next book, aren't you?"

"Maybe. Sometimes I don't know myself until I see it. Maybe the book and the case are the same thing now—you solve one and you have the plot of the other."

Stepping out of the elevator on the 27th floor of the Landmark Tower, Rebecca found herself in a mahogany-paneled vestibule without windows, facing a pair of matching entry doors, no longer crossed by strips of yellow crime scene tape. A large Chinese vase with dry feathery fountain grass guarded them on both sides. She knew that the objects she was seeing now were nearly the last things Mark Sands had seen as he walked into an ambush of some kind, possibly seeming harmless until it was too late to react or flee. Ken Abrams moved past her and unlocked the doors.

"You realize we wouldn't be coming back here if Megan Sands weren't still in France," he said.

Rebecca had wanted to attend the funeral and was disappointed, but not surprised, to find it was private. The story Jeremy had heard was that Megan didn't want to be plagued with questions from Mark's clients, something that Rebecca readily understood. She would have had to restrain herself to keep from being one of the questioners.

"Anything on the security tapes?" Rebecca asked.

"From the lobby there was no one we couldn't account for."

She turned back to the elevator door. "That's interesting. How about this one?" An unobtrusive wall-mounted camera covered both the elevator doors and those of the condo.

"We got that one too. Mark Sands leaves at 8:14 A.M. carrying a briefcase, dressed in the same suit he died in. Megan Sands leaves at 12:56 P.M. Mark returns at 3:31 and dies outside at 3:38. That's the total traffic for the day. Megan was intercepted on the sidewalk coming home around 4:15. Their apartment had already been secured and she went to the St. Paul Hotel that night, right next door."

"So the murderer entered and departed how?"

"That's the prize-winning question," he said.

Not waiting for an answer, Ken opened the door and stepped aside for her. She noticed the polished marble floor inside, thinking this was what real money looked like. The high ceiling was coffered and the surfaces had the dull mellow gleam of lacquered silver leaf. For the moment she forgot about her eagerness to see Sands' Cantú.

81

"Is she still a suspect? Megan Sands, I mean," she asked after looking around for a moment.

"Everyone's a suspect." Something he must have said many times before, she thought. It was a line she had even used in *Grunge*. Or was it *Grunge II?* Probably in both.

She turned to him with a frank look to find him looking back at her. "Meaning that you have no one else yet?"

"Right. Not even you, now."

Rebecca let this pass. "How old is Megan?"

"Twenty-eight."

"That's about right." She studied Abrams' reaction to this. "I know he was married before, but it was over by the time I started using Outremer. He was in his mid-fifties, right?"

"Fifty-four."

"Not quite two-to-one. How does she look?"

"Drop-dead gorgeous," he said, shrugging and moving farther into the foyer. "About five-seven, dark hair and dark eyes. Great figure. Big dimples when she smiles, which hasn't been very often lately, at least when I've seen her. I think she must have one Asian parent because of her features. Wears her hair . . ."

"I meant how does she look as a suspect, Ken," Rebecca interrupted, tired of waiting for an opening.

He flushed slightly. "Ah, that. It's possible, I guess." His voice became more official. "Naturally we always look at the beneficiary first. Even if there are no substantial assets, it's still usually the spouse who's the best suspect. I looked through Mark's will and there's nothing odd about it. Other than a few charitable bequests, none of them surprising, she gets it all, since there were no kids from his first marriage. Anyway, her background is clean and there's no sign she's been messing around."

"Any old boyfriends who might have been upset by her marriage?"

"She lived with a labor relations lawyer for more than two years, but it ended a year before she took up with Mark. The lawyer was the one who ended it. Megan says they haven't had any further contact. She didn't seem reluctant to talk about it, and I didn't detect any bitterness on her part. I had a sense that if the lawyer hadn't ended it she would have. Some things just peter out that way. I'm not getting anything strange off her at all. I still don't know where this is going. Maybe you can tell me."

He stood in front of an antique commode that held a Chinese vase in blue, orange and gold. "I've never understood this ceramic stuff," he said.

"Any alibi?"

"Shopping." He turned to face her now, hands behind him against the commode. "No surprise there. We couldn't verify it. She hadn't bought anything and no one remembered her at the stores she said she'd visited. Maybe if there'd been a lot of men behind the counters we could verify it."

"What's her background?"

"She was a securities analyst with Piper Jaffrey. Mark Sands met her at a conference in Honolulu three years ago."

"Wasn't she a little young for a position like that?" Rebecca was thinking she wouldn't want someone her own age making investment recommendations for her own portfolio.

"Her specialty was the high-fashion clothing

chains. I asked the same question myself to some other people in the industry and it turns out there's no analyst in that area more than thirty-seven years old. I was told that middle-aged people don't understand retail. And she's got a degree in finance."

"Right. That fits. So she was doing OK before they got married."

"She was making about $150,000 a year. Seems all right to me, but she wasn't in his league." Abrams shrugged.

"Not many women would be."

"Still, he could have married one of his young widow clients who brought in a ton of insurance money. There were a few of those. Now she's in France. Took off the day after the funeral, still wearing black."

"You had a chance to talk to her again."

"Of course. I didn't get anything useful."

"I don't suppose she could have pushed him over the parapet?" Rebecca was trying to visualize it, and before the question was out of her mouth she knew the answer.

Abrams shook his head slowly. "You knew him. Six-foot-two, 190 pounds. I don't see it, unless she had some help. But the problem with having help is that it lays her open to blackmail by her helper. If she did it alone, the only way was to douse Mark with the propofol right at the edge of the parapet and push him over as he collapsed. Her timing would have to be perfect, because if he just dropped to the veranda deck, she wouldn't have been able to lift him over by herself. Limp bodies are awkward to handle, and the railing is at forty-two inches, which meets St. Paul building codes. Then when he wakes up, and that wouldn't take long, she has to explain to him what she was doing by blowing that stuff in his face for no reason, which would take some fancy footwork on her part. It's thin."

"It didn't happen that way, did it?"

"No. We knew that from the surveillance tape. Megan wasn't in the building. Anyway, it's clear that Mark inhaled the propofol in the dining room. But then you have the additional problem of getting him to the rail. The spot where he went over is twenty-nine feet from where he inhaled the propofol. So he had to be carried over to it, which would require at least two people, and probably more. Maybe he had a lot of enemies with small feet we haven't identified yet. I don't like Megan Sands for it. I'm still not ready to take her off my list, but maybe I should."

"How about the propofol itself?" she asked. "Can you get it at a pharmacy?"

"No. There's no prescription application for it, but hospitals have it. A nurse anesthetist could get it, or the doctor she works with, but they track it just like all the other narcotics. We checked the local hospitals and there's none unaccounted for. Besides, you still have to convert it to powder form, which means you have access to a lab, and there aren't that many around here. We made the rounds and we couldn't connect her."

The octagonal foyer opened before them in several directions. Directly ahead was the living room laid out along a bank of windows facing Rice Park, the trees in late March still skeletal far below. The furniture was similar to what Rebecca remembered from Mark's office; chrome, leather, onyx, dark wood here and there. Touches of polished steel. He must have been fixated on late modern, and it seemed like Megan, coming into his life at a point where his tastes were well developed, hadn't had much influence on the decor. On the right, a pair of glass doors led to the veranda. Rebecca looked through them toward the railing, shuddered involuntarily, and looked away. She would not be going out there. They moved into the dining room.

A long refectory table dominated the room. Here the dated modern gave way to antiques; perhaps they were more Megan's taste. The table looked genuinely worn and from the patina and style possibly several hundred years old, but Rebecca was guessing. The buffet also made her think Jacobean, with knobby turned feet, but she didn't know the styles well enough to be sure. Instead of a back rising behind to accommodate plate rails, there was a painting that stopped Rebecca immediately. This was what she had come for, and involuntarily she put her hand over her mouth.

"My God!" she muttered. "It's Cantú's *Last Supper*. Edward called me about it last summer, and I saw it on his website, but by the time I got back to Santa Fe again he'd already sold it. I never knew Mark bought it. Naturally Edward wouldn't say where it went. It really fits here."

"Does Cantú have some special meaning for you?" Abrams was studying her face rather than the painting.

"I've been enjoying his pictures for years, that's all. When *Grunge* started to make money, the first thing I thought was that now I could own one myself."

He didn't reply for a minute. "I don't think I understand it. I found it unpleasant to look at when I was here before and I still do. Besides, I really don't see how it has any bearing on the case. I know you think otherwise. Isn't it just the kind of detail that sells books, but doesn't enter into the evidence in any important way on a real case?"

Absorbed by the painting, Rebecca didn't answer. It was the largest Cantú she had ever seen, and the most complex composition. It was as if the painter were asserting his claim to be ranked with the old masters. As long as the buffet, the painting showed thirteen figures, nine facing the viewer and two at each end of the long table. On the Christ figure's right, taller than the men and leaning into his shoulder, was one of Cantú's nude girls. Rebecca leaned forward over the buffet to get a closer look, but she couldn't get close enough to tell whether the girl's eyes were violet or not, and it seemed that this girl's face was subtly different from the one in Rebecca's own painting. All the other figures were dressed in the scuffed medieval outfits he always used.

Rebecca moved around the table and regarded the painting from across the room. Unusual for a Cantú figure, the hairless Christ was staring back at the viewer, one ear enormously enlarged, the look of pensive sadness on his face that Rebecca had seen so many times at Born & Born. There was a suggestion of a military sensibility in his tattered leather clothes; something like an epaulet was still perched on his left shoulder, although the surrounding fabric had fallen away. It was held to the bare skin by a rivet, perhaps hinting at the suffering to come.

Her eyes went down the row and scanned each figure. The longer she looked, the more she was invaded by a sense of chaos, a level of disorder so extreme it at once mocked both civilization and religion. For the first time, she felt there might be something truly evil in the private vision of Rafael Cantú, something with the intent of undermining society, and she recalled the slogan above the gallery room at Born and Born about the end of the world. Absurd, she said to herself, moving back around the table again. That was only the perverse painter jacking up the level of discomfort. But did the eyes of Christ suddenly move to follow her?

Back at the buffet she leaned forward again, this time focused on the eyes of the man about to die. They looked back at her calmly, unmoving. Her breath came out suddenly in a long wavering sigh; she hadn't realized she'd stopped breathing.

Abrams was next to her. "Are you all right?"

She nodded.

Below the banquet table, in the foreground two dogs struggled over a stringy scrap of grayish meat, glaring at each other. Both with long, ferret-like muzzles, they looked like mutilated war veterans, one with rusty misshapen wheels instead of back feet, the other with a square steel plate riveted to his ribs at two corners.

"I really don't like this much," said Abrams, taking a step backward and bumping against the dining table. "It makes me uncomfortable. I don't know what I'm looking at."

"It's supposed to make you uncomfortable," she said, feeling like this didn't begin to describe it. "Cantu's specialty is alternative reality. It's never what you're used to."

"What do you mean?"

"Would you want to see art that made you feel

relaxed, self-satisfied, even complacent when you came home from work?" She turned from the picture to look at him, feeling like she had to defend the painting but at the same time thinking it might have gone too far.

"With my job, I think I would. I've got a LeRoy Neiman horse racing print, not signed, of course. That's good to come home to, but I surely wouldn't want to see something like this. I've got whole file cabinets full of alternative reality right behind me in the office. The morgue is full of it downstairs. I'm always happy to leave it all behind when I go home. Sometimes simple can be good."

"Not the case with my job," she said, still studying the picture. "I like edgy. This is a great painting." Abruptly she thought of the one on her own wall at home. Never a comfortable picture, now it was even less so. So be it, she thought. If it's connected to Mark Sands' murder, then it will drive the book. Ken Abrams was not going to get this, but it seemed perfectly clear to her.

She wouldn't have guessed Mark Sands owned a Cantú; but then, what was the typical Cantú owner like? Besides a taste for the uncomfortable, there was probably no common characteristic other than the means to buy one. She didn't know much about the financial markets, but she had a suspicion that Mark Sands had been successful there because of his ability to think outside the box. She was about to move into the kitchen when Ken Abrams placed a hand on her shoulder and she turned, pleasantly surprised at his touch.

"Before we go on I want to show you something else. It was on the floor right here that we found the powder, all along the front of the buffet."

"You said it was disturbed like in Born's gallery?"

She went down on one knee, but of course, no trace of it remained now.

"That was odd. There were two clear footprints of Sands, and a big disturbance in the coating of the powder from when he must have fallen into it, and then twelve or fourteen much smaller prints, but soft, without heel or sole patterns, as if they were cloth or leather just wrapped around a normal foot. Maybe they were sock prints, but there were no real weave marks that we could make out, and the photos we took had extremely high resolution. Since it's a hardwood floor, you'd think we could have picked up something. Judging from the measurements, they were made by a number of different people, or probably kids, from the sizes. But why would kids be involved in this?"

Rebecca pondered this, staring at the feet of the "apostles" under the long table in the painting.

"Were they like this?" she said, pointing to the feet of the Christ figure.

Abrams moved closer to the picture. "They could be. Isn't that ironic. Go figure." But he said nothing more.

Rebecca moved on, turning back once to look at the picture again, wishing she owned it now. Maybe Megan would sell it when she returned from France; it was probably not her taste. But then Rebecca would have to explain how she knew about it. "This is kind of overwhelming," she said as they went into the kitchen, "I almost feel as if he's looking over my shoulder. Do you feel Mark's presence here at all?"

"No, I was at his funeral. We always go if it's a murder victim, just because the killer is often in the crowd too, like a voyeur. But I don't feel Mark Sands here or anywhere. Anyway, aside from the painting, you said you wanted to get a feel for him at home, the lower-powered Mark, without the market trappings and the $3,000 suits."

"That's right."

They went into the kitchen, all stainless steel appliances and granite counters: cold, but polished and stylish. Rebecca didn't care for a look she felt was institutional, no matter how high end. For her it said nothing about cooking. She didn't do much of it herself, but she liked to feel her kitchen would welcome it if she did. The other exit led back into the foyer, where three more doors led to the bedrooms and a powder room. In the master suite, a wall of windows looked out over Kellogg Boulevard and the river, and two dressing rooms flanked the bath. She opened the door to one of the dressing rooms. It was empty, except for dozens of expensive wooden hangers with no clothes.

"I guess Megan couldn't stand to look at his clothes anymore," said Abrams.

"In any case, she didn't waste much time. Interesting that she kept the hangers."

"Maybe she has a frugal streak," Ken said, "not that she needs to."

Rebecca didn't open the other dressing room, knowing what she'd find—better clothes than what she was wearing. On each side of the bed were Western landscapes, and on the entry wall a low black lacquer cabinet supporting a wide flat-screen TV. She picked up the remote and turned it on. CNBC came on, the financial channel. The Dow Industrials were up forty-one points. "I think I've seen enough," she said. "I haven't noticed anything personal of his around, except the art, which must have been mostly his. She didn't stop with his clothes, did she?"

Abrams shrugged. "Some people don't want any reminders. When you're gone, they want you to be all gone."

"Harsh," she said.

"I'm just saying what I've observed. Maybe having no reminders let's you move on faster. I think she didn't want to come back from Europe and have it all waiting for her."

"If moving on is your main goal," she said, not sure what hers would be.

"It depends on whether you've got something waiting for you."

Back in his car, the unmarked brown Ford sedan with no extras other than a spotlight on the driver's side that only a person blind from birth would fail to identify as a police vehicle, he turned to look at her as they stopped for a traffic light on Wabasha Street. "What did I miss? Did you learn anything up there?" he said.

"Only that there was nothing in the apartment to suggest why he was killed. Maybe it was only because he was descended from the Arenas family, and I can't see any connection there with Edward Born, other than Mark's purchase of the picture."

"We could run a family background on Born."

"I'll have Jeremy do it. He came up with the other stuff."

Back in Abram's office there were two faxed photos of the ligatures waiting on his desk. They both bent over and looked at them closely. Rebecca found herself aware of his shoulder next to hers.

"If I didn't know the Houston one was locked up in their evidence room, said Abrams, "I'd say that they could almost be the same one, but this one from Santa Fe is longer. What do you think?"

"Edward had a bigger neck, I guess. They must come in different sizes. Same colors in the braid, same amber bead on the end. These people are not doing much to cover their tracks. What does that say to you?" she asked, trying to think what it would say to Lester Grunge. He'd have some cynical, but revealing, comment.

"A simple thing: that they don't care."

"What kind of killer doesn't care?" she said.

"Two possibilities. One, these things could be part of a ritual, so they're significant in themselves, and using them in each murder is more important than the fact that they also link the murders in an obvious way for the police."

"Wouldn't there be a common link among the victims then? Something that made them desirable as victims?"

"You'd think so, but I'm not seeing it apart from the Arenas name. The other thing might be that the killers don't care because they're arrogant and they don't think they can be caught. I hope it's that one because it means they won't be careful about other things, either, like the propofol. There are probably more parts to this we haven't spotted yet, as well. Details. Nothing I plan to miss, though." He gave her a look.

Later Rebecca walked down Shepherd Road back to her condo, wondering what to wear that evening when she had dinner with Ken Abrams.

CHAPTER 5

Things began to turn for Jeremy Wyman when he was no more than five steps inside the double oak doors of Antoine's, his normal Friday night, or any night, watering hole. The fact that it was a Monday simply meant it would be less crowded. The decor was sandblasted yellow brick, with a tin ceiling and droopy Boston ferns, that in the name of romantic ambience and low, people-flattering illumination, never got quite enough light. The tired Victorian nudes on the walls tempted the glance of no one who'd seen them more than once. They were like faded wallpaper in frames. Jeremy was pulling off his puffy down jacket when his scan of the room paused on the girl seated near the outside wall. He did not at first realize what a beauty she was.

Alone at a white marble-topped table near a window, she was small, with a narrow face, dark hair and eyes. Her hands were together on the table, one over the other as if for warmth. That was understandable, since outside, the puddles were beginning to ice over again from the afternoon thaw. A few large snowflakes fell without much conviction, as if they were only dropping from the bare trees, not the sky. Drifting slowly to the damp pavement with a sideways swirling motion, they shimmered briefly under the old-fashioned streetlights and disappeared. It was a historic neighborhood, and period details mattered.

On the girl's chair hung a greenish jacket, possibly suede, but Jeremy was too far away to be sure. Although she looked at no one in the room, her gaze seemed intense and focused. She wore a turtleneck sweater in a darker color, something he thought might be called heather in a more certain light. An almost melancholy look had settled over the girl's face. She looked like someone's unassertive younger sister, reluctantly brought along to a party, then abandoned to her own resources once inside the door. She didn't look at him as he took a stool at the end of the horseshoe-shaped bar, at an angle where he could see her in the space between two other couples. He liked her unthreatening look and tried to imagine what her smile might be like if only she would turn toward him.

The bartender set a black and tan in front of him and followed his gaze back to the girl.

"Haven't seen her in here before, Jeremy. She came in alone about half an hour ago. She could be waiting for someone, I don't know."

Jeremy was flattered Dick had noticed his interest in the girl, as if he were some well-known stud sniffing at a new prospect, but the truth was that Jeremy had never been a ladies' man. A near genius with research, as intuitive as a ferret in digging out reluctant facts, he had never been able to translate these skills into sex appeal, although he had researched that too.

He liked girls, but they didn't seem to respond to him much. His pale skin, the color of not quite fresh skim milk, the reddish orange hair so fine that even when it was too long it didn't completely mask the pink tone of his scalp, his eyes of an indeterminate color that might have been blue in the right light but usually just read as dull gray, did not add up to a compelling picture of manhood. The fine dusting of freckles on his face and neck also covered most of his body. No woman aside from his mother knew this first hand.

He took a long draft of the beer. Eventually he was going to have to make a move toward some girl like this. Maybe she was the one, or maybe not. There was no hurry: he was only twenty-five.

Jeremy had never been a natural athlete. Graceless in adolescence, moving abruptly as if caught by surprise, even to the startled look on his face, during high school he was inevitably one of the last few unchosen for any team. As the others moved off to the playing field he'd be shifting about on one foot or the other, looking pathetic among the chess players and computer nerds. The tragic truth was that at twenty-five, Jeremy was still a virgin and there was no relief in view. It was as if he'd been handed a bad script at birth, one tense with abstinence and top-heavy with frustration.

His closest near miss had happened in his last year of college, when a girl he worked with in the computer lab had allowed him to remove her top and bra and nuzzle her breasts for five minutes before she put her top back on without comment, scanning her email as she snapped her bra behind. He felt he had simply filled a few moments of empty time for her, with no obvious result for either of them. Going over it again and again in his mind, he decided she was nothing but a tease.

Even though her indifference was powerful, this incident remained his main sexual fantasy three years later because of its uniqueness. Constantly exploring in his mind a further move with her that had never materialized, or the clever line that would have made it happen, he still did not understand why it had stopped at that point. After all, she could have teased him more, could have practically enslaved him by taking it a step further. The only thing he could think of was that she must have been expecting something important in her email and it had suddenly arrived. If there was a lesson for him in this, it was that girls have priorities too, but he wasn't one of them.

Jeremy felt he had never been able to project the warmth he felt for women, even as he matured. Lately he had been focusing on the thought that it would only take one to bring him along. The girl at the window turned so he could see her face almost fully. She was beautiful. Was she also the one who would change everything? She took a sip of her drink, something tall with a straw in it, and briefly looked his way with no special expression on her face, then returned to staring out at the street.

She must be waiting for someone, he thought, someone luckier than I'll ever be. Maybe she sensed that I've been staring at her. Maybe she knows I'd like to come up beside her and plant a kiss on the side of her neck, just below the ear, and then she'd get up and put her arms around me, her hair falling across my cheek, her breath like roses, while I . . . . The thought evaporated in futility, a familiar sensation.

He looked down at his khaki pants, where a brown drip of dried spaghetti sauce had fallen some time ago near the right pocket, and at his shirt, tonight a short-sleeved seersucker in pink and white that had never been his color and was too light for the weather. It was laundry time again and he was running short of everything. The truth was that most people who knew Jeremy and bothered to think about it believed he was a nice guy, competent and determined in his work. He wondered whether "nice" in this context might be equivalent to pathetic, a form of praise so feeble as to mean almost the opposite.

He knew that Rebecca, although she spent hours composing emails and could find any fashion website in the world in a matter of seconds, would have been lost and bogged down doing her own research. Her issue was patience. She regarded him as a living extension of the Internet, with the ability to play it like a cello, coaxing endless fluid streams of information from it in ways she could never imagine. He felt certain it hadn't occurred to her that he had never mentioned his personal life. His chummy and familiar manner with her was his nice guy facade, one that he wore every day in lieu of a suit, which he did not own anyway.

Rebecca had never even physically touched him, except to shake hands the first time they met. He had no idea if she was aware of the way he sometimes looked at her, at the superfine blond down on her neck below her hairline, at her great legs, her wonderful butt. The way her breasts thrust up against the snug tee shirts she favored, especially the one that said, BITE ME. Jeremy would have eagerly bitten her anywhere. He could go on and on, but what was the point? A girl like that, gorgeous and now wealthy and famous to boot, would never give him the time of day if he didn't work for her, and rightly so. He'd never even tried to friend her on Facebook, where she probably had 8,000 friends. All but six, men.

Maybe this girl at the table wouldn't give him the

time of day, either. In a different way, more smoky and seductive, she was exotic as well, where Rebecca looked like the best of a large group of Midwestern blondes. The more he looked at the window girl, the better she looked. Yet grounded in his own experience, he had no expectations.

Dick set a menu down in front of him. "What do you think?"

"I think she's gorgeous." He made a gesture of hopeless dismissal, but even to his own ear, his voice sounded soft and wistful, almost mushy.

"She's kind of small, though, you know?" Dick wrinkled his nose.

"Yeah, but that's all right. Petite is good." Anything is good, he thought.

Personally, Jeremy was clean, and besides that single dry spot of spaghetti sauce, no larger than a pea in diameter, well groomed, and his fingernails were immaculate and closely trimmed so that they didn't clatter on his keyboard, something he considered unprofessional. He had a ready smile that showed his even teeth, and went a long way to help him do the research that involved personal contact, although not much did. Personal contact was usually a fantasy.

The problem was that he was simply clueless about women, and they could easily sense it. He gave off the aura to girls his own age that he was somehow much younger than they were, much less experienced, and in the end, far less interesting than they themselves were. He wouldn't have disagreed with this, and for the most part, neither would they. What he needed was someone to make a point of taking him on like a science project, a psychology lab experiment in personal relations. It was possible that he could help prove someone's theory about something, but what? Did anyone major in shyness? Was anyone working on a vaccine?

So it was with an air of sadness that Jeremy now regarded the girl at the table by the window, knowing that his record of failure would remain intact, not even challenged, and that nothing would ever happen. Yet she had a certain look he could relate to, as if she were different enough to also be one of the unchosen. Probably she was not someone who sparked much interest from ordinary men, particularly those who could not see in her the angular beauty that Jeremy saw. It was something he could not quite articulate, possibly because there was no research behind it. What was coming, if anything at all, would all be based on his own experience, something as thin as a butterfly's wing.

Perhaps she had been isolated in a suspended adolescence like he had, endlessly waiting it out. Waiting to be acted upon, rather than acting. His interest was now tinged with sympathy. Jeremy himself had partly moved on and now regarded that difficult period of his high school years with some amusement, but perhaps she never had. He ordered a plate of corned beef hash and another beer. It could be that she needed his help resolving it. He grinned at the thought of himself as a big brother figure, a mentor, authoritative but not totally disinterested, bringing this girl along. With him she could bloom, if only she would try. Without realizing it, he'd made a decision.

"What's she drinking?" he asked Dick impulsively, when he returned with his order.

"Lemonade. She's got a sandwich coming, too,

the veggie club, mayo on the side. Extra mushrooms."

"Send along another lemonade with it and put it on my tab," he said with startling bravado. It was a bold move for him, one he hoped wouldn't be misinterpreted, but how many interpretations could there be?

When her food came with another drink, she gave the waitress an enquiring look. The waitress turned and gestured toward Jeremy, who felt an unwelcome flush descend from the roots of his hair continuously into his white socks as he nodded in her direction. He immediately wished he hadn't sent the lemonade, but when the waitress moved on to the next table, the girl turned and gave him a welcoming smile instead of a look of scorn, and gestured with her hand toward the chair opposite. He was once again struck by her beauty—why was no one else hitting on her?

Instantly on his feet, Jeremy's napkin drifted unnoticed to the floor. His left shoe caught briefly on the leg of the barstool as he picked up his plate and glass and moved to join her, but no person of good will would have called it a stumble. Jeremy hoped it looked more like a tentative dance step he was trying to learn or remember, a bit of rarely-seen rumba, not very common in St. Paul nightlife. Why he'd chosen that moment to attempt it was not something he could have explained. Now he sat opposite her, tongue-tied, breathing hard from traveling the seven steps to her table. It was longest trip he'd made in some time.

"My name is Luisa," she said. "You're very nice. Thank you for the lemonade."

There was that word again, nice, but she didn't seem to give it anything other than its normal meaning.

She put out her hand to him and he took it gingerly, as if she were offering him a small bird. Her voice carried the hint of an accent, but not one that was familiar. The intonation was also different, surprisingly deep for a girl of no great size. There was a breathy quality to it that intrigued him. At this point, anything she did would have.

"I'm Jeremy Wyman," he managed, looking now at the details of her face, her fine skin, the small mouth with rosebud lips, the way the unusual length of her nose did not detract from her looks, perhaps because it was delicate and finely formed, almost sculptural, harmoniously echoing the narrowness of her face. Her eyelashes were long and thick.

She turned suddenly, reacting to a loud outburst of laughter at the bar. Holding her hair in place at the back of her head was a clasp framing a scorpion in amber.

His glance traveled to her fingers, where he saw a ring made from some twisted fiber on the middle finger of her right hand, ending in a stylized flower bud. It was dark brown and resembled the skin of a mummy. Although her hand was warm to the touch, her nails were bluish and oddly translucent.

Luisa smiled again, her eyes leaving his after a moment to scan the room. As they caught the light from the bar he was startled to see that her irises were violet. Was she looking for someone else after all? Then why invite him to sit with her? "I've never seen you in here before," he continued, uncertain whether she was still listening. Was this even going that well? He had no experience to compare it to. In his entire life he'd never picked up more than the mail.

"No," she answered, as she continued to look

toward the entrance. "I've never been here before." She looked back at him suddenly, the same smile on her lips. "But I'm glad I came, because now we're going to get to know each other," she said, brightening.

Jeremy nodded slowly, disconcerted. He couldn't read her—no surprise, but he knew she'd read him.

At the same moment, a mile and a half down the hill from Antoine's, at the edge of downtown St. Paul and fronting the same magical view of Rice Park as the late Mark Sands' condo, a man entered the St. Paul Grill. It was a clubby restaurant paneled in dark wood and much favored by the city's business elite. Across the park it faced the Ordway Theater, a sparkling venue for Broadway shows and concerts, and to the right the restored nineteenth century Federal Courts building.

The Grill was a place rarely patronized by Detective Abrams, but tonight he was about to have dinner with an important, or more accurately, trendy, mystery writer whose net worth, he knew from his investigation, went easily into seven figures, and that wasn't even her principle appeal. There was also the possibility that she would mop the floor with him on the Sands investigation, and he would end up supplying the background material for her to do it. If this gave him mixed feelings, it did not give him pause. He'd still get credit at headquarters for solving the case. After all, she was gorgeous in a spiky way, and she could not be easily ignored because of the skills she'd shown him so far. Best of all, he enjoyed being with her.

With a little effort, he could see them as a team on

a TV detective show, offbeat and off kilter, one of them committed to conventional means or detection, the other about six degrees out of plumb. He'd be the straight man to her snappy comments. Together, they'd knock down cases one after another.

Oddly, Abrams' neck was causing him no problems tonight. As he was shown to their booth, he was preoccupied with what might be the connection among all the propofol victims popping up in his latest murder investigation. The most interesting link was now turning out to be Rafael Cantú, although a call to the Houston and the Trenton Police departments had revealed no more of his paintings among the possessions of either victim. No surprise there; Abrams didn't see an auxiliary bishop or a student teacher collecting a painter whose work always brought five figures at gallery prices. But when Rebecca brought in the murder of Edward Born, with its propofol and leather thong elements, another door had opened. It was a chance kind of thing, but often murder cases turned on just such an occurrence, and she had promised she'd be able to pick up on what he missed.

A few minutes before Abrams had left his office, Detective Shapiro of Santa Fe called with another element. The deleted emails recovered from the Born & Born Gallery computer hard drive showed a series of messages from Rafael Cantú. They were almost all of a business nature. However the last one, received within the same time frame as Born's estimated time of death, could be interpreted as threatening, and departed from the normal pattern. In Abrams' mind, the fact that these words had been deleted represented an equivocal clue. Either Born had deleted it himself after reading it, or it had been deleted by the murderer. There was no way to tell.

No fingerprints other than Born's had been found on the keyboard, although one of the arrow keys and the delete key held no prints at all. Of course, they might have been wiped clean by some random gesture, a handkerchief in Born's fingers passing over the keyboard surface, for example. Abrams tended to think the murderer had deleted the message because it linked Born's death to Rafael Cantú. There was no clear reason why Born would have deleted it himself, although it was possible, even though five or six earlier messages from Cantú remained. The next step in the investigation was to find the painter and have a quiet conversation.

"You're deep in thought." The voice came from the edge of the table. Abrams scrambled to his feet, nearly tipping over his water glass. It was a bad habit of his to get so deeply into sorting through the pieces of a case that he lost track of everything around him. It worked OK in his office, not so well elsewhere.

"Please, please sit down, Rebecca," he said.

Abrams' eyes remained on her face as he apologized for not seeing her come up to the table. "Just mulling over the case. You know how it is."

"So its a working date," Rebecca said as she slid into the booth and set her small purse on the seat next to her. "That's fine with me, but I wasn't sure what to wear. I don't have a dressy shoulder holster like you do. Although looking at your face I think you might have shaved since I saw you this morning. Is that a clue?"

"I wasn't sure myself, I was trying to cover all the bases." He gave her a crooked smile.

The dress she had chosen was black, scoop necked

and fitted. Sleeveless and belted, it came just above knee length. Ken thought it said that she was partying in a modest way, but nothing about her availability. She showed no cleavage, but her bare shoulders were eye-catching. The perfect statement, confident but ambiguous; she had topped it with a sterling silver heart pendant and matching hoop earrings. He noticed her looking at his blue suit and red tie. The suit was fresh and a good weave. Like her dress, it didn't say much about his intentions. It was scheduled to enter his normal work lineup in a week or two, replacing one he was about to give to Goodwill.

She leaned forward on the table. "Is there more now?" Her voice was slightly breathless.

"There's a lot more. You really look great tonight, for starters."

She appeared confused and blushed a little, but didn't seem displeased with the complement.

"Thank you, I meant about the case."

As a waiter delivered water for her and menus, he filled her in on Ira Shapiro's call. Rebecca refused a cocktail, so he didn't order one either, but she asked to see the wine list.

"I hear what you're saying about the email message," she said, her eyes moving down the Pinot Noir section, "but I just can't see Rafael Cantú as a murderer. Why would he kill one of his main gallery owners—a cash cow? For a painter to get loyal representation is often harder than painting the pictures themselves."

"Think of the email; 'You have asked the wrong question. You will not try again.' Doesn't that sound threatening to you?"

"Possibly," she said, "but it could also be a lot of

other things, since we don't know what the question was. Suppose Born had asked, 'How many pictures of yours does the Geneva gallery sell?' Then maybe Cantú is offended because he thinks Born should only be focused on how many Born & Born sells. Do you see that? The answer could fit a variety of questions. You might be missing it." She shot him a smile that he didn't miss.

He was thinking that this was weak, and that it came from nothing more than being unable to accept the idea that Cantú might act against Born & Born. The waiter brought two glasses of an Australian pinot noir.

"According to Shapiro," Abrams said, "every other email from the artist had both a salutation and a signature. This one is alone in having neither. I think that's what makes it seem sinister. There's a level of rudeness in it that departs from Cantú's normal polite style. From what I've heard, Méxicans are particular about observing the niceties of good manners. If . . ."

Abrams's cell phone vibrated suddenly. He pulled it out with an apology, glancing at the screen.

"Sorry. I have to take this, it's Shapiro again." He opened the line. "Abrams. You're still at the office?"

"It's only six-thirty here," said Shapiro. "Something else came up on Born's computer and I thought you'd want to know. Our tech broke down the keyboard and guess what he found?"

"Our favorite pixie dust?"

Across the table Rebecca's eyebrows went up.

"It looks like what you described to me. They've got minute traces of white powder surrounding the delete key. We won't have the lab results on it until midmorning, but get this; they also came up with seven particles of glitter around the same two wiped keys. Under the micro-scope they match what we picked up from the floor in the gallery. We got that ourselves without the lab; it's a much larger particle."

"So the message was deleted by the killer," Abrams said, "not by Born. That's what I've been think-ing all along."

"I was too, and this locks it up. I'll give you twenty-to-one that the powder comes back as propofol. I'll let you know either way, and there's one more thing. The source of the emails from Cantú is in Santa Elena, México. Are you going to try to talk to him?"

"I think so."

"Maybe I'll run into you down there. I'm going as well. You owe me a drink, Abrams."

When he pocketed the cell phone Rebecca was taking a slow sip of her wine.

"Physical evidence on the keyboard?" she asked.

She's sharp, he thought, looking at her lips and the edges of her teeth.

"The same stuff. The killer must have had it on his fingers when he deleted the message."

"Do you see a contradiction here?" she asked, leaning across the table. "The killers leave their leather garrotes around everywhere, as well as this propofol-glitter mixture, and they make no attempt to cover their tracks, except for fingerprints on the keyboard. But then they delete the message from Cantú. What does that say? Because that's the exact kind of conflicting information I like to use when I'm developing a plot. It can send you off in two directions."

"It says they need to cover the tracks of their

chief," said Abrams, "but no one else matters, right?"

"So Cantú is behind this?"

"That's how it looks to me."

"My God!" she said, setting her glass down on the table too hard. Her other hand pressed against her chest. "I wonder if I set this in motion when I asked Edward for a photo of him? Maybe the wrong question he referred to was, 'Can you send me a photo for one of my clients?'"

"There's no way you can know that." Shaking his head slowly, he wanted to reach for her hand, but it was still pressed to the neckline of her dress.

"Of course I can!" she said. "Shapiro's computer people can recover the deleted sent messages as well as the received ones, can't they? That would tell us exactly what Edward e-mailed to him."

Abrams nodded reluctantly. "I'll get back to Shapiro about it in the morning. Let's order something to eat." He had actually thought of this angle already, but wanted to protect Rebecca from thinking she'd indirectly caused Born's death, although it was starting to look that way to him too.

"I've scanned Cantú's work on the Internet for years," she said after the waiter went off with their order, "and I've never seen a self-portrait. It's traditional to do at least one. So why would he not want anyone to know what he looks like? Isn't that the real question here? Has he got a record? Is he really someone else?"

"It could be anything," said Abrams. "Is he hiding because someone would like to kill him? Does he have enemies who'd recognize his picture but not necessarily know him under the name of Rafael Cantú?"

"I'm going to put Jeremy on this when I get home."

"Maybe there are other sources for a photo. Like when he went to art school, there could be a class picture."

Dinner came a few minutes later.

"I feel like you're digesting this carefully," he said after they'd started.

"The halibut? It's great with the tarragon."

"No, the twists in this case. Is this how you develop your plots?"

"To tell you the truth, I don't usually pay much attention to the news as a story source, and I don't read the papers very often. That's why I have Jeremy, my researcher." She lifted her glass and took a sip. "Most of my material is made up out of nothing. Most of the time I don't even base my characters on real people. My theory is that Cantú gets his painting subjects the same way. When I asked for that photo, I was thinking he might have that odd look himself, and then he paints the world as if it were like him. I never said that to Edward Born. He would probably have told me that I had a superficial take on Cantú's work. Maybe it is."

"Do you ever get material from your dreams?"

"It's rarely worth anything," she said. "It's usually too tame."

"How do you know when some of it is good, you know, usable?" His eyes were fixed on the silver heart at her neck, moving as she spoke.

"I filter it, I try it on for size. If there's any dialogue in it I speak it out loud, and if it's useless or silly, I can hear that right away."

Chewing slowly, he gave her a long look and moved his fork over his steak, thinking about whether he could trust her. Of course he couldn't, he only wanted to trust her. Just three days earlier she'd been a suspect. Next she'd be solving the case before he could. Then she'd never talk to him again. He'd be over, out of her life, reduced to a sentence when she told someone else about the case, or even just a name, one of a series on the acknowledgment page of her next book. Part of a crowd scene in her memory, his face would be indistinct. Then he'd run into her downtown one day and she wouldn't recognize him. Even when he said his name to her she'd have to think for a moment.

"I've had some strange dreams," he said, launching into it without planning to. Was it a way of making himself more memorable to her? It was if someone else was standing behind him and operating his mouth by a tiny lever behind his ear. He was starting to regret speaking when he realized how tired he was of being guarded all the time in what he said. Why wasn't there anyone he could talk to about how he felt at work? About how his engagement with his job was fading daily. Of course there was the department's staff psychologist who nobody wanted to talk to because it went on their record, although they say it didn't.

"We all have them," she said, studying his face. "Strange dreams can be good."

"Not for me. In my dreams I kill people." To avoid looking at her, he refilled their glasses.

"But that's your job, isn't it, Ken, in a way?"

"I don't do it for my job. In my waking life, I've never fired my gun at a suspect, just in the required annual target practice. I only kill people in my dreams."

"So . . . you're kind of kinky," she said, setting her fork on the edge of her plate, where it made a small metallic clink that punctuated her comment. He saw no discomfort in her look; in fact, there was a trace of a smile.

"Something like that. I don't know if that's the exact word. I don't feel kinky when I pull the trigger." He realized he had always avoided assigning any word to it.

Rebecca leaned forward over the table and her voice grew hushed. "Now that we're sharing secrets, I'll tell you one. I've got a tattoo."

"What is it?" he said automatically, disappointed that she thought this was an equivalent confidence.

"Yin and yang." She waited for his reaction with a sly grin.

He'd heard the words, but couldn't connect any image with them. "What's that again?"

"An Asian symbol, red and black, like two teardrops interlocking to form a circle. There's some long bit of theory about how it represents the two halves of reality. I think of it as meaning it takes two to tango."

"Where is it?" he asked after a moment, unsure whether he should have said this.

"I'll just let you imagine where it is," she said softly, with her chin on her hands, giving him a smoky look.

A darkened room, two miles down the Mississippi River from where Ken and Rebecca are sharing secrets. Lights from the river traffic along the shoreline road dance on the restored pale yellow limestone walls of an old Great Northern Railroad warehouse. Inside, within the painting titled *Girl with Three Players*, a small male figure sitting on a table begins to move. Slowly lifting his hairless head as if coming awake, he scans the darkened room, before he touches the ace of hearts before him with blunt fingertips. The card lifts slightly, then falls back when he pulls his finger away, as if his skin is slightly sticky. When he sees no one, he flips the card over with an impatient gesture, then turns it back.

One short, hairless leg comes out over the lower edge of the picture frame, swings briefly above the left side of Rebecca's desktop, then slowly returns to its original position. It's as if the player were waiting for her to return. Beneath his extended foot was, for a moment, a stack of her notes on the Mark Sands murder. It's unfortunate that our friend doesn't read English, having studied Russian and Chinese instead. From beneath the tablecloth he sits on, a small dog thrusts his nose out, sniffs the air tentatively, and then withdraws. The girl in the picture does not move, because she's occupied elsewhere at the moment, seated at a table in a bar called Antoine's, connecting with a new friend.

CHAPTER 6

A t Antoine's, their conversation at dinner had been mostly about Jeremy, with Luisa leading the way. "I love your red hair," she said. "I don't think I've ever seen it on anyone before."

Although he wondered how this could be, he found her intelligent and easy to talk to, surprised at how well he was doing with someone he'd never met before. Perhaps he was amazed that he was talking to a girl in a bar at all. He couldn't remember when it last happened. She was especially interested in the people he was doing research for, finding his offbeat job fascinating, making it seem as if being self-employed was a sign of remarkable courage.

"I could tell right away you're a self-starter," she said, rubbing the back of his hand with two small, warm fingers.

In fact he had found it difficult to even apply for a job since he'd finished college, thinking it felt like bleakly offering himself for a sports team in high school. He saw it as little more than another opportunity for rejection, and he'd been unable to bear any more rejection for years. Being a self-employed researcher looked to him more like the easy way out than being courageous, and being shy made him a better researcher. He found it easier to work alone. He had reached the point now where he enjoyed it, the independence it gave him and the demand for creativity in his thinking, but until this evening it hadn't helped with his social life. Nothing ever did. Every time he thought about it, a sense of isolation and regret washed over him. He'd lived in St. Paul all his life, but was still only at the fringes of it. The connection among young people was there, he could see it happening, but it was like being on the other side of a plate glass window. Jeremy was a perpetual observer of other people who led the life he wanted. He tried not analyze himself in detail, but he knew he was totally bored with his life.

He needed some kind of violent shock to break him loose from what was holding him back—himself. He had no family left in St. Paul; his parents had moved to Florida two years before. He had a few friends from college, but none were that close. If only he could move out and take a chance, something with real scale and dimension.

Whenever he paused for breath, Luisa was staring into his eyes. She had stopped glancing around the room altogether now. She was more focused, more engaged. Suddenly needing to touch her, he seized her right hand in both of his, finding her odd ring between his fingertips. This startled him as much as Luisa.

"What is this ring?" he asked, thinking more of the smooth texture of her skin, "I've never seen anything like it. Is it leather?" Touching her hand sent a wave of pleasure through his whole body. He felt he could sit there with her for hours.

Jeremy drew her hand closer into the light from the candle in the center of the table, and looked at the ring more carefully. Luisa's fingers curved around his. He could see that the ring had an odd, gnarly texture, but on a fine scale. The material was twisted, not woven, and hard to the touch, although it resembled leather. Perhaps it was made of a single fine strip of rawhide that had been varnished or soaked in resin before it was formed into a ring. The flower bud at the top was made from tiny closed loops of the same material.

"It's just a reminder, a memento, you could say."

"Of what?"

"Of who I am and where I came from." The violet eyes regarded him calmly, offering nothing else. He waited for her to say more, but she didn't. She had a way of watching him passively, yet he wondered now if she were quite as inexperienced as he first thought. If the ball was in his court it was because she had placed it there.

Finally she continued. "It was made from my umbilical cord." Her face was expressionless. "It's a link with my past. You look surprised."

Although he didn't think of himself as squeamish, the beer and corned beef hash mixture in Jeremy's stomach now came back to life and began to ferment with a sudden lurch. He felt like it was seeking a means of escape, and he didn't like either of the possible exit options. This is no time to be shy, he told himself. When you meet someone new, they're not likely to be just the same as everyone else you know. That's the point.

"I'm a little startled, that's all."

Once he had researched the hippie period of the 60s and 70s and he tried to recall now whether trinkets made from fetal materials were a feature of that era, but nothing came to mind. The only comparable thing he could think of was the Victorian jewelry made from the braided hair of the dead.

"Do you like it?" she went on, smiling now, her clear, guileless eyes fixed on his. "My mother made it for me. It's one of our customs. In our part of México, every child has one." Jeremy slowly released her hand, his fingers moving over her exquisite skin.

"It is unique," he said, not wanting to appear put off, but not caring to pursue it any further either, afraid there might be necklaces, bracelets, hair ornaments, brooches made from God knows what other discarded body parts. Even earrings, looping through pierced earlobes, dead flesh against the living. The beer and the corned beef hash in his stomach had drawn up battle lines and were now preparing for war. He shuddered involuntarily and she noticed it. Get a grip, he thought. This is the biggest opportunity of your life.

"Don't be put off by it," she said with a smile. "Would you like to go to my place for a drink?" It was not the smoothest of segues, but Jeremy's interest was captured more by the content than the style.

When they emerged from Antoine's they found a light dusting of snow had fallen while they had dinner. Although there was little wind, she drew her shoulders together against the cold. Coarse flakes were scattered over his windshield and the sidewalk, not enough to affect traffic, but sufficient to remind him that spring was not quite there. As they drove off in his rusty white Toyota Camry, she directed him toward her rooming house on West Dexter St.

They had driven only a block when she leaned her head on his shoulder.

"I'm glad you came into Antoine's tonight, Jeremy," she said. Hearing her say his name made his heart beat faster.

"Really? Why?" He felt there might be a compliment on the way. The last one he'd had from a woman came from his mother, concerning his grades.

"Because of all the men who were there tonight I picked you to spend the night with. I'm very happy with the choice." She turned her face upward and gave him a charming smile, but the news hit him like an unexpected shock, and his vision narrowed almost to a point. He realized that he could passionately desire something for a long time and still not be ready for it when it came. Even though the heater had not yet warmed, up he began to sweat again as he struggled to avoid hitting parked cars. He gripped the wheel in rigid silence. How could you respond to that? Here was his breakout opportunity looming, and it only filled him with terror.

"It's all right," Luisa said, placing her gloved hand on his leg. She pointed to a house on the right. "It's the one at the corner. My room is above the porch."

It was the largest house on a block of fading middle class bungalows that must have been a great place to live, Jeremy thought, even fashionable, ninety years before. He was happy to focus on something other than what was coming. The restoration junkies hadn't discovered the area yet, still occupied with Victorian properties closer to downtown. There was a cast-iron park bench in the front yard next to a streetlight of a discontinued pattern, but it still worked. At the opposite end of the bench sat a large rock, as high as the armrest. Someone's idea of landscaping, fifty years earlier.

Most windows of the house were unlit, but a bulb

over the deep porch lit the door enough to make the lock visible. The porch held several pieces of upholstered furniture that had been weathering for years. When they got to the door she struggled with the key. "I've been here only two days," she said. "I'm not used to it yet."

Inside the house, Luisa guided him up the front stairs, softened with a dusty brown runner, and paused on the second floor landing to search her purse for another key. Still trembling slightly, Jeremy could hear the impatient movements of an animal awaiting them on the other side of the door.

"I'm more comfortable at night, so I don't go out much during the day," she said. "Usually the light hurts my eyes, especially if it's coming off the snow. I don't think I'll be here long enough to get used to it."

"I always think of México as a bright, sunny place," he said, thinking of the winter light in Minnesota as nothing more than a pale glimmer making brief cameo appearances along the horizon at three-day intervals. "Tons of people from the Midwest go there in the winter, especially to Cancun."

"We don't have any beaches where I'm from, although there are lots of sands, and where I live the sun rarely shines. It's not much like the coast."

"You're just teasing me, aren't you?" he said with a smile. He was starting to really like her. He wasn't sure why, but she seemed unlike any girl he'd ever met. Luisa made him hope that his lifelong shyness had only been a passing phase, now receding. His hands were no longer trembling. He almost put a hand on her shoulder.

"No, it's true. You could even say that my people were driven underground many years ago."

"By an evil tyrant, I suppose," Jeremy said, and began to giggle nervously, but then stopped when she offered no response. Standing behind her, he couldn't stop looking at the fine skin of her neck as she finally located the room key and put it in the lock. Hadn't he noticed before on his own college trip to Cancun that Méxicans had exquisite skin? But Luisa's was paler than most. Maybe he'd never gotten this close before.

Inside, a fussy, overweight brown dog greeted her, ran over to slurp at its water bowl, and then, giving him a morose look, disappeared under the kitchen table. Jeremy sat down but then stood up immediately and removed his jacket. The animal emerged again from under the long tablecloth and began to sniff Jeremy's cuffs. It was a short-haired dog, with a flat narrow face like a pit bull, but smaller in scale. It had an expression of benign resignation, oddly like that of Luisa herself.

"That's Ortíz," she said. "I just call him Tease." Tease's left front leg was partly wrapped in something like leather, a rusty greenish color, rolled around what must have been an injured knee, then pinned at the top with a sharpened, but refined and polished piece of wood about four inches long. The wood looked like something that might once have been part of a hair ornament. Luisa was watching Jeremy.

"In this dry climate he's been nibbling at the skin on his leg, so I had to wrap it up. He doesn't like the taste of that suede material, so he leaves it alone, but he's not happy about it."

Tease turned to look up at Jeremy with a melancholy air and then went back under the table, now limping slightly as if he understood what she said. Jeremy heard him turn in a circle two or three times, then drop to the floor with a grunt and a sigh.

The room played too many roles, none of them well. Besides the kitchen table where they sat there was a single bed, a small television on a dresser with curved-front drawers, and a microwave on a counter near the window. Cotton print curtains framed a view of the park bench in the yard. Near the door, a sink hung on the wall with a towel bar next to it, the worn brown hand towel neatly folded. Everything Jeremy could see was worn, but immaculate. If Jeremy had been researching Luisa's life, he would have noted that she was a person of simple tastes, but he was almost too jittery to notice.

From under the patchy carpet, linoleum in a pink and green pattern extended to the baseboards, ribbed as it telegraphed the edges of old wood flooring beneath. It spoke of patching, but not replacing. Luisa didn't seem to notice. She appeared to be waiting for Jeremy to respond to her invitation to spend the night. Thinking of this conversation as well, which had not left his mind for an instant, he struggled to form a sentence.

"Luisa, I feel like I have to tell you something." He folded his hands on the table, feeling the cold sweat congealing like bacon fat in his armpits. "You probably don't realize this, but I'm not very experienced with women. In fact, I'm not experienced at all. I just don't know that I'll be very good with you. And I want to be."

He felt like he was hearing someone else's voice, a person much more detached and cool than he had ever been. His resolve was stretched thin between raging desire and stark panic.

"You must have had a bad experience in the

past," she said. "I could sense it. Am I right?"

Startled, he looked into her sympathetic eyes. The whole experience was something he could rarely bring himself to think about, far less talk about it. Naturally he had been careful never to research his problem.

"Worse than bad," he said, after a while, reminding himself of his resolve to take a chance of great magnitude.

"Tell me. It was a woman, right?"

"A girl."

"How old were you?"

"Sixteen. She was sixteen as well. It was my first date." He couldn't believe he was speaking about it. This was more than he'd ever said to anyone before. "I tried for months to get the courage to ask her to a dance, just a dumb unimportant high school dance. It wasn't the prom or anything like that. I could never have asked her to the prom."

"And then you did ask her, and she turned you down?"

"No! She said yes. I was shocked, and I agonized all week about what to wear, like a girl would do."

Jeremy began to sweat bullets. The memory had been buried for years.

"She left the dance with someone else," said Luisa calmly, when he didn't appear able to go on.

"How did you know that?"

"She was sixteen, you said. She was only testing her power. It happens all the time because it's what girls that age do. It wasn't anything about you. But you've always thought it was."

"I don't understand. . ."

"I can tell it by your face. You're seeing it again now."

He felt tears forming in his eyes and he turned away. Jeremy had never been the target of some great crime after all, only the victim of his own vulnerability, which he now realized was worse, since for years it had made him an accessory in his own victimhood.

"And that was the end of your social life," Luisa said matter-of-factly.

"The beginning and the end. It was my first and last date. Now every time when I think I might approach a woman I have the same reaction. That's why when I go out now it's mainly to not be alone. I'm having it again now, Luisa."

"But don't think that. This is your second date, to-night, right now. It's going better than you ever imagined it could. And you initiated things, remember? You picked me up."

Luisa leaned forward, smiling. Turning his face toward her, she placed her finger to his lips.

"It's all right, Jeremy, don't you see? We're scav-engers." As if this made sense of it. The "we" didn't seem to include him and there was no one else present. Or was it the dog? That might fit.

"We?" he said, not able to understand what the scavenger part might mean.

"The group that I'm part of," she said. "We're collectors of the discarded, experts of reuse. Do you know what I mean? Your situation is like a lot of other things. It's only a matter of finding the right niche for you. There's nothing wrong with you, Jeremy. I want to underline that. You've only been a bad fit until now. You need to go somewhere else, a place where you'll fit in as if you were meant to be there." She made a vague gesture with her hands that didn't clarify it any further. "Don't you see? You can have what you want. Let's talk." She nodded vigorously.

The idea that his problem was mainly geographic, one of dislocation rather than personality, was not something he'd ever considered. It had always seemed to wrap around him like a shroud, traveling where he did, often even in the lead.

But hope could be anywhere, except St. Paul, apparently.

"What group is it that you're part of?" he asked, still trying to wrap his mind around this idea, which had a strangely promising aura. Was it a religion, or even a union of militant recyclers who went about announcing themselves as scavengers? Was there a secret handshake when they met to sort through old cans? A private high sign for aluminum or copper? His researcher's mind rapidly ticked off the options. Research had often been his hiding place as well as his livelihood. There was a comfort in facts that reality did not often possess.

"Kiss me," she said suddenly. She pulled him closer, and moved her chair toward his, drawing his head down to hers. Her arms encircled his neck and he felt himself pulled into her kiss. Her tongue suddenly gripped his in a way he didn't understand and had never encountered in the literature, much less in person. It didn't seem possible; and yet it was a thrilling sensation. He drew back, but she held on to his wrists with her small hands.

"Luisa, let me see your tongue," he said, surprising himself at the firmness of his tone. She shook her head slowly and drew back. "You won't like it."

"I liked it, I really did, but I want to see it, too."

She opened her mouth slightly and thrust her tongue out between her lips. It was forked for an inch at the end, otherwise pink and healthy-looking. Vigorous. As he stared at it she made the two tips touch side to side, then divided them vertically, one up, one down. She closed her mouth and grinned.

"Jesus Christ!" he said, trying hard not to react, but feeling himself pulling back in the chair, retreating into his fear. "Why is that?" As if body parts required explanations. He had not kissed many girls, perhaps two, but surely this was not right.

"It's connected to our diet, I guess, or evolution," she said steadily, and paused, calmly watching his response. None of this seemed to agitate her. "Why not? We have two nostrils, two ears, why not two tips to the tongue? I said that I was a little different, remember? But it sounds like different might be right for you, since normal hasn't been working that well."

Jeremy considered this. Luisa had also said she was from México, and he knew that many different indigenous groups made up the population. Who knew what variety lay within their gene pool? A small difference like this could be completely normal, even in someone as beautiful as Luisa. She was right; he was different himself, and maybe the problem had been that he was trying to connect with women who weren't different enough for him.

He was still pondering this when she stood up, and, loosening her skirt, stepped out of it, letting it slip to the floor. Suppressing a gasp, Jeremy watched it fall, embarrassed, feeling the sweat break out on his forehead, trying not to look at her body, yet compelled to do so.

She was beautiful, well made in a way that, to him, suggested a work of art. Could the end of his misery be rushing toward him? Everything she had said was meant to be encouraging. But her willingness to bring him along trumped everything. After his initial queasiness he now found excitement. They had come this far, and there was still no rejection from her. He'd been honest with her, something he found it hard to be with any other girl. Soon it would be too late to turn him away. He put his hands on the sides of his head, feeling the throb of his pulse even in the back of his eyes.

To keep his fingers from touching her, he picked up the skirt, immediately noticing the fine hand of the fabric, which didn't seem to be a weave. It was not thin or sheer, but thick to the touch, yet oddly soft and pliant. Somehow silky and not like any cloth he'd ever felt. Every time he got close to her he found something new to digest. She saw his look.

"This is my best skirt. I wore it for tonight. It's bat fur," she said. "A luxury with us, but because the fiber is so short, it can't be woven, it's felted."

"You mean it's pressed together like a hat?"

She only nodded.

Luisa pulled off her sweater and he looked at her body again, naked but for dark stockings that came just above her knees. Very sensible, he thought idiotically, not yet able to fully come to grips with the idea that here was a nearly naked girl standing next to him.

Luisa sat down again, and crossing one leg over the other, she began to pull the stockings off too. She seemed much like pictures he'd seen on the Internet, but only the classier ones. Perhaps they'd just gotten off to an awkward start because of his inexperience. He wasn't seeing anything else that seemed strange. Maybe it was time to cut the girl a little slack. His own strength was growing. Jeremy suddenly realized that his gut panic reaction at being so close to making love to her was gone. In its place was a feeling he could barely recognize. It was almost recklessness, a term he'd only encountered before in researching other people.

She smiled at his intent look. "You have to realize," she said, "that I'm still very young."

Please God, he thought, not that young. She must be eighteen at least, maybe even twenty.

His momentum was immediately replaced by a chill. So there it was, now that he was coming out of himself, as startling and unwelcome as a missionary ringing the doorbell during dinner. Now that he had come this far, he knew something like that would appear to stop him, and of course, it would crop up right at the end when they were almost in bed. He felt himself deflating like a hot air balloon with the propane flame gone out.

Yet, he thought, she's filled out like a grown-up. Worst case, she could be what? Sixteen? He tried to remember if that was the legal age in Minnesota. It was an issue he had never researched because it seemed to have no possible bearing on his life.

"Just as you told me about your greatest disaster, I'm going to be frank with you. I'm not yet seventy," she went on. "Not until spring. Another month. Please don't think I'm too young for you." The corners of her mouth turned downward, yet at the same time he sensed she was somehow teasing him. For just a moment, Jeremy felt his stomach churn again, but then it went away. She was only making a joke. It relaxed him that Luisa was taking this so lightly. Perhaps she was prompting him to do the same.

"I don't think I understand," he mumbled. "Help me with this. You look like you couldn't be more than twenty." And why wouldn't this be flattering, if she were really sixty-nine? Without realizing it, Jeremy was having his first insights into women.

Her violet eyes stared back at him with sympathy and compassion. You have so much to learn, they seemed to say. This part was no surprise. She pressed a small hand to his cheek. He briefly wondered whether she might be not completely sane to be behaving so differently from other women, but put the thought aside. He really liked her, and he needed her to be completely, totally, sane, especially in her insights into his situation. After all, she appeared to be making allowances for him, why not reciprocate?

"The people I come from live longer than you do, Jeremy. It's not very scary, but we're more like a racial subgroup. Because of this, our childhood and youth are both longer. We have more time to learn. Trust me, it's a good thing. I've had more than forty years of schooling, and I speak nine languages. I've had two years devoted exclusively to English slang. In college I had four majors and twelve minors. I'm even a terrific welder, which is my job back home. All of us do this, or other things like it. Should I say something to you in Croatian?"

"Maybe later. I often try to speak Croatian myself just before closing time at Antoine's." He waited for her to laugh, but she didn't seem to get it. "Right now I'm trying to keep up with everything you've said in English. The group you come from, are these people the scavengers you mentioned?" he said, now looking at her frankly. She had made no attempt to cover herself.

"You could say that. There have been only six generations of us." She pulled his head closer to her breast, offering him a choice of two exquisite nipples. They did not remind him of his earlier experience in the computer lab.

"Six generations," he repeated, staring at her breasts, thinking with the 10% of his brain still operating that six normal generations would take her family back to about the 1840s. Was it somehow a new branch line of evolution? He knew from his research that this could happen.

"We're all descended from one man in México, Juan de Arenas, and his wife, Elena. They were first cousins. She was an Arenas too. Her father was Juan's uncle, his father's brother. It was not that unusual at the time, especially among noble families in Spain."

"So you're an Arenas as well?" he said, startled, thinking of Mark Sands and the bishop and the student teacher. This was making no sense at all. What possible connection could there be with Luisa, and why was that name still turning up?

"Of course. We all are. It's the only family name among us. There has been some breeding among outsiders, but not much. Pregnancies are difficult to achieve. In the few cases when they happen with people . . . like you, the names are usually lost, or just never mentioned again. They don't matter much."

She seemed to be suggesting that Jeremy's genes were not of the highest quality, his name not worth recalling. The last part he already knew from other women.

All right, he thought. It made sense that pregnancies could be difficult at seventy. A shock of fear suddenly went through him. If Luisa was an Arenas, then she could be on someone's murder list too. There must be a plot to kill them all, and he felt a sudden need to protect her.

"But I did some research on the family," he said. "Juan de Arenas, if it's the same one you're talking about, came to México with Hernan Cortés in 1519. He was given what became the Santa Elena region to govern in 1529, subject to being able to bring it under control. How could you be only six generations away from him? That's almost five hundred years ago."

"It's the long childhood, Jeremy, as I said." Luisa placed her elbows on the table and leaned toward him. "There is much to prepare for in being an adult. Surely you've seen people in your own genetic group reach the proper age and yet not be ready for what was expected of them."

"Often, it's almost the norm now. So you were born in 1941?" Jeremy was born in 1986.

"Yes, in April. Now I'm approaching my fertile years. This could be an important time for you. I'm very excited and I think you ought to be too." For the first time she gave him a look he thought was coy. "Of course," he said, not at all certain that he was excited about her fertility. "How long does that last, your fertile period?"

"Perhaps another sixty years. It varies."

He nodded. "So you could have many children?"

"In theory, but most likely only one. As I said, it is difficult to become pregnant. Most women never do. You have to try constantly, night after night. That's where you come in." She gave him a glowing smile that showed her small, even teeth. "Of course, not many children are needed. We live long lives and our environment doesn't support a large population."

"What do you mean, your environment?"

"Perhaps it's better not to say too much more at this point. I sense you're becoming uncomfortable."

"Uncomfortable? You're kidding, right? Luisa, you're very pretty in a different sort of way, and I do like you a lot." His voice became squeaky here, "but I'm not sure I can do this. It's kind of strange."

"Just come along with me. I can take you to a new world."

Jeremy was starting to warm to this, wondering whether one of her minors had been psychology, but there was another bend or two in the trail.

"My hesitation is nothing about you, OK? There's nothing wrong with the way you are. I'm just not sure I can get used to this. I've never seen it before. There's nothing in the research that . . . " He sensed himself chattering.

She placed her hand on his wrist and he stopped. "Jeremy, that's not it. It's only that you've never done it before because you haven't found the right woman. But that's over now, and here's a simple insight. I'm the right woman. I know I can help you, if you'll only let me."

"How?" Here it was, the real thing. Yet an uneasy sensation in his abdomen suggested the problem was not entirely over.

"Like this." She reached into the pocket on the front of her skirt where it lay folded across a chair, then opened her hand palm upward in front of his face and blew into it. Her own face, still smiling, quickly blurred and he frowned as he started to rise and lurched toward the bed. It seemed to be slowly rotating away from him as he fell face down on the tattered quilt. It would have smelled musty if he'd still been fully conscious. An alarmed grunt came from Tease under the table, and the last thing Jeremy was aware of was that someone was turning him over onto his back and loosening his belt. Then there was darkness, or bliss.

He regained consciousness several times over the next ten minutes, each time finding Luisa straddling him, and both of them engaged in a passionate moment of a kind that was new to him. Whenever his eyes opened she blew more pixie dust into his face. It made for a surreal experience, like opening and closing a door repeatedly on a scene he urgently wanted to view in its entirety, and from the beginning. Details count, he would have thought, if he had been at all coherent.

Later, Luisa lay on her stomach, naked on the narrow bed. It was over. From under the tablecloth Tease put out his head and watched them with a sorrowful look, hurt and confused. Jeremy, now continuously conscious and enjoying a fragmented afterglow, looked at her body, how finely made she was. The soft pale skin. The odd delicate line of short hair that ran from the back of her neck down her vertebrae, ending at the base of her spine, just where her buttocks began to divide.

He began to see her as a member of a different, but closely related, race, perhaps one that had never been classified and named. Just as if her ancestors had come from Africa or China, Luisa's had come from somewhere in México, which was not nearly as foreign, he felt.

His own Luisa was still human, or at least de-

scended from more familiar humans a mere six generations back, and the picture he was getting was that she
was part of an isolated group, begun by inbreeding and
still inbred, coming from a tragic situation that had somehow started with Juan de Arenas and his first-cousin wife.
The fact that it went on with subsequent generations—as
a researcher, he'd seen this before—was what happened
when a group had no contact with the main population
for a while, like Darwin found in the Galapagos Islands.
She did say that pregnancies were difficult to achieve.

Yet there was no doubt she was now his woman.
He was glad she had forced him into it. They would be
doing it again soon, and this time he planned to remain
awake through it. A sudden recollection crossed his mind
of the powder on Mark Sands' dining room floor, but it
was the wrong moment to bring it up.

His eyes now traveled downward along her thigh,
past the hollow behind her normal-looking knee, over the
curve of her calf muscle, and past her ankle to the bottom
of her foot. Unconsciously he counted her toes. Excellent!
There were only five of them on each foot! How strange
could this be? He felt his doubts evaporating.

She turned and faced him with a satisfied smile.
As a great wave of emotion passed over him, he realized
once again how lovely she was.

"Jeremy, you were great," she said, beaming. "I
probably won't even have to put you out next time, will I?"

He shook his head slowly, looking at her with a
steady gaze. At nearly seventy, she looked fresh and innocent, and she was certainly his girl in a way no girl had
ever cared to be.

"What was that stuff you blew in my face?" he

asked, more comfortable now, almost ready for a cigarette, although he had never smoked, but still keeping the sheet over his chest. "I know it was to relax me."

"Just our standard party mix; an anesthetic with a dash of glitter." She shook her long hair out and ran her fingers through it, not returning his gaze. She had taken off the scorpion-in-amber hair clasp when she undressed.

"But it put me right out; how could I party?"

"It was so *I* could party," she said, giving him a sly grin.

"So where do you get it, and why the glitter?"

"We make it up in our lab right—well, I'll tell you later. The glitter is our reference to sand. You know that Arenas means sands, right? It's like our signature, our calling card. It says, maybe you forced us underground, baby, but we're still here and we're thriving. Better watch your back." The last sentence had a peculiar emphasis, and her sly grin disappeared, replaced by a look of commitment.

What a girl, he thought, looking at the graceful yet fierce determination in her face. This was going to be an unusual relationship, but different was good, it stretched your capabilities; a new thought for him. Breakout had begun; in fact, it was finished and behind him. The main thing was to just relax and let it flow, take whatever came next. This was something Rebecca had once said to him and he'd placed it in his notes without quite believing it.

He wondered what Luisa might like for her birthday, now looming on the horizon. How did you buy a present for someone this special? It was clearly the appropriate thing to do. She might like something else in bat fur, something tailored if he could find it. Maybe a beret would be a possibility, or even a blazer. Although he'd never been in one of their stores, he'd heard that Talbot's was good for smaller sizes. What colors did she like besides mouse and heather? And couldn't almost anyone wear black? Maybe just stick to accessories, gloves or a belt perhaps. Play it safe, go slowly, even as his life took wing.

This looked like it could be something unique and wonderful.

CHAPTER 7

Rebecca spent the next three days on her computer roughing out scenes from the Mark Sands murder mystery, trying to imagine situations in which Ken Abrams and Lester Grunge were partners, but it wasn't working. On the page, Lester was much more real to her than Ken, and he didn't have any of the back and neck problems she had noticed with the St. Paul detective.

She realized she had forgotten to contact Jeremy about researching Cantú, but when she opened her email, she leaped up from her computer in a state of shock. After reading it on the screen twice, she printed Jeremy's incoming message and held the copy in her hand, scanning it word by word for hidden meanings, for anything that would make sense of it.

Rebecca—I've gone to Santa Elena, México. There's no other way to start this note but to state it flat out. I'll be staying here with a girl named Luisa. I've fallen in love with her. Yes, I know this is a shock. It is to me too. I've never mentioned her to you because I just met her. There is literally no way to describe her except to say that she's not like anyone I've ever known. I believe she loves me too.

I have reason to believe that she is somehow connected to this situation with Mark Sands and the others because her last name is also Arenas (!), but I'm not sure yet what the connection is. It can't be in any sinister way, so don't think that, and she may even be able to help us. You can see why I feel protective of her, since this may be a plot to wipe out her family.

And here is a surprise! She actually knows your painter Rafael Cantú! I have my laptop with me—in fact, I'm sending this from the Santa Elena airport right now—they have wi-fi—and I'll still be able to continue with any research you need. Please let me know you received this because Luisa told me communications here can sometimes be spotty. Life is great if you just seize the initiative!
Jeremy Wyman

Rebecca sat down at her desk again, shaking her head. Seize the initiative? Was this the same Jeremy Wyman who did research for her? He sounded bewitched. Vague as they were, the possible implications of Jeremy's email were flooding her mind and the wind seemed to go out of her as she hit the chair. She hadn't brought him up to speed on what she and Abrams had learned because she properly felt that, as police business, it was meant to be kept confidential, even though Abrams had not said this outright. She was privileged to be in on it herself, but it was only because she'd committed to seeing things he missed, she thought, as she hit the reply command.

Hi Jeremy, got your note. More to follow later, once I talk to Ken Abrams. My first reaction, though, is BE CAREFUL! This is bigger than you think. Locate Cantú if you can. It seems he may be down there, but DO NOT approach him. It's looking more and more as if he could be dangerous.
Rebecca

She paused for a moment before hitting send,

wondering if she should also warn him against the girl, Luisa, or against anyone who was in contact with Rafael Cantú, but thought better of it. Obviously, given his new relationship, Jeremy would not be in a state of mind to hear anything against her. She recalled her old boyfriend Matt when she'd first started sleeping with him. His focus in life had quickly shrunk to a small area between her knees and her waistband—the sap had been unable to think of anything else. "I have a face, too, and a brain," she'd said to him one evening at dinner. When he struggled to find a response, she saw the end of their relationship come into view, distant, but inevitable.

She dialed Ken Abrams.

"I don't have any idea what to make of this. I don't know him," he said, after listening to her read the email. "It seems strange that he would run across someone here who not only knows Cantú but is also named Arenas, just at the time we're investigating this case. This feels like he's being setup."

"That's what alarms me. That this girl claims to know Cantú is bad enough, but Jeremy's suddenly being impulsive as well. It's not like him. I don't think he's ever had a girlfriend, or if he has he's never mentioned it to me. The fact that he says he's in love with her suggests he's been swept away, that he's got no experience. Besides, other than mentioning the bishop and the student teacher, I kept him out of the loop on everything else you and I came up with. He's walking into this a complete innocent, and God knows what this girl is up to. I'm going after him. I feel responsible now."

"I'm glad you said that. I just got clearance an hour ago to set up a Cantú interview myself, if it can be done. There's a flight in the morning. I wonder if you'd like to go down to México with me?"

Jeremy had arrived in Santa Elena on an early evening flight. He sent the email to Rebecca, then killed some time at the airport digging into the research he had printed out before he left. He was appreciative of Luisa's gift of a guidebook and he read the parts relating to Santa Elena history on the plane, but he was more trusting of his own intuition to root out the Internet sources that might have a different slant. He started with the obvious.

Once the standard historical guide, R. F. Polanski's book on northern México had been out of print for years, but Jeremy was able to find lengthy excerpts on someone else's travel site. Writing in the early 70s, Polanski hadn't been taken seriously by some travelers because of his irreverent style and fondness for gossip and unproven anecdote, but Jeremy knew his habit of connecting individual families with events might prove interesting. In Polanski's chapter on the second wave of conquest Jeremy found the following:

It is unfortunate that Juan de Arenas left behind no notes tracing his thinking in choosing the site for his capital, Santa Elena, but part of it must have been a concern about security. The local Pichancha Indians had never been subject to the nearby Aztec empire, and had only on rare occasions been persuaded to pay the Aztecs tribute, and then only for brief periods. When Montezuma and his court fell to Cortés, the Indians around Santa Elena shed no tears and simply went about their business, yet always keeping a wary eye on the Conquistadores.

Heading northwest from the mostly pacified Aztec territory in 1529 with an escort of 420 Spaniards, just over 200 Tlaxcalan Indians—mostly men—and 165 horses, Arenas found the route to his new domains blocked at every point by these implacable Pichanchas. They fought from ambush with deadly accuracy, poisoning streams, and rolling boulders into his encampments at night in the narrow arroyos, where they fractured horses' legs and crushed men's bodies as they slept. On one occasion they diverted a stream that became an inundation sweeping through Arenas' camp, carrying away part of his baggage train. Two days were lost while they tried to recover their gear miles downstream, as the Pichanchas picked them off from the cliffs above. Just nine days out of México City the invaders' numbers had been reduced by nearly twenty percent, and Juan de Arenas was woefully rethinking his strategy. Meanwhile unrest grew within his ranks because after the first few days he hadn't paused to bury any more of the dead. The Pichanchas just disinterred the ones they had buried during the first few days and fed them to their dogs.

According to the diary of his third in command, Pedro Alvarez Olvido, a decision was made to attempt to capture, and if possible level, the great fortified Pichancha capital at what the Spanish invaders called Monte Tres Reyes. No security seemed likely for the settlers without the immediate subjugation of the Pichanchas.

Two days later Juan de Arenas deployed his forces on the plain before Monte Tres Reyes, carefully avoiding the thousands of lethally spiked agave plants smeared with coyote dung. Either Olvido chose not to describe the ensuing battle itself, or the pages from his unbound journal that dealt with it have been removed from the archives in Spain. It is known from brief references in other sources, however, that Arenas's forces had four small cannon with them and, in a three-day battle, the hilltop fortress was taken and the surviving Pichanchas put to the sword, except for the younger women. .

The Spaniards and their Indian allies found themselves in

possession of a table-like mountaintop ideally suited for defense—except against cannon—and broad enough to accommodate a substantial city. A shallow depression roughly in the center held a small lake that was spring fed from within the mountain itself. There was an ample supply of water there, while the surrounding country had little. In the weeks that followed, dozens of additional Pichanchas emerged from tunnels and warrens within the mountain, only to be put to death on sight. Several generations passed, however, before the Tres Reyes mountain was recognized for what it was; a long extinct volcano with a thick mantle of silted-over lava ideal for agriculture on the surface, quarrying building materials, or tunneling inside, just as various springs and rivers had already done naturally.

Today, urbanization, highway construction, and the simple passage of time have all taken their toll on the Tres Reyes mountain, now known officially as Ciudad Santa Elena de la Vera Cruz—City of St. Helena of the True Cross. The great mound itself was long ago swallowed up by the hungry reach of the city, and the environs of Santa Elena, now with a population of more than four million, extend outward onto the surrounding plain. It is México's third largest city, a business and banking center, a major agricultural marketing hub for the northwest central part of the country. It is the largest grain and meat packing center in the nation, and distributes tequila to a grateful world. Two Japanese and one European auto manufacturer have plants there. Although no longer overtly active politically, the large and powerful Arenas family still manages much of the city's economy from behind the scenes. Through their agents, they serve as landlords for the twenty-nine per cent of Santa Elena real estate they still own. Prudently, the aristocratic "de" was dropped from their name during the 1910 Revolution. However, few were fooled at the time, nor is anyone now.

In Googling Arenas in conjunction with modern Santa Elena, Jeremy then came up with the following in

141

a (translated) magazine article about upcoming Méxican society weddings, particularly in families with a long history or a breath of scandal. This writer had done a bit of digging and obviously had sources within the Santa Elena police.

At its head (that of the Arenas family) presently stands the white haired but still vigorous patriarch Enrique Arenas, sixty-three years old, ruling from behind the gates of the 14,000 acre Hacienda Milagro. He is rarely, if ever, seen outside the grounds, which begin just six kilometers from the autopista that encircles Santa Elena. He would be the first to acknowledge that he owes his longevity to luck, having survived four assassination attempts. Yet he would be surprised to learn that, according to some sources, he has also survived two others that failed less spectacularly, and therefore never came to light. But the thing that nearly drives him over the edge is that he does not know who his enemies are, or why they are so determined to kill him and his family.

Naturally, heavy security is anticipated at the wedding of Enrique Arenas' daughter Angelina, to, if you can imagine, one her father's bodyguards. With a guest list of more than 200 notables from as far away as Buenos Aires and Madrid, it is scheduled for two o'clock on March 27.

Enrique Arenas is known as a religious man, and within the 9,000-square-foot residence portion of the hacienda is a private family chapel which replicates to the last detail the chapel in the original Arenas fortified palace that once stood within the old citadel of Santa Elena. This chapel was destroyed in the 1656 earthquake, which also brought down the adjacent cathedral just fifteen years after its completion. Fortunately, the original Arenas chapel drawings survived in a Spanish archive.

Construction of a new cathedral, based on Baroque designs, was begun one year to the day later, March 26, 1657, but the Arenas family had already moved their main residence to their primary hacienda in the countryside, where it has been ever since.

The ruins of the original cathedral, and the adjacent citadel that held the first Arenas Palace, were never cleared because of a pronouncement by the bishop that since God had decreed their destruction, it would be sacrilegious to reverse His judgment, and the ruins ought to stand for all time as a reminder of the folly of human pride. The bishop was no doubt thinking of the Arenases, with whom he had crossed swords several times in the past.

Now, consecrated as a memorial, portions of the old cathedral's nave still stand, as well as the lower walls of the citadel and the Arenas Palace, in a preserve directly behind the new cathedral, dedicated this time to God's mercy. This complex of ruins, fenced elaborately in wrought iron and open to processions on only a few major church feast days, is now one of the most popular tourist attractions in Santa Elena. Seeing it fills the heads of visitors with pious thoughts and inspires numerous donations, which partly accounts for its continued survival.

Oddly, in recent years, seismologists and students of plate tectonics who have studied the area have unanimously concluded that no such earthquake as the one recorded in 1656 ever occurred, despite the physical evidence presented by the ruins. According to their opinion, the caldera of the ancient volcano on which Santa Elena rests was effectively just a random blow-hole in an otherwise solid tectonic plate of considerable thickness, hundreds of miles in from its edge. It was only one of nature's pressure valves from a much earlier geological era, somewhat like a pimple on the smooth cheek of an adolescent earth. The conditions at the time of the Conquest and following were simply not right for an earthquake. The experts attribute the collapse of the cathedral and citadel to faulty building techniques, or design flaws.

The Catholic Church has summarily dismissed these con-

clusions as vain and secular in nature.

As Jeremy finished these articles, he sat in the uncomfortable black leather and chrome airport chair thinking about the odd chain of events that had gotten him to this point. It was the first time since it began in Antoine's that he'd really had the time or the distance to examine it seriously. Being in another country helped give it perspective.

Jeremy had made love to Luisa twice more during that first night, neither time requiring anesthesia from the pixie dust, and aside from some irritating particles remaining in his airways, he felt that his entire life had been heading toward this single point of bliss.

He was preparing to go back home in the morning and about to ask her when they would see each other again, when she told him that because the St. Paul climate was damaging to her health, she had to return to México almost immediately, and that she wanted him to come with her. There was nothing shy in the expression on her face as she said this. As startled as he was by it, the idea of staying behind and losing touch with her was impossible to contemplate.

Since everything else in his personal life was already moving at light speed, it didn't seem like an unusual request. Luisa had already upended his existence. He could go home and boot his computer, but he could never return to what his life had been. As far as his job went, there was no reason he couldn't do his research from México, or anywhere else that she might wish to go. He could even brush up on his Spanish online.

Jeremy paused for a mental inventory. What kind of life did he have in St. Paul anyway? Up until now he'd had no love life and hardly any social life. He hated the weather, when everything was battened down and driven inside for five months a year. It was a life that felt safe and almost comfortable, but certainly unfulfilling. But being safe wasn't taking him anywhere. Worst of all, it didn't hold the tiniest seed of change. It promised to be exactly what it was now ten years down the road. He could see nothing holding him in St. Paul but mindless inertia. A life where he was looking through a window and watching himself go through the motions. All this passed through his head in a flash as he stared back at Luisa, who awaited his answer.

He took a step forward and pressed her to his chest. "Luisa, I'm ready to go."

As she wrapped herself around him, a brief look of satisfaction crossed her face that he didn't see.

She then told him they wouldn't be traveling to Santa Elena together. It was something about Ortiz, she said. Because he had started life as a street dog, Tease didn't take to those little plastic boxes they used for animals in planes; they made him start to gnaw at other parts of his body, and he was now too old to survive much more self-abuse of that kind. His skin had become fragile and easily infected; witness the current problem on his leg. Instead, she would meet Jeremy behind the Santa Elena Cathedral, at the main gate to the ruins in two days time, at three in the morning. Anyone could find it. She handed him a current guidebook to Santa Elena, saying he could read it on the plane trip down. How considerate of her that it was in English. Jeremy was amazed at how pre-pared she was for things that were obviously the product of pure chance, like their meeting at Antoine's.

"Pay particular attention to the history of the place, so that what I tell you when we're there will make sense."

If Jeremy had thought about it, which he was not in a frame of mind to do, he might also have wondered how Luisa was going to join him in less than forty hours at a point in a foreign country that was more than 2,000 miles away from where they now stood, and without fly-ing. If she had told him that later that day, she and Tease would be returning to Rebecca's condo, where one of the figures in the Cantú painting would let them in, and they would pass back into the image within the frame, and from there to Santa Elena, he would have laughed.

It's possible that Jeremy's head was simply filled with ecstatic thoughts of his new love, and instead of ana-lyzing it, he only reacted to the idea that they wouldn't be together for a couple of days. It was disappointing, but if he thought this was odd, it was less so than many other things about Luisa, and he raised no protest. He had the sense of blindly feeling his way into a relationship, the first real one he'd ever had, and if that meant he'd be more tentative than he was about most other things, then so be it. She had kissed him sweetly as they parted, and he was left with the unique sensation of his entire life filled with moments like this.

"Don't get a hotel room when you arrive," was the last thing she said. "You can stay with me." She gave him a promising wink.

In the airport, Jeremy had awakened with a start sometime after one o'clock, stiff all over and with a cramp in his knee. After a walk around the terminal and a cup of bad coffee, he checked his email and then took a cab to centro, shocked into alertness by the insane violence of the traffic, even at that hour. Now, still trembling from the experience, his throat and eyes burning, he stood at the locked gate of the ruins, looking through the ornate bars into dark, incoherent masses of masonry clotted with weeds. Remnants of a wall with buttresses faced him, but most of it was not more than six or eight feet high, and in places nothing remained. Within those gaps the darkness was intense. There were a few ground lights around the periphery, but deep in the interior all he could see clearly was the chaotic black silhouette against the city-lit night sky, where he could look through the high empty windows of the single remaining wall of the old cathedral, emerging in silent warning from the rubble beneath it.

Why had Luisa wanted to meet here? Was it because it was such a dramatic setting for his first night in Santa Elena? She definitely had her romantic side.

As he stood at the fence, he tried to imagine the great dome falling, according to some reports, turning as it crumbled, which destabilized the thick adjoining walls, except for the single one that remained. The curved walls behind the altar had been pushed outward into the citadel behind, causing it to collapse as well, domino-like, into the old Arenas Palace at the end of the complex. On the Internet Jeremy had done some additional work on the controversy regarding the cause of the collapse, reading both more views of the church and those of scientists, and concluded that since it happened about 350 years before, there wasn't going to be any easy solution to it now. Even skillful research had its limits, but in this case, he tended to favor the view of the scientists, who drew no moral lessons from it, rather than the churchmen.

There was a slight chill to the windless night, but it was still much warmer than at home in St. Paul. He heard no one approach, but suddenly a small warm hand slipped into his and then Luisa was in his arms. There was no sign of Tease.

He looked at her in the glow from the ground lights. Her hair was pulled back into a ponytail and tied with a braided leather thong with beads on the ends. She wore snug jeans with rhinestones on the back pockets and a shirt of indeterminate color with flapped pockets on the front. He wondered briefly if she weren't dressing too young, but then dismissed the thought. She knew her own culture, and in her heart she was twenty. She was in Jeremy's mind as well.

"I've missed you very much," she said into his ear, as he bent to kiss her. "Come with me, darling, I'm taking you home."

It didn't occur to him to be alarmed at this, and his fingers traveled over her spine, caressing the perfect texture of her skin.

Soon I'm going to meet the family, he thought. I hope we can find a moment to be alone afterward. An entire night didn't seem likely, although how much supervision did she really need at her age? The family members were probably much like her, their genetic differences would be more or less obvious. He suddenly felt queasy because he'd never been introduced as the boyfriend before. It would be even more awkward because he wasn't one of them. Having a flash of panic, he suddenly felt like an Eastern European immigrant with poor language skills showing up for a date with the daughter of a well-established family, in this case a noble one. Maybe on the surface they would be formally polite, and only after the door had closed behind him would they bend over double, hooting with laughter at his crude manners and cheap funny clothes, his stumbling ineptitude with their language. The way he mispronounced everyone's names. They would dance about, mocking him and mimicking his mistakes. So be it: he had been an outsider before with no payoff. This time it was worth it. The single fact of being with Luisa would make him invulnerable to whatever the future offered.

As she led him around the outside of the complex, he towed his red suitcase, with its broken zipper and plastic wheels, crunching over the gravel walk. Although there was no one around to disturb, he felt like a noisy intruder. After about fifty yards they stopped. He thought they were about the go back down the gentle slope and leave the plaza. Instead, she handed him a piece of fabric she pulled from her sleeve, just as the nuns in grade school used to pull out a tissue. As he touched her hand to take it, he felt the umbilical ring again. She had never been without it since he met her. Jeremy had come too far to feel squeamish about it anymore.

"Put this on for a blindfold," she said. "I can't show you the way in, and I'll explain later. We've got a few rules about security here. I don't make them, but they do seem to keep people from wandering in by accident."

"What? Wandering in?" he said, as he tied it

behind his head. "Isn't this just our meeting place? I thought we were going back into the city? How am I going to navigate all that traffic blindfolded? It's crazy once you leave the Plaza."

Luisa placed a firm hand on his wrist. He hadn't known her grip could be so strong.

"Jeremy, listen to me. We're going under the ruins. That's where I live. You'll find it perfectly civilized, more so, in fact, than out here, believe me."

"Your family is underground?" He felt suddenly breathless.

"I told you that in St. Paul."

"When you said that I thought it was just a metaphor, like the Underground Railway. It was a series of safe houses." He wished now he could see her. "Why would anyone live underground?"

"Because of our small differences, we've been victims of discrimination in the past. It's safer there."

Finding himself at a crossroads, Jeremy hesitated. The scene he had imagined as breaking out from his old life featured vistas of bright sunlight, lacy trees rustling in the breeze above a picnic lunch, possibly with Luisa in a sundress, running barefoot in slow-motion through grassy meadows, like in a deodorant commercial at home.

Living below ancient ruins sounded more like what he'd left behind in St. Paul, at least psychologically. It was a kind of emotional winter, followed by no spring. He realized he was not going to go from having nothing to having everything. Now, on one side of the scale was life with Luisa in what looked like a difficult setting. On the other side there was only his difficult past without her. The choice was still clear, but since he'd paid his dues so thoroughly, over and over again, why wasn't the outcome perfect? He was fighting back a sense of panic again.

Luisa put her hand on his cheek and a sense of calm swept over him. Her touch was magical.

"Jeremy, do you know what I sense about you? Why I brought you here? You're just like us! A little bit off the main road sometimes, but still OK. That's why I like you, and I like you a lot! I feel like I got lucky!"

No woman had ever said this to him before. He made his choice. After all, he could always leave if he found it intolerable. If that happened, and they'd been together for a while, she might go with him.

The traffic noise was far away, at the edges of the plaza. Jeremy pulled the blindfold down from one eye and took a last look at the pale night sky, starless from the reflected city lights, then pulled the cloth back over his eyes. It had a musty smell, as if it had been buried for a long time and recently exhumed. Luisa's people probably didn't have many visitors, so it didn't get much use. So far this was not making much sense, but he'd been having far better luck lately with things that didn't than anything that did, so he was more than ready to go with it. At this point he'd accumulated a certain amount of confidence in her. Luisa's instincts had been right ever since she met him in Antoine's. For example, she had sensed that he was ready to embrace someone like her. The fact that he now felt like a man rather than a hapless exile trapped in an extended childhood was all her doing, and although he was beginning to suspect she had planned their connection for reasons that were obscure to him, it didn't matter. It was what it was; his life was now in motion.

Was this how the sad story ended? The hard-boiled realist investigator saunters away from his frustrating life with a woman on his arm that makes him the envy of any man who sees them. He doesn't bother to glance back at them. It might be time to redesign his web page.

Luisa guided him farther down the fence line. "Just a bit more," she said. His free hand gripped each upright as they passed. Then, "Stop here."

He set the suitcase down and put his arms out blindly, his right hand connecting with a gate, more irregular on the barred surface, perhaps hammered out long ago in some colonial smithy. A latch was thrown and a pivot moved, old metal on metal, more shudder than squeak. She guided him forward a few steps. Metal pivoted on metal again behind him as she took his hand and said, "There are five steps here, with a hand rail on the right." She placed his fingers around it. "When we get to the bottom, give me your suitcase so you can have both your hands free, and I'll come back for you."

He waited for a moment at the base of the steps, a breeze stirring now within the unseen ruins, hearing the crunch of gravel underfoot, the creak of hinges. Her footsteps moved farther away, the suitcase skittering along behind her, and then after a moment they returned. The air was now cooler, as if he stood within a place the sun had never found. The chill froze some of his resolve. Of course, he told himself, trust is part of this, and who had trusted him more than Luisa, to make him her lover, and now to bring him to her secret home? His task was now to trust her.

Something rushed at him from nowhere and flew past his face. Under the blindfold he instinctively blinked, although his eyes were already closed. The flutter of wings, not entirely soundless, sent a current of air moving over his cheek. He knew that any birds would have settled in at dusk, hours ago. Then Luisa's hands were on his head and the blindfold came away. It was as dark around him as before it came off. He blinked again, rapidly, but nothing changed. Her hand found his.

"Just follow me, darling."

"I can't see anything. How do you know where you're going?"

"I'm used to it, that's all. I can still see well enough to find my way. You'll get used to it too after a while. Once we're inside we'll have some lights. Just enough."

They moved along, Luisa's hand in his. From somewhere behind came the fluttering of wings again. Jeremy cringed, one hand protecting his eyes, but said nothing, thinking of her felt skirt that first night, their only night. Would the interior be full of creatures of darkness? Luisa had said in Antoine's that she was more comfortable after dark. What else had she told him that he'd glossed over without examining?

Most of the time between their first night and now he had spent going over everything they had done, what he could remember through the gaps of consciousness, at least. There were a thousand questions he wanted to ask her but thought it more sensible to pay attention to navigating this entrance. There would be plenty of time later.

"More steps now," she said, after a pair of turns. "There are fifteen, somewhat steep."

There was no rail this time and he found it hard to keep his balance when he couldn't see where he was going, even though she was holding his hand. He miscounted and stepped down hard off the last one, jarring his spine. Her hands came up to his chest suddenly.

"Stop and recover your balance," she said quietly. "Wait here for a moment." Luisa moved off and he heard a low rasp of hinges that sounded like they didn't get much use. She returned to pull him forward and now he could see she had silently lifted a trapdoor as well, and another long flight of steps opened below, lit by a dim unseen source toward the bottom.

Jeremy's mouth went dry. Was this the gate of doom? The sound had crystallized the image. He was going down to the underworld. What did he know about Orpheus and Euridice. It was the same story. Orpheus had followed her to save her. For a moment, Jeremy's feet froze in place. But wasn't he there to save himself?

Luisa again drew him forward. He knew she didn't grasp his feelings. His suitcase was next to the opening, and he pulled it along. Once they were inside she drew the trap closed above them. It moved on a well-maintained pivot. The temperature was about the same as outside but the air smelled closed in and unused, as if there were in a closet that hadn't been opened in years.

Here the floor was roughly paved, and under his shoes he felt the irregular edges of the stones, as if some had shifted higher or lower over time His suitcase clattered along, bumping over the changing levels. There was enough light to make out broad arches with ribbed vaults as they passed, one after another for a long way, twelve in all. The construction looked medieval, although he knew it couldn't be that early.

"Where are we?" he asked her.

"Under the old cathedral, approaching the crypt.

Isn't it great?"

"You mean all this is still intact? I thought it collapsed in the seventeenth century."

"Some of the underground parts survived," she
said. "The area directly under the old dome is mostly
gone so we don't try to go in there, but here we're moving
along the right side."

Ahead they passed through a smaller arch and
Luisa reached behind a stone casing and the lights behind
them went out, as low lights within the crypt ahead went
on.

In the center of the cavernous room, supported in
the dimness by vaults and arches, two tall white stone sar-
cophagi stood next to each other, the sides paneled in stone
rectangles with vaguely Islamic arabesques in the corners.
On the tops, about five feet above the floor, each held a
carved effigy. On the first one lay the elaborate armored
figure of Juan de Arenas, one hand on the scabbard of
his sheathed sword, the other on his heart. A crested hel-
met waited at his side. Even in death, Jeremy thought, he's
ready in case the Pichanchas return. He moved forward
and read the lettering carved at the foot. Besides Juan, de
Arenas had six or seven additional names Jeremy hadn't
seen in the sources. At the bottom of the inscription were
the dates; 1495 - 1552, with a few Latin words below.

Arenas had already been buried elsewhere and
transferred to the cathedral when it was built, he thought.

"Is that his wife, Elena, next to him?"

"Yes," Luisa said. "She died in 1571."

The image was of a woman dressed simply in the
garments of death, wearing a long robe gathered at the
waist, in her arms a bouquet of calla lilies, carved as limp

and wilted. Jeremy stared at them for a long moment, then his eyes made out other dark forms beyond them in the dim light under the vaults. He took a few steps forward. Toward the rear of the crypt, resting on the floor, three rows of black coffins with ridged lids ranged in formation, more than twenty in all.

"The other children and their children, until the time of the collapse," she said, seeing his look. "Their names are on the ends of each casket if you're interested, but now I think we should go down. There's something else I want to show you. You can always come back later if you want to study this."

Jeremy thought about the first thing she said, and he didn't move. "What do you mean, the other children?"

"The first two children of Juan de Arenas, Tomás and Maria, were born with what was thought at the time to be a curse. The governor's agents located a Pichancha girl out in the hills who was said to be a bruja, and quite naturally the Inquisition ordered her burned at the stake for using the power of the devil to place a curse on the governor's children. Tomás was small, hairless, his ears enlarged. The court physicians were stumped. Finally, word was given out that he had died in early infancy, a highly plausible occurrence at the time. Since it was thought that he wasn't really human, he was never baptized. Instead, quarters were created below ground in the citadel for him, as well as his tutor and guards."

"Guards?"

"Although he couldn't be eliminated, Tomás was never allowed to return to the surface. It would have been humiliating to the Arenas family honor. When Maria was born two years after him, she was brought to the lower levels as well. She was different from Tomás, not as small, more like normal people, but not quite so. Rather like me, I like to think. There are small differences, as you now know. Nonetheless, she was confined as well. Soon they found another bruja to burn. Tomás and Maria are buried in the citadel in unnamed graves with only the date of death. At that time, the rulers above were the grandchildren and great grandchildren of Juan and Elena. The story had not been made public, so they didn't know who had passed on. Our information came from the journal kept by a priest at the time.

"So after their births, the other children of Juan and Elena were normal? The ones buried here in those black coffins?"

"Yes, these offspring took on the role of firstborn and so on, and Tomás and Maria were never acknowledged, in fact, any record of their existence was actively suppressed."

"What happened to them? How did they live?"

She tugged at his hand. "I think you can see where this goes, Jeremy. Being a race unto themselves, they also became a couple and eventually had their own children who, not surprisingly, were like they were. Of course, they never married. They didn't have to and they made their own rules that didn't relate to any church. The Arenases above ground simply turned their backs on the whole thing. Eventually they were forgotten and gradually, with the help of their guards, became self-sufficient. Those early times are not very clear and other than a few pages of the priest's journal, there are no records of this period other than an oral tradition. But we are all descended from Tomás and Maria."

They were like Adam and Eve, Jeremy thought, pioneers in a new game of life. Tomás and Maria had gone on in a strange environment and created their own family. Now, not that many generations further on, there was Luisa. There were the Arenases underground and those above. He knew nothing about the ones above, except for three of them, and of those three, Mark Sands and the bishop were dead and the other had been assaulted in her drugged sleep. This much Rebecca had told him for his family tree search, then nothing more, as she got further into the case. Now he wondered what else there was that she hadn't told him. Drawing this close to Luisa was starting to give him some insight into Rebecca as well. Clearly, there were things she wanted him to know, and other things she didn't.

He turned to Luisa, who stood waiting for him next to Juan de Arenas' sarcophagus, and watched as she pressed the edge of one of the tall side panels and slid it effortlessly to the left. She stepped into the opening, beckoning for him to follow. He stuck his head inside doubtfully. "But isn't there still a body in here somewhere?" His voice echoed in the small, hard space as he wrinkled his nose, but once inside, it smelled no different.

Luisa shook her head. "Many years ago, on a very dark night, all their bones were thrown into the river. We recovered their jewels first, of course. Now this is our front door. Isn't it great? We only use it for special guests, not that there are many. It's a way of showing contempt for what they did to us." She reached for his hand and drew him further in. Her hand was warm and inviting; much, Jeremy thought, like her heart.

CHAPTER 8

The entrance through the sarcophagus led to another series of steps, no surprise, carved, as far as Jeremy could tell in the minimal light, from a black material resembling lava, and faced on the treads and edges with something harder and less porous, like limestone. The walls and ceiling were black as well. After the elaborate stonework of the crypt and the corridor leading to it, the area they were in seemed severe and unadorned. Luisa lives inside an extinct volcano, he thought. At least, I hope it's extinct. I guess her rooming house in St. Paul wasn't so great either.

Everything was silent; the city noise did not penetrate this far down. Jeremy lifted the suitcase and held it by the side handle so it wouldn't bounce on the steps. Now and then circular openings about five or six inches wide appeared in the ceiling. As they passed under these Jeremy could feel a current of air on his head. At the landing of the flight of stairs they entered a hub with eight passages radiating into the mountain like spokes on a wheel. Luisa unerringly selected one, although they were not marked, and switched off the lights behind them as they moved through the corridor.

Occasionally a drip fell from the ceiling and landed on his neck. These ceilings were only a few inches above his head, designed for a race of much shorter people. Although there seemed to be no danger of bumping his forehead, the awareness of the stone just a hand's breadth above his scalp was disconcerting. It intruded on his space and pressed him down psychologically. I'll get used to it, he thought.

Contrary to his expectations, Jeremy had not met Luisa's family on the way in after all. He had expected to find them rising from their chairs to shake his hand or offer him a glass of wine; but there had been no chairs and no reception. Maybe there was no family, either, or perhaps all of them were family, since there had only been a few generations. He was not able to imagine what they might be like. Luisa's parents would almost certainly be between 130 and 150 years old. What kind of work did people do in a place like this anyway? How did they feed themselves? Once he had the time and knew a little more about it, he decided to try to work out an economic model of an underground city with no official surface contact. It was the kind of research project that appealed to him. The extended life spans would throw off any conventional models.

Although she'd promised she would make him comfortable once they were inside, Luisa was vague about giving him any more information. "The others are busy now," or, "This isn't a good time," she said. "Let's settle in first. I missed you. Why don't we go to bed for a while? This is the first time I've had my own room, we should take advantage of it."

"Do you have to be seventy to get your own room here?" Jeremy thought suddenly this sounded a little peevish, then realized he was only nervous.

"No, you only have to have a boyfriend, silly." She took his hand again. "I know this is strange for you, but try to relax. Think about all the different worlds you come across in your research. Think of Islam in the time of the Crusades, or Rome during the Republic. Many of them no longer exist, but this one does, and it's not known to the people from the Outside. Think of yourself as an explorer, like Cortés, who hooked up with a native girl when he arrived. I'll be your Malinche, your guide and translator, there for you every night. You'll need me to explain the customs of the locals so you don't commit some stumbling faux pas and embarrass both of us."

"You've already been my guide." He touched her cheek.

"I know. You're coming along nicely." She paused and turned to him, kissing his neck. Although she sometimes seemed forceful and even inflexible, there was something deeply sensuous about her in the right mood, and she often was. Whether this was her human side, or more the subterranean, he couldn't tell. It was not something he'd encountered above ground before he met Luisa. Maybe normal girls were never like this.

"You're very conservation-conscious, turning the lights off behind us," he said, trying to make sense of where they were. "Electricity must be expensive here."

"It would be, but we don't pay for it. How could we ever get a bill? We don't receive mail; no one knows we exist. Our electric power down here is all stolen, and much of it comes from the new cathedral. We're tapped into their lines. Rafael calls it the power of God. He has kind of a crude sense of humor. Naturally we try to keep consumption down so no one notices. Some of it comes from the hospital, too, across the plaza. Of course, they don't care how much they use."

Jeremy digested this for a moment. He assumed Rafael referred to Cantú. "Is there any natural light?"

"There are several light shafts in the ruins of the citadel and the old palace, but they're structured so that even if you were standing outside directly above you couldn't see in very far. Mirrors inside reflect the light into the interior."

"I suppose that's important."

"It is if we don't want the bishop thinking too hard about how much power he uses." She stopped suddenly. "I want to show you something as long as we're passing this way. I don't normally use that entrance."

She led him into a small room one level below the crypt. Inside, the four black walls and a coved ceiling had no trace of decoration. Jeremy was not sophisticated about decor, but so far the underground seemed soulless and utilitarian. There was no door or grill at the room's entry, and the only furniture inside was a plain trestle table made of wooden planks and a bench next to it in the same style.

On one wall, a group of recesses carved into the stone held boxes of varying sizes. Each had a notation in a script Jeremy didn't recognize. It might have been old Spanish, since the lettering was crabbed and archaic. It reminded him of antique German, the letters full of spiky Gothic corners. At the bottom shelf, Luisa bent over a rectangular wooden box. It held no carving or decoration, but the construction appeared to be nothing recent. The corners and edges were worn and rounded over.

"Can you help me with this?"

Jeremy lifted one end and they set it on the table. Luisa switched on a wall sconce lamp near the end.

"As a researcher, I think you're going to enjoy this. Lift off the lid." He touched the nails that held the sides together. They all had square heads.

Sitting on the bench, Jeremy opened the box and looked inside, suppressing a gasp.

"Beautiful, isn't it?" she said from over his shoulder. "We call it the Relic."

"Aren't you afraid someone will steal it?"

"Where would they take it, and why would they? We are all family here. We don't go in much for individual possessions, other than clothing and toothbrushes. And boyfriends, now."

He almost thought she was blushing, but he couldn't be sure in the dim light.

"But what if someone else got in here?"

"No one ever has, uninvited, in more than 450 years. It's our treasury. These other boxes have the altar service from the old cathedral, the chalices and so on. One of them has the jewels Juan and Elena were buried with. But this is the prize, I guess."

"Can I touch it?"

"Of course. Take it out. It's no big deal to us."

Jeremy lifted the heavy Relic out and Luisa slid the wooden box aside to make room for it on the table. In his hands was a silver reliquary shaped like a cross with equal arms, each of them about seven inches high by seven wide in section, and measuring a little more than three feet long from top to bottom and from side to side.

"A Greek cross," he said. "It looks Byzantine, I can see that right away. Am I right?"

"Yes, the type of halo around the heads of the saint figures places it in the first half of the ninth century." She said this without pretension, as if it was probably something he had once known himself and forgotten over time. Perhaps it didn't come up much, and her statement was just a reminder.

He looked at her in surprise. "How would you know that?"

"We studied it in World Art 17. I went to school for more than forty years, remember? Anyway, part of that course was a cross-cultural analysis using the iconoclastic movement as a focus to compare mid-Byzantine with early Islamic art, basically the period from about the last three hundred years of the first millennium. Iconoclasm was an idea that was popular in both civilizations. We were lucky to have this to pass around."

"You passed this around?" His mouth was hanging open.

"Well, not literally, we lined up to look at it."

The surface of the cross was covered with low-relief figures in four distinct scenes illustrating the tale of the discovery of the True Cross in the early fourth century by St. Helena, the mother of the Roman emperor Constantine. The first showed its discovery in Jerusalem; then the transportation of it to Constantinople; the installation in the cathedral there; and finally the veneration of it by the Emperor Constantine, St. Helena and the other saints who had been summoned for the occasion. On all four ends were empty damaged bezels where rows of gemstones had once been mounted and later pried away.

Jeremy ran his fingers over the reliefs, amazed at the fineness of the workmanship and the excellent condition of the entire piece, aside from the loss of the gems.

"I see now why Juan de Arenas called this place Santa Elena. He obviously knew about this treasure. Where did it come from?" he asked. His mind was racing because he thought he knew the story behind what was in his hands.

"Initially it was under the high altar in the old cathedral. You know how they always have a relic under every altar, right? Usually it's a small piece of stone with a saint's bone fragment embedded in it, something like that. Maybe a tooth or a fingertip."

"I know, I was raised Catholic. I spent five years as an altar boy. In fact, I think our church had a toenail clipping from St. Anselm."

She didn't smile. "They believed this was a piece of the True Cross."

"A piece? Luisa, I think I know what this is. I wrote a paper once in college called Research Methods: Separating Myth from Reality in Older Sources. I used the True Cross as one of my examples of the pitfalls in research. I'm almost certain that what you have here is the Helena Fragment. It's the largest surviving piece of the True Cross after it was broken up and distributed among dozens of churches in the fifth century." His heart was pounding rapidly now, his gestures as broad as the reliquary itself. "Didn't you get into that in your class? I feel like I'm an archaeologist making a big score here." He was getting fired up now and out of breath. Research could get him going like nothing else, particularly when the sources went back over a thousand years.

She shook her head slowly. "There was just no interest in that part of it. It was an art class. We saw it as a major example of Byzantine silverwork. We dealt only with stylistic elements, not their religious meaning. Would you react with reverence in front of a Mayan sculpture? Awe, maybe, but you wouldn't drop to your knees."

He scored one for Luisa and couldn't answer this directly. "How could there be no interest in the religious aspect of it? That's what it's all about," he said, trying to look into her eyes in the dim light.

"Simply because it was religious." She looked back at him now as if he'd asked a dumb question. "We should get moving and bring your suitcase down to my room."

"So? I don't see how. . ."

"Jeremy, I've gotten to like you very much, but you need to consider where I'm coming from. We were sent into exile underground by religious people, pious people. They went to mass every day. They did it all by the book so they could go to heaven like their saints did. Then they also cursed us and cast us out like demons, or like Adam and Eve, just because we had a slight genetic problem, one that originally came from them. I don't think there's the slightest interest in religion now among any of us, except as a cultural phenomenon. There never has been."

He saw the pain in her face, but he couldn't let go of what he'd discovered.

"Even though," he said in his most measured tone, "you have in your storeroom here the greatest surviving relic of Christianity? That's why it's different from a Mayan sculpture. Christianity lives!"

"In St. Paul, maybe, or in Rome, but it doesn't live down here. Anyway, if that's what it is. How do we know? Ask yourself for a moment why you would even think that. Is it just the elegant presentation? Rafael would be the first one to tell you that the right frame does wonders for any picture, even one that's not very good." She shrugged elaborately in the Méxican fashion, thumbs pointed outward, eyebrows raised, mouth twisted, and looked down at the Relic.

"Especially one that's not very good," she went on. "Where was the True Cross for that first three hundred years before your St. Helena claimed to have found it. Where's the chain of custody, as your cops would say, like we're seeing on American cable TV now? Who signed off each time it changed hands? Why couldn't this piece be something some merchant just sold St. Helena in the bazaar in Jerusalem? Maybe he found out ahead of time that she was coming to town looking for it and had it prepared for her. The desire to believe can sanctify anything. You must have seen that in your research too."

"I don't know. There is a lot of faith involved, I guess." Some of these questions he hadn't ever tried to look at in the research.

"Not down here. There's been no faith down here for a long time, like since day one." She shook her head as she looked down at the reliquary. Her index finger moved up and down on the haloed figure of St. Helena.

"OK," he said. "Let's put the early provenance aside. How did you get this?" He knew that if it had been in the old cathedral's altar, it must have disappeared in the 1656 collapse.

"After the cathedral fell our people began to look for it, burrowing into the ruins, knowing it was of great value to the Arenases above ground. It took us almost seven years to find it, since the high altar, standing directly under the dome, was obliterated. A number of our diggers were killed when the rubble collapsed as they tunneled in. It was very unstable at first. The oral tradition tells us a lot about this."

"You know, this reliquary has been lost for centuries. It was last seen," he said, "when the Turks captured Constantinople in 1453. It would have been part of their booty."

"Well, that's not quite true, is it? We've been seeing it ever since we recovered it seven years after the cathedral fell, and the Arenases in Spain clearly knew about it before that because they must have had it. It just wasn't reported to the outside."

"So how did it get to Santa Elena?" he asked.

"If it was considered infidel loot when Constantinople was sacked, it was probably sold and resold throughout the Islamic world. After all, to them, Christ was a prophet. It's not a stretch to think it might have made its way to Spain, which in that period was still mostly dominated by Islam. Why couldn't the Arenases, who were already a prominent family, have picked it up when they were looting Moorish properties in Cordoba in the years right before Columbus set sail?"

"I've never seen anything about this online."

"Of course not! One theory I heard was that it was part of Elena de Arenas' dowry when she married Juan in the 1530s. Perhaps her father had acquired it because she was St. Helena's namesake, or maybe she was given that name because he already had it. Who can tell now? But clearly, by the time Juan de Arenas named the city, it was already in the family's possession."

"I have to see it," he said. Now he could hardly

hold himself back.

"Go ahead. The top lifts off, I think, if it still works. There are little pins on the sides that slide into tubes along the edges."

"Have you ever looked inside it?"

"Never. It's probably just an old chunk of wood. It was only the case we were interested in, not the contents, since it was an art class. I think you're making way too much of this, but go ahead."

Knowing he looked like he had a backward Outsider mentality, Jeremy moved the reliquary closer into the light at the end of the table and began to work the stiff silver pins loose until they were all free. The lid lifted with the resistance of a vacuum being released.

Inside, the object was covered by rotting silk, a mottled brownish red and in some places disintegrated. He brushed the powdery fragments away with his fingertips and found himself staring at a round length of wood shaped like a section of fence post, nearly as long as the cross-shaped container, and about six inches in diameter. The surface, nearly black in color, was deeply scored by cracks and furrows, patchy and shiny in some areas as if there were still the residues of ancient fluids on it. Near the center began a number of holes that penetrated the surface deeply. He lifted the fragment out of its case and rotated it to get a better look. The holes went all around the circumference of it. Within a distance of about six inches in length, where they were all concentrated, he counted twenty-two holes. Each one was approximately square, and as Jeremy studied them he realized they occurred in pairs slightly less than two inches apart.

"This must have been used a number of times,"

he said in an awestruck tone. "Multiple men died on this thing." He could hardly believe what he was holding in his hands.

"Perhaps you thought they would have given him a new cross?" Luisa asked, in a tone that suggested she had little patience with his interest. He was not surprised to hear her say it. Although Luisa was not a very big person, she tended to express herself forcefully; perhaps she did even because of this, in compensation for her size. "I don't think everyone would have gotten a fresh one, Jeremy. The Romans were a practical people. Wood was probably no more plentiful then in Israel than it is today."

"I guess I never thought about it, but it had to have been a big deal at the time, though. Didn't it? Don't you think? Or do you?"

"I think that to them, he was just another prisoner. It was one more political execution for crimes against the state. Remember, the Jews passed the buck to Pontius Pilate."

Jeremy was getting so little confirmation from her that he was starting to ask himself how much of what he had always believed about it was just propaganda or preconception. Or worse, just lore, an ephemeral term that, as a researcher, he didn't respect much. Lore was a surface layer, almost like accumulated grit, never more than a starting point for real research.

"Maybe to the executioners," she continued, "it was just another day up on the hill. They come home, wash the blood off in the stone sink, and the wife puts dinner on the table. Who did you kill today, sweetheart? Another Jewish visionary? Or was it just a political rabble-rouser this time? Or maybe a couple of thieves?"

"You seem a little cynical," he said, trying without success not to be shocked. "I don't think you appreciate what you're looking at here."

"Maybe I've been underground too long. It's bound to influence your viewpoint. It's hard to be a visionary when you can't see more than a few feet in front of you. Here, we're more focused on not stumbling. Think about it. It's no picnic down in this place. We've only had television for the last four years. Rafael still doesn't give us Internet access."

He placed the timber back in the reliquary and lifted the rotting silk from within the two shorter arms. The cloth from the left arm contained nothing. It fell to pieces in his hands. From the other arm, his fingers pulled a strip of wrought iron about a quarter of an inch thick and square in cross section, tapered and filed to a sharp point at both ends. It was shaped like a U, so that the points were about two inches apart. Six or seven inches long, the surface was black like the wood. Suddenly getting an idea, he inserted the pointed ends into one of the pairs of holes. They fit perfectly.

"Oh my God!" he said, shaking his head in disbelief. "If it was him, Christ was stapled to this cross, and counting the pairs of holes, so was everyone else, eleven in all. I can't believe this!"

Luisa moved closer and took the hand-forged iron staple out of his hand. "It makes sense, though, doesn't it? If the victim was thrashing about, he might tear his wrist loose from a nail between the bones, but he would never get free from a staple once they pounded it in. One point would go in between his wrist bones, and the other directly into the wood outside them." She touched a finger to one of the points. "The Romans were practical people. Isn't this just the kind of thing they'd have around the prison? What better way to attach a length of chain to a beam or a post than with something like this? How easy to string a rope through it. Maybe this is the real thing after all, I don't know."

A chill went through Jeremy, reaching all the way to his fingertips. He placed the staple back into the powdery silk.

"So now you're a believer?" he said, giving her a tentative smile.

"Not really," she shook her head, as if almost bored with it. "I like the questions you're asking, but it still doesn't matter in the end."

He looked at her blankly for a moment. "What *does* matter, then?"

She looked up at him gravely, eye to eye.

"The same thing that matters to you: survival. We're no different in that way."

He wanted to think there was more to life than that. Instead, he simply asked, "How many of you are there?"

"I don't know exactly, but surely, not more than 300. Births aren't common, but on the other hand, people don't die here very often. It's a fairly stable population."

Survival, he thought, in the ensuing silence between them. Their whole race depended on less than 300 members--not much of a gene pool. In the States, Luisa's group would be protected as an endangered species.

Jeremy moved the cover back over the box, sliding it into place and pushing the silver pins back into position. He couldn't bear to look at the piece of wood anymore, standing next to his dear Luisa with her utter lack of faith or even much interest in the Relic. Since he wasn't religious, he wasn't certain what he felt himself, other than that he had touched something momentous, something that had inspired centuries of wars and pilgrimages. Yet it was an artifact with no clear pedigree. Maybe she was right after all; it was all about faith, and that was the only certain thing about it. No one would ever know any more about it than that, no matter how good the research.

After he helped her replace the Relic in the shelves, Luisa took his hand and led him from the room. They had gone only a few steps before he stopped next to his worn red suitcase, which now seemed ridiculous after what he'd been holding in his hands, and looked back to the plank table and the shelf wall.

"So are your feelings about religion and religious people really that bad?"

She sighed quietly, as if it was an emotional question for her, or she may have just run out of patience. "Jeremy, don't you get it yet? I didn't think I'd have to spell it out." Luisa shook her head in the dim light, then peered into his face. In that light her eyes were not violet but black and empty in her narrow face. "There was never an earthquake in Santa Elena, OK? It was *our* people who brought down the old cathedral in 1656. It was on March 26. Ever since then it's been our national holiday down here."

With his mouth open he stared back at her, then placed his hands on her shoulders and drew her closer against him, almost able to feel her fine skin through the moleskin shirt. His fingertips found the line of soft hair that began at the top of her neck and traveled downward beneath her collar.

"Luisa, if you have less than three hundred people now, how many could there have been then? I mean, to take down the whole cathedral?"

"It was the Forty-One. They were enough to undermine one of the four main piers under the dome. They are legendary, as close as we have to saints here, if you want to think of it like that."

"So no one above ground ever figured it out?"

"Never. That's our secret. Now you're family." She gave him an impish smile, placed her index finger over her lips, and moved away as he slowly shook his head.

CHAPTER 9

Rebecca and Ken Abrams had both nearly been late for the plane, and after the long line at security ended up sprinting to the gate separately once they got their shoes back on. Her cab had run into heavy freeway traffic because of a sleety storm of mixed rain and snow, and it was not until they took off that she felt relaxed enough to think about business again. An ongoing problem on her book tour had been that she was a white-knuckle flyer, and it was never until she was finally airborne with the plane leveling out that the tension dissipated. Early on she'd gotten into the habit of flying first class but, of course, Abrams' police budget didn't allow it.

"I'm OK now, so tell me what Shapiro said about the emails to Cantú from Edward Born," she said as they began to level off, the pitch of the engines changing. She pushed off her shoes and drew her legs up beneath her on the seat. It brought her shoulders level with his.

"That the final message Born sent to the artist was simply the results from the show opening. It went out on Saturday afternoon. Nine pictures were sold, one of them to you, and two were on hold. Six remained. So that tells us nothing, but it doesn't require a response from Cantú, either, unless he wanted to say how gratified he was, and apparently he didn't. It was Born's previous message to him, from Friday night when you were there, that tells the story. It went something like, 'Can you send me a photo of yourself for one of my clients? It could guarantee a sale.' It went out during the opening itself."

"Right," she nodded, "I just wanted to see what a man who painted like that would look like. Edward must have sent it while I was outside taking the news from Jeremy that Mark Sands was dead."

"It wasn't until nearly a week later that Cantú responded with, 'You have asked the wrong question.'"

She shook her head slowly and folded her arms. "I still feel like I killed Edward."

"Don't beat yourself up over it. I'm not sure there's any connection. That was an absolutely harmless request, Rebecca. Anyone could have asked for a photo, and I'm surprised no one had in the past." He took her hand, but didn't say any more. After a moment, he almost let it go, but then he didn't, keeping it awkwardly on the arm rail between them.

She fell silent for a while, peering through layers of oval Plexiglas to the neat squares of Midwestern farmland, some bare and blackish brown, others still partly covered with a layer of late snow. It somehow made sense, unlike the death of Edward Born. Ken's index finger was moving on her palm. It didn't feel like sympathy. In the context of the conversation it didn't seem like romance, either. She wasn't sure what it was, maybe just connectedness. Perhaps he was getting absent-minded and didn't know either.

Of course her request had been perfectly harmless, as Abrams said, but Edward was still dead. She tried not to picture him in his coffin. Did he even own a conservative suit to be buried in? Maybe he'd been cremated.

She wanted to believe there was no connection between her question and Edward's death, as Ken had suggested. There was a disconnect between the trivial reality of her question and the violent response of Cantú, if it was Cantú who had caused Edward's death.

"Did Shapiro say who's taking the unsold inventory?" she asked after a while. The cabin attendants were setting up drinks in the aisle.

"It's going back to Mentor Gallery, where Cantú showed for years before he went to Born & Born, but don't get your hopes up there. Born didn't have it on consignment. Shapiro said he'd purchased it all outright. So Mentor will now have it to liquidate on consignment from Born's estate, once probate begins. There won't be any payments going to Cantú."

"So you know what I was thinking."

"Yes, that the successor gallery to Born would be contact with Cantú, but it doesn't work out that way. I called Mentor and they don't know how to reach him, either. I thought about giving them Cantú's email address, but then, considering what happened to Born, I didn't."

"We'll just have to find him ourselves," she said.

"That's the way it usually shakes out when you're a cop."

"What have we got?"

"The usual, nothing much. Shapiro's got shipping cases from some of the pictures. We know they came up to Santa Fe through Red Hat out of Santa Elena."

"So we can contact Red Hat when we get there, right?" she said, brightening.

"I already did. The return address Cantú used is a fake; they checked it out for me. The street exists but the number doesn't. I had their St. Paul office check with them, and no one remembered who brought the paintings into their Santa Elena office. It was weeks ago."

"How about bank records for remittances going to Cantú from Edward? They had a long history."

"They've all been wire transfers through Citibank, which owns Banamex, where Cantú has his account. We're dead-ended there. The Méxican government doesn't allow transaction or account ownership information to be reported out of Méxican banks, even if they're U.S. owned subsidiaries. They told me it was a firewall, whatever that means."

"This is going to be fun. How's your Spanish?" she asked.

"High school junior level, twenty-three years back, but I have used it a little since. St. Paul's got a lot of Hispanics. I've run into a couple of them in the course of my job."

"Mine's no better."

"I'm still glad to have you with me, although I couldn't tell my boss you were coming."

"Why not? Are your intentions dishonorable?"

"That wouldn't have come up. But what if you're killed or injured? Everything is about insurance these days."

"You don't mind taking a chance on me?"

Abrams squeezed her hand in response. "You're taking a chance on me."

St. Paul, Minnesota had rapidly fallen away behind them. A middletown sort of place in the Midwest, it's no longer in its prime, but aging gracefully and holding up well. There, a reasonable person can drive the streets downtown during rush hour without breaking a sweat or making rude hand signals. There the residents have forgotten, or more likely, never even imagined, the kind of traffic mayhem that is the norm for Santa Elena. In that town, the words hora pico, rush hour, have long since fallen out of use, since there is no time of day that this term does not describe.

Two moderately weary souls on the cusp of a life-changing experience emerged from Customs and Immigration at the Santa Elena airport with luggage in tow, entered a waiting yellow and black taxi, and within ten seconds were plunged into the hungry chaos of the freeway heading into town. This was traffic on the scale of Istanbul or Cairo, Caracas or Rio, where the very substance of it is fluid, raw, and angry; a matrix of distorted energy so palpable in its density that they felt they'd entered a black hole. Any thought of escape was simply crushed by its gravity.

The motion was constant and unpredictable. It was not the movement of individual vehicles, single buses, trucks, or automobiles, but more like liquid under multiple atmospheres of pressure. Rebecca could feel it in her mouth, although she hadn't opened it, and almost in her pores. Yet the cab driver kept an average of three tires on the pavement at any given moment, while giving the appearance of someone long brain dead behind the wheel, eyes still open but apparently coated thickly with dust.

Thinking that, during her book tour, even Boston or New York had been nothing like this, and New Orleans had been a cakewalk, Rebecca stared longingly at the exits as they flew past in a blur. She peered through adjacent cars inches away, looking past the brown moles on people's necks, the sweat pooling in the pouches under their eyes, the petulant, clammy, dark-eyed children staring back at her with their fingers halfway up their noses, ready to cry. It was an unasked-for intimacy with the tortured, the newly damned. This to the backdrop of a thousand horns in discordant tones ebbing and flowing in nonstop crescendo, while semi trucks and buses belched clouds of black, vaporous lungdeath. Breathing it was like inhaling charred and shredded burlap as the taxi flew along in breakneck gridlock.

"It's probably going to need to be amputated," yelled Ken suddenly over the chaos.

"What! What?" She was leaning into his face to be heard.

"My arm, the way you're gripping it. I think one of the bones is broken, and there's no circulation, no feeling in my fingers anymore. Thank God it's not my gun hand."

She relaxed her grip, then pulled her hands away entirely, settling back into the seat without looking at him, having the sense of being in a life-or-death situation with someone she didn't know well enough to hear her last words. "Sorry. There are no seat belts," she said in what she felt was a reasonable tone of voice. It was a statement that didn't explain everything, and he probably hadn't heard it.

But he had. "Of course not," he said. "They'd only delay cutting your body out of the wreckage."

A space opened beside them about half the length

of the taxi, and the driver shoehorned the cab into it in less than a second, the space stretching to accommodate them, but not an inch more. Oddly, there was no screech of tortured metal, and only a small, muted gasp from Rebecca. Two more such maneuvers executed at blinding speed and they were in the right lane.

Suddenly, without slowing, they lurched onto an exit and landed among the second-string players, those who, perhaps already maimed or only partially disabled or possibly just blinded, were unable to drive in lockstep at eighty miles an hour, and were now moving at a leisurely fifty on the narrow streets. They were still bouncing over curbs and speed bumps, slowing imperceptibly or not at all at intersections, shooting through red traffic lights as if they were gentle hints, mere suggestions.

Not exactly the land of *mariachis* harmonizing gentle candlelight melodies of love, or that of exotic *señoritas* with flowers in their hair, or even that of laid-back Latin Americans with plenty of time to get where they were going. *Mañana* would do just fine, but somewhere other than Santa Elena, where good manners, common sense, courtesy and simple humanity had all disappeared within days of the introduction of gasoline. Anyone who was old enough to remember them had also departed long go.

"I've come up with a title for my next book," Rebecca said, as they screeched to a stop at a major intersection behind a bus that looked like a junkyard escapee. "I'm calling it *Gringos in Paradise.* It's about two people who meet on a murder case in México and . . . "

"Don't tell me," he said. "You'll spoil the suspense. I'm guessing that the main characters were probably killed instantly in a traffic accident before they could get anywhere on the case. Any other outcome would be impossible."

"Maybe it should just be a short story."

The Santa Elena police headquarters, where Abrams paid his professional courtesy call the following morning, was unlike any police building he had ever seen. A quadrangle with a massive interior courtyard occupied almost the entire city block. In the entry, buffered by four marble staircases, one on each side, was an immense fountain with a statue of a woman he assumed represented justice. Water streamed from both her outstretched hands.

He'd called his mother to say goodbye the night before he left St. Paul. She had cautioned him to wash his hands whenever he had the chance, drink beer instead of water, although not too much, and stay away from the "native" girls. He wondered whether she thought they wore grass skirts. He didn't mention that he'd brought one of St. Paul's native girls with him.

Although he'd left his gun at the hotel, for this official visit he was armed with a letter of introduction from the St. Paul chief of police, another letter from the mayor of St. Paul with an embossed gold seal trailing a tiny green ribbon at the bottom, a notarized copy of his detective certificate, a photocopy of his college diploma, and his passport in a buttoned hip pocket. Ken had been told before he left St. Paul that Méxicans loved official papers, and he had no intention of letting them down.

Sensing she would never be able to take it seriously, he suggested none of the detail of this to Rebecca before he left the hotel, but only left a short note at the desk. He had detected an ironic look in her eyes more than once when they'd talked about police administrative matters, and he knew she was seeing it through a writer's filter, one with more flexibility than his reality ever had.

He picked one of the four grand staircases at random and climbed to the second floor, where he was stopped by a uniformed receptionist. Unsure of the proper protocol, he saluted the man and said, "Teniente Ricardo Montes de Oca, por favor." He opened his slender briefcase and began to lift out the papers to demonstrate the seriousness of his visit.

Abrams had been coached by a Spanish-speaking patrolman on the St. Paul force and was reasonably sure he'd gotten it right. Montes de Oca was senior staff liaison with other police forces throughout México, as well as abroad. It was a position of considerable flexibility, as well as a profit center, since the Santa Elena police had little interest in cooperating with other police forces, or with anyone else, for that matter, who didn't make it worth their while.

The reception officer shrugged and pointed to a large waiting area where more than two dozen people were already seated. They appeared to represent all kinds of Méxican civilians. None of them looked like visiting police officers from other jurisdictions, and it seemed to Abrams that they must be waiting for someone other than Montes de Oca. With his fairly exalted position, Montes de Oca would most likely not be conducting routine business with ordinary citizens, which Abrams took to mean, people without gold seals and green ribbons on their documents. The hall had to be a central waiting room for the whole department, a staging area for people of all ranks and missions. He began to relax; this was not going to be so bad.

It was five minutes after nine in the morning. Abrams gathered his papers and moved toward the seat closest to the inner office door, facing another officer on duty. As he lowered himself into the chair, the officer rapped sharply on the desktop with a ruler, then pointed first at Abrams and then to an empty seat in the back of the room, shaking his head with some degree of irritation. Abrams thought of turning around to see if the man could possibly be pointing to someone else, but decided against it. It could only be him. With an inaudible sigh, but keeping his face blank, he rose and moved to the back of the room, feeling dozens of eyes on his back, watching him in triumph. The officer at the door waited until he was seated, and then, looking Abrams in the eye, beckoned elegantly to the man first in line to come forward to the desk.

A quick study, Abrams realized that etiquette was key. I'll just have to get a handle on business manners here, he thought. It isn't enough to be an important visitor working a major multiple homicide case; it's a matter of the approach, of showing the proper respect. It's probably critical to come up through channels like everybody else. Then, once you're eye to eye with the people in authority, things will get less formal, you'll be treated like one of them, which of course I am. Abrams settled in for a long wait. The officer sitting up front with the lucky visitor was now stamping papers. He had first looked carefully at the three rubber stamps before him as if he'd never seen any of them before and they were possibly booby-trapped by al Qaida, rigged to explode on the first impact. Finally he picked up the center one, examined the date portion of it and made an adjustment. Then he opened the file folder the man had brought with him and began stamping each paper, first on the front, then on the back, as if the two halves might spontaneously delaminate at some point, and in their separated state, each side would need to retain its official mark. When he finished, he leaned back in his chair and began to peruse each one, occasionally holding them up to the light to check the watermark. About halfway through the stack he moved his chair back from the desk, rose without speaking or even looking at his client, and stepped away, disappearing through a door at the front of the room, and closing it firmly behind him.

Once the man was gone Abrams looked at his watch. The hands no longer seemed to be moving, so he shook it. He wondered what Rebecca was doing. It had to be much more interesting, even if she was still asleep.

Even in her running shoes, Rebecca unaccountably slipped and went down hard for the second time, raking the other bare knee against the sharp edge of the curb, as she skidded across the wet stone sidewalk and slammed her shoulder into the wall. Shaking her head to clear it, she was up again in an instant, but now both knees streamed blood down her shins. She knew it was seeping into her socks, but she couldn't stop to look, because her pursuers weren't far behind now. She didn't have to hear them to know it.

As she sprinted down the street, she fished in the

tiny inside pocket in the waistband of her running shorts for the key and had it ready in her hand as she slammed against the door. Halfway through the turn of the lock it always found resistance at a sticky spot, and her heart paused as well, then the key traveled the rest of the way and the plank door swung open and instantly flew shut again behind her. Throwing the bolt, she didn't look back.

Rebecca collapsed sideways onto a bench just inside, closing her tear-flooded eyes and pulling her legs up to her chest, trying to catch her breath. Sometimes it was like this coming home. Often she thought she wouldn't make it.

She had never seen them. That ultimate horror was being withheld from her, saved for the right moment, whenever that might be, for them. She only knew it would be the worst possible time when it came: a time when she was helpless, vulnerable, incapable of handling it—a time like now. Her breathing was just beginning to slow toward normal when she felt small sticky fingers on her bare thighs, her skin lifting under their touch. Her legs and arms thrust outward in panic, and her body recoiled backward, slamming against the slats of the bench and banging her sweating head.

Suddenly Rebecca sat upright in bed at the Hotel Estrella, blinking and not recognizing the room for a moment, then drew her legs up to her chest again and looked at her knees. They were smooth and unmarked. No blood ran down her shins.

The tee shirt she slept in, long enough to reach her upper thighs when she was standing, was hiked up and twisted tightly around her ribs, as if she'd been spinning as she slept. The clock read 7:35. With both hands, she massaged her scalp at the back, where her head had slammed the headboard. She found only a small bump, and rubbing it helped with reentry. In her dreams she was not usually the victim. She wondered now why she had so often said that uncomfortable paintings were good. Certainly the matching dreams were losing their charm.

Soaping down in the shower, with special attention to her knees and upper shins, even checking her ankles, she went through the dream moment by moment. It looked like it had something to do with Cantú, but it was not anything she could use in the book. With her hair dry half an hour later when she dialed Ken's room, she was still debating whether to mention it to him, but when he didn't answer she decided to keep it to herself.

Checking at the desk, she found he'd left a note for her saying only, "Official business—back shortly."

Shortly? Feeling out of the loop and wondering whether this was how it was going to be now that they'd arrived in Santa Elena, she waited for Abrams another half an hour after breakfast, composing a follow-up email to Jeremy, notifying him that they had arrived in Santa Elena as well and warning him again to be careful. Could he meet them—without Luisa Arenas—somewhere, anywhere, soon? She considered whether she wanted to put the Luisa part into the message, but since there was no way to reach Jeremy by phone, she'd have to take a chance that Luisa might see it. But when she hit send, and waited for the familiar whooshing sound indicating it had gone, nothing happened. A moment later the screen displayed a message saying it was undeliverable.

Rebecca shut down the laptop, sensing a bad trend already to the day's developments, and then caught a cab to *centro*. The running dream lingered in her mind, but with less force now. If this was going to be nothing more than a business trip, then she had some business of her own to do.

She was not surprised this time at the density of the traffic, the constant noise like fabric ripping beside her head, and kept a handkerchief over her nose and mouth when they were behind buses. She even remembered to ask the cabdriver in advance to commit to what the trip would cost, using a phrase from her travel dictionary. She mentally shut out the din and turned away from cars thrusting their noses out into the traffic flow.

After studying the guidebook at breakfast, her idea to was to orient herself to the four plazas surrounding the cathedral, and the peculiar ruins behind it, that of the old cathedral and citadel, left uncleared after the great earthquake of 1656. What an odd thing, to leave the ruins like that, but now, apparently, they were overgrown with vines and creepers in many places, gently mounding over and forming their own bizarre landscape, almost like the swallowed-up Mayan cities of the Yucatan.

About twenty-five minutes later the driver pulled up at a great plaza bounded on three sides by buildings of the colonial period. In a city that had no word for mellow, Rebecca found herself facing the calm, weathered limestone facades of seventeenth and eighteenth century México—New Spain when they were built. As she advanced through the plaza in comfortable shoes that also gave her some lift, the traffic fell away, leaving her in what seemed an island of the untroubled past.

It was a cool sunny morning that promised a much warmer finish, but for now the sun lay lightly on the ancient stones. México had not participated in the world wars of the last century, she knew, or the police actions, the Vietnams and Koreas, the Iraqs and Afghanistans, and so had no massive cemeteries to shelter its war dead, no monuments to the maimed and shell-shocked. No veterans' hospitals warehoused the old soldiers in their discarded state where they, the forgotten, could drink themselves into their own kind of forgetting. The buildings before her were etched with the restful patina of wind and weather, the graceful, blurred abrasive of time.

Inside the police building, Ken Abrams squirmed in his chair. He did not have an appointment with Ricardo Montes de Oca, which now looked like a mistake, and he did not know how to express his business to the reception officer. He realized he had assumed they spoke at least some English, enough, at least, to get the gist of his mission. It was too soon to know for sure, but this was possibly mistake number two and was most likely going to be seen as another example of Yankee arrogance, which it may have been. As an investigator, he had observed in the past that arrogance is always undetectable in themselves by the people who practice it, only noticed by others who were its object. Meanwhile, the officer did not return.

Abrams had no way of knowing that at that moment, Ricardo Montes de Oca was pulling up a chair in the Cafe del Teatro, in a corner just out of direct sunlight, and removing his backgammon board from its tooled leather case. His opponent, a judge deeply engaged in a murder case in the nearby law courts building, was approaching from across the square. Couples strolled lazily over the pavement as flower vendors called to them. Another beautiful day in Santa Elena.

To amuse himself while waiting, Ken began looking at a series of large-scale murals that covered three walls of the room. They depicted a narrative of the early days of the Santa Elena region. He had not bothered to research any history of the place; this was a working trip, and all he wanted was for the local police to help him locate Rafael Cantú after he'd signed in. He and Rebecca had made only a two-day reservation at the Hotel Estrella, figuring that after they talked to the painter on the first morning they could fill in the remainder of their time with some limited sightseeing. The only iffy thing was to find him fairly fast, but how hard could that be? Ken had seen the Born & Born website, and even if it hadn't shown a photo of him, Cantú was well known, even in Europe. No problem.

What he was now seeing on these upper walls was a mellow illustration of the first official meeting of Juan de Arenas with the Pichancha Indians in 1529. Three Indian children were spreading flower petals at his feet. Their leader, Xochilaxtlac, extends a manly hand in greeting, while with the other he offers his eldest daughter in marriage to the conquering hero. Far from shrinking in terror from their strange armored visitor, she leans toward Arenas with unveiled interest, looking fetchingly nubile in a rather minimal outfit. Because this mural was painted in 1934, the daughter's costume had been more influenced by movies featuring Radio City Music Hall performances than by anything one of the Pichancha girls would really have worn, even on an important blind date like this.

Behind Xochilaxtlac, the other Pichanchas bend
their knees to the Spaniards. Juan de Arenas bows slightly
in minimal respect to the native leader, meanwhile eyeing
the daughter, and if Abrams had been able to read any
of the inscription coming from Arenas' mouth on a me-
andering white band, he would have been gratified at the
promises of perpetual peace and cooperation expressed
by the great pioneer. As it was, Abrams only had the impression that the locals and their new friends knew how
to get things done. Have patience, he counseled himself,
for when the officer returns. Clearly manners count here.
Obviously they had gotten things off on the right foot
back in 1529. After a few more minutes the officer reappeared and sat down.

By the time four hours had passed, Ken Abrams
had surveyed everyone in the seats around him, analyzing
them in terms of occupation, age, marital status, gender
preference, IQ, and what they'd eaten for breakfast. Some
of this had necessarily been speculative. He'd studied every figure in the great mural and concluded that although
there were twenty-three human figures depicted, the
painter had used only eleven models, possibly ten, since
one was turned away from the viewer. The same equine
model had served for all seven horses. Abrams was in the
midst of counting the light bulbs in the eight bronze ceiling fixtures when another tap on the desktop caught his
attention and he realized he was next. He moved confi-
dently to the desk and sat down, opening his briefcase and
spreading out his papers.

The officer leafed through them for a while without looking at Abrams, then pulled out his rubber stamp
and stamped each one on both sides. So far it was working,

and Abrams' self-esteem was returning. When this was finished the officer uttered a series of sentences in Spanish, the last word of which seemed to be something like passport. Was it *passoporto? Passaporta?* Or *passo el porta?* It didn't matter. No greenhorn gringo anymore, with a modest smile of satisfaction Ken quickly pulled it out, opening it to the photo page, and pushed it toward the officer, then snatched it back abruptly and handed it to him. He'd been warned about this. Good manners required that you place things in people's hands. The man shook his head and held it up by one corner as if it were a particularly ripe piece of trash.

"*Copia,*" he said, now leafing roughly through each page one by one and pointing to each side of it, "*copia, copia, copia.*" Nodding at each word.

Abrams suddenly realized that to get copies, he would have to leave his position in the room, which would lose him his place in line. His shoulders slumped and a flash of pain shot through his neck from top to bottom as he placed the passport back in his pocket and gathered up the other papers. Now he regretted not bringing Rebecca with him. She could have worn one of her short skirts and they would both have been waved right through.

The officer placed his hand on Abrams' wrist, saying, "And when you have copied all of it, *señor*—the place is just across the square, ask for Roberto Moreno—bring it back to me directly, and I'll stamp it. You won't have to wait in line again." This in perfect unaccented English. The man could have grown up in Cleveland.

Ken Abrams was thinking glumly about bureaucracy as he came back across the square with his copies, which he believed had cost him twenty-six pesos. It was really thirty-six because Roberto Moreno had taken advantage of his lack of familiarity with the coinage to shortchange him by ten.

Ken also believed he understood the police department version of government bureaucracy, at least in St. Paul. Its main function was to ensure that in every case procedures were followed that made the accumulated evidence vulnerable to as few court challenges as possible. That made sense. The rest of it was about making people feel that their jobs mattered, because if their jobs mattered then they did as well. The version he was encountering now seemed to fall entirely in the second category.

Back in the waiting room, his footsteps echoing on the marble floor, he walked briskly up to the desk and set the sheaf of passport copies before the officer, who at that moment was on the phone and between clients. However, from behind his back Ken heard a collective muted hiss of unrest from the waiting. . . what? They all were potential stampees like he'd been. Once you'd been stamped, there would be nothing more to do. The meaning was the process and the process was the meaning. He didn't bother to turn around.

With a flourish and an expression of benign fairness on his face, the officer hung up the phone and stamped the passport copies front and back and handed them back, pointing to a door beyond where the other stampees had disappeared over the course of the day. Abrams thanked him in English and walked through upright, a survivor, if not yet a winner, thinking hopefully, now we get to meet Ricardo Montes de Oca at last. It better be worth it.

After the wilting chaos of her taxi ride, Rebecca relaxed as she walked through the square. In the airbrushed presentation surrounding her, she could not see the pockmarks of bullets and the craters of cannon balls from the 1810 War of Independence. The effect of these and subsequent revolutions had long ago been repaired by the stone carver's expert hand. Scrub brushes and generations of rainwater had washed away the blackening left by the fires of the Revolution of 1910. Fortunately the Yankees hadn't come to Santa Elena after they smashed México City and Vera Cruz in the 1840s, or there would have been much more to repair.

Such reminders of class struggle made the local powers nervous, and foremost among those powers was the Arenas family, now bunkered in their walled and patrolled Hacienda Milagro, just outside of town. The family patriarch, Enrique Arenas, was waiting for the next attack. In a matter of days his youngest daughter, Angelina, would marry one of his own bodyguards in the cathedral, and the level of exposure this represented was giving Enrique ulcers.

Attractive, but short and fleshy, now pregnant and not bothering to pretend otherwise, Angelina Arenas had dreamed of a big family wedding in the cathedral since she was five years old. There was no way she would have settled for anything less, and although she was the youngest girl in the family, she had not grown up as a peacemaker. No one other than her doctor had ever dared to refer to her current condition in her presence. With her hair-trigger personality and smoldering black eyes, Angelina had been a handful since her toddler days, fond of pulling off her diaper and hitting her sisters in the face with it. Her nickname given by these two older sisters was "Bloodbath." It had stuck.

She had changed schools in fourth grade after she thrust an umbrella into the front wheel spokes of a bicycle ridden by a boy who loved to harass her. In protecting his head as he went over the handlebars he fractured his arm. Enrique had thought for some time that if he ever found out who was trying to kill him, he would give Angelina a gun and turn her loose on them first. In all likelihood, no follow-up would be required.

Rebecca, out of touch with her researcher now, knew nothing whatever of Enrique Arenas. Her thoughts ran more to orienting herself to Santa Elena, and using this oasis of calm to absorb a sense of it for her book. The campus-like setting of four plazas and their attendant government buildings and cathedral seemed perfect. She pulled out her map and tried to locate the precise spot on which she was standing. Since it was all background material, she could write the trip off on her taxes.

By mid-afternoon she had mastered the area around the cathedral, had been impressed as she circumnavigated the fenced-in ruins, taken a leisurely lunch, and discovered that the shopping in the area surrounding the plaza did not meet her expectations. In the immediate vicinity she found five art galleries and enquired in each, using her phrase book in a stumbling way, about a painter named Rafael Cantú. Oddly, no one had heard of him, but in one, a girl located a pocket directory of Santa Elena artists and studios, where there was no listing for him, either. She was gracious enough to give Rebecca a copy.

How could this be? she thought. Cantú sells in South America and Europe as well. With her digital camera, Rebecca photographed dozens of locations in and around the connected plazas to use in her Mark Sands book, and updated her expense notes to make sure what she spent was covered. On the southern portion of the four plazas, she moved toward a sculpture group set in a circle slightly recessed into the pavement. It consisted of four bronze chairs made from a variety of not quite chair-like components: castings of human feet, shoes, odd draperies and hardware. She spent some time looking at each part of it, and then backed off twenty feet or so to get a better sense of the group and the way each piece interacted with the others. Stepping a few paces farther back still, she discovered herself in the midst of three more small sculptures.

These diverse figures stood apart, past the opposite edge of the circle, as if silently absorbing the collective impression, just as Rebecca was. They were smaller, cast in bronze like the chair set, alone and unconnected to each other except by their task. She had the sense that, unlike the chairs, these figures were each made by a different artist. The first was an elderly woman with an umbrella, the tip planted squarely between her blunt mannish shoes. She stared back at the chairs with a perplexed look as if determined not to understand. Was she a tourist? Her glasses, slid halfway down her nose, may or may not have helped.

The second observer was a small girl in a two-piece bathing suit, meant to be about four or five years old, seated as if playing in the sand, one leg tucked under the other and one arm raised with an empty shovel pointed at the chairs. Rebecca sensed that the sand had just poured out. The girl's expression was one of amazement. An unseen breeze lifted the bronze curls from her forehead. Although it had a certain sense of motion, Rebecca thought the work only moderately interesting, but not up to the chairs themselves.

The third figure stopped her immediately. As she approached, she first thought it was a young boy, turned slightly away from her with an arm outstretched, the elbow at an angle. But as she came around to face it she realized she was looking at a sculptural representation of one of Rafael Cantú's little people. The vague stare, the enlarged ear facing her, the other one covered by an archaic cap; it was everything she had seen in the paintings, and her heartbeat raced.

Moving from side to side, she could find no position where the figure's gaze connected with her directly. The outstretched hand pointed approximately at the chairs, the wrist loose and somehow gracefully arched in a curve not possible in the real world. The facial expression expressed a tentative interest, yet also remained uncommitted. The lips were slightly pursed. One hand was raised palm upward, and the angle of the figure's head suggested that he might be just about to blow into it for no obvious reason. The long nose was there, the vaguely medieval clothes, and on its feet, the figure wore what appeared to be soft, half-formed leather footwear. They were not really shoes, but something that might have been worn on the feet before the concept of shoes had been fully worked out. Proto-shoes, she thought, imagining the small, amorphous prints they might make as they moved through some powdery floor residue. She recalled the twelve shabby "apostles" in Mark Sands' dining room painting, Cantú's *The Last Supper.*

Thinking she must have looked like an idiot standing transfixed before a minor part of the installation, she photographed it carefully, including the recessed rectangle on the figure's lower back that framed the signature. "C Morris," it said, with the lower arm of the C reaching under the Morris and beyond, a flourish that may have been pointing to a bigger and brighter future in art over the hill.

"Bingo!" said Rebecca to herself. Her first thought was that Rafael Cantú might be simply a cover identity for the person named C. Morris. This would account not only for his reluctance to supply a photograph, but the scarcity of information about his personal life as well, beyond a list of group exhibitions and one-man shows.

Remembering the artist directory and pulling it out of her purse, she flipped it open to M and there he was, Carlos Morris at Cruz Verde 32, Sculptor. This was easy, she thought, but what was the Morris connection going to be? At a minimum, Morris must know Cantú, and perhaps had used the image with the painter's permission. That would be enough, because one way or another they would get Cantú's address out of Morris. Ken was full of interrogation tricks. She could invent some phony story herself about having seen the painter's work in the States and desperately wanting to buy a picture. It wouldn't even have to be that phony.

When Rebecca headed for the edge of the plaza to catch a cab, it was past mid-afternoon. Ken's disappearance was problematic, but at least she had come up with an important lead herself, something she had promised to do. The case was now starting to point to a brilliant revival of her career in book three. She thought of trying to call the hotel to reach Abrams but decided that by the time she found a phone it would be just as fast to head back there. Naturally, her cell phone wasn't working in Santa Elena.

Abrams felt he was now in the endgame, but on the other side of the door he found himself in another waiting room much like the first. Inside were essentially the same two dozen people who'd been ahead of him in the first room. Now facing the seats were two desks, side by side, instead of one, with two officers, implying that they could handle the crowd in half the time, although that degree of efficiency had apparently not yet developed. Maybe they both took twice as long with each client. One of them looked up as he came in, and narrowly watched him as Ken carefully chose the appropriate seat in the back of the room, then continued with his current business.

Two and a half hours later Abrams had concluded that there really was no person named Teniente Ricardo Montes de Oca at all. It was really a verb of some weight and uncertain conjugation, *tenientericardomontesdeoca*, that described a process of grinding people down into a sad, uniform paste, pale brown in color, that on close inspection smelled strongly of defeat. At this moment he was summoned by a sharp rap of a pencil on the desk on the right, where, as he sat down with an attempt at a modest smile, the officer rose and slowly walked away without looking at him again.

Had Abrams looked out the window at this moment he would have seen Ricardo Montes de Oca win his third game of backgammon and pack the pieces into their sleek case as he watched the swinging hips of a visiting teacher from México City while she navigated the plaza in a striped dress and sun hat. Aware of his interest, she waited until she was well past him before she turned and looked back.

Twelve minutes later the officer returned, gave Abrams a kindly smile, and released a stream of Spanish that meant nothing whatever to him, then sat awaiting his response. Ken moved the folder toward the man and said, "My credentials," his voice slightly too loud, tapping the papers solemnly with his index finger and nodding. Thinking this would cue whatever English the man possessed, it didn't. Perhaps with this man there was none to cue. Instead, the officer carefully examined the stamped marks on both sides of each page, and finishing, pushed the stack back to Abrams with finality.

"*Español*," he said, "*no ingles*."

He opened his top drawer and drew out a business card, laying it on top of the documents. Ken picked it up. "Translation of the Documants, in the english oficial," it said, followed by, "Pedro Avila P." A phone number appeared below. Abrams nodded encouragingly as he thrust it in his shirt pocket, trying without success to manage a smile, then slid all the papers back into the file folder, now dog-eared and floppy. He didn't look back as he descended the grand marble staircase slowly, even thoughtfully. He waited until he was back in the plaza fronting the police headquarters before venting his feelings, which echoed back and forth among the elegant colonial facades, couched in a language he was certain few of the locals understood, but in a tone that must have been familiar to all. How smart he felt now to have left his gun back at the hotel. Sometimes you just have to trust your instincts, because he could have gone postal and shot everyone in sight.

As Rebecca passed the police headquarters she was arrested by the sight of a familiar-looking man standing in front of a nearby trash receptacle tearing a series of documents into tiny pieces. There was a focused violence in his gestures as he doubled over each wad until it was too thick to rip in half anymore. Countless minute pieces escaped from his hands, swirling through the air around the barrel. He didn't bother to pick them up, even though littering in Santa Elena was a crime. There were signs throughout each of the plazas to that effect.

She rushed over to the trashcan. "Ken, what's wrong?"

He looked up as if caught doing something shameful and spat out the Méxican verb he had just learned, "*Tenientericardomontesdeoca!*"

"OK," she said, calmly, now slipping instinctively into the role of a woman bracing up her man. "I haven't heard that word here before, but I know it must be something bad. Let me just look it up."

Rebecca pulled out her pocket dictionary, opening it to T, but of course there was no entry; the book didn't include obscenities. She flipped it shut and shoved it back into her purse, and glancing at his red face, took his hand comfortingly and put her arm around his waist as they slowly walked away. He suddenly had the stride of a much older person, and there seemed to be something strange about his neck.

"Give me a minute," he said. "I'll get this right. I've just never seen that kind of bureaucracy before." Without looking at her, he began to roll his head around on his shoulders as if releasing a kink, or a demon.

"We both can do this right if we join forces. I want to show you what I found." She guided him toward *The Witness* sculpture, for the first time feeling like they were a team, and planning to play up the strictly accidental way in which she had found it.

CHAPTER 10

Cruz Verde 32 was a two-story stucco house wider than most on the block, dusty rose in color, with trim in a muddy violet suggesting rotten grapes, and fronting, as usual, right up to the uneven slate sidewalk. At the street level, a garage door took up a third of the width. An iron grill covered the inexpensive stamped sheet-metal entry door. Abrams pressed the buzzer and they waited. Over the bell, a rectangular ceramic plaque bearing the words, "Casa Morris," was set into the stucco. Rebecca glanced up and down the street. Across from them a shoe store was opening, rows of girls' pink sneakers on view near the front. Next to it, a tiny *tienda* sold orange juice by the plastic bag, straw included, as well as toothpaste, bottled water, tamales and other sundries. A pair of speed bumps in the street dropped traffic velocity below thirty miles an hour, briefly.

"Somehow this doesn't look like the house of a well known sculptor," she said, biting her lower lip. She had worn jeans today with boots and a safari jacket over a tank top, hoping it was the right thing for a working sculptor's studio. The top showed enough cleavage to tempt Morris to talk, if cleavage was what made him talk. It had worked before.

"Maybe he's not that well known," Ken said. "I never heard of him."

She reflected for a moment on the fact that there was probably not a single sculptor's name that he could have summoned without some research. "It's not that I was expecting Rodin," she said, "but he had to be somebody of consequence to do that the piece on the plaza, it's so prominent."

"In the cluster of sculptural figures, he was only the witness, not the star. Maybe that was what the runner-ups got to do in the competition, if there was one. A consolation prize. Morris is just an also-ran, not a headliner."

There was the sound of a bolt sliding back and the inner door opened. A middle aged Méxican woman with her hair in a bun gave them an enquiring look.

Abrams leaned into the grill. "Carlos Morris?" He didn't attempt to ask whether Morris was at home.

"Charlie," she said. "He's here but I don't know if he can talk to you," she went on in English. "He isn't up yet. I'm Lupita."

Rebecca looked at her watch. It was two minutes after ten.

"Pleased to meet you. I'm Rebecca Stuart and this is my friend Ken Abrams. We want to talk to Mr. Morris about his sculpture in the plaza. It's very important. I want to know whether he's done any more like that. We might be interested."

Ken added, "I thought it was remarkable."

The woman put a key in the grill door and opened it. Inside they passed a door open to a room that faced the inner court, and then went up a flight of concrete stairs. The house design looked like it dated from the fifties. It had a utilitarian feeling, not something they expected from someone in the arts. At the top of the stairs the woman took off her apron. "I'm going to make some coffee," she said. "Would you like some?"

"Please don't go to any trouble," Rebecca said.

"It's no trouble. It's really for Charlie. He should be getting up now anyway. If I don't get him going he sleeps all day. Then he's up all night."

Rebecca gave Abrams a look; it sounded like Charlie was a child or an incompetent in this woman's care. Was he perhaps like an idiot savant, brilliant in sculpture but incapable of taking care of himself in routine ways? Maybe he also did formidable math problems in his head or juggled Coke bottles ten at a time, but couldn't dress himself.

"You can go on down to the studio," the woman went on, gesturing to a flight of industrial steel stairs that descended into the central courtyard. "I'll bring the coffee when it's ready. Charlie will be on one of the sofas. You can start waking him up, if you want. It may take a while." She spoke with an easy command of English, not quite as if she'd grown up speaking it, but more as though she'd lived for some years in the States.

Ken led the way down the stairs into a working courtyard, not the often elegant arcaded space found throughout México, but a drab utilitarian rectangle faced on three sides by the second floor of Morris' own house held up by reinforced concrete beams, and on the fourth by the rough brick wall of his neighbor's property. No stands of bamboo or bromeliad softened the edges; no palms, no split leaf philodendrons.

Looking toward the front of the house they could see into the garage, where a dusty Dodge pickup sat. The courtyard floor where they stood was concrete with overlapping chemical stains, the roof rusty corrugated steel covering half the space, the rest left open to the light and weather.

They walked among several worktables with clay projects underway, some of them beginning to express the subtle grace they'd seen in the witness figure in the plaza. Rebecca paused before several of them, examining the detail. There was no doubt that Charlie Morris had a solid grip on his materials and a refined touch. It was often centered on the open hand, similar to the hand of the Cantú figure they'd seen in the plaza, where the turn of the wrist was as elegant as the invitation of a geisha. It expressed a subtle insight, the comment of an observer perhaps detached, but not entirely withdrawn, far enough away to get a careful perspective, and also to remain uninvolved.

"Charlie Morris must know Cantú," said Rebecca. "He captured so much of that. . ."

A cavernous snore interrupted her, so loud that Abrams nearly went for his gun. Somewhere in the dark rooms recessed under the second floor, a pile of rags twitched as if a family of animals was running beneath it. A further snort, less startling, then silence. Nothing more moved.

"The Great Man," whispered Rebecca. "I believe we've found him. Let's do some type casting. I'll be the art connoisseur, you be the Philistine."

"This is just good cop/bad cop," he said, "I don't want to be the Philistine. It's not enough of a challenge."

"I know. Isn't it fun?"

In the room farthest from the street they found a brown plush sofa bearing a mound covered by two frayed and stained wool blankets, one green, one blue. A dark head protruded from one end, nearly covered with hair, shoulder length, with a thick beard and mustache. On a table nearby were two bottles of Havana Club rum, one nearly empty and the other unopened, a short thick glass pinched in the middle, an empty package of Camels, and an ashtray that hadn't been emptied in a while. Altogether they made a still life of late hours creativity. Rebecca leaned over the man and shook his shoulder.

"Mr. Morris! Mr. Morris, we saw your work on the plaza. It was called *The Witness*."

Nothing. The cloud of vaporized rum hanging over the sofa was possibly a fire hazard, but somewhat less offensive than the bus exhaust they had lived with on the streets since they arrived in Santa Elena. Abrams took a turn with the same result.

"He can't be drunk at this hour, can he?" he said. "It's only a little after ten."

Lupita's voice came from behind them. "He probably had his last drink about six-thirty or seven this morning."

"So he works through the night?"

"He's got it totally turned around now. He sleeps during the day off and on, then works at night. Soon he won't be able to do anything but work and sleep, and then the work part will start to fail too."

"What happens then?" asked Rebecca.

"He won't be able to tolerate that, because he's serious about what he does. So he'll go in for treatment again. I'd give it maybe five or six weeks. Charlie! Get up! You've got company. She placed her tray on the table and then shoved his thigh expertly with one foot.

"You've seen this cycle before?" said Rebecca.

"I've been with him almost ten years. This would be about the eighth or ninth time."

"How can he go through that cycle over and over again?"

"Well, we all have our life patterns, don't we?" There was no dismay in her voice.

Rebecca regarded her for a moment, wondering what Lupita's patterns might be. They had to form a set that integrated fairly well with those of Charlie Morris for her to have stayed around that long.

Morris sat up blinking, and pulled a blanket around his shoulders as if he thought he was naked. Patches of gray sprouted in his beard, and his eyes were pouchy, but not devoid of humor. He looked like Saddam Hussein immediately after his capture by U.S. forces in Iraq, only a degree or two more Hispanic. "I'll have the coffee now," he said, looking at his guests. "You guys have a cup too. What time is it?"

"Ten-fifteen," said Lupita. "These folks saw your work in the plaza. They wanted to meet you."

"*The Witness?*" he said, taking a slow sip as he pulled the hair back off his cheek with his left hand.

"Exactly," said Rebecca and introduced them. "I'm a collector and I was struck by it right away." Collector, as she knew from experience, was the magic word to any artist. "There was something about the expression and the gesture of the hand. What can you tell me about it?" Come at this slowly, she thought. Ken was looking at her with approval, saying nothing.

Morris made a loose gesture with his left hand, then dragged it over his eyes. "It was just second place in a competition, that's all. There was a request to submit a proposal for the plaza piece, and I did a miniature of the three graces, but in my own style, because they wanted it to be multiple figures. Jose Ferrante won with those chair things. Then they came back and said they wanted three witnesses to be set back from the Ferrante pieces, but looking at them, maybe as if they were just walking by or something." He paused, drew a long sip of coffee, and wiped his face vigorously with a corner of the blanket. "The idea was that they would mix with the real people passing on the plaza, like it was a continuously changing installation that included the tourists. It turned out I had that piece already made. I was ready to find a home for it and they liked it. It had been kicking around for a couple years and no one else had ever been interested in it. I guess nobody understood it. I'm not sure I do myself. End of story."

Rebecca now sensed the impatience coming off Ken like a cheap cologne, probably something with a sports theme and a macho name.

"Umm," he said, "but there must have been some inspiration behind that little figure, because when I look at it and I see the way he's, ah, looking so intently back at the chairs, it's almost like you planned it for exactly that position. Isn't it?"

Ken Abrams the art maven, Rebecca thought. It took him quite a few vague gestures to get through this statement. She wondered if she occasionally sounded like that herself. Probably not. Or if she did, only Edward Born would have noticed it.

Charlie Morris looked back at Abrams with a vague expression, and took another swig of his coffee. Setting it down, he shook his head. "Not really."

"It must have been intended for a different location, then, right?" Rebecca said, feeling like she needed to jump in before Ken blew this totally off the map. "Because it's so individual, so particular."

"It's so specific!" said Abrams triumphantly, grinning.

"To tell you guys the truth, I don't even remember," said Morris, starting to drift away from the conversation and gesturing to Lupita to refill his coffee cup. "I had that thing around the studio for several years, like I said. I mean, I liked it, but I can't remember why I made it. Doesn't that ever happen to you?" He finished by scratching his neck at the edge of his beard with a long fingernail.

Rebecca and Ken looked at each other blankly, Rebecca thinking that to connect to this thought she would have had to have written a novel without recalling why.

"Well, here's the thing," said Ken finally, now edging toward bad cop. "That little guy reminded me of the work of another artist, but this time a painter, named Rafael Cantú. Ever heard of him? I think it might even be a Méxican name. Someone told me he often spends some time here in Santa Elena."

Lupita was moving about in the background, getting a little impatient. It was as if the conversation seemed threatening in some way. Rebecca grinned and nodded at her reassuringly. Morris only shook his head.

"No, I don't think I have. You're saying he paints figures like my *Witness*? He must have seen it. Maybe he was here as a tourist. I don't know." He tilted his head back and took a long swallow of the coffee.

Rebecca nodded. "I even have one of his pictures myself," she said. "It came from a gallery in Santa Fe. That's why we were so struck by your work when we saw it on the plaza. We were just walking by."

"Cantú is an unusual name. I just don't remember it, but then, I don't try to remember everything." Charlie Morris's grin expressed a kind of calm resignation to this.

"And that peculiar grace," Abrams said, "that hand gesture, the way it. . . "

"Holy shit!" said Morris, standing up unsteadily and setting the cup on a table nearby. "I do remember now! It was in the cathedral." He paused for a moment, looking at the floor, then off at the brick wall of the neighboring house, as at a scene unrolling. "Sometimes it takes me a while. I haven't thought about this in a long time."

"In what they call the 'new' cathedral here?" asked Ken. "Not the ruined one behind it."

"Yes! I was there to look at that stuffed saint they've got in a glass cabinet on the left where you come in. I was thinking of using that image, but more twisted, you know? And I was sitting in a pew nearby waiting for a crowd of school kids to move on so I could get a better look at it." He began to cough harshly, as if clearing his mind required that his throat be cleared as well.

"But that saint couldn't have been the inspiration for this image, because she doesn't look anything like that," Rebecca said when he finished. She had already read in the guidebook about the bones of a Roman girl of the third century that had been found in the Vatican Catacombs in the 1880s and given to the Cathedral of Santa Elena. The story came with them that she was twelve years old at the time of her death and was trying to protect her virginity. Now what remained of her was packaged in the nineteenth century image of a smiling china doll of almost dime-store quality.

"No, no, it had nothing to do with that, but as I was sitting there, this little guy came out from under the pew in front of me, right next to a column. He was like a kid in size, but with a much more mature look on his face, yet hairless. It startled the hell out of me. When he saw me he was really surprised too, and when I took out my cell phone to snap a picture of him, he dipped his hand in his pocket and blew into it. God, it's so funny that you came here about it because it just all came back to me. I haven't thought of that for a long time."

"What happened then?" said Rebecca quietly, digesting this as she recalled the pixie dust on Mark Sands' dining room floor.

"Well, I really don't remember anything after that, not even leaving, but I had the picture on my phone and when I found it later, I used that for the sculpture. That's where it ends, I mean. I really hadn't ever thought about the rest of it other than the sculpture itself until you guys started asking me about it. You know how it is sometimes? There are things you don't remember. I'd probably had a few drinks that night. Maybe it didn't even happen that way." He stared off toward the garage as if he'd seen something moving there. Rebecca followed his gaze, pulling her jacket more closely about her.

Ken nodded patiently. "Really," he said without irony. "I can see that."

"Yeah," said Morris, still thinking about it.

"Yet the image of that little guy stayed with you," said Rebecca, "and you probably kept the picture on your phone, right? It was that remarkable. I know I would've."

"Yeah, I guess, of course. Well, no, actually. That was two phones ago, I think."

"And you never saw anything like that again?" said Ken.

"No. I'm not sure now that I saw it the first time, although there was that picture, and then the sculpture, so I must have." Shrugging, Morris shook his head and sat down, staring at one of the blank walls. His right hand probed the curly hairs of an eyebrow. "I think I'm going to get back to work now, after I go to the bathroom. Thanks for coming by. 'Preciate it." He didn't offer to shake hands. Lupita watched him walk away.

"That's the way he is now. You did well getting that memory out of him. It's more than I can usually do."

"Did he ever do anything else based on that image?" Rebecca asked her.

"Nothing. Sometimes he'll have an idea and it turns into a long series, one he can't get out of his head, and he'll run variations on it for months, but The Witness was not that way. Of course it wasn't called The Witness then. I liked it, but it was as if, after he did it, he didn't want to think about it again."

"Do you recall what he titled it originally?"

"Yes, he called it *The Other*. Later, when it was kicking around the studio all that time he started calling it Shorty. He'd talk to it. He'd say, 'Hey Shorty, when is someone going to take you off my hands?'"

Ken and Rebecca exchanged glances as they followed her back up the steel staircase and then out the front door.

Standing outside on the sidewalk, Rebecca said,

"It wasn't the booze that made him see *The Witness* that night. There's a long tradition of dwarfs in Spanish painting, think of Velasquez. But *The Witness* was clearly not a dwarf. The proportions aren't right."

"No," said Abrams. "I have the feeling Charlie Morris was working from life, more or less."

"And he saw the figure coming out from under the pews? What did he say again?"

"He said, 'This little thing came out from under the pew in front of me, right next to a column.' Those were his exact words. Sometimes you can't write things down in front of people. When you're a cop, you just have to memorize what they say." He pulled out a notebook and began writing.

"I think it's time for us to pay a visit to the cathedral," said Rebecca. "I heard there's an interesting saint there who died protecting her virtue." Not a problem I've been having lately, she thought to herself.

Ken and Rebecca took a twenty-five minute cab ride from Casa Morris and stood at the Victorian bandstand on the square before the Santa Elena Cathedral entrance. Neither said much during the ride, unable to make themselves heard over the traffic. The exterior of the church was an orgy of Baroque extravagance, reflecting the fundamental principle of design of that period: life is short—if you have any ideas about architecture, preferably borrowed from past styles, use them all on the same building, because you may not live long enough to do another one. A Gothic spire can be very effective next to a Renaissance dome over a Greek temple pediment.

For Rebecca it meant that enthusiasm trumped coherence. "What do you think of the cathedral?" she asked.

Abrams shrugged. "I'm not usually interested in things religious except when they have some bearing on a case. To me it's just a big building where one of Rafael Cantú's pals was once seen and might possibly be seen again."

"What was it that you think he saw?"

"I can't put a name to it, but I don't have to at this point. Seeing *The Witness* after seeing your painting and Cantú's *Last Supper*, I know there are small people out there and he's got access to them. I wish now that I'd requested photos of the crime scene floor from Trenton, Houston, and Santa Fe." He pulled out his notebook and scribbled in it. "I'd like to see what their footprints were like, if there were any. We know there was propofol and glitter used."

"I think México's been a little difficult for you so far," she said, thinking of the scene in front of the police building. "Maybe you should cut yourself some slack, after all, it's a foreign country. You probably don't travel much, right?"

"Not that much. There's the problem of trying to use your investigative discipline when you don't know what you're looking at."

"So for you a foreign country might usually be somewhat closer to home, something more like Louisiana or Utah. Or New York City, for example."

He looked at her for a moment, his face creased but holding, then laughed as they climbed the cathedral steps. "I'm glad you're here to set me straight Rebecca. Anyway, the tell was in that sculpture. Think about the crime scene footprints."

She stopped at the door. "Of course. Tiny, child-like, and from your photos, no weave, no defined heel or toe. Just what these folks would wear, if they existed. He couldn't have known that, unless. . ."

"Charlie Morris really saw one in the cathedral."

"Just imagine what else he's seen. It must be like the sixties all over again for him some nights, especially when it's time for him to go back into treatment again."

"I don't think he's old enough to remember the sixties, but here's the bottom line." Ken started gesturing now because it was beginning to come together. "You can believe one of two things. Either Morris saw one or more of Cantú's pictures and decided to rip off the image for his own work, or he saw one of those real life Cantú characters somewhere, probably just a few steps away from us inside."

"Then let's look at the first possibility," Rebecca said. "It's interesting that no one seems to know Cantú or his work here."

"And don't most painters try to keep their name before the public?"

"Where did Morris see Cantú's work then, if he's ripping him off? It doesn't look like he's able to travel much. He could have gone to a gallery website, but how would he have known the name? Cantú obviously doesn't show here and he's not listed in the art guide. He can show in Santa Fe, in Geneva, God knows where else, but according to Edward Born, he was never seen in person at his openings, and his photo is never shown. He's a painter with a strong reputation but no image, and he gets away with it."

"That leaves us with option two," Ken said, "and I don't like this one, but it's what we're left with. Morris must have seen the real Cantú character."

"My sense was that when he finally found his way back into that memory, he was telling us the truth," she said, "and there's one more thing as well. The little guy on the plaza was about to blow into his hand, and Morris seemed to recall that too. I know what I thought of when I saw that, and it's nothing that Charlie Morris could have gotten from one of Cantú's paintings. I've looked at as much of his work as anyone, and I've never seen it."

"It could be the last thing Charlie saw in the cathedral, and when he snapped the photo, he caught the little guy in the act. But I don't think he knew what it meant when he made the sculpture, it was just a gesture that the picture recorded. When he passed out in the pew, it was nothing new and he took no special notice of it because it probably happened to him several times a day."

Inside the cathedral, expecting the pale ochre of limestone, the standard building material of México, they saw instead an interior of gleaming white with gold trim.

Ken immediately began looking for the 12-year-old saint, but Rebecca's eyes sought the dome, thinking of the first one going down, and wondering if these builders had somehow reinforced the construction to compensate for the possibility of earthquakes. As she walked up the main aisle the dome came slowly into view.

It was, she thought, a simple concept. There were four massive columns—or piers—at the corners of a square, connected by four huge arches. The bottom of the dome, which was circular and went straight up for a small distance, forming a drum, rested on the top center of each arch. The arches alternated with a curved, triangular section that supported the rest of the drum and the dome above as it moved around the circle. If an earthquake destabilized any one of the piers, the whole thing would come down. How reassuring that now, at least, seismologists all over the world worked to detect instability anywhere in the earth's crust. If there were a problem developing, at least the cathedral could probably be cleared of people in time.

A hand came to rest on her shoulder, the fingers lingering for an instant on her neck, giving her a small tingle. "That better not be the priest," she said, "or I'm telling."

"I think I've found the place," Ken's said softly. "Come and take a look."

They moved down the main aisle toward the back, where, in a wide choir loft above the doors, an immense pipe organ filled the space. At the last pew they turned right and walked to the corner. Here, behind the glass in confectionery splendor, lay the remains of the third century saint, her face a pale pink bisque above a white satin party dress. Tiny blue bows edged the puffed sleeves.

Ken was leaning over the glass case. "I think she must have looked a little bit like you," he said, "in her prime."

"And what exactly are we looking at?" asked Rebecca.

"I really don't know," said Abrams, "but this figure is what Carlos Morris came to see that night."

"How can this image be so bland if she died so

violently?"

"Maybe what's on offer here is the reassurance of triumph over that kind of victimhood," he said. "The violence is short-lived, the victory is eternal."

"I didn't know you were a believer," she said, turning to look at him.

"I'm not. I'm just an observer, and that's the message I see. Now let's observe this." He led her to the last row of pews across the side aisle, which ended just short of a pier at the left, not continuing behind it because the view toward the altar would have been blocked. "Here's where Morris was sitting, because if he were farther up, even in the next row, he couldn't have seen the martyred girl as he waited for the school kids to move on. He was here in the last pew."

"Then he sees the *Witness* figure under the seat ahead and takes the phone picture," Rebecca said. "The figure blows pixie dust in Morris' face, he passes out, and when he wakes up, there's no one there. What does that tell us?"

"Not much. It's more what it doesn't tell us. For example, where did the little guy come from? I don't think he lives under the pews. There's something we're not seeing, but anyway, the little guy apparently does not feel he can mix with the crowd. The pixie dust response says that. So he must not have just walked in here looking like himself—he'd stand out too much."

"So he can't be seen by anyone, but why take the risk of being here?"

"I don't know," Ken said. "This time yesterday I didn't even know his kind existed. Maybe he's religious but he can't tolerate crowds so he views the services from under the pews."

"I think that's thin. What if he's a thief, going through purses while their owners are singing hymns or taking communion?"

"That's plausible, but the guy is more than a purse snatcher, and judging from the evidence at the other crime locations, there must be more than one of his kind." Abrams dropped to his knees and stuck his head under the next pew. Rebecca leaned over to watch.

"Sudden conversion?" she said. "I think it's finally getting to you."

He was bent over now close to the base of the pier, reaching in his pocket. "I just want to take a sample from the floor."

"But hasn't it been four years or so?"

"Yes, but I'm betting that nothing has been cleaned between the edges of the marble floor tiles and the base of the pier during that time. Maybe even since this place was built." He pulled a handkerchief out and opened his penknife. Wrapping the cloth around the back edge of the blade, he inserted it into the space against the pier base and dragged it along through the crack. When he finished, he folded it over and over on itself with the trapped particles inside.

"We'll see what the lab in St. Paul has to say about this. If it comes up pixie dust, then we'll have proof of Morris' story. Since we know from his emails that Cantú operates from here too, I think we might have to extend our visit. Let's find a courier service that can overnight this, maybe Red Hat. With a little luck we might know something for certain in forty-eight hours."

"Wait a minute. Why didn't the little guy from

under the pew take Charlie's cell phone after he took the picture?"

"Did he even know Charlie took his picture with the phone?"

"I wonder if he knew what it was. If he can't go out much in public, he might be living such an isolated life that he doesn't know much about current technology. Could that be?"

CHAPTER 11

As Abrams and Rebecca left the cathedral they passed within 200 feet of Jeremy, below and off to the right, who was at that moment lying in bed with Luisa in her small private room three levels beneath the rubble.

Luisa's room was dark except for what little light leaked in around the edges of the curtain from the floor lighting in the corridor. Jeremy's fingertips located his glasses on the night stand, and he swung his legs over the side of the platform bed. There was just enough light to pull on his pants and shirt, and locate his shoes. As he turned toward the curtain his foot lodged against something soft, and there was a low growl as a mouthful of teeth closed lightly around his ankle, then released it. He had offended Tease again; it was inevitable. The dog hadn't accepted him yet and probably never would.

When he awakened earlier—he'd misplaced his watch somewhere in Luisa's room so he couldn't tell just how late it was—he found himself in the mood for some independent exploration. Besides helping him with his coming of age, Luisa had been a wonderful guide through some of the mysteries of the underground colony, as in the case of the Relic, but now he was in the mood to form his own impression of things. It was the researcher in him.

Somewhere there had to be a dedicated infrastructure that furnished all the essentials for a small town. Without the Internet, which he hadn't been able to connect with from his laptop, he would find it himself. He couldn't hear Luisa's breathing, but by placing his hand on the thin line of hair on her back, he knew she was asleep because it didn't rise under his fingers.

He had met no other residents of the Aldea, as Luisa called it, saying the word meant village. Her reluctance to introduce him was puzzling. He had considered at first whether she might be ashamed of him, but then remembered she had chosen him from a large pool of possible mates, so it couldn't be that. Surely, most men would envy him now. As he swung his feet over the side of the bed he recalled all the little differences he had at first only accommodated but now positively embraced.

Jeremy waited until he was in the corridor to put his shoes on, bracing his back against the grainy wall. Lighting was provided by a thin strip along the floor at both sides, like in a movie theater. He knew he and Luisa had come in from the left so he turned right. Immediately beyond her room was another curtained doorway. He hesitated for a moment, then slid the fabric an inch or so away from the edge. He could see nothing inside, but realized that he was probably visible to whoever occupied the room. Jeremy hastened on, feeling like a prowler.

The other side of the corridor held no openings, and he began to sense he must be at the edge of the Aldea in a dormitory area, and that at any time, when the population required it, new rooms could be cut into the stone opposite Luisa's. This prompted a further thought. What was being done with the debris when they carved out a new room? With nearly 300 residents, there must be at least a hundred sleeping rooms, plus all the utilities and common areas. Was it like being in a POW camp movie where the prisoners all had their pockets full of dirt from the tunnel they were digging, and they shuffled around each day sprinkling it out through their pants legs?

Coming down with Luisa, he had found the plan to be a stairwell with a hub of radiating corridors at each new level. It didn't seem logical to Jeremy that there would be only one such stack of hubs, given the size of the Aldea. He continued to the right, thinking that the hubs would be linked. His only concern was that if he came to another hub, how could he mark the corridor he had come from? There were no signs. He moved along, counting his steps. He had memorized the pattern of the fabric that covered Luisa's door, since these draperies were the only individual elements he'd seen.

At forty-four steps from Luisa's room he reached the next hub, where he pulled a pen from his shirt pocket, one of three he always carried, and marked this on an expense receipt from Office Max from his wallet. There were seven other corridor openings in view. Reluctantly he removed his left shoe and tapped one of his precious pens into the soft porous lava about two inches from the floor at the opening he'd emerged from, thinking it was not likely to be seen by anyone else and removed. Crossing the center, he entered the stairwell and discovered to his huge surprise that the stairs only went up. If he was truly just four or five levels down, he was still at the bottom of this hub. He did the only thing he could do, he went up the stairs, pausing at each level and looking out at the center. He still saw no one.

There were five levels exactly like the ones he had come down in, but then Jeremy arrived at the bottom of a rectangular shaft with steel rungs climbing one side. Testing each one for firmness, he began to ascend. At each rung, set oddly close together, the light was dimmer since the floor lighting did not travel far up the shaft.

At the fifteenth rung, the wall surface changed, detectable only because it was no longer the black lava, and gave off marginally more of the limited reflected light. To his touch, it was smoother, not grainy. He did not know what this meant.

After two more rungs the shaft widened out onto a narrow platform on all four sides. He stood gradually, pressing his hands against the wall and found that he could not quite stand fully up; his head was still bent over. He raised his hands and pushed against the surface above him. It yielded slightly as if it were not firmly anchored, and he lowered his hands. Clearly it was not stone. In the semidarkness he smiled grimly—he was onto them now. It was obviously a trap door, the same kind of device Luisa had opened on their way in after meeting him at the iron fence. How these crude coverings had kept their secret for hundreds of years was a mystery to him. He considered the idea that the inhabitants of Santa Elena might not be that smart, but then rejected it. Maybe it was more a case of hide in plain sight.

He was determined to go on now, to continue to the surface no matter where it might be. Luisa had said they had entered through the "guest" entrance when they came down through the Arenas sarcophagus. Later she had also called it the front door. The one he stood in now must be the staff entrance. Listening for a moment, he thought he could hear low conversation nearby. With one mighty thrust that briefly but fondly reminded him of his latest encounter with Luisa, he lifted against the ceiling panel with both hands and his head, expecting it to pivot on one side and hinge back out of the way, revealing either daylight or the night sky. He felt it yield, subtly at first, but then with a nasty unexpected crack. Suddenly the panel buckled in the middle and a cascade of rubbish fell over him and down through the shaft, bouncing and echoing against the rungs and walls in the stairwell below. He had no idea what time it was, since the shaft hadn't gotten lighter, and he hadn't been able to locate his watch in Luisa's room before he left without turning on a light.

Jeremy slid down the wall into a sitting position, happy to have avoided falling down the shaft, even as he listened to the banging and crashing of large and small objects below him, from the sound, some continuing down all five levels. His eyes were blinded with dust, and at the end, a large object, smooth and rounded, had careened off his shoulder and landed in his lap, like some kind of ball. His hands stroked the surface until he found two of his fingers in the eye sockets of a small human skull.

His immediate instinct was to thrust it away from him and let it fall with the rest of the debris, apparently the entire contents of some forgotten grave, possibly a burial lost within the old cathedral. But there was also the noise to consider; he had already made enough racket. He set the skull on the ledge. Besides, he was covered with filth of a kind he didn't want to think about. Although it was dry to the touch, it smelled musty and was dense with earthy overtones, complex, almost meaty. To his touch, the surfaces around him were powdery and scattered with textile fragments that reminded him of the rotted silk packed with the Relic. As he sat there considering his next move, he noticed light at the edges of the enclosure opposite him where it joined a stone wall. It looked like the enclosure where he sat could move outward. Had he only disturbed some covering display at the top of it? Jeremy didn't feel, with all the disruption he'd already caused, that he could explore it any further at this moment. Perhaps as he worked on the layout of this place further, he could revisit it. He shuddered and shook himself off as well as he could, then started down the rungs, his hands closing over the dusting of debris on each one.

At the bottom he dragged his fingers through his hair and shook it like a dog coming out of a pool. Residue had collected in both his ears, and on his eyebrows, and he peeled off his shirt and shook it out as well.

His first thought as he threaded his way along the corridor was to find some paper and start a map once he was cleaned up. The second was how he was going to explain this to Luisa.

CHAPTER 12

Even during his earliest efforts in painting Rafael Cantú Arenas had never used Arenas, his mother's family name, when signing his canvases. Instead, he tried to emphasize his otherness, his distance from the small common gene pool that had solely determined the physical makeup of most of the people who lived inside the Aldea, the Village. Inside, no reference was ever made to Santa Elena, the city founded and still dominated by the other branch of the Arenases, other than calling it the Outside.

Young Rafael was a good-looking kid, one of few in the Aldea who shared ancestry with the big people of the Outside who were not of the Arenas family. This accounted for his impressive stature. He was nearly five feet tall, as tall or taller even than most of the women under the mountain. Even as an untried youth in his late fifties, it had given him an unaccustomed feeling of equality with them. He knew that the other men, mostly one meter tall or less, envied him. Who wouldn't? There was even a touch of curl in his hair.

In fourth year Mores and Taboos class, his mother had studied the courtship protocols of the Scottish Highland clans, which required young men to find mates outside their own extended family groups. She had observed with concern the effects of inbreeding in the Aldea. It turned her into a pioneer advocate of exogamy, the practice of choosing your spouse from family groups entirely outside your own.

To make her point, in her mid seventies she had picked up and seduced in his sleeper car a traveling businessman from Morelia in the later part of 1910, just as the first phase of the Revolution was getting underway. This man, Jorge Cantú, played no further role in her life once she got off three stops later, or in that of her son Rafael, who was born of this brief union in June of 1911. The name given him by his mother would prove to be prophetic. She had thought it referred only to an angel, but he, early on, knew otherwise.

The ease with which she became pregnant suggested that her interest in Outsiders was well founded, although it had not started a trend, perhaps because the women residents of the Aldea tended to be shy, and reluctant to spend extended periods in the Outside. It was even worse for the men, who, being easy to spot, almost never went out, and certainly not during daylight. In either case, the Aldeans had a tendency to sunburn even after short periods of exposure.

Growing up, Rafael found himself strongly drawn to art, especially the painters of the northern European Renaissance: Hieronymus Bosch, Jan van Eyck, and others who saw an apocalyptic vision latent on their canvases. He began to identify the Aldeans with the lost and outcast figures that peopled this universe, and he studied the techniques of these painters carefully with an eye to developing a similar style and polish. Surely the twentieth century was no stranger to apocalypse, and their manner of painting could be made to feel current. Rafael had experienced it locally for the first nine years of his life as the Revolution went on above them, and he felt early on that he might be able to extend and even burnish the concept in his work. To one who lived underground because of the oppression of others, the chaos afflicting those above had some appeal.

When he began to paint seriously he didn't have to look far for his subjects, selecting from among his first cousins those who most clearly showed the characteristics that the original Juan de Arenas had found disturbing about his two first-born children. In the small family museum in the ruined citadel he was able to examine the shabby garments worn by little Tomás de Arenas and his sister Julia when they were first confined there. This group of tattered and disintegrating items became the inspiration for all the clothing he subsequently used in his pictures.

These ideas were evolving about the same time as World War II was demolishing Europe and Asia piecemeal. The poster images of the maimed and psychologically ruined men returning from the trenches that he witnessed on his occasional trips above ground inspired him to create improvised prosthetic devices as props. They were aids that the people of the Aldea might have been able to manufacture themselves from the wood scraps and other cast off materials in their warehouse beneath the old citadel. Later he adapted these to animals as well.

Because he was so much taller than his male relatives, during this period and for some time following, Rafael was able to appear in public on the surface of the mountain, arousing a moderate but still tolerable amount of attention from the normal residents of Santa

Elena. Most Outsiders mistook him for a dwarf, although his proportions were reasonable for someone his height. Over time he became known by sight in the art supply stores, but with that implicit shyness of a persecuted race, he never gave his name and always paid in cash.

Although the stature of other Aldean males confined them to mostly labor and service positions, as Cantú matured, he rose to a leadership role, partly because of his (relatively) great height and his ability to move about freely in the outside world. This was something that normally only the girls were able to do. It was a role somewhat informal, since there was no regular government in the Aldea. In the past, residents with critical skills, like the women who operated the clothing manufacturing workshop, or the ones who managed food production or ran the educational programs, had often found themselves with as much power as anyone who was an elected leader on the Outside. But titles of leadership were never used.

As his painting evolved and he became more deeply engaged in the situation of the Aldeans, Rafael Cantú grew increasingly bitter about the role fate had assigned his people. In the limited archives, he had researched the early history of the Arenases, and soon realized that the present holders of the family assets and power had no right to either, being descended from Juan de Arenas' third-born and following children. In the perpetual night of the subterranean corridors of the Aldea, he began to plot his revenge.

During this period he painted Luisa a number of times, always nude or nearly so, once alone but usually with other figures. This included the work titled *Girl with Three Players*. She had also appeared in his *Last Supper* as the nude Mary Magdalene, one of his most ambitious works. For this Rafael had given her hair a reddish tint and some loose curl. Edward Born had sold it much later for $54,000. Born believed that the buyer's name had been kept confidential, but it didn't take Cantú—curious about who would pay so much for one of his paintings—more than a day after its delivery in St. Paul to discover Mark Sands' identity. The apostle who'd posed as St. Thomas had simply climbed out of his seat next to St. Peter, hopped off the buffet, and examined Mark's Sands' mail on the dining table.

Through the painting, Luisa and the twelve others had, on another occasion, watched unmoving from the wall over Sands' buffet as the maid served dinner to a trio of business clients. The model who had posed for the Christ figure was later heard to remark that Megan Sands looked pretty hot for an Outsider chick, although somewhat out of scale. He was the same one who had blown pixie dust in Mark Sands' face during the last moments of his life.

Rafael himself, with eight years of English study in his background, was intrigued by the name Sands. He soon discovered online that Mark Sands was a distant relative. This was the startling coincidence that sealed the money manager's fate.

For a year or two, Luisa was Cantú's favorite model, although he often modified her features slightly so the viewer wouldn't recognize her from picture to picture. He painted other girls from the Aldea nude as well, always in a pose that emphasized their apparent humanity, concealing other features, like the additional hair on their spines, which might suggest they had unresolved genetic issues. Their mouths were never open because of their forked tongues, for example, although Cantú didn't try to alter their violet eyes. As one of these models was passing behind the canvas one morning and paused to say something to him, he was greatly startled to see her nearly finished image on the canvas move as she spoke. Although considerable thought on his part yielded no plausible explanation for this, like most residents of the Aldea, he was a utilitarian at heart, and a period of protracted experimentation with this new feature immediately followed.

What emerged was that anyone portrayed in his canvases could climb out and back in if the real person were standing behind it, even if the canvas were placed some distance away (even thousands of miles away), provided that the models were dressed the same—or undressed the same—as in the painting. Rafael Cantu was not able to explain any of these protocols, but he immediately saw their nearly infinite possibilities for abuse, something that, as he aged, was developing more appeal for him. He felt like he'd been handed a new tool in his campaign to wreak havoc on his usurping kin in the Outside.

Additional research online convinced him that the process was related to crystals embedded in the volcanic structure of the mountain. Not being a fan of New Age elements, he let it go at that.

It was also during this period that he broke through and obtained major representation for his work. Besides Born & Born, he began showing at Bergen & Fils in Geneva, which specialized in quirky central European painters who were not represented in the Paris or London markets. He also sold through La Jugaretta, a fashion-forward space in downtown Buenos Aires, all white walls and odd angles within a confectionery French Beaux Arts building, where his work stood out starkly in its unreality. The backgrounds of these paintings, most often olive brown verging on black, beckoned the viewer into an otherworldly space that created the same kind of discomfort the residents of the Aldea felt when they ventured into the Outside. This was an important part of Cantú's message, as was his subjects' obvious sense of isolation.

As his status within the international art community grew, there was not only the sudden gratification as his work began to sell, but also the greatly increased access to hard currency. Aldean girls who were the tallest and looked the most normal could be sent outside with cash to purchase much needed things that couldn't be made underground, like paper, pharmaceuticals, tools, and the tiny light bulbs for the carefully controlled low-voltage lighting system that had been salvaged from a demolished movie theater.

Pharmaceuticals were critically important because salves and ointments to combat the multitude of rashes and skin fungi that grew in the absence of sunlight were indispensable. They couldn't be made in-house. Without remedies like this, within a matter of months, people's toes tended to fuse into a solid gummy mass. Eventually this problem was resolved by placing one of the girls in a job with a firm that distributed wholesale pharmaceuticals. There she had access to a variety of samples that, unlike product inventory, were never tracked. One of these samples was propofol.

Embarking on a series of experiments with a each sample as it came in, Aldean chemists quickly discovered a use for propofol, and the minimally equipped in-house lab developed a way to dry it. Mixing it with glitter that they made from grinding up old CDs was a nice touch, suggestive to Rafael of the sand in each of their names. For this purpose Cantú especially favored rap CDs, as being grittier than most other kinds.

Unfortunately, as these positive developments were happening, Rafael Cantú was also gaining weight. At first he thought he was only entering a sedentary maturity. After all, painting didn't provide much exercise. But the weight gain continued unabated even though he tried to eat less. He didn't know that the same thing had happened to his father, who had blown up so badly toward the end of his life that he could no longer get through the doors of his beloved sleeper cars. He had ultimately died of heart failure in 1926 at the age of fifty-one. Because Rafael didn't know this, it also did not occur to him that the gene pool outside the mountain might be fraught with risk as well, that it did not always represent the ideal way to be, in ways other than just the observed fact that lifetimes were shorter in the Outside.

Gradually Rafael became increasingly pear-shaped, and as his flesh sagged in pendulous rolls around his body, bell shaped, so much so that it was often difficult to get close enough to the easel for the fine detail that his pictorial style demanded. Constantly leaning over caused chronic back problems. Although his lowered center of gravity made it unlikely he would capsize, he still found himself using brushes with longer handles. These called for a steadier hand, ironically, something harder to achieve as he aged.

He had lengthened and broadened his usual painter's smocks into tent-like garments that caused the clothing workshop to complain that they required too much fabric, always at a premium underground. Cotton especially, was prone to rot, especially when stored near the porous walls that often permitted water to seep in from the Outside.

During this period, Cantú also stopped shaving, the very necessity of which had always been a point of pride for him, even though razor blades were hard to find, since no one else underground had needed to. As his patchy beard grew he found it was becoming more uneven and mottled in color, as if his DNA were separating into its two constituent halves, each giving different instructions to his body. His reaction to this was mixed anger and despair, for like most residents of the Aldea, he had a horror of genetic problems. In the end he did what any painter would do when faced with these issues, he kept on painting as if it were his salvation, as it was.

None of this process improved his already thorny disposition.

Because of his deterioration, the paintings became darker, the characters more distant and unconnected, and he began to brood more about revenge against the Outsider Arenases. They were all usurpers, and they would all pay.

It was after several years of this kind of thinking that he began to make attempts on the life of Enrique Arenas, the local head of the above-ground family, and later, Alvaro Arenas, the auxiliary bishop in Houston, and soon after, Mark Sands. It was not that Rafael was evil or inherently vicious, like a character in a Lester Grunge mystery, only that his sense of ongoing injustice gradually became unendurable. The assault on the student teacher in New Jersey was no more than an attempt to see if breeding would work with selected Outsider females, in this case, one conveniently part of the family. It didn't. At five-foot-ten, the attackers had all found their intended victim too large and intimidating to deal with, even after liberal doses of pixie dust.

At this point, already mounting toward crisis, Rafael Cantú was abruptly thrown into a panic by the message from Edward Born requesting his photo. It was not his first such request (Cantú had ignored two others), but now it began to feel like a gratuitous betrayal, coming from a man who had helped him get his start and nourished the price levels of his pictures to the point where they were the primary source of cash for the community.

Perhaps there was also a paranoid strain among the genes passed to him from Jorge Cantú, another defect. In any case Rafael saw the photo request as an effort to penetrate the carefully controlled shield he'd erected around his identity. After brooding about it for several days, he reluctantly took action against the art dealer. He wondered later if he'd overreacted, but by then the deed was done and his small cousins had climbed back into their canvases. The Geneva and Buenos Aires galleries were always requesting more paintings, and it seemed unlikely that his sales would suffer.

Cantú sat in his studio in the former comedor, the dining room, of the old Arenas Palace. Because the building had been constructed in anticipation of Juan de Arenas' wedding in 1535, a time when defensive considerations were still part of any major structure in Santa Elena, the room was on a lower level facing an inner courtyard. Here the outer wall was part of the foundation and earthworks, necessarily windowless. Although the Pichanchas had been reduced by military action and disease to one tenth their original number, and confined to servitude as well, the occasional straggler could still pop up with revenge in his heart.

Now blooming with cracks, the comedor's barrel vault ceiling had easily held during the collapse above, some distance from the fallen dome. While the decorative painting had mostly faded with time or flaked away from seepage, nonetheless the room still held an inviting feel for the painter, now even more so because he'd done so many disturbing pictures there. It had a comfortable history.

Within the courtyard beyond, nearly filled with masonry rubble, passages had been cleared here and there to allow natural light to penetrate with the aid of a set of cleverly placed mirrors. With subtle adjustments during the day and larger ones throughout the year, Cantú was able to approximate and maintain the diffuse indirect quality of the north light any painter needs.

His mountainous form was no longer able to fit within the arms of any chair available in the Aldea, so he sat on a bench that, even though it was backless, gave him the comforting width he required as he worked. But on this particular morning, he was not working, although there was a picture on his easel that looked promising as far as it went. Rafael was beginning to feel that his weight was dragging him down. He was only ninety-six, a time of life that within the mountain should have been part of a vigorous middle age. It felt more like the onset of a great weariness, possibly the slide toward an early death, and he had so much yet to do. Besides all the unpainted pictures queued up in his head, there was the largely unresolved matter of the surface Arenases.

Now he was brooding because the genes of his father that had given him his great height had also robbed him of years from his life expectancy. How ironic it was. At the top of his mental and creative powers, he was to be cut off in his prime. It was time to consider his successor. Once chosen, there would hopefully be a training period during which Cantú would also have time to achieve his triumph over Enrique Arenas and his family.

No one was available to take over the painting workshop because he was its only member. He had never even been able to recruit an apprentice because, in a world with little ambient light, visuals were few people's priority. Although able to distinguish among a vast range of grays, other colors represented a challenge too formidable for some. Naturally there was no audience for his paintings underground. He was as unappreciated among his own people as van Gogh had been. Cantú's early creative development would probably have been stunted too, if he hadn't been able to go out so often in his youth, and because he spent so much time there, he developed a tolerance for the intense sunlight that stayed with him after he no longer was able to show himself in the Outside.

Of course there was no question but that the community would suffer a major hit when the painting income stopped. The utilities, clothing, leather, food raising, metal work, pharmacy, health care, construction, education, and social workshops all had tall women leaders of commanding presence, many of them reaching five feet in height, any of whom might naturally emerge to take his place, even though the utility workshop was chiefly involved in the theft of electricity, cable television, and sewer connections, and didn't produce anything itself.

As he was going through their names one by one he had a sudden thought. He had always taken pride in his own Outsider blood; what if he took a look at Jeremy Wyman, whom Luisa had recently recruited with Cantú's permission, and who had recently arrived in the Aldea? One of Luisa's arguments for bringing him in was the same attribute that his mother had found so appealing about Jorge Cantú—a different set of genes and an eagerness to share them.

Rafael had partly agreed because he knew from information gleaned by the watchers in the painting on Rebecca Stuart's wall that Jeremy was working as a researcher on issues related to Mark Sands' death. If he could gradually be brought into the life of the Aldea, made sympathetic through his attachment to Luisa, then the people under the mountain would have an informant who could brief them on what the other camp was up to. Rafael Cantú was not greatly drawn to symmetry in his pictures, but he liked the symmetry of this idea. He pulled at his patchy beard as he thought about it. A simple interview would suffice. The man would either be malleable or not. If not, he could simply be discarded once Luisa was pregnant, although that could take a while. Naturally, once that happened, his name would be forgotten. Their child would be an Arenas of the legitimate line, not of the usurpers above.

In any case, Jeremy Wyman would never be leaving the Aldea alive.

CHAPTER 13

Jeremy felt like he was at the top of the world, even though he was sixty feet below the surface. He could have used a Havana cigar, although where he would find one in that maze-like warren was not clear. Probably they didn't want anyone smoking there anyway. It appeared that the renewal of the air supply had been a carefully thought-out solution to a knotty problem.

His aborted exploratory mission during the night had not resulted in a scolding from Luisa. Upon his return covered with ancient grime, she had sniffed him briefly then turned away because, when she curled her lip in distaste, her two tongue tips were exposed, and she thought Jeremy was still sensitive about this.

"I suppose you've been in the compost beds," she said, "although I can't imagine why. I spent a few years there in my late fifties. I may still have a callus or two from the shovel handles." She looked at her palms briefly.

He hadn't contradicted her as she led him down the corridor to a group bathing area where he showered in an empty room with twelve showerheads, none of which had much pressure. He had to drop to his knees to wash his hair and his armpits. When he came out she was gone, but a clean set of clothes from his suitcase awaited him on the sink counter. He had needed a shower anyway, even before being covered with vintage corpse residues. The fact that they were holy was no consolation.

A small fingertip now traced the line of his vertebrae downward starting at his neck. He picked up her other hand and looked at the nails. They were still bluish. It had not been from the hostile St. Paul climate after all; it was part of her genetic package.

"You're so bare back here," Luisa said, "like a child. It's almost like you shaved it all off."

"We all have our little differences," he said, hoping to sound expansive and tolerant. The truth was that he was now deeply engaged by these differences and the thought of being with a normal girl of his own age seemed vaguely repellent, perhaps morally wrong or even somewhat perverse. In any case, it was a disturbing idea, and he hoped it was not something he'd ever have to face. He leaned over and kissed her neck, then his mouth found hers. He could feel the two ends of her tongue probing his and she was linking her legs around him. At that moment a buzzer rang at the side of the bed, jarring him upright, his heart pounding.

"You've got a doorbell in here?" he said. "Who would know to ring it?"

"That's just Rafael. He's calling us. I think he might want to meet you. It's no big deal."

Right, he thought, like the Relic was no big deal, either. In 500 years of separation, some definitions had migrated, as well as the genes. "Meet me? How would he even know about me?" The email message from Rebecca flashed through his mind again—Do Not Approach, now coming to life in crimson neon.

"He makes a point of knowing what goes on with

all of us. Before I went up to St. Paul, I had to ask his permission to bring you here. Don't worry; he's very nice, almost like our father. It's different, better, I think, because fathers here usually don't count for much. They just set things in motion, if they can, and then move on." She turned to the side for a moment and a less sanguine look came over her features, as if she had additional thoughts about Cantú she didn't wish to alarm him with.

Jeremy himself had not thought any more about Rafael Cantú. There was the warning message from Rebecca about finding the painter that he'd gotten before he left the airport, but in general, his attitude then was that Cantú was a part of his job, and now he was deeply involved in his life, and perhaps for the first time it was more than just his job that informed his life. It now had actual interesting content of its own. Priorities were shifting, the footing was unfamiliar, and the difficulty of keeping his balance required most of his attention. The subject of Méxican artists and the problem of Mark Sands' death could wait. After all, Rebecca had Ken Abrams and the St. Paul Police Department behind her, with whatever resources they could bring to bear. Jeremy had a hot new girlfriend, the first one of his life, and was therefore off duty. He thought of himself, like Elvis, as having left the building. When he might return was unclear. Maybe never, but whenever it was, he would decide that for himself.

It was true that Luisa had told him Cantú was somewhere in the Aldea, and if he could only connect to the Internet, he could give Rebecca a heads-up if their paths crossed. Although he had more than come to terms with the small genetic differences he had discovered in Luisa, he didn't feel like sharing them with Rebecca or giving

away the fact that Luisa lived under the old cathedral ruins in Santa Elena. Certainly a major painter would have
concerns other than what Luisa was doing with her love
life. Quite possibly he didn't even know her. Jeremy hadn't
thought to ask whether she'd ever posed for him. He'd
never seen a Cantú picture or looked at them online; the
man could be painting landscapes or abstracts for all he
knew. *The Girl with Three Players* painting of Rebecca's had
arrived after Jeremy's last visit to her condo. There had
been no more messages from her, and it was possible she
didn't need anything else from him at the moment. It was
just as well.

Now he was alarmed. Jeremy swung his legs over
the side of the bed and began pulling on his clothes. He
was going to meet the family after all and he found himself dreading it and wishing he knew more about what
Cantú's role in this might be. He had thought it odd that
he'd seen few others but Luisa since his arrival, and wondered whether she was somehow isolating him from the
rest of the community, perhaps preparing a meeting she
could manage. This was apparently it.

Outside her room, they moved along in the same
direction he had taken before on his way to the grave disaster, until they reached the familiar hub. This time they
passed five or six small men carrying boxes, and two girls
who gave him an interested look, but none gave him a real
greeting. This was progress, he thought.

"Should I be saying something to people? What's
the custom here?"

"You don't have to if you haven't been introduced. Everybody knew you were coming. They're giving
you some time to adapt."

In the stairway they went up two flights and at that hub Luisa chose a corridor somewhat wider than the rest. He noticed that the bones and other debris in the stairwell had been cleaned up. She'd pulled on a robe that looked like the same material as the skirt she'd been wearing when they met. On her feet were soft moccasin-like coverings that didn't have much definition. They whispered against the lava floor as she moved.

"Where does he live?" he asked. Even though her stride was shorter, he was panting to keep up with her. Maybe it was the altitude, although it was hard to think about altitude when you were underground.

"Like a lot of people who work all the time, he lives in his studio. It's in the dining room of the old palace. We're not allowed to go there unless we're summoned, because he doesn't like to be interrupted as he works. His paintings supply most of our money. As you can imagine, it's hard to get cash down here."

"Where is everyone else? Is this normal?"

"In their rooms mostly, when they're not working, or in the new dining hall. They can watch TV there. We have cable now and the reality shows are very popular. There's been a big upswing in the popularity of singing and dancing lessons because of American Idol. The younger ones are in the classrooms, of course, and you haven't been on that level yet."

Jeremy thought this could mean anyone up to about sixty-five or even seventy if they were doing graduate work, although who would want to after forty years of schooling? He found his heart was pounding as they hurried along. Several times small people turned away on seeing them, waiting until they passed. After five minutes of threading their way through the corridors, they paused before a pair of studded steel doors. Above them a sign read, Comedor, the first sign he'd seen. At the bottom edge of the door, normal-looking daylight crept out along the floor.

"How did he get these doors?"

"They were from the treasury in the old cathedral. We salvaged them and hung them here. We're scavengers, remember? That's how I found you." Of course, she had picked him out of the crowd in Antoine's—how long ago that now seemed, half his life, at least. He thought of it as the meaningful half, the rest he could barely remember. It seemed that without Luisa, the rest of it had no context. She leaned on it with her shoulder to push one of the doors open. Jeremy blinked in the sudden normal light.

In the huge room, with a barrel vault ceiling more than thirty feet high, an easel stood in the center, flanked by a bench and a heavy worktable. Drying canvases leaned against the arched ends of the room. On the bench sat a squat figure draped in folds of cloth dragging on the floor. A mottled beard covered most of his face, and on his head perched a conical cap. Jeremy could see he was well below normal height, but still much taller than other males he'd glimpsed in the corridors. Luisa wasn't quite five feet tall. The man on the bench looked up as they came in. The cap added a foot to his stature.

"I won't be needing you, Luisa, thank you. We'll only be a few minutes." The voice was low and power-ful, accustomed to command. It possessed a strong lower range, as if it could easily growl as well.

Luisa faded from view and Jeremy heard the steel doors close with the sound of two slabs of great mass coming together behind him, followed by an echo tracking the barrel vault above his head. He could think of nothing to say, and he shoved his hands into the pockets of his khaki pants and waited, shifting his weight from one foot to the other, wondering whether he should speak first. He began to chew on his lower lip. The man on the bench regarded him without comment for a while and Jeremy felt he was being examined with great care. Maybe painters really saw things differently. If this one did, he wasn't giving much away.

"I am Rafael Cantú, a painter, and the closest we have to a leader here. So you are with our Luisa now, I understand."

"Yes." In his own ears Jeremy's voice sounded squeaky, as if he hadn't used it in some time.

"I hope you're treating her well. She's a valued member of this community as well as one of my favorite models."

"Yes." He nodded vigorously. Now he knew he was going to have to check the painter's website to see what he had done with her, if he could ever get his computer to work online down there. He had tried several times but there was never any wi-fi. The place needed updating. They didn't seem to know it was the twenty-first century. Looking at Cantú, he felt they may have missed the twentieth as well.

"Has she told you our history?"

"Yes, I have a sense of it anyway. Should I be calling you sir?"

"There is no need. We are all equals here, victims of history. None is more important than another."

His English was flawless and held only the merest

trace of a Méxican accent. Jeremy thought of the forty years of schooling Luisa had mentioned.

"I've heard that you do research, mostly on the Internet. You will find that we are not connected to it here except for a few uses that I control. You will not be able to go online unless I specifically authorize it and give you access to a connection, which is unlikely. I hope that won't be too great an inconvenience."

"I'll manage OK. I have nothing much going on right now."

"Not with your laptop, anyway, I imagine."

Jeremy felt himself blush. If Cantú was expecting a response, he couldn't think what it might be, and didn't wish to share any details of his relationship with Luisa. It was still exotic and mystical in his own mind, and he knew it would take months or years to work out. He had felt himself an outsider most of his life, but never to this degree, and never before with a capital O.

He began to focus on the finished painting on the easel. It showed a small hairless boy wearing a leathery-looking diaper fastened with an oversize straight pin. He held a stick in one hand, apparently trying to persuade a brown dog to do some kind of trick. The dog looked much like Tease, but his rear legs had been amputated. A small, wheeled platform, lashed on above his hips with a braided rawhide thong, supported the rear part of his body. Each end of the thong was finished with a translucent amber bead.

The device itself lay on a table near Cantú, but no dog model was present. The studio space was widely lit by several mirrors on the lower walls facing the rubble-filled court that picked up light from obscure sources outside. This accounted for the natural-looking glow Jeremy had seen under the doors. Rubble completely blocked the windows above, with timbers holding back the fractured slabs of masonry beyond. Other than the mirrors, the walls were undecorated, no more than plaster painted in a pale color that reflected the light evenly, with no glare.

The boy in the picture had a long nose like that of Luisa, and a mature look for his size. The ear visible to the viewer, as he faced the dog, was definitely too large. It was possible he was listening for something from outside the canvas, but no ambient noise reached the interior of the mountain.

"Are you able to stay with us for a while?" Cantú's voice was still low, but softer, less commanding now.

"Oh, yes, of course, I'm sure I can stay."

"Being here won't adversely affect your work?"

There was an odd emphasis on the word work, and Jeremy began to wonder whether there wasn't a probing quality to this question, something beyond simple courtesy.

"Not really. As I said, there's not much going on right now. You see, Luisa and I have sort of found each other. . ." He paused, giving Cantú a self-deprecating smile, then found he was unwilling to go on, and the smile faded. The painter responded with a shrewd look.

"I know. You like her, I'm sure. If you wish, there are other girls here who would want to sleep with you too. We are not monogamous in the Aldea. Maintaining our population is a higher priority, and anyway, our values are somewhat different from those in the Outside." He made an expansive gesture, indicating, perhaps, that Jeremy had the run of the community. The painter seemed to imply it was possible Jeremy could be the master of his own harem of maybe sixty or seventy girls between the ages of seventy to a hundred, a lusty and accommodating group, ready to party and eager to get pregnant. He could learn salsa dancing, something he'd always been too shy to attempt in St. Paul, where it had seemed subtly out of place. Probably somewhere above ground in Santa Elena, he could find the right shirts for it, something with ruffled sleeves. Cantú looked at him as if expecting shouts of glee. His look seemed to say, yes, girls just want to have fun, like the song says. It's all true, down here anyway.

Jeremy now blushed a color that he felt the artist would readily know how to mix. "I'll have to let you know on that one," he stuttered, "but right now Luisa is fine, just enough, I mean. It's OK, really."

"Are you quite certain? I spent much time in the Outside myself when I was younger, and I know that the girls are not as liberal there."

For Jeremy this greatly understated things. Liberal and girl were two words that his experience had never prompted him to use in the same sentence, or connect in the same thought until quite recently, and then only in a single instance. He was not prepared to generalize.

As he struggled to find a polite answer, he felt a subtle vibration beneath his feet, a sense of cargo in motion, perhaps on rails as in a mine. It quickly passed, yet it left him with a momentary revival of his researcher's curiosity. Surely there was no space for a train beneath him. What he was hearing had to be smaller, yet he had unmistakably sensed the rhythm of an irregularity, or perhaps a narrow gap in the rails as pairs of wheels passed over them in succession, somewhat like a snick, snick, snick.

What were they carrying? He shifted his weight from one foot to the other, flexing his knees a bit, but the floor didn't move. He realized Cantú was regarding him intently, his head thrust forward.

"You are sensing our agricultural operations beneath you, I think. They are moving finished products about down there. Ask Luisa to show you some time. As you might imagine, living underground requires certain adaptations in the cultivation of food. For example, we don't grow many sunflowers here." He leaned his heavy body forward with his head cocked to one side as he said this, and the bench creaked. His lips, parting in a grin, revealed the stubby ends of worn grayish teeth, somewhat less than a full set.

The pose reminded Jeremy of the male figure in the picture behind him, and he couldn't decide whether he was expected to laugh at the sunflower line or not. Probably not, the man wasn't joking much, although there was some pendulous movement beneath his vast robe, as if a beaver or an otter might be trapped inside and getting restive. Overall, Rafael Cantú seemed to take himself very seriously.

"You may go back to Luisa now," he said, when it became clear Jeremy had no response, "please excuse me if I don't see you out. Ask her to give you a tour of the Aldea. Some areas are restricted, but most are not. I hope we may soon talk again." This was followed by something like a smile, but Jeremy thought there was a look in Cantú's eyes that others might have found a little demented.

"My pleasure," said Jeremy, backing away toward the steel doors. He turned and pulled at one of the lever handles. It didn't move, but the other one did, and then he was in the corridor running toward Luisa, panting as usual. He had missed the sardonic look on Cantú's face as he fiddled with the doors. Had he been able to read it, it would have said, "Limited mechanical aptitude."

The look left his face as Rafael Cantú sat thoughtfully facing the exit for a moment, disappointed in Jeremy's subservient manner. Perhaps the painter had been expecting too much this soon. Luisa's new lover lacked confidence, and seemed much too focused on her and their relationship to promise many skills in the way of leadership. In any case, he would bear watching. It might be that his only use, aside from servicing Luisa, would be as an information source about the other side. For example, where were Ken Abrams and Rebecca Stuart at this moment? Had they arrived yet? The players watching from the painting on her condo wall had reported a complete absence of activity there for a while. It might be time to allow Jeremy to connect to the Internet. But then, how to control what he did with it? Besides Cantú, no one else in the Aldea had a computer.

He was about to turn back to the easel when the door opened again, and a small figure entered the studio. She was shorter than Luisa, only about four-foot-six, with a boy's shorter haircut. Her schoolboy's uniform consisted of dark green workout pants and jacket, both with narrow white stripes down the arms and legs. She did not look like a woman, nor did she look to Outsiders like her nearly sixty years. He greeted her and waved her inside.

"The cop and the writer are both here now, and they've found Carlos Morris already," she said in a voice that betrayed the fact that she was not a 10-year-old boy. She stuck her hands in her pockets and put most of her weight on one leg, keeping the mannerisms of a schoolboy going even underground. Conscientious about her job, she worked at staying in character. It was hard enough to be on the Outside in the constant glare of the Méxican sun, let alone pretending to be a male only a sixth her age.

"The writer girl took the cop to *The Witness* statue yesterday afternoon, and they went to see Morris this morning."

Cantú shifted on his bench, favoring his back. "Did he remember anything? I don't suppose you would know."

"He must have, because they went on to the cathedral afterward and sat in the back corner where it happened. The cop took a scraping of some kind at the base of the column. They were interested in the martyr too, but they didn't examine the case closely. I think we're safe there. They were more concerned with the presentation, then they left."

Cantú nodded slowly. "You didn't follow them?"

"No, they went in a cab and I didn't want to abandon my bike." She was the only person in the Aldea with a bicycle, and it conferred on her an obscure but unique prestige. Riding through the dim corridors always got her noticed, and she had many suitors, but it was awkward getting the bike in and out. She always had to bring it through the front door at the sarcophagus, which meant lugging it up two flights of stairs.

"Thank you, Ana. Watch the cathedral and the plaza again tomorrow." She nodded and left. As she turned, he watched the movement of her body inside the schoolboy's uniform. He couldn't recall when he had last painted anyone dressed in anything but the beaten medieval outfits he was known for, aside from nudes. It had been forty or fifty years. It's a good look for her, he thought, no one notices an Outsider kid that age.

He turned again to the easel and pulled out a long brush, flexing the bristled end between his blunt fingers. Ana was an attractive girl, even more so than Luisa, and not so tall and domineering. He had always suspected Luisa of having a rebellious streak. Something in her tone when she spoke to him made him wonder whether she was fully behind his plan for revenge against the above-ground part of the family. He put the thought aside. It was too late now to object.

Somehow Ana's boyish looks lent her a certain spice, although at only fifty-nine she was still somewhat underage. It was a shame he was too deteriorated to do anything about it any more, because he liked his girls on the young side, and a dash of gender ambiguity didn't hurt either. Oh, to be eighty once again, even eighty-five. Of course, he could always just paint her. That was mostly what he did in his current state anyway.

"How did it go?" Luisa asked Jeremy.

"Good, I guess," he said without enthusiasm. "I think he might be interested in what I'm doing, my work, that is."

"Of course he is."

He thought there was a subtle pride in her smile. "Why would he care?"

"Because you're with me, silly." She looked up at him with an expression of affectionate possessiveness. Her small hand slipped into his palm.

Jeremy's insights may have been at a low point during the brief period that he'd been underground, perhaps because his blood flow had recently been concentrated more in his pelvis than in his brain. Nonetheless a small alarm began to sound in a distant part of his consciousness.

"He said you should give me a tour of the grounds." Jeremy wasn't sure if this was the correct term, but since they were below grade it seemed plausible.

"Did he mention to you that some areas are forbidden?"

"Yes, but he didn't say why or which ones."

"We have some new technologies. You might say they're proprietary, I guess." It was as if she were discussing plastics or electronics. Perhaps missile-guidance systems.

"You don't want any other underground colonies to catch up?" Too late he realized there was a trace of a smirk on his face.

She stopped abruptly and turned, putting her palm flat against his chest. It halted him more from the character of the gesture itself than the strength behind it.

"You may think that was a funny thing to say, but we've been confined down here since 1537. According to my calculations, that adds up to 474 years. Think about it for a moment." In that light her violet eyes were black.

"I'm sorry, Luisa. It's hard for me to put myself in your position, but did you ever think of just coming up and out? The way some people come out of the closet when they're gay? I realize it would be hard to be so obviously different, and scientists would want to study the genetic changes you've been through, but in the end you'd be accepted because they'd have to accept you. You could even sue the Arenas family for a share of their wealth, since you're descended from the rightful heirs of Juan de Arenas and the others aren't."

She looked at him for a moment and then lowered her hand from his chest.

"I know you said that sincerely, but I also know history. I know how minorities are treated in your country, and in México as well. My own family nearly destroyed the Pichanchas simply to seize their land. The descendants of the survivors now sell little straw dolls dressed in native costumes down by the cathedral doors not a hundred meters from where we're standing. First we destroyed their citadel and their fighting men, then we obliterated their culture, and then eliminated their self-respect and trained them to be peons on our haciendas. This is the treatment that awaits us if we come out of the closet as you suggest."

"So where is justice for you? Can it even happen?" He began to guide her by the shoulder farther along the corridor, lest Rafael Cantú emerge from his studio and hear some of this. She didn't answer immediately, but when she did, her voice was emphatic.

"I am not part of that," she said finally as they approached the hub, shaking her head vigorously and not looking at him anymore.

"I don't understand."

"Only that, the justice part. It's the job of others to make it right. All of us down here have our jobs. That one is not mine. I'm only a welder and I'm happy with that. Don't you have a job?"

Besides gathering information, part of Jeremy's job was to think, and he'd been neglecting that aspect of it lately along with all the rest of it. He'd at first assumed that what Rebecca and Ken Abrams had uncovered was a plot against the Arenas family, all the Arenases. He now realized it was a plot of one branch against the other, and the appeal of revenge may have made the underground branch deeply invested in their victimhood, to the point of choosing it in preference to simple justice. He had no way of knowing whether that was only the thinking of Cantú, or of others in the Aldea as well.

"Yes," he said, remembering her question, "yes, I do have a job, but let me ask you a question too, a historical one. In all those 474 years has anyone ever tried to lead you out of here, or even raised the issue for discussion? To come out into the light and tell what happened so many years ago? No one knows the facts but you."

Luisa answered immediately, emphatically, as if he had touched on a taboo that, as an Outsider, he could not have known existed. "No, never." Her hands came out in front of her and described a horizontal line like a barrier.

Jeremy did not ask the follow-up question, which was simply, "Why not?" It didn't matter now because he had another idea, one that almost made him catch his breath in its boldness. A grave look came over his face.

"I could do it, Luisa," he said quietly, looking

back at the studio doors again. "I could make it happen. I believe I can see how." Ideas were coming one after the other now. He had never been an actor on any stage of events, even as a walk-on; instead hanging about in the wings trying to learn his lines. It seemed that he'd always been content to report on the effects of what the real actors had done long after the curtain had fallen. Now the simple lack of interaction between the two halves of the family pointed the way to some interesting possibilities. The most compelling of these was that the underground Arenases possessed the Relic, but placed no value on it, when the others would value it highly. Perhaps a deal could be made; someone on the Outside might trade something of great importance for it. "Here's how it could work" he went on. "First, we get hold of the Relic. . ."

She reached up and put two fingers to his lips and began to shake her head slowly, a pained look on her face. "Don't even *think* about it, Jeremy. If you even bring it up they will kill you." He looked around sharply at Cantú's studio doors again, some distance down the hall, as she took his hand and led him into the hub, not wanting to glance back at the shocked look on his face.

CHAPTER 14

The seven-meter high iron gates of Hacienda Milagro swung open without warning and three polished black Suburbans sped through, moving in close formation down the highway in the glare of the afternoon sun. It was more than eight kilometers before they left the border of Enrique Arenas' land, streaming past on both sides of the cars. Just as they did, a battered twelve-year-old Toyota pickup belonging to the ranch foreman's son emerged from the gates and turned down the highway in the same direction.

Each of the Suburbans contained an armed passenger as well as the driver. The Toyota was occupied by the driver alone, behind the tinted glass, dressed in a ranch hand's dusty jeans and stained Western shirt. A straw hat was crushed onto his head to cover most of his white hair. It was Enrique Arenas, the patriarch of the above-ground family. His face, neck and hands were darkened with makeup, and he whistled a tune as he drove. It was the only way he felt safe leaving the hacienda, eight kilometers behind his decoy convoy, which he felt, given his experience, might be taken out with a bazooka at any time. But people expected a man of his stature to travel with an escort, so being the sole occupant of an anonymous Toyota pickup was the perfect cover. He resisted the impulse to speed up to see if anyone was following the others, the Toyota couldn't have escaped them, anyway. Hide in plain sight, he thought.

Another six kilometers down the highway, the convoy took the first exit and followed a series of back streets to the main plaza cluster. Enrique came into Santa Elena every day now at varying times, just to examine the cathedral, studying it for changes that might conceal traps. This time he had selected late afternoon. He still hated leaving the Hacienda Milagro compound, but his daughter Angelina's wedding was in less than twenty-four hours, and he wasn't sleeping much anymore. With his wife dead the last four years, the entire burden of the wedding had fallen on him. His sister had stepped in to help, but she didn't feel the exposure that he did.

At the underground car park next to the police building, he eased in next to his Suburbans in a cluster of four reserved spaces. Four of his six guards had already distributed themselves along the route to the cathedral. One waited at the entrance for Enrique to leave so he could trail him from twenty meters back, and the last one remained guarding the cars, the same distribution they always used. When Enrique reached the cathedral grounds, he took a slow circuit around it before going inside, keeping the man ahead of him in view, not looking at the man behind. As with each previous day he saw nothing unusual and took a position inside. Removing his hat, he spotted one of his men toward the front, another in the rear. The third was out of sight, most likely up in the choir loft. Two remained outside covering the entrances.

Rebecca and Ken had been in the cathedral all day and she felt if she ever saw one more square inch of gold leaf in her entire life she would scream. She planned to sell all her gold jewelry when she returned to St. Paul. Her cell phone reached no one here, so she didn't even have the consolation of text-messaging her friends as she waited. Ideas kept coming to her about the new book on the Mark Sands case, but she had no means of writing them down, and she tried not to think about it in fear that she would get an especially good one and then forget it.

She'd watched for hours as Ken did a microscopic examination of the interior masonry, as if he was working down some invisible checklist. There had not yet been enough time for the crime lab in St. Paul to respond to his sample, so he simply assumed they would find pixie dust and went ahead with his search of the cathedral. He had told her he was now convinced the little people came and went from within the building. First he began by sneaking into the priests' rooms at the front because the low level of traffic might have made it easier for the trespassers to come and go from that area. Now he was out of sight within one of the side chapels.

The crowd had thinned, and Rebecca scanned the remaining visitors. There were seven women kneeling at prayer, two with small children, and three unaccompanied school kids, two girls and a boy, all in uniforms, but not of the same school. Not far from Rebecca, near the center but closer to the wall, an older farmer type with a heavy tan and white hair sat without praying, a ratty straw hat on his lap. Two beefy guys, one in front, one in the rear, who both looked broad enough to hold up the cathedral themselves if another earthquake should occur, seemed to be loitering. It was a slow day for the faithful, she thought.

Get inside the plot, she said to herself. What are the little people up to? Even if she was not in a position to write it down as usual, maybe she could live it instead, and if she lived it, she'd remember it. This cathedral interior was the last link with Rafael Cantú, other than the paintings themselves. She had spent most of the day there as Abrams poked and prodded at the walls and panels. This was a part of police procedure she'd ignored in her books as deadly boring. Watching Abrams proved the reality was no more interesting.

Rebecca covered her mouth and yawned, deciding she was finished for the day. She got up and walked along the outer aisles until she saw Ken behind the side altar, then nodded briefly before he gave her a small wave. This was a signal they had arranged beforehand, knowing that he was going to conceal himself inside the cathedral and keep watch overnight. Rebecca would return in the morning at 6:30 when it opened for early mass. She went out through the side entrance without looking back. Seated on the steps another beefy Méxican looked up at her, then turned away. She decided this must be cattle country.

At the Hotel Estrella she checked messages and found one from Detective Ira Shapiro from Santa Fe. It simply said he had arrived. He left a number in Santa Elena where he could be reached. The desk had received it at 9:30 AM, eight hours earlier, just after Ken and Rebecca left for centro. She debated whether to use the hotel phone and call Shapiro herself, but since the message was left for Ken and she didn't think he would have told Shapiro she was in on the case, she put it in her purse to give to Ken in the morning. There would be plenty of time to touch base with Shapiro tomorrow. She didn't think it likely he could have come up with anything as important as the Witness and Charlie Morris' narrative.

At seven she changed her clothes and walked a few blocks down to a pedestrian street called Avenida Independencia, where she had dinner in an old mansion. While she ate, a mariachi band was playing that featured small boys on two of the instruments. She didn't attempt any Spanish and merely pointed at the items on the menu that she wanted. No one bothered her while she had a margarita with her dinner. She decided that Santa Elena was not such a bad place after all, if you could avoid the traffic. Mostly she thought about Ken trying to keep from nodding off in the cathedral.

From his position near the last side altar toward the front, Ken heard a door near the main altar open and close at five minutes before nine P.M., so he slipped to the floor and rolled under a pew as footsteps came down the main aisle. When they stopped he heard the two small doors at the front being closed and locked, and then the sacristan moved to the side and secured that door as well. Ken had found nothing in his search, but that was the way most searches were. Sometimes they only revealed what wasn't there, and that was often valuable too. It didn't matter which way it went; he paced himself in these things.

A minute passed and the lights began to go out, but not all of them. A row of small lanterns along both sides of the nave remained lit, as well as a sanctuary light near the main altar, and larger clusters at the front and side entrances. Ken felt relieved when they stopped going out.

He waited until the sacristy door closed and listened for any other movement for about five minutes, hearing nothing. He already knew what his vantage point would be, having spotted a series of three connected wooden booths about halfway down on one side. The center booth was wider and higher than the flanking ones, enclosed by a door with a screen in the upper half. The two side entries were covered by drapes. It would be perfect for looking out into the church while remaining nearly invisible to anyone who was not standing directly in front of him. When Cantú's little people emerged, Abrams would at last find out what they were up to and where they came and went from. With any luck they would lead him to the painter himself.

Abrams was not religious, nor was he familiar with Catholic ritual, but he did have some sense that his intended spy hole was what was called a confessional. Sliding around the corner of the side altar area, he scanned the nave, and seeing no one, walked down the side aisle and slipped inside the center booth. The seat had a comfortable cushion, arm rests, and a view from behind the wooden screen that cut off the high altar and the front entrance, but still provided an excellent perspective on nearly everything else. As he sat down he realized that for a while he hadn't had any recurrence of the back and neck pain he'd had in St. Paul. Was it the climate? Or was it that this case now felt more meaningful than the others, despite still being incomprehensible?

On both sides of his seat were sliding screens that opened to the flanking booths. The only problem would be trying to stay awake through the night. He thought for a while about Rebecca, what she might be doing now. Surely she hadn't stayed at the hotel, she would have found some smart cafe where she could have dinner, possibly connecting with some interesting Méxican guy. Fortunately she didn't speak much Spanish, and although she could often be outrageous, she didn't seem easy. Not to him anyway. Her signals were always mixed. He was thinking about how sweet her mouth sometimes looked when she had that certain expression, part disdain and part amusement, when she was really in doubt about how she felt and was trying to mask it. He'd seen it a dozen times since they'd arrived in Santa Elena.

A subtle noise interrupted his thoughts, a low creak as if someone had shifted his weight in a pew outside. Abrams had not brought his gun, thinking it unlikely he'd be involved in a shootout inside the cathedral. His police ID he'd also left at the hotel. It was useless since he hadn't registered with the police liaison and he couldn't bring himself to pronounce the words Montes de Oca again. He leaned forward to broaden his view over and between the pews, and saw no one, but doing this caused his own seat to creak. Having a sudden insight, he leaned back and slid open the screen on his left side, peering into the next booth. What he saw in the dim light was the blunt barrel of a .38 revolver pointed at his forehead. Behind it a broad smiling Méxican face said, in English, "Bless me father, for I am about to sin."

At six o'clock the following morning Santa Elena traffic was no quieter than twelve hours earlier. Rebecca was not surprised. After getting up at five to get ready, a time she was more accustomed to approaching from the other direction, she managed to find a cab outside the hotel. There was no light on the horizon or any hint of it. The cab driver understood the word "plaza" and twenty-five minutes later let her off on the southern end, only overcharging her by thirty pesos.

She found herself on a narrow extension of the plaza system, flanked by rows of shops offering jewelry, all still dark at this hour. No one else was in view, but the area was decently lit and she felt somewhat safe. As she climbed a broad flight of stairs she realized she was approaching the group of chair sculptures from behind, and she could make out between them the Witness of Charlie Morris facing her. Ground lights outside the circle caught the small figure from behind, lacing the edges with a strange glow but leaving the front unlit. She came around behind it and faced the chairs. A breeze came across the pavement at this higher level and she pulled her jacket collar more closely about her. The bronze chairs were now lit from behind just as *The Witness* had been earlier. Suddenly she made out a new figure seated in the left chair, leaning against the armrest, his head tilted over and resting on his own shoulder.

How sad, Rebecca thought, but it didn't really surprise her. It was simply the first homeless person she'd seen in Santa Elena. She reached into her purse and pulled out a hundred-peso note, thinking it would buy the man breakfast and lunch. As she came closer, she could see he wore a lightweight suit and tie with a trench coat.

Light from the ground bulbs glinted on his polished shoes. Perhaps he was not homeless, but only a middle class person down on his luck, or maybe his wife had thrown him out. Oddly, he had male pattern baldness, something she hadn't seen much on Méxican men. It was when she leaned over to offer him the money that she noticed the end of a braided leather garrote emerging from the deep crease in his neck and hanging down in front, the amber bead reaching below his collar to the center of his tie. Catching her breath, instinctively she leaped backward, staggering but not falling. As she struggled to stay upright she was able to suppress a scream. Her left foot crushed a pair of glasses on the pavement. Rebecca's next thought was that in better light she would have also seen the sparkle of glitter around his nose and mouth.

She also thought she knew who this man was, even though she'd never met him. Looking around and composing herself, she cautiously advanced again toward the body and put two fingers on the back of one of his hands. This took enormous courage and she felt Ken would have been proud of her. The skin was as cold as the bronze chair the body sat in. A glance at her watch told her it would be at least five minutes before the cathedral opened and Ken would be able to get out. Now the horizon began to glow along the buildings on the plaza. She couldn't wait.

After first refusing to talk about it, Ken had finally told her about his failed attempt to register his credentials with the police. Since he therefore had no standing in Santa Elena, she knew the local police would be no help. If she called them she'd be detained endlessly and unable to tell Ken anything. He wouldn't even know where she was. Cringing, she reached around to the body's back pockets and then the jacket pockets. There was no wallet, but in the inner breast pocket of the trench coat she found a notebook, and flipping it open at random saw the name, "Cantú." She shoved it into her purse and pulled out her cell phone. Not knowing whether the light was sufficient, she snapped a photo of what she already knew was Ira Shapiro's body, and ran off toward the cathedral.

Rebecca moved quickly past the police building, where the only illumination was at the entrance and a few random windows on the upper floor, then sprinted diagonally cross the plaza in front and, threading her way through the traffic, crossed to the next square and stopped at the front doors of the cathedral. By her watch it was now 6:28. Thinking it imprudent to be standing in front of the entry waiting for someone who had hidden inside all night, she moved away toward the wrought iron band-stand in the center of the square and took a seat on the steps where she could watch.

At 6:35 the door opened and the sacristan went back inside. No one came out. Ten or twelve people were already crossing the plaza behind her and moving toward the cathedral. Rebecca rushed to the steps and went in-side. At the head of the main aisle, the sacristan turned to the left and went back behind the altar. She stood waiting, bursting with the news about Shapiro's murder, thinking that Ken would not leave his hiding place until the sacris-tan was well out of sight.

When nothing happened and people began mov-ing up the aisle behind her, she sat down in a pew, want-ing to scan Shapiro's notebook, but afraid she'd miss Ken when he appeared. At ten minutes to seven, she pulled out her cell phone and looked at the picture she'd taken. The dead man was about forty-five, with dark hair in a fringe around the sides and back of his head, and a thick mustache. His eyes were nearly closed and his lips slightly parted. The loose trench coat screened his body, but she estimated that he was about twenty-five pounds over-weight, and something like average height, although this was more of a guess, since he was seated.

The mouth was pouchy at the corners and the facial expression vacant. It was possible that the tip of his tongue protruded between his lips. In the photograph the man looked somehow more obviously dead than in person. She had studied crime scene photos while re-searching both the *Grunge* books and she knew that dead people didn't photograph well, but she didn't understand why. The camera seemed to catch a kind of dull slack-ness about them that the eye often missed in person. She wouldn't have walked up to Shapiro's body if she'd seen the photo first.

Rebecca was beginning to fidget now. She flipped the phone shut with more force than necessary and bit her lip. Where the hell was Abrams? If he had slipped out somehow during the night, why not let her know? There was a phone in her room and the lobby desk was staffed without interruption. There were nearly a hundred peo-ple in the cathedral now and she knew she was suffering more than any of them, no matter what their woes might be. A good-looking guy with a kind of layered look in em-broidered robes was coming out to the altar. Seven o'clock mass had begun.

"Shit," she said to herself, wondering if anyone had heard her. From the rear someone said softly, "Amen."

CHAPTER 15

The gaunt pale man was a waiter in his mid-twenties, wearing a soiled black jacket and striped pants, when they arrested him for killing the restaurant owner. Avoiding his bug-eyed stare, Abrams read him his rights before they went out the kitchen entrance at the back. The pavement was icy, and slippery as well from garbage. Grease with ice was a bad combination. He held the man's arm. As they approached the car Abrams drew his revolver and shot him in the back of the head, inserting his fingers in his collar a moment before and shifting him away from the open car door first so that the rear of the police sedan wouldn't be sprayed with blood and tissue. As Abrams' eyes opened, he saw the waiter fall in the alley next to the rear tire of the patrol car. The dream was over and he got to his feet. Usually these dreams haunted him for hours, but this time, something else immediately caught his attention.

It was only a half-inch strip of tentative daylight beneath the door that suggested dawn had arrived. Abrams' first thought was that it was enough space to admit a scorpion. The windowless room was chilly, the single mattress covered with a thin wool blanket and no linens or pillow. He hadn't expected to sleep but he knew from the dream that he had. The dream was number seventeen, the first one he'd had in México. It was a bad sign that they'd returned. At least his neck was still OK.

They had taken his wallet and watch when they blindfolded him and shoved him into a waiting Suburban in the parking ramp. He still had a pen in his shirt pocket and a small notebook in his jeans. Apparently they thought neither was any threat. The one who had taken him out of the cathedral was twice as big as Abrams, and he had his own key to the front door of the building. At least they had overlooked Rebecca earlier.

He had no idea where he was, but he had a few clues. He estimated it had been a twenty-five minute ride from the parking ramp where they blindfolded him, but it was possible they had circled for part of that, except near the end when they were moving faster, possibly because of lighter traffic. Ever since he opened his eyes he'd been hearing cocks crowing, periodic horse noises, and the occasional barking dog. Overlaying it all was the smell of manure. As for who these people were, he had no idea.

Because of an additional dimension that other recent cases hadn't had, this one had now become much more interesting: they were probably going to kill him. What he couldn't figure out was why they weren't small. Judging from the ones he'd seen, they weren't even average in size. It didn't fit.

Ken had brought no identification to the cathedral other than his driver's license, which did not show he was a detective, merely giving his home address in St. Paul and a physical description under his photo. It also noted that he was an organ donor, something he hoped wouldn't come up. He'd left his cell phone behind at the hotel. He could have left it in St. Paul for all the use he was getting from it, since he hadn't bought the expanded service.

As the thin line of daylight grew in intensity at the bottom of the door he began a search of his surroundings, mainly still by touch, but partly aided now by the dimly lit edges of the sparse furniture. Pacing off the room revealed it was about twelve by fourteen feet. The walls were a bare, soft adobe brick. On the short wall opposite the bed were a sink and an unenclosed toilet. Thick planks made up the door, and the floor was made from crude, uneven tiles. On the small table next to the bed sat a bottle of water. At no point had he been tied up, and he still had his shoes. He thought that this might have been an error by his captors. It suggested they didn't have much experience at kidnapping. Ken didn't either.

He had seen only the burly guy in the confessional and the driver of the van. They could have been brothers. No one had spoken during the ride, suggesting that they didn't know whether he spoke Spanish, and didn't want to take the chance that he did, which in turn meant they didn't know anything about him. This raised the question of motive. Ransom was doubtful. Had he interfered with something they were doing or about to do in the cathedral? It was not clear, but it gave him latitude in what he could put together when he talked to them. That had to be soon. Knowing nothing about how they would come at him, everything would have to be improvised.

He paced off the room in tight passes, finding only a small table near the bed, the bed itself, and an armless upholstered chair. No lamp. Nothing was loose and lying about waiting to be used as a weapon, and the chair was too heavy and awkward to use in a fight. He sat down to wait. With only the crack at the bottom of the door as a light source, the room didn't get any brighter as the morning progressed. Rebecca was probably wandering the cathedral now looking for him. Until he could figure this out, it was all going to be on her. It seemed like it had been going this way for a while, but he resisted reading anything into this. She usually seemed to be up to it. After a while someone pounded on the door.

"*Señor* Abrams! Please move back from the door so I can see you when I open it. You will remember that I have a gun." The voice spoke in English. They would have analyzed the contents of his wallet by now.

Ken moved back to the bed and sat down. There was the sound of a stout bolt being thrown and the door swung outward. Daylight flooded the room and Ken shaded his eyes. Several steps back from the opening stood the wide man from the confessional, wearing jeans with well-used boots, and a blue shirt fronted with embroidered pocket flaps. He gestured with a revolver.

Abrams came out blinking. When his eyes adjusted, he took everything in as rapidly as he could. He had emerged from a flat-roofed adobe building at the edge of a corral holding ten or a dozen horses. Ken knew nothing about horseflesh but they looked strong and spirited. As two approached him tossing their heads, he moved off in the direction of his captor's gesture, walking along the fence line toward a much larger building with barred windows. The low hills ahead sprouted three or four kinds of cactus. A steel water tower stood on a trestle next to the building they were approaching, and a trough led down to a tank inside the corral. He looked back to see one of the horses turn away, showing a brand on its hind quarter, a circle with an inverted V, with the point touching the top of the curve and the space between the two arms open at the bottom.

When seven o'clock mass was finished, Rebecca walked through the cathedral looking along each aisle for Ken's dead body under one of the pews. Nothing. After finding the chilly corpse of Ira Shapiro she could think of only one reason that Ken hadn't appeared. The only possible source of hope was that his body had not been in the chair circle with Shapiro's, but that was thin. Certainly it didn't mean he was alive.

She was still holding onto a shred of calm, but it was getting harder. At nearly eight she left the cathedral and went back to the bandstand to think. What would Lester Grunge do? This was no different from plotting a detective novel. One thing always led directly to another.

"Live the book," she said to herself aloud. Ken had been locked into the cathedral on the theory that concealed somewhere inside, the little people had a way of getting in and out. If he didn't come out in the morning, then it could only mean he'd found it, and left by the same route himself. How simple! He wasn't dead, probably only lost underground or in some passageway within the walls. If he were Lester Grunge he would have left something behind at the exit point as a sign for her, since he couldn't get hold of her by phone. Of course, Ken was not Lester Grunge, and her estimate of his competence had been diminished back in St. Paul when he briefly thought of her as a suspect. She hadn't been able to avoid the sense that he was stumbling in México as well. She jumped up and ran back inside anyway.

The seven o'clock mass crowd had largely dispersed and initially she walked the walls, studying the intersection of floor and marble base with care, not knowing what to look for, but she had seen Ken do the same thing yesterday. She checked the fronts and sides of the altars in the side chapels. Then she moved on to the columns, getting strange looks from the few remaining worshippers. A check of the Roman saint's display revealed nothing, and as an object of some reverence she didn't want to start pounding on it. There remained now only the main altar itself, and Rebecca didn't feel that she could simply walk up and check it out without causing an incident. Perhaps the best plan was to be in position nearby and if the moment came when there was no one in the cathedral, to slip inside the communion rail. She moved up the side aisle.

When she reached the confessional she realized she'd been so focused on the wall and base panels that she'd ignored the triple booth, simply walked around it as if it could have no relevance. She sat down in a pew opposite the confessional for a moment, not thinking any more about solving the case before Ken and feeling very much alone in a strange place, one more hostile than she'd expected. Something had changed when she found Shapiro's body. The deaths of Edward Born and Mark Sands had been more abstract, even though she'd known both of them. The difference was that she'd seen neither of their bodies.

The sad tilted mass of Ira Shapiro on the bronze chair, with a pale glimmer from the ground lights behind coming off the bald center of his head like a halo, had a different kind of immediacy. Was it because she had touched his cold hand? It hadn't felt human anymore, the skin stiff and leathery. It was like touching putty, there was no resilience. If she'd made a fingernail mark on his skin it would have stayed there; he'd be buried with it. She felt his glasses shatter beneath her foot again, shuddering now to think of it, wondering if he had a family. At some point they would have to make an anonymous call to the Santa Elena police, as she would if Ken was gone too. She wondered who to call for him back home. The St. Paul Police would handle it.

Rebecca got up, thinking she was down to the wire now, and her last resource was Lester Grunge. There were only three women left in the cathedral, all of them closer to the altar, none looking back. She drew aside the curtain on the right confessional booth and looked inside. It held nothing but smooth walls and a kneeler. Pressing on the back wall revealed no passageway.

At the center booth she opened the door and saw the message immediately, a white business card lying on the tufted red cushion. Thinking it would be Ken's card she glanced around before she stepped inside and picked it up, pulling the door shut behind her. In black letters it read, Hotel Estrella. They had both taken one to show cab drivers, not wanting to limp through their miserable Spanish to give the address each time they returned to the hotel. Nothing was handwritten on it. Ken must have been in a hurry.

Rebecca stuffed the card in her jeans pocket and pulled the cushion off the bench, expecting to find a trap door beneath, but the wood was seamless and solid. The walls around it felt normal, the sliding screen on each side looked into the adjacent booths. She knelt and pushed on the panel below the seat and found it yielded a fraction of an inch. This had to be it. She began to work the panel back and forth, making a creaking noise, but she didn't care at that point. Finally the panel gave with a crack and fell into the space beneath the seat. Sitting above the opening with her knees apart she bent over and looked inside. She was sitting on an empty box. There was nothing inside but the loose panel lying on the floor.

She leaned back and nearly began to cry. How could this be a dead end? Ken had obviously left the card there for her and it had to mean this was his exit point. She stood up and put her hand on the door, but it opened before she could push on it. In the opening stood a priest in a black cassock with half a smile on his handsome young face, the same one who had said mass earlier. Her first thought was, What would Lester Grunge do now? With a reliable instinct, Rebecca threw herself into the priest's arms, which without hesitation closed around her and pressed her closer. He smelled of sweat and incense and after-shave, and he felt as solid as eternity when her breasts flattened against his welcoming chest.

The revolver from the confessional lay on the desk in front of him, the barrel pointing off to the left. "I am called Diego," said the man with the big face.

Abrams was not tied up, but faced the broad man from the back of the room, too far away to even think of making a move, but not so distant he wouldn't take a bullet in the center of his chest if he tried. He sat in a brown leather armchair, comfortably worn and covered with fine cracks, like the wrinkles marking the face of an aged friend. Behind the desk, a wide window with steel mullions framed the view beyond the deep porch to the corral and beyond, with green fields moving slowly up and down over low hills as far as he could see. On the left the land was dry, spiked with agave and struggling shrubs. In some places the prickly pear was nearly twenty feet high anchored on trunks like a tree.

Abrams was recording everything. He knew there had to be a substantial irrigation system. From the beamed ceiling hung two wrought iron chandeliers. In the corner near the desk stood a stand with a flat-screen computer and a printer. Next to them sat two tall file cabinets. From the absence of the sun in the sky, he knew the windows faced roughly west, but he didn't know whether Santa Elena also lay in that direction.

The rest of the wall space in the office was taken up with dozens of photos of prize-winning horses. Light-skinned men with big mustaches and suits posed with them.

"You seem to have had much interest in the cathedral yesterday, *Señor* Abrams."

"Your English is very good, Diego."

"Like many Méxicans, I have spent some time in the States. But perhaps you can tell me now about the cathedral."

"A fine example, mid-seventeenth century in design, strong Baroque influence. It's the largest one in north central México, and it replaces the one that fell earlier in an earthquake, ah, in the 1650s, I believe." Abrams had seen this on a plaque in five languages near the entry.

"So, you are a student of history? Because I have

read that too." Diego placed his elbows on the desk and rested his chin on his hands. His look did not appear threatening, only inquisitive. They might have just met on a bus pulling into Santa Elena and begun to get acquainted by speaking about their children. He reached in his shirt pocket for a cigarette pack and shook one loose, tapping it briefly on the desktop before he lit it.

"I'm an architect. Naturally a great historic structure like that would interest me," said Abrams, trying to sound erudite. "There are no large churches of that period in the States." This was a guess, but he didn't think Diego would know this either.

"So your work is mainly with churches?" The wide man expelled a long plume of smoke that settled up between the chandeliers as he slid the matchbox closed.

This guy's got big lungs too, Ken thought. "Not at all, I mainly do residential design. But of course, architecture is architecture, anywhere. I'm sure you'll agree."

"Of course. So it was the architecture of the confessional that you were investigating when we met?" With his index finger Diego pushed the gun slightly to the right, in the process turning it so the barrel now pointed more directly toward Abrams. The benign expression on his face did not change. Beneath his upper lip, his tongue probed against his teeth for an errant fleck of tobacco.

Abrams gave a modest shrug. "Sometimes these fine points, these details, if you will, can have an unexpected impact on the overall design."

"They say God is in the details," said Diego, crossing himself. "I have heard this too. And quite naturally you find it is better to explore them after the cathedral closes for the night?"

"Easier to concentrate without the crowds." Abrams smiled, nodding. "There's a lot of detail to observe, even though the light may not be as good."

Diego looked at him for a long minute. "There is a phrase I learned when I lived in Bakersfield, let me see if I can get it right now, it's been a few years. I think it was, 'You are pulling on my legs?' Isn't that it?"

"Close enough," he said, nodding again, more cordially.

Diego leaned forward on the old-fashioned green baize blotter, his elbows spread across the front edge. His shoulders were so huge they seemed nearly as wide as the desk itself. For the first time a sour and frustrated look appeared on his face. "Señor Abrams, I think you will understand that my patience is not. . ."

It was a subtle sound at first, rhythmic and measured, but growing in intensity, and Abrams could immediately see that the other man recognized it sooner than he did. It was not until Diego was up and out the door screaming, "*Madre de Dios!*" that Abrams saw the first horse charge past the window at a gallop, followed by a dozen or so others in a blurred stream of motion, reminding him of his own LeRoy Neimann horse print at home in St. Paul. A moment later, the thirteenth figure, two legged and enveloped in the dust of their hoof-beats, was Diego himself, rapidly falling behind as the horses moved off toward the low hills.

Abrams leapt forward and recovered his wallet and Diego's pistol from the desktop at the same moment, and moved out through the door. He was poised for an instant on the deep porch, considering which direction to head in, when a guttural roar interrupted his thoughts, already none too clear, about which way the highway might be. A dusty red four-wheeler paused in front of him, with a dusty blond woman at the controls, a big smile on her face.

"Climb aboard, babe, we're outa here," Rebecca yelled over the engine noise. Abrams leaped on behind her and wrapped his arms around her waistband. They roared off along the side of the corral and down the lane past the end of a green field. There had been times when he wanted to put his arms around her before, but never as much as now.

"You're good," he said into her ear, as they swung left onto the paved road.

"Bet on it. All I did was open the corral. The horses did the rest."

"I think I was betting on it. Nothing else was coming to me." Once again he had the thought that she would simply hand him this case. It didn't matter now. Only winning mattered.

Rebecca twisted the handle-grip control to the maximum speed. It topped out at sixty kilometers, about thirty-five miles an hour, maybe a little more. He wondered how long it would be before the ranch people came after them. They would all have cell phones, of course, and Diego would soon give up on the horses. The fields along the road alternated between grazing land and green crops, mostly corn. Obviously some ranchers had irrigation and some did not, and tall corn in March meant two crops a year. It might give some cover.

Neither had looked at the odometer, but it could have been ten or twelve kilometers later when Ken angled his head to look in the rear view mirror and saw the black

Suburban behind them screaming down the highway, gaining fast.

"Get off the road!" he yelled at her. "Here they come!"

"Hang on!" she yelled. He gripped her more closely. Unhesitatingly she veered off into a tall stand of corn, bouncing into and through the shallow ditch, then out of sight, mowing down the rows of stalks. They slowed to about thirty kilometers per hour, the corn stalks slapping to the ground beneath them and severed ears sailing over their heads.

"I've got a gun now," he yelled, not certain she could hear him. "Stop and get away from this thing. Our track is too visible." Behind them a lengthening three-foot wide swath of shredded plants pointed to their exact location. She cut the engine, and they leaped off and ran through the corn, stopping four rows back from the ditch.

The Suburban slowed, crawling along the edge of the road nearly even with them, then stopped. Two men jumped out, crouched and fired at the four-wheeler. Shots ricocheted off the metal as Ken took slow aim at the Suburban and fired, hitting first the front tire on the passenger side, then on the driver's side. The front of the vehicle slumped and settled. The two men jumped back behind it. Silence.

"I've got only four shots left," Ken said in her ear, "but they have to come out in the open to get at us. They're not both going to make it."

Five minutes passed. One man emerged in a crouching run from the rear of the Suburban, but dropped to the tarmac and rolled onto his back at the same instant Ken fired. The man didn't move again.

"Their first mistake," Ken said. "Their only chance was to both come at once. I think they're amateurs." What he did not say was that this was the first time he'd ever fired any gun in anger, and it was different from the seventeen dreams where he'd killed prisoners in his custody. In the dreams, the gun had never had a kick in his hand. He was now certain that the department's required annual target practice was worth doing more than once a year. He'd be recommending the change if he lived through this.

A long silence followed. Then the Suburban roared to life, shot forward a car length, then backed up off the road on the edge of the ditch, coming to rest at an angle. The fallen man's head, now the only part of him in view, disappeared as his body was dragged backward a moment later.

"Come on!" she said.

Ken fired one more precious round into the vehicle, shattering the front window on the passenger side, and they ran for the four-wheeler.

"That last one was just machismo," she said as the ATV leaped forward.

"I couldn't help myself," he yelled back, but she didn't appear to hear him.

One final shot trailed them as they zigzagged through the corn, then nothing more. The Suburban stayed where it was.

No one paid any attention to them as they drove through Santa Elena and parked two streets over from the

Rio San Pedro, a small restaurant south of Independencia, where Abrams took some time using his handkerchief to wipe all the fingerprints off the red four-wheeler. None of the bullets had hit the gas tank, but the seat was pierced through, and although there were three holes in the fenders, the tires were intact. Anyone passing by would have thought he was trying to get the dust off. Perhaps they found it strange that the wheels and motor were still filthy when he finished, but they were both gringos and may not have understood how to keep a vehicle clean. In the States people probably had staff to do that.

In the restaurant, their dusty clothing didn't stand out much because it was still morning and no one else was there yet, but Abrams was starving. Rebecca looked down at her dirty jeans and soiled Grunge Tee shirt and shrugged. When the waiter left with their order Rebecca pulled out Ira Shapiro's notebook and slid it across the table.

"What is this?" Abrams said, his smile fading.

"I think you'll see. Shapiro's dead, Ken. When I was on the way to meet you this morning, I found his body by the Witness, seated in one of those bronze chairs. He'd been dead for a while, maybe all night. The body was cold to the touch. No ID or badge, just this notebook in his trench coat."

Abrams didn't respond immediately, and a look of distress came over his face.

"Cause of death? I know you're not the coroner, but was it obvious?" He stared at her for a moment. She seemed calm enough, although a little grubby around the edges.

"It was that same garrote thing with an amber

bead at the ends. I didn't touch it. The only thing that would hold my prints is this notebook. It was still too dark to see if there was any glitter. I didn't call the police, they would have found him anyway when it was daylight." She pulled out her cell phone and opened the photo, sliding it across the table to him. "We're going to have to help them with his identity, though, his wallet was gone."

Abrams looked at the dead man's image, peering closely at the neck, then shut the phone, shaking his head. "He said he'd see me here, said I owed him a drink. I'm glad you took the notebook, the police here wouldn't know what to do with it." He was thinking they'd stamp both sides of every page in it first, send it out to be translated, then stamp every page of the translation when it came back. Then they'd quit for the day without looking at it."

"Get over it. We're the only ones working this case now. We do what we have to do." She gave him a stern look.

"You're channeling Lester Grunge, right?"

"Pretty much. How was it?"

"Not bad. Any other marks on the body?"

"I didn't stick around. There was light starting up on the horizon and I didn't feel like answering any questions. I never do."

As lunch arrived Abrams flipped through the notebook, scanned the entries on Born and Rafael Cantú, and closed it again, sticking it in his back pocket. "This is Shapiro, all right. I want to study it when I'm not so hungry. I can't think on an empty stomach."

"They didn't give you any breakfast," she said.

He shook his head. "I was the only thing being

grilled."

They were sitting with their backs to the wall in a rear corner with a clear view of the room and the entry. It was going to be like that for a while now.

"You were absolutely wonderful," he said, as he worked over the *huevos rancheros* a few minutes later "You can be my backup any time."

"Were? When did it stop? I've been your backup all along, even when I was a suspect. You just didn't know it yet."

Abrams knew this was true but he didn't want a backup with a big head, and she was sounding like her hat size had recently increased.

"How did you know where I was?"

"The priest told me, after he busted me in the confessional when I came to find you in the morning. I found your hotel card, by the way, but I assumed you'd left it because you'd followed the little people out through the priest's chair. He charged me 200 pesos for the damage I caused trying to find the exit." She passed the card across to him.

"But still. . .?"

"Padre Roberto stayed late last night and he saw you leave with a very big guy that he knew from seeing him in the cathedral every day. The big guy always came to check it out with his boss, Enrique."

Abrams made a gimme motion with his left hand as he took a forkful of the *huevos rancheros*. "You're holding out on me."

"Enrique Arenas, who's also a big guy around here, has keys to the cathedral. He inspects the place every day at different times. The padre wouldn't tell me any more. It was only when I said you hadn't left willingly that he told me I would probably find you at Hacienda Milagro, where Arenas lives. Be very polite if you go out there, he said, and don't say I told you. He was still holding my hand at that point."

"Another Arenas; it's like they ran out of names here. And then?"

"I took a cab. When we got to those big iron gates I knew they'd never let me in. My driver spoke some English so I asked him if there was a service entry that was easier. It was just down the road a bit where all the ranch hands go in. It cost me only fifty pesos more for the information. It turns out the heavy security is mainly around the residential compound."

"OK. Now who is Enrique Arenas, and why is he so spooked?"

"The padre wouldn't talk about it. All he would say is that Arenas is a big deal in this town and that he does a lot for the community."

"Sounds contradictory after the other stuff he told you."

"He was conflicted about talking, and I was flirting with him. Anyway, the lane I came in on led to that big corral. I headed to the only building in sight, besides a little bunker kind of thing with no windows. That's when I saw you through that big window in front. There were four of those ATVs out behind it so I knew what I had to do. An old boyfriend of mine had one, so I'd driven them before."

"I think you're incredible, but then I'm not so hungry now. I can focus on other things."

"Of course, but don't get all sloppy on me. I'm

still not going to show you my tattoo."

Abrams pulled out a pen and made a quick sketch on a paper napkin, a circle with an open bottom, an inverted V inside. "That reminds me. I saw this on one of the horses and I assumed this was an inverted V, but it must be an A with a short bar that I didn't make out."

"Arenas," she said.

"I don't get it. Why are the Arenases after me? We're trying to help them, or avenge them, at least."

"They don't know who you were, that's all."

"Something was bothering them about what I was doing in the cathedral. They were just starting out on me when you showed up."

"What if they think someone's trying to kill this Enrique?" she asked. "Maybe they found out about the murdered bishop in Houston. That would make them want to talk to you."

"Even more so now that I shot their guy. He could be dead. That would only confirm their theory about me."

Rebecca thought for a moment. "So now Enrique Arenas takes a story to the police about his people being ambushed on the highway when they chased a couple who had stolen a four-wheeler from the ranch. Maybe he's got the clout to bring the whole force in on it. Everybody in Santa Elena is going to be looking for us. Aren't you glad now you didn't get to register with the authorities?"

"I think it's time we went underground."

After the late breakfast, they caught a cab in front of the restaurant. As they drove off, a block away they saw a Transito tow truck pulling the four-wheeler up onto its flatbed.

"Were we illegally parked?" asked Rebecca,

watching the process through the rear window.

"Actually, parking there was probably our last legal act in México. We better locate Jeremy and Cantú fast or this thing is going to overtake us."

"I think I can already hear heavy breathing behind me," she said, nodding slowly. "Just like on the four-wheeler."

CHAPTER 16

For Jeremy it was hard to think of the person looking up at him as a man, but he was clearly male and not young. From where they stood in one of the hubs with eight corridors branching off, he could see dozens of others going about their business, occasionally glancing his way, but not approaching. Most looked like blue-collar workers. They were all around him now. The women in the crowd were all head and shoulders above the men. For the first time Jeremy felt like he was in a city. Before, all the others he'd seen had kept their distance. Luisa admitted that initially they'd concealed themselves on Rafael's orders to allow Jeremy to adapt better to his new life. But now he was ready for it, the other side of the Aldea.

He shook the small rough hand that was offered him. The skin was mostly dry and not entirely clean, possibly even a little sticky on the fingertips, but this one, whose name was Eugenio, did not work in food service; he was a librarian. He was about three feet tall and hairless, and while he resembled the small person in the painting in Cantú's studio, he was not dressed in battered medieval castoffs. Luisa towered over him as he looked up at her with respect.

Eugenio wore children's sneakers and shorts, and

a dark blue tee shirt with no lettering. Both his ears were large and seemed to align themselves toward Jeremy like miniature radar dishes quivering to receive a distant signal from above. Other than the ears, his proportions were normal for his height.

"How old is he?" Jeremy said to Luisa.

"You can ask him yourself. His English is as good as mine."

"I'm ninety-one," Eugenio said with a proud smile framing uneven teeth, one of which was the color of tobacco juice and shorter than the others. It suggested that dentistry hadn't yet entered the Aldea's portfolio of skills. "I have a son who just turned eleven. He'll be weaned soon."

Jeremy hadn't thought of this before, but in a disturbing way it did fit with the long childhood. He tried not to picture a child of eleven nursing, but didn't succeed. And wouldn't the kid have a lot of teeth by then? He shuddered.

"Still in diapers?" he asked impulsively, thinking to make conversation, then realized he didn't want to know the answer.

"Just another year, more or less," Eugenio said, with an indulgent shrug. "You never know. It always has to be their own idea, so we don't push him about it."

Jeremy nodded in sympathy, then glanced at Luisa, who as she listened to this was clasping both hands over her abdomen like the Virgin Mary during the Annunciation, a beatific smile on her face. Twelve years of diapers, Jeremy thought, puts a different spin on parenthood. As they moved on, Luisa leaned into his shoulder. "My middle name is Maria," she said, looking up at him hopefully. "One of them, anyway."

"How can that be if everybody down here is anti-religious?" He thought he had her now.

"Take away all the saints' names in México and the kids would have to be named X and Y. There wouldn't be anything left. Although I suppose we could name them Amber and Tiffany, or maybe Lance and Derek."

By Thursday night, Jeremy was far along on his map of the Aldea. During the day, not that there was any difference, Luisa had shown him the mushroom beds with their vital but vaporous compost pits in the adjoining rooms. The ripe humid heat they generated was apparent halfway down the corridor. Maybe she'd only pretended to think he'd already found them on his own. Then there were the grub farms, which fed the chickens because grain was scarce, the weaving and tailor shops, the classrooms and recreation halls, the main dining room, the library and a few other places where the small people looked at him politely as if he were a harmless alien. There were four corridors of fish tanks, where long concrete troughs held a dozen varieties. Paper drums of dry fish food lined the walls.

"They're all deep-water types," Luisa said, gesturing broadly, "so they don't need much light. Some of them even avoid it." A few of these areas, like the grub farm, he had quickly forgotten after he marked them on the map.

He also hadn't been fond of the bat-breeding cages outside the felting room, where wire baskets full of flapping and fluttering airborne mice filled the air with their ultra high-pitched squeals of excitement. She said she found it amusing that he was fitting these stations together with the hubs and stairways and corridors, making notes everywhere they went. He asked her to mark the place where they'd come in, saying he'd always been fascinated by maps, and what he loved about the Aldea was the multiple layers, so that the maps could be stacked one over the other in three dimensions. She hesitated at first, but then pointed it out.

"I'm not going anywhere," he told her. "None of this is likely to fall into the wrong hands."

"There are times when I wonder, though, how long I'll be here myself," she said. "I'm not sure I can stand to be ruled by Rafael forever."

"What do you mean?"

"I really can't talk about it, but what he's planning is especially upsetting, and there's no way to challenge him, except by confronting him directly."

This left Jeremy confused and apprehensive. Even as he moved toward a fuller acceptance of living underground, he wanted less and less to be under the thumb of a marginal personality. When Luisa would say no more about it, he had put together his gear and moved off to his next exploration.

Besides his compass, which he never traveled without, in his luggage Jeremy had brought Luisa's pocket guide to Santa Elena, which had a detailed enlargement of the central district, which was focused on the four connecting plazas. He recalled that the night they came in they had traveled under twelve arches before they reached the crypt. He made his Aldea maps to the same scale as the guide's detail page of the plazas. Now, by overlaying one on the other, he knew exactly where they were in relation to the Outside. He also knew where the old palace dining hall was, now Rafael's studio. The treasury where the Relic was kept was easy, just off the first hub coming in from the sarcophagus in the old crypt.

Most important of all, he had identified the areas of forbidden access, which he kept blank on the map, as if tacitly accepting the official line that they didn't exist. The truth was that he was accepting what he was told about the Aldea less and less every day. All these taboo areas were in a wedge-shaped slab with one long curved side, five levels deep (he believed) that, in a shape like a baseball field, was partly extended under the new cathedral. One of the straight sides of this area, roughly along the first base line, also passed under Rafael Cantú's studio near home plate.

It was from this area that Jeremy had heard the sounds of cargo moving over rails, but he soon dismissed Rafael's statement that the noise was from agriculture. For Jeremy, the entire Aldea was a warren of ongoing tunnels, but why secret excavations might be going on under the cathedral, when the structure itself had to be so immensely heavy, made no sense to him. With their extensive educational system, didn't they have engineers who could inform them of the risk?

When he placed the street overlay on top of the baseball field wedge and aligned it properly, the four piers supporting the great cathedral dome formed a diamond with one point approximately over the pitcher's mound, another at deep center field, and the remaining two at center right and center left fields.

Jeremy was lying in bed thinking about the complexities of removing all this debris, when the sensation of a small forked tongue traveling up his indecently bare spine derailed his thoughts. "You're so naked without any back hair," Luisa said. "You don't even seem aware of it. Now there's only one way for me to tell when you're turned on."

"We're not aware of it at all back in St. Paul," he said, rolling onto his back and pulling her to his chest. "I suppose it's like when women reporters go to Islamic countries without covering their faces or hair. The local guys are all thinking, 'Wow! She's hot. Look at how much that babe is showing, and she doesn't even care. I bet she's easy.'"

"I'm easy, too," Luisa said with a pouty look. "Disgracefully easy. Lucky you."

But Jeremy's mind was again on the map, his finger mentally tracing a line from somewhere in center field through second base and then home plate, just about the point where he'd been standing when he'd spoken to Cantú, and felt or heard the narrow-gage cart moving on rails below. He imagined himself boring through solid rock to lay tracks. Very tough, but people did it. Lava would be easier than most kinds of stone, because it was so porous. What they did not do was meander around as they worked. The borers went the shortest way, which was a straight line, unless they hit some compelling reason not to. If the track went under the art studio to dump tunneling residues, there must be an exit on the far end of the citadel mound, opposite the cathedral. His maps were not far enough along to show where these routes might go.

Luisa had said the population was relatively stable, which argued there was no need for new facilities. By now he had seen most of the agricultural operation, and although he'd noticed many handcarts, there had been no rails. Cantú really had been misleading him. The real produce was all carried on those carts. Beyond the fact that the Aldea itself existed in secrecy, what was there within it that required another, higher level of security? Surely they didn't have a nuclear weapons program. H wondered if it was connected to Cantú's plan that Luisa had mentioned.

As much as he was worn down by his recent sexual acrobatics, Jeremy had not been sleeping well. It was partly because his mind was working at a rapid pace. His newfound potency was like opening a long-sealed door, and it suggested that his mind might have been dormant in other areas as well, one of them, surprisingly, being diplomacy.

It was not something he'd ever thought of, until he emerged from the Cantú interview. As a young guy of Irish ancestry, he was steeped in the self-deprecating culture of the Midwest. St. Paul had produced no one of international stature since F. Scott Fitzgerald left for Paris after World War I. It seemed normal that Jeremy Wyman was modest in demeanor and held no elevated ambitions beyond hoisting a few at Antoine's when the spirit moved him, and one day losing his unlamented cherry to a girl of average appeal, but above-average willingness.

Now that things were in motion, however, Jeremy planned to soon contact the Vatican and make their day. It was unfortunate he hadn't seen a phone in the

Aldea. Maybe he could email the Pope once he figured out how to get on the Internet. It was obvious that poor communications might be one of the things holding this community back.

It was good, in a way, that the Polish pope was already gone. A nice guy, of course, even saintly in his way, but he'd seemed too worn out and tilted for the gritty realities of a tough negotiation. Possibly he had still been carrying around some bullet fragments from that Turkish crackpot who'd tried to kill him.

The new pope had been in Hitler Youth, and in the German army during the War, and although he seemed rather small and fluffy now, age can do that, and Jeremy's research suggested that even fluffy Germans were likely to have a practical turn of mind. By contrast, the Poles obviously did not, since in 1939 they'd met the Nazi Panzer divisions on their border with horse cavalry.

Offering Pope Benedict XVI the largest remaining fragment of the True Cross would get his attention. It would be a simple trade. One seriously historic chunk of wood, with accompanying iron staple, all in a damn fine silver case, in exchange for the liberation and restored fortunes of the Aldea clan. No questions asked. How handy that México was a Catholic country, where the Pope's influence would be strong. Benedict would be able to make it happen. Of course the nuts and bolts of it would be worked out with a lesser functionary, possibly the Vatican secretary of state, whatever he was called. But Jeremy would insist on being present himself at the signing of the final agreement with the little guy in white. If he'd had Internet access, he would have pulled up his German dictionary at this point.

He had cast off Luisa's warning about not mentioning any emergence from underground. There was clearly a crisis on the way because of Rafael, and the Aldeans needed to be ready with some serious cards to play. He did not plan to become an ineffective quixotic hero, like the Irish (his ancestors) who had struggled unsuccessfully to liberate their country from England. He knew what to do. First he had to find out what was happening in the forbidden area so he could gauge what he was up against, and then contact Rome. With the message he was now blocking out, they couldn't fail to listen.

It was time to begin. This was the real function of the maps. Initially he'd felt guilty about holding it back from Luisa, but he didn't feel that she was always frank with him either. He didn't have enough relationship experience to know yet whether this was normal.

"Exercise," Jeremy said to her, breaking a long silence. "I'm not getting enough of it down here. When I'm home in St. Paul, I'm out constantly, pounding the pavement, staying in shape."

"I can see that," Luisa said without looking up from her book. Her chin rested on one hand, the elbow on a small table near her bed. "Your muscle tone is amazing, in some places, anyway. Why don't you take a hike?"

He stood in the curtained doorway for a moment, thinking about her two years of English slang courses, the six years of grammar. He sensed no irony in her tone, yet there was some nuance there. . .

When he didn't respond, she set the book facedown on the bed, regarding him calmly, naked as usual when she was in her new bedroom, twisting her hair into a thick cable that she knotted behind her head. He loved

the way her breasts moved when she had her hands behind her neck. It's too bad you can't screw twenty-four
hours a day, he was thinking, but you just can't. You have
to talk sometimes too. I should have spent a little more
time on the Internet checking out the relationship thing,
like how to be in one without always saying the wrong
thing, or having some of those long silences. He knew
there was someone who had written a bunch of books
about it, but he couldn't remember her name. Now it was
too late. Without the Internet he was helpless. Maybe he
could check the Aldea library. It was marked somewhere
on his map.

Originally he had pictured himself and Luisa
having marvelous conversations, and they did have some,
to a point. The problem was that when they got deeply into any subject, she simply blew him away with her
knowledge of the detail and her understanding of its implications. It seemed like she'd already been through all
the ramifications of everything, even subjects he thought
of as strictly candidates for research on a slow day. These
exchanges were often followed by periods of silence when
he felt he would never be able to keep up with her without
being online. Of course in the Aldea, that was over.

"OK," he said to her suddenly. "How about asex-
ual reproduction in carrots?" He had no idea if it was
even possible, but if it was, surely no one cared about it.
Sometimes he tried to catch her off guard by throwing
things out at random that he had just plucked out of the
air. Luisa rarely failed to have a response, and this one
didn't give her pause at all.

"You can do it with individual phloem cells in an
agar medium, but why would you want to? It's boring.

Our way is more fun." She gave him an impudent look, placing one slender finger along her nose.

Luisa also had the startling ability to connect things that he never realized had any relationship at all. Yesterday she'd shown him how the Vietnam War debt had caused the energy crisis of the seventies because it forced Richard Nixon to remove the silver support from the dollar, effectively reducing the price of a barrel of oil as the dollar then dropped in value. OPEC had responded with massive price increases. When she was finished, his mouth was open but nothing came out. She sometimes made him feel like there were vast empty spaces in his head, connected by thin quavery clumps of active brain cells that were stretched to their capacity, but still short on coverage. How ironic now that he couldn't let her in on his liberation plan for the Aldea. Then her mouth could have hung open for a while, exposing that odd little tongue that he had grown to love.

"Why don't you work on your map?" she asked. "Go pace some things off. You don't have the water and sewer works on there yet, or the recreation room. Or should I teach you welding? It would give you something to do. It's not that hard."

He felt like it was the tone she might have used with a fourth grader toward the end of a three-day car trip. She picked up volume two of Gibbon's Decline and Fall of the Roman Empire again, and opened it to her satin bookmark. "To think I once had this almost entirely memorized. Of course, that was thirty years ago," she said, shaking her head without looking up again.

Five years before I was born, he thought. He'd always thought Edward Gibbon had an anti-Christian bias anyway, but of course, that would have been taken for objectivity in the Aldea. Dismissed, and rather sad that Luisa was so complacent in the face of what was brewing, Jeremy adjusted his backpack and moved off down the corridor. What could he do? She had sealed his lips with her statement that people would kill him if they knew what he was plotting.

He moved back this time in the direction they'd used coming in. That first stack of hubs he had now named Cluster I, and in terms of his baseball field floor plan, it stood on the third base line, closer to third than home plate. Luisa's room was on level three, and the level below her was largely fish tanks and mushrooms, and usually quiet. She had taken him through all this earlier, but now he intended to explore some of the other levels, while avoiding classrooms and other population centers. Somewhere out there were the tracks, which he now believed were the key, because people were being deceptive about them. As a researcher, Jeremy knew deception better than most. Most of the time, the truth lay directly behind it.

At the Cluster I hub he discovered a crowd. This time, no one looked at him much except for three or four girls who reminded him of Luisa, although they weren't quite as tall. They had the same rosebud mouth and long nose, not projecting much, but closely held and delicate, as if it were a treasure they were leery of sharing. Jeremy knew why. However, their densely violet eyes lit up as he approached and suggested they might make an exception for him. More than might, it looked like a virtual certainty. He could almost sense their back hair beginning to stand up, but he didn't touch any of them.

Experienced now, he estimated they might be in

their mid-seventies and, from their manner, kind of wild. Possibly they were even part of a rough crowd, but still superbly educated. As always, when in a foreign country Jeremy remained aware of his surroundings, even though until now this had only included a brief foray into western Ontario. It hadn't seemed that threatening, aside from the occasional moose, which were alarmingly big. When the girls weren't looking, he moved his wallet to his front pocket, closing his hand over it as he went down another flight of steps. He looked back when he reached the bottom, but thankfully none of them had followed.

His watch said it was a little after six, which explained the rush hour crowd. He no longer knew whether six meant A.M. or P.M. He was in a corridor of public rooms, and the first was the dining room. It was unoccupied now and he stepped inside. He had been in this room earlier in the day, or yesterday? It wasn't clear, and then the crowd of small people eating, mostly working men, made him uneasy and ready to flee. Now he could survey it in detail. The walls and floor were the same lava, the ceiling a shallow vault. It was furnished with long tables and plastic chairs that could have been discarded from an elementary school.

On one long wall at the corner were two black steel doors with ventilation grills near the top that Jeremy hadn't noticed on his earlier visit. Below one, water and waste pipes entered the wall, and below the other, electrical conduit. Both meant the same thing to him—these were utility chases, vertical passages in the wall going from floor to floor and room to room. The black doors allowed access for repairs. He pulled the map stack from his backpack and marked the chases on the lunchroom wall.

Farther along the corridor, a series of classrooms all held a similar chase access, but only one, for electrical conduit. Two bathrooms had both. He marveled at the small toilets and the low sink counters in the men's.

For three hours Jeremy moved through the levels and corridors adding the utility chase locations to the rooms on his map. Together they formed a separate system of internal movement. He got a few strange looks, but smiled and waved in response; he was getting used to it. He was nearing Cluster II when he saw the first set of chase doors on a corridor wall, and neither had pipes or conduit below. Looking both ways and seeing no one, he opened one of the doors, much like that of a high school gym locker, and looked inside. It contained a steel ladder on the wall and no floor. The other locker contained a steel ladder on the wall and no ceiling. It was evidently some kind of junction or transfer point.

His face betraying nothing, he moved down the hallway a hundred feet like any other casual tourist savoring the marvels of tunneled lava construction. Pulling out his maps, he marked the pair of passage doors on the corridor. The location was at the extreme edge of the known Aldea, close to the forbidden zone, where he had left a blank wedge on the map. He knew the steel doors led into danger in both directions. He mentally flipped a coin and chose the one on the right. Jeremy was going up.

With a backpack and the twenty pounds he didn't need, clearance was tight in a passage designed for much smaller people. Had there been pipes inside it wouldn't have worked. The rungs were close together as in the grave shaft on Tuesday. Once the door was shut behind him there was virtually no light, so he used his hand to measure the distance between rungs. It was close to one span of his spread fingers, which he decided to call ten inches.

Twelve rungs put him at the next door, ten feet up, he thought. It was plausible if the corridors had a ceiling height of about six-foot-four or six. It left around three and a half feet of lava between floors. At the next level the rungs ended.

By twisting around, he could see through the grill to the floor and several feet in each direction, feeling like a hot dog in a square metal and lava bun. He waited for a moment, listening and hearing nothing before he slowly opened the door and slipped out. No one was in view. On his left, the corridor ended. Across from him was a lunchroom with washroom attached. Long low tables and orange plastic chairs suggested the scale of fourth grade students. To the right the corridor veered away at a forty-five degree angle.

He began to hear that odd noise again now. It was the sound he thought of before as a snick, the impact of steel wheels repeatedly hitting the tiny space between two lengths of rail that weren't quite touching. It was the same sound he had heard, or perhaps only felt, beneath his feet in Cantú's studio. Although, as he thought about it, if there was no space and the rails heated up for some reason, then they'd expand and buckle. The spaces had to be intentional; they were expansion gaps.

His map was precise in terms of geography, although in this area it showed no individual features, and the next step he took put him in the forbidden zone. The real problem, here as anywhere in the Aldea, was exposure. There was virtually no place to hide when he was off limits. He was out of the bedroom area, and would have to risk walking the corridor, alone, or hiding in some very public room, if anyone appeared. A crowd of three-foot Aldeans would never provide cover. Even with his average height, Jeremy already felt like a giraffe in a herd of sheep. Putting a smile on his face that would convince no one, he advanced down the corridor toward a T-shaped junction ahead. He was about halfway there when he saw a pair of rails with a taut cable about a foot above. After another five steps the first cars came into view, moving slowly to the left, toward center field on his map.

They reminded him of the scaled-down railway he had ridden often in Como Park on the western side of St. Paul when he was a kid. He saw himself with a yellow ticket stub in one hand and an ice cream cone in the other as his mother fastened the safety belt around his waist. Suddenly at the edges of his tongue he could taste the damp rotting smell of fallen leaves in October. How far away that was from the Aldea and this moment.

Instead of having seats, the cars before him now were all open hoppers. There was a string of fourteen, dark green in color, with bulging sides and a multitude of scars from hard use. All they lacked was graffiti.

There was no driver at the far end, and there had been none at the front when it passed, only the cable pulling it. The cars must be gravity-driven, he thought. They would have gone out full, rolling slowly downhill, restrained by the cable, then emptied. Now they were being towed back for refill, as if being rewound. They were not moving very fast as he waited for the last one, then swung his weight over the side and crouched below the top edge. He could feel as well as hear the *snick* noise beneath his kneecaps and elbows as the wheels hit the tiny gaps between rails. As he moved farther into the mountain he had the sensation of being under home plate and Rafael Cantú standing directly above in his studio, looking downward through the floor at him.

Before he climbed aboard, the upper edges of the cars had been just above waist-high for him, which meant they were higher than eye level for the small people, the men anyway. None of the men standing next to the rails or even on them would be able to look in at him, and he doubted the women would be working on the rail line. The cable meant that the track was straight, or nearly so, because the friction it would cause scraping the walls going around corners would rapidly wear it away.

The floor of his car was covered with coarse black grit that pitted his hands and knees. Jeremy was on his way to a dig, and from his angle of travel he estimated that he would pass under the pitcher's mound and second base, if he went that far. He raised his head to the front edge of the car and looked up the line.

Like most places in the Aldea, it was not well lit, but at about 150 feet ahead the tunnel opened out into a taller, brighter space, with columns or other supports. It may have been a waiting room of some kind, but he had seen no passenger cars. The train slowed to a crawl.

Soon he could make out a central column about twenty feet high and four feet in diameter. Near the top, carved arches spread away from it and merged upward into the ceiling. The track traveled eight or ten feet past the column base. Strangely, near the floor the column thinned in diameter for the length of a couple of feet, then resumed its normal width above and below. Beyond, the first cars in the string stopped near a horizontal wheel operated by a dozen small men, winding up the cable like on a capstan. On the other side of the cars were mounds of debris awaiting removal. Jeremy didn't want to get any closer.

Coming up on the left was a recess in the wall, and at the rear of it, a gym locker door like the others he'd seen. Jeremy scanned the chamber quickly, and finding no one looking in his direction, slipped over the side of the car and flattened himself within the recess. Inside the door, which creaked as he opened it, he found a set of rungs on the wall. When he shut the door behind him and began to climb, he heard a low throbbing sound, followed a second later by a half dozen shouts in whiny, but oddly low-pitched voices. He turned and pulled himself up the rungs as fast as he could. Below, he heard the door thrown open once again and grunts mixed with Spanish as people mounted the rungs below him.

He was prone to panting anyway, and now he began to sweat from every pore. His hands were wet and slippery on the metal bars. Three levels up from the track he burst from the door into a corridor, and pulling the next to last ball point pen from his pocket, slipped it into the hasp made for a padlock and rushed toward the hub. It wouldn't hold for long, but it would give him a start.

He was in an area of sleeping rooms now, but more than that he didn't know. Entering the hub, he encountered a group of Aldeans heading straight toward him, each with a determined look, and he made a hairpin turn into the next corridor. It was only his much longer stride that helped him outdistance them, and breathless as he was, he beat them to the end where there was a connecting route to the next corridor.

Rounding the corner, he saw another group far down at the hub. He paused in confusion. They were coming now from both directions. Soon he'd be able to hear the soft shuffling sound of their undefined footwear, no more than an insistent whisper on the rough lava floor. There were doorways on both sides, all covered with drapes, and as he considered whether he ought to slip inside one at random, the light strip at his feet went dark.

Of course, he thought, they can see better in here than I can, although how they could see at all in the absence of any light was something he couldn't answer. A pale afterimage remained in his eyes and he found the nearest opening with his hands and slipped inside, his heart pounding. With any luck the room would be empty. He put out both hands and cautiously edged forward into deeper darkness, pushing one foot slowly ahead of the other. There was no sound until suddenly, one of his hands was seized by two others, and he uttered a soft grunt of surprise. The hands easily pulled him off balance and he stumbled forward. Hitting his shins, fell onto a mattress supported by a platform like the one in Luisa's room.

It was hard to think clearly with his heart pounding against his ribs, filling his head with its noise. Was it possible he might have come back to her room without realizing it? He'd been running hard and paying more attention to his pursuers than to geography. The lights had gone out before he had a chance to notice the pattern of the curtain. But if this person was Luisa, wouldn't she have said his name or some other greeting? Suddenly a pair of lips were pressed against his and the familiar sensation returned of a small moist forked tongue gripping his, this time with a considerable degree of passion. It worked its way up and down on both sides of his tongue, creating small dimples of compression. Love dots, Luisa called them.

His hands found the head facing his, and below, only skin, smooth, pliant, and he knew from experience, quite pale. This time the body seemed smaller than Luisa's, although it was difficult to judge the height of a person who is lying on top of you, especially in total darkness. As he tried to trace the outline with his hands the lips drew away and a palm was clamped tightly over his mouth, the other gripping the back of his neck. Thinking of the small searchers outside, he didn't struggle. In the corridor muffled footsteps passed the doorway, the whisper of many small bags of rags dragged over worn sandpaper.

Initially Jeremy had been dripping and motionless, frozen with a sense of the last minutes of his life ticking away. Then as the sound of the searchers receded, his hands came alive again. She was definitely smaller in shoulder and limb than Luisa, and her hair was shorter, almost like a boy's. Her skin was soft and inviting, her breasts small and the nipples erect. Her hands moved back to his neck and she pulled his face to her breast. She had not said a word.

Doesn't she speak English? he thought, and what am I doing? He pulled back a bit as he began to unbutton his shirt. It was not as if he could leave before the crowd outside dispersed, anyway. But where's my loyalty to Luisa? She said they don't share boyfriends, but yet Cantú said there would be other girls who might be interested.

He felt like a priest or monk who had repudiated his vow of chastity when he met Luisa, but had he now acquired a different vow, one of commitment to her, just because she had released him from the first one? Was the liberation she'd given him only a new species of bondage, a more attractive set of shackles? With so little experience it was confusing. He was in favor of ethical behavior, but in the Aldea, what exactly was the correct thing to do in this situation? Different worlds had different rules; he knew this from his research.

Jeremy was trying to sort this out when the girl's small thigh moved between his legs, sliding back and forth, and her hands began working on his belt buckle. He decided to postpone a decision until he could think more clearly. Suddenly the lights came back on, and he paused to look at her face, boyish and more youthful than Luisa's, although possibly even prettier. She may have been only in her fifties, but he couldn't worry about that now. As he started to courteously ask her name—it seemed only right since he was in her bed—the doorway curtain was yanked aside and six small figures rushed into the room. The girl quickly pulled a blanket over herself, and Jeremy regarded them with surprise, his fingers frozen on his shirt buttons. They were the same kind of small males he had been meeting in the corridors and public rooms, the same kind that had been laboring down by the track and collecting in the hub. This close they could have been brothers to Eugenio. But they were dressed more formally, wearing matching olive uniforms, tee shirts over shorts with a lot of pockets. They didn't seem formidable, but they were clearly not there for any good purpose.

There was a moment of silence as they all stared at each other, then a sly grin as the one closest to him drew his hand from his pocket and blew something fine and sparkling into Jeremy's face. It had a familiar gritty sour taste as it entered his mouth and nose, and a familiar effect as he pitched forward onto the mattress at the spot where the girl had just been. She had already pulled away, drawing her body close against the black wall, covering her mouth and nose as well with the blanket. As the pixie dust settled in the dimly lit room, she did not breathe. Nor did she reach out to touch Jeremy's body in farewell as, grunting, the security detail muscled him onto their narrow shoulders and carted him off.

CHAPTER 17

Ken Abrams turned over a page in Shapiro's notebook as he sat at a small writing table next to the window in his room. Rebecca looked past him to a view of the pool they had never used. "What does *boda* mean?" he said. "Most of his notes are in English but here it says, '*boda el 27 M. a las dos.* Cat. Sta. E." I suppose he must have known some Spanish to be a detective in Santa Fe."

Rebecca sat on his bed, cross-legged and for once barefoot, and flipped through her dictionary. "It's a wedding, and dos is two. You must have known that part." Her toenails were a pearly coral color. They looked great although she was not quite comfortable without her shoes, but she could hardly have worn them on his bed and there was nowhere else to sit.

"So Shapiro was here for a wedding at two on the twenty-seventh? That's today, apparently at the cathedral," he said.

"I don't know. Maybe he was multitasking? He seemed competent when you talked to him on the phone, right?"

"I thought so at the time. Does M stand for March? Because if it isn't it would have to be May, and that'd be too far off. Or are the months named something different here? I can't remember."

"Not that different. There's a chart here. Any-thing else in there?" she asked.

"Nothing we don't already know."

"He'd only been here less than a day. How much could he accomplish? And he didn't have any expert help."

"Like Lester Grunge?" he asked.

"Laugh if you want, but we're both still alive. I feel terrible for Shapiro. That makes four people they've killed now."

"Well, aside from more detail on the death of Born, this *boda* note is the only thing that might be of use. But who's getting married? This seems to be a major point of interest for him."

"How about checking the banns?" she said. "They post them here too, I saw some at the cathedral but I didn't read them."

"Like a wedding announcement?"

"Right. They post them at the church entry for several weeks in advance, and it gives people a chance to protest the wedding."

Abrams looked at his watch. "We've got time to check out the banns before the crowd gathers."

Twenty-five minutes later a taxi dropped them back at the edge of the cathedral plaza. On the side far-thest from the ruins, a stretch limousine and five Lincoln Town Cars waited in a roped-off area. This time Rebecca and Abrams entered by the side door and moved back along the aisle toward the main entry. Both scanned the workers in the pews and side chapels. The end of each pew on the main aisle was decorated with a stand of flowers bundled with ribbons. Two men were bringing bouquets up the main aisle for the altar and setting them up between elaborate wrought iron candle stands. In the choir, the organist was limbering up and a string quartet was setting up chairs and music stands.

"What did the guy who kidnapped you look like?" Rebecca asked, studying the people decorating.

"Diego? I thought you saw him at the ranch? He was as wide as a bus, but not as tall."

"He was at the back of a cloud of dust. I never saw much of him. Besides, I was looking for you. Here are the banns."

She paused at a framed and glass-covered announcement board within the entry, running her finger down the list of impending marriages. "Bingo," she said. "Angelina Arenas Mendoza and Justo Toledano Campos. March 27 at two. This has got to be it. How many Arenases can there be?"

"Half the town, apparently," Abrams said. "But isn't Arenas her middle name?"

"No, that's her father's name. Mendoza is her mother's name. An occasion like this is one of the few times she'd use both of them. I've been studying this stuff online. Normally I'd have Jeremy doing it."

As she turned to look at Abrams, the color went out of her face and the corners of her mouth turned down. "They're going to kill her," she said. "Isn't it clear that Angelina Arenas is next? Somehow Shapiro figured it out—he was going to attend this wedding. Maybe this is why the Arenases kidnapped you. They think something is coming and you might be part of it. We've got to stop it."

Cautious now, she pulled him away from the

doors and they stood at the last row of pews where Charlie Morris had seen the model for *The Witness*.

"Get real, Rebecca, Shapiro couldn't have stopped anything, and we're not going to be able to either. Think about this—we're already at the wedding," Abrams said, "where in a little while there will be more security than for a presidential inauguration. All the delivery and set up people will be gone and they'll start by sweeping the place from top to bottom. They'll know both of us by sight because of the four-wheeler episode and we'll probably be the only ones here who aren't Méxican. There'll be dozens of police wanting to charge us with attempted murder and vehicle theft at a minimum. The bodyguards will gun us down even before we can be arrested, and we'll be shipped back to the States in body bags. No one will say they didn't act properly, because we'd already shot one of them. My mother will write to her congressman and then not live long enough to get a response."

"If we're lucky," she said, putting her hands on her hips. "Any other problems with it? You sound like your cup is half empty. At least we know what's coming, sort of. Sometimes you're just too realistic, Ken. It doesn't always help."

"And maybe you're not realistic enough. This isn't fiction, although it seems like it. I'm afraid Angelina Arenas is going to have to take her chances without us. We just don't have the firepower to stop whatever is coming. All I've got is a .38 with three rounds left in it."

She watched as Abrams scanned the marble floor for ideas, remembering he'd told her he'd never been fired at until the cornfield. He'd stayed cool enough then, but she hoped he wasn't thinking they could hide in the confessional again. Suddenly he moved toward the saint's display and dropped to his hands and knees.

"Look at this."

Rebecca knelt beside him, seeing two subtle tracks, hardly more than parallel rub marks on the floor, moving outward from the base of the saint's enclosure. "It looks like this thing might slide out from the wall."

Abrams got to his feet and looked over the cathedral interior. Six women moved among the pews, dusting, all in the front half. "Check the plaza and tell me if anyone is coming toward the entry. I'm going to see if this thing is their exit." He moved his hands along the bottom edge of the molding under the glass. The china face of the saint gazed up at him in eternal delight.

Rebecca crossed to the cathedral entrance and immediately jumped back into shadow when she glimpsed three police cars speeding over the plaza toward them. Converging from different directions, they were silent but with lights flashing. A cloud of pigeons rose in panic and swirled in unison toward the bandstand roof. She ran back to Abrams, who had pulled the saint's case forward about eighteen inches out from the wall. He was crouched along the side away from the pews and looking back behind it. She touched his shoulder.

"It's open back here beneath the display," he said in a voice that couldn't be heard more than two pews away. "I can see dim light below."

"Then get in, NOW. The plaza's full of cops."

Inside they found a rectangular opening with a ledge about two feet wide all around. It was stone like the floor and scattered with debris. Some of it appeared to be rags mixed with small bones. Rebecca brushed some of it aside to make a place for herself, careful not to push it over the edge. They both found a seat and Abrams reached up and pulled the case back to the wall. Below them, dimly lit steel rungs were anchored in the stone, which changed color inches below their feet from buff to black. The rungs ended at the top of a staircase below.

A moment later a clatter of footsteps passed the saint and dispersed out of earshot.

"What's all this stuff we're sitting in?" Rebecca whispered, taking hold of his hand, and wondering what the back of her jeans was going to look like.

"I think it's the remains of our saint, plus some of her packaging. It's not plastic peanuts though."

"Yuck."

"Think of it as forensic evidence," he said. "I'm going down. Why not come along? I could use another set of eyes. Maybe we'll find the model for our Witness down there."

"And his family as well," she said, peering grimly into the stairwell. "Maybe we'll find Cantú." And the finish to my book plot, she thought.

Abrams swung over the side and hooked onto the rungs. Rebecca, wondering what awaited them below, noticed for the first time a slight thinning area in his hair toward the back of the top of his head. She hadn't seen this before, and she didn't think he knew it was there. It seemed somehow touching at a moment when they were heading into something they might never come back from. She also saw that he had his gun as she followed him down.

When the rungs ended they descended through a conventional stairwell, except that the walls and ceiling were black and coarsely porous, and the ceilings unusually low. She'd been expecting some ancient construction contemporary with the cathedral itself, but what she found had no character. It could have been carved last week or 300 years ago, but with no decoration or style. Utilitarian is timeless, she thought. When the stairs ended, Abrams stopped and put his hand out behind him, looking around the doorway into a circular open space about thirty feet across. There was no one in view.

"It looks like some kind of utility area," said Abrams. "But why is there so much of it?"

Rebecca felt slightly dizzy and her heart was beating too fast, much like during an unforgettable sixth-grade class trip to some caves in western Wisconsin. She had lost her lunch halfway through it.

While Rebecca and Abrams were feeling their way into the Aldea, Luisa, locked in her own disturbing thoughts, slipped down to the lowest level and entered the machine shop. No one saw her go in. She had never suggested it to anyone, other than a general hint to Jeremy regarding Cantú, but she was less than comfortable taking orders from a man, even an unusually tall and accomplished one like Rafael. Men had always had a lower status in the Aldea, and although she couldn't recall exactly why, there had to be some good reason for it beyond tradition. The men, well educated as they were, generally were assigned menial positions, and rarely were promoted to management roles. Rafael was the shining exception, thought to be a role model for aspiring men, but few had come forward. He remained an anomaly. Until the arrival of Jeremy had required Rafael's approval, it had seemed manageable, but now it was already excessive. The painter seemed to have his fingers in every corner of her life. Maybe this was why men had always been kept in their place.

The Aldea had no constitution, no formal government of any kind, but within living memory, which was considerable, there had always been an informal understanding that it would be "guided" by a *junta* of the women who ran the individual departments. (Usually little guidance was necessary.) Luisa felt that Cantú was exercising power on an ad hoc basis, almost as if there had been a coup, and the source of his authority was only his height, and as time went on, his ability to bring in hard currency. These were impressive characteristics, but still not enough for Luisa. There was no tradition of political discourse in the Aldea. Politics as such hardly existed, and there was no sense of party. The implicit hostility of the outside had made unity below easy and natural throughout their history.

To her there was no need for Cantú's increasingly heavy-handed grip on the community. It paralleled what he was doing in her life. There had been no crisis of any importance since 1656, when the first dome came down. It had been known as the time of "the holding of the breath," a period of anticipating that there might be some kind of retaliation, when someone might have guessed what had happened. But at the time, the bishop's decree that the rubble remain uncleared, guaranteed that the cause of the collapse would never be discovered.

Luisa's locker was fronted by a black steel door

exactly like those on the utility chases throughout the Aldea. These doors had been liberated from a high school demolition in the 1980s. She pulled out a dark blue coverall and sat down on a bench to pull it over her legs.

Jeremy's question about justice for the Aldeans had touched a nerve, and her denial that it was her job to think about it had been instantaneous. She had carefully kept herself separate from any plots against the Arenases of the Outside, but she could hardly avoid modeling. Rafael's revenge program was known to everyone in the Aldea, and it was difficult to maintain to herself that she was entirely uninvolved. She had watched from The Last Supper painting as Mark Sands was drugged, dropped to the floor, and carried off. She saw the look of consternation on his face as the party mix sparkled and swirled around his head. Although she stayed within the frame and hadn't helped to carry him to the parapet, this still made her an accessory. She had also reported back to Cantú on several conversations between Ken Abrams and Rebecca Stuart, and between Rebecca and Jeremy. This was how he had first caught her eye. She had observed them from Rebecca's condo wall within the Girl with Three Players painting, and forwarded the information to Rafael that they were planning to come to Santa Elena. By now she was barely able to continue rationalizing her role, and it was getting more difficult as Rafael's surprise approached. Any thought of maintaining her distance had ended with Jeremy's arrest.

She pulled up the zipper on the coverall, knotted her hair into a bun and donned the brimless cap that covered it, and pulled the leather gloves and the facemask out of the locker.

Luisa had been uncertain at first about Jeremy, having chosen him—aside from his connection to those investigating the Mark Sands murder—as malleable and sexually naive, but she now found him growing on her. His great feeling for her was undeniable, and his occasional bungling uncertainty about how to act with her was still somehow endearing. It also left him open to her guidance, and to her this seemed comfortable and natural. It was true he was gawky and tiresome now and then, but Luisa, being so young, up until this time had had only a few tentative attachments herself, all of them with much older and shorter men who had spent years in menial jobs and had little personality or conversational skills. She wondered whether their years of education were wasted, even mostly forgotten. While working in the compost beds, she'd observed that a detailed knowledge of classical Greek theater seemed of little use, nor was a ready hand with calculus. These suitors of hers were stunted in more ways than height: to her they had nothing much to say. At least Jeremy was full of raw intelligence. His mind was intuitive and his questions were constant. For the most part, Luisa was ready with the answers.

Jeremy also brought something to the relationship that Luisa could not. Whether or not she thought it was valid, gringos somehow had more status. She would have sworn in Outsider court (they all watched Law and Order in the Aldea) that all people were equal, yet, the gringos' pale (aristocratic) skin, their history of smashing México and kicking its neutered remains aside several times in the past, their successful consumerism—simultaneously envied and resented by most of the world—made it a less than subtle plus to have an American boyfriend. It didn't hurt that he was nearly twice as tall as anyone else's. She hated all this in the way that one only hated the facts, and she understood it perfectly.

Even the least interesting moments of their connection seemed lively and intimate in comparison with her other suitors. She was now thinking they might have a future if she could get him a little more education and keep the other women away from him. She knew that sexual awakenings of the kind he had undergone with her were dangerous, capable of spreading like a virus. Especially within the Aldea, he would discover how easy it was to be a Casanova once he got started. There would be no shortage of willing accomplices, and of course at five-ten, his great height made him fascinating to most of the women. Without clearly analyzing it any further than this, she knew she'd made a decision. She would take Jeremy to the Outside, and they would somehow make a life. It would be a hazardous existence out there, like moving to the jungle with only a pocketknife and a damp book of matches, but she could see no other options.

With a key from her coverall pocket Luisa opened a storage room at the end of the lockers and rolled out a two-wheel trolley holding a pair of gas tanks, oxygen and acetylene, with the torch and spark lighter in a bracket at the back. Dropping the mask over her face, she peered around the corner into the corridor. There was no one in sight, and she quickly moved out, pulling the trolley toward the hub, where an adjacent hallway led to the infirmary, the old age ward, and the punishment cell.

For some time, she'd been able to convince herself that Cantú would be able to get away with his current plan, but the more she allowed herself to think about it, the less likely it now seemed. She knew that Jeremy had told Rebecca and Abrams that Mark Sands was an Arenas. When the painter summoned her and said that Jeremy had been apprehended by security forces after entering the forbidden zone, she couldn't dodge the issue anymore, and with an imperious gesture he had swept aside her argument that Jeremy had merely been working on his mapping project and may have blundered off course. For him, Cantú said, it was a simple matter of obedience. There could be no excuses. To Luisa it was the voice of authority run wild, and unbelievably, this was from a man! It had to be the lack of any experience in wielding power that made his actions so crude and offensive. It would probably take him another thirty or forty years to develop any finesse at all.

She passed the window of the old age ward, where Paco Morales, 197 years old and the oldest person in the Aldea, waved feebly to her from his bunk. He was no longer able to move much and this was his only amusement. She waved back. Several nurses in the room behind him paid no attention to her. Few people ever visited down there.

The punishment cell, the only one for the entire population, was at the end of the corridor, fronted by a guardroom with a small desk, now unoccupied. The cell was almost never used.

As she wheeled in the trolley, Jeremy leaped up from his bunk in alarm. She flipped up the mask, realizing he didn't know who she was.

"My God! It's you Luisa, thank you, thank you, thank you!"

"Be quiet and turn around. You can't look at this,

so cover your eyes." She knew she must have sounded irritated, but what she was about to do would signal the end of their stay in the Aldea, the end of her life as she had known it for nearly seventy years. Now she wouldn't be there for her birthday. Seventy was always a big celebration, a coming of age, like the *quinceañera* of the fifteen-year-old girls in the Outside. She couldn't imagine what it would be like out there, where seventy usually occurred during retirement. Of course, the people in the Outside were so poorly educated they didn't know any better. Compulsory education in the Outside ended at twelve.

The cell door was made from wrought iron bars, salvaged from another cell somewhere on the hilltop, possibly from the old citadel, although no one remembered for certain, but the lock and strike were much newer and well made. She had welded the two together initially and she knew that Rafael held the only keys.

She turned on the tank valves, adjusted the regulators, and then flipped down her mask as she sparked the blue flame to life. As she pulled on her long leather gloves, Jeremy was facing the back corner of the cell. He looks like a schoolboy caught misbehaving, she thought.

"What were you doing in Ana's room?" she asked without prologue. "Ramon said she was naked."

"Who is Ramon?"

Thinking this was a diversion, she tuned the flame to a fine edge and brought it down on the bar at the top of the lock. The white paint blackened and blistered on the metal, and after a moment, the lock edge and the bar glowed red. Then sparks began to fly in a fan-shaped arc backward into the cell.

"He's the chief of security. He and his boys picked

you up, remember? Or perhaps you don't. Your mind was elsewhere, I think. Otherwise engaged, as they say."

"I was hiding. Really! They spotted me down by the tracks. I was running and I picked a room at random. I didn't think there was anyone in there."

"Well you picked one of the village hotties. Ana doesn't have the best reputation, even though she's not quite of age." The top bar burned through and Luisa moved the torch to the next one down. "Did she kiss you?" Luisa was glad to have the mask covering her face as she said this so he couldn't turn and witness her ugly look.

"Yes, but I couldn't help it, really, Luisa. The lights went off and I didn't see it coming. Honest. I would have turned my head." He was still facing the corner of the tiny cell. A kerf began to open up in the bar, and the sparks of glowing metal flew toward his heels.

"What else happened? Did you touch her with your hands?" Her voice was neutral.

"I didn't."

"Only because they came too soon." It wasn't a question. They were just in time, she said to herself.

He made no response to this. The steel lock box sagged backward into the cell as the glowing support bar beneath gave way. With one gloved hand Luisa caught the lock neatly on a cool edge as it came free, and set it on the floor. She dialed the torch off and hung it on the trolley. "You can turn around now." She flipped the mask up and pulled the cell door open, then walked out of the room towing the tank trolley behind her. Jeremy moved through the acrid metallic cloud in the air and followed her down the hall. She said nothing about how she was going to ex-plain to Cantú what she had done. Of course, there could be no explanation. Jeremy had become a fugitive the moment he was discovered down at the tracks and now they both were.

In the tool room he sat on a bench with his elbows on his knees while she pulled off the coverall and the welding cap. Her coiled hair fell back down on her shoulders and she shook it out with a toss of her head, tying it with a leather thong.

"It's over now, isn't it?" he said. "We have to leave."

She wasn't sure whether she heard regret or relief in his voice.

"There's no other way. We can't stay after what I just did. Besides, Rafael's surprise party is about to start. It's better not to be here. You'll see what I mean."

"I'm sorry. I know I caused this."

She came over and touched his shoulder. "This goes back way before you, it's older than any of us. Don't worry about it. I think I saw my part in this coming too."

"What do you mean?"

"There's an ethical issue here, a huge one. Even without your problem it would be time for me to leave. I can't stand this anymore. You've made me see it."

"Has anyone ever left the Aldea before? I mean for good?"

"Never. I'll have to get used to the light. It's much brighter out there than in St. Paul."

"Will they come after us?"

"I don't think so, once we get out. They'll have their hands full here."

"What do you mean?"

"I can't say any more. Just be ready to go when I

tell you. It won't be long. Not days, but hours."

Everything was back in place. She closed the locker and locked the storage room. It didn't matter that she would never see it again; Luisa was an orderly person. She put her tools away when the job was finished so she knew where to find them again. She had never been able to abide chaos and that was why she so resented Rafael's usurpation of power. Her extensive reading of history had showed her that it was always that way; chaos appeared in the guise of order. It was the big lie, and often it worked.

Rafael had brought on what was about to happen. She knew art history as well; she'd had nine years of it. This was what artists did. Interested only in breakthroughs, they acted without care for the consequences. Society properly regarded them with suspicion. She looked at Jeremy, still waiting for her on the bench, and came over and put her hands behind his head, drawing him closer to her breast. He reached behind her and clasped his hands. Where would she find her life again? It was unlikely they could remain in Santa Elena. She knew she couldn't survive the arctic climate of St. Paul, where Jeremy was comfortable. She didn't know any other place. None of the Aldeans had ever tried to live for long in the Outside. It had an evil reputation, and rightly so.

Besides the fact that the light was too strong, even on a cloudy day, the people were mostly too big and unattractive, with skin and hair of different colors. There was no order to it. They all died young, but they didn't look young. The outside temperatures were wildly inconsistent. You had to pay money for everything and prices were high. Yet, at the same time these were the people who had written all of her beloved books. No one in the

Aldea had ever written one, except for a single pamphlet on mushroom cultivation. Maybe she would understand things better once she was out there. It would all have to be dealt with somehow, but what she had to do now was get the two of them back out through the front door. It was a good thing she was still young and had the energy to start a new life.

Luisa didn't know whether Rafael had instituted additional security because of his pending surprise. Probably he had, this was why Jeremy had been caught so quickly when he violated the forbidden zone border. She took his hand and they climbed back in the direction of their room. As they went he was subdued, even confused, sometimes muttering to himself and unwilling to share with her what he was thinking. She knew the leadership that would save them would have to come from her. She was used to it. It was what women did, here or anywhere. She knew from her reading that this was true even in the Outside, although they pretended not to realize it.

CHAPTER 18

Ana Arenas had shed her schoolboy's uniform and slipped into the cathedral sacristy earlier in the day to collect a black cassock and a lacy white surplice. Now she could circulate freely as an altar boy while the flower people decorated the sanctuary and set up the candles. Looking down the long center aisle from behind the altar she could see the crowd thickening outside on the plaza. A few men smoked on the bandstand. It was a well-dressed crowd. She quietly moved down a side aisle and climbed the steps inside a column to take her place in the pulpit. It would not be in use during the service. Enrique Arenas' security detail began to circulate before taking positions at the corners, side chapels and front.

Ana had already done a dry run with a previous wedding and she knew that once the priest appeared before the altar the guests would begin to enter and be seated. As she calmly watched the preparations there was a sudden explosion of activity at the entrance and six police officers rushed in with guns drawn, spreading out to the sides as they moved toward the altar. The security detail converged on them at the same time. Five minutes of conference followed and then all of them spread out though the cathedral and side chapels, making a thorough search. She glimpsed the priest stick his head out at the sacristy door, and seeing the problem, draw it back in. Just a small delay, she thought. They have good reason to be nervous, more than they know.

Ken Abrams not only felt Rebecca's presence immediately behind him, more than that, he felt the risk he'd placed her in by allowing her to come with him to Santa Elena. He had even invited her. He felt that all of his professional instincts had been flaking away like old paint from a rusting car fender. What remained didn't look like much. What had he been thinking? Or had he been thinking at all? Going over the immediate past, it seemed muddy, incoherent, one thing leading to another without much structure. Rather than being proactive, he'd been led by events, drifting since his back and neck pains appeared. Although they had now disappeared, his cool logic had not returned. He'd lost the initiative. Serendipity was not a detective skill. Luck was undependable. He felt like giving Rebecca his badge.

This was a perfect example. He didn't believe he would have allowed her to accompany him underground if it had been a simple choice, but the arrival of the police at the cathedral left no other option. There was no way they could have stayed in the building to protect Angelina Arenas. Maybe the police and her own security could. He had no authority here, therefore no backup would appear if they found themselves in a tough spot. He began to feel an increasing sense of urgency with no idea what they could do to change things above them.

The end of the staircase told him they were on the lowest level. Around them in the adjacent hub, seven more openings diverged into the black lava, each lit by low voltage strings of lights along the bases of the walls. The air was heavy with the feel of moisture and damp earth, and oddly warm. The silence was dense and eerie. Abrams stepped out into the circle and slipped into the first corridor on his right, pulling Rebecca with him. About thirty feet down, an arched opening pierced the black wall. They stepped inside to find three long rows of mushroom beds, the white caps giving off a ghostly glow in the dim light. The beds were less than four feet wide and about twenty inches above the floor.

"Who would want to pick these at that height?" said Ken in a whisper. "It would kill your back." He was doing some rapid mental calculations.

"Not if you were three feet tall," she said. "Think about it."

"This room is about sixty feet long. Three beds about four feet wide makes twelve feet times sixty. What kind of colony needs 720 square feet of mushrooms? What is this place, anyway?"

"That's a lot of soup," she said.

Abrams was picturing the Witness figure of Charlie Morris bent over the beds snipping off mushrooms when his ear caught the muffled sound of something soft moving over the floor outside, not far away. A guttural voice said something in Spanish. Another voice answered, moving closer. Abrams pulled Rebecca's arm and they moved quickly past the last raised bed, where they dropped to the floor, head to head, pressing themselves against the brick frame. This close to the floor he could see that the lava had layers of inclusions, as if thin sheets of shale or slate had broken up and then were separated by the flow of molten lava. It had a grain, and with enough stress could probably be parted along these visible lines. Did it act as reinforcement for the porous, lightweight lava, like straw in bricks? Or was it a structural risk, a source of parting lines like perforations in a sheet of paper?

The shuffling footsteps entered the room and a single strip of florescent lights went on in the center of the arched ceiling. Wooden containers scuffed against the lava as they were set on the floor. Neither Abrams or Rebecca could see anything without lifting their heads and being seen themselves, but it seemed that the newcomers were cutting mushrooms from the bed nearest the door and dropping them into the baskets. Twenty minutes passed. After some scraping and lifting sounds the workers moved back out into the corridor.

Arbrams waited three or four minutes before he rose and went to the entrance, looking narrowly around the frame. The two workers were just about to disappear through a doorway next to the hub.

"Look at them. It wasn't from his dreams," said Rebecca in a normal tone of voice from just behind him. "Cantú's been painting his day to day reality. All those characters in his pictures are his neighbors."

"You think he's down here too?"

"Of course. He must be one of them himself. This is why he couldn't send his picture to Edward. He must have thought Edward was onto him when he requested it."

"So what are they?" He had turned to face her, putting his hands on her shoulders.

She shook her head. "I don't know, but they're beyond uncomfortable."

"You liked them well enough when you thought they were only Cantú's fantasy."

"This is different. I like my fantasy and my reality separate."

"I'm sorry I brought you in on this," he said. "Clearly they killed Mark Sands, but I still can't figure out how they got into his condo. Obviously they killed Edward Born as well."

"In any case, Cantú isn't going to talk to us, and you don't have the authority to arrest him. We've got to get out of here and find Jeremy. He must be still with that girl Luisa Arenas somewhere."

"Maybe she's at the wedding?" he said. "But there's no way we can go back up there."

There was also no way to gauge the extent of the underground village, no way to know which routes were more likely to furnish an exit, other than back through the cathedral, so they simply followed in the direction of the mushroom harvesters, who had eventually disappeared into a kitchen. Abrams looked around a corner and saw them go into a walk-in cooler made from lava blocks.

"It's big enough to be a hotel kitchen. There must be a dozen or more of them in here."

"Either that or they have a catering business," she joked. Down at the other end, three small figures with their backs to them were bent over a low sink.

Crossing through the hub, most of the other rooms they passed had an agricultural or warehousing function and they saw no one else working. After a while the room entrances ceased but the corridor continued, leading to a single brightly lit point, shining like a gem at the end of the dimly lit tunnel.

"Not much cover here," said Abrams. "If some-one sees us, it's over."

Rebecca looked back over her shoulder. The lighted end grew larger, and after a while the walls ended. They were in a loading area overlooking a long mound of lava refuse accumulating against an old stone wall opposite. A considerable overhang sheltered the opening where they stood, but beyond it blinding natural sunlight streamed down. The exit they were standing in couldn't be seen from above or from the top of the wall opposite.

"Construction debris," said Abrams, "or excavation debris might be a better word."

Behind them was a narrow gauge railroad track heading straight back into the mountainside, terminating in a stop at their end made from angled steel beams. Several small handcarts with rubber wheels were lined up on one side, a row of shovels and other tools next to them.

"We can get out here," said Rebecca. "What do you think?"

Abrams moved toward the edge. "It's a drop into all this lava trash, then a sheer stone wall opposite. There's no sign that this would lead us out, and if we go down we may not get back up. Let's see where these tracks go first." The light on the rails darkened to nearly nothing as they followed them. "This feels better," he said. "We were kind of exposed."

It was nearly half a mile before they found the first car. Abrams walked the length of the train while Rebecca kept watch. He examined the line of fourteen cars, each filled with lava rubble mixed with slate and shale fragments. At the front of the lead car, a makeshift brake on the cast iron wheel prevented the train from moving forward toward the hillside opening. A single blow from a large hammer would knock it free, releasing the train to move down the track under gravity, gathering momentum. Looking down the rails the way they'd come, all he could see was a diminishing tunnel where the lighting faded to nothing, but for the single point of daylight in the center.

At the other end, nearest the column, a coil of steel cable was stacked on the track. One end was attached to the closest car, the other snaked out from the bottom of the coil and was secured to the narrowest part of the roof support column just above rail height. Abrams took this to be a back-up safety device, should the brake at the front car fail. As for why these excavations continued, or why the safety cable was attached at the narrowest part of the column, he could think of no reason. It didn't make sense. Maybe this underground community had an employment problem and make-work projects were the order of the day. No one appeared as he walked back toward Rebecca.

"What time is it?" she asked. "Could it be lunch hour? Is that why no one's here?"

"It's a little before two o'clock," he said.

"I guess we're going to miss the wedding. What is all this about?"

"Rubbish removal? I don't know. Anyway, we were always going to miss the wedding."

"I still think they're going to kill Angelina."

"Think of all the security she'll have. Even if they can get to her, it'll cost them their own lives."

"Maybe they don't care."

Behind the column they found a narrow staircase and, climbing it, began walking back through the upper level, pausing at each turn, but no one else appeared.

At first the walls were blank, then doorways flanked the corridor on both sides, covered with drapes of differing patterns. Abrams stuck his head through now and then but saw no one. Ahead was another hub. As they left, from behind a pair of handcarts, a small figure had raised his head and watched them go.

Luisa watched as Jeremy collected a few scattered things from their room and stuffed them in his red suitcase. First was the seersucker shirt he'd been wearing when they met in Antoine's. Clean and neatly folded, it was one that he hadn't had a chance to wear yet in the Aldea. She knew he'd brought it along for a celebration, thinking they'd go out for dinner in Santa Elena. The sandals he'd foolishly brought, thinking of the sunny Méxican skies. He was paler now than when he'd arrived. The city guidebook and his unfinished set of maps he placed on top. It didn't look like he'd ever get back to them now. She thought his face expressed relief and dashed hopes all at once.

Luisa had filled a backpack with a few skirts and tops, two pair of her soft little pod-like shoes. She didn't have much underwear or cosmetics, and only one pair of street shoes. These she had already put on her feet with a grimace. She hadn't worn them since St. Paul, and she'd never gotten used to them there. She owned only one pair of socks besides the leggings she'd worn on that trip.

There was no question of bringing any of her books. Her Minnesota visit was the only time in her life she'd ever had any money, and she'd had to return the unspent portion to Rafael on her return, even the odd-looking coins. She'd held back a single Lincoln penny—no one in the Aldea had a beard except Rafael, and his looked like a briar patch.

Luisa didn't stop to reflect on how little she owned; it had always been that way. The Aldea had never been about what you owned, it was about where you were, what you were part of. Belonging, not possessing. In leaving, she would not only have nothing, she would be nothing, because she had broken trust with her home and her people in a way no one had ever done before.

"My laptop!" Jeremy said suddenly, speaking too loud in the small space. "Where is it?"

"Rafael's got it." She backed away from Jeremy a step or two, sighing. She knew this would come up.

"What! Are you serious?"

"He wanted to see your files after they took you to the lockup. He made me bring it to him. If I'd refused he would have had me locked up too. We'd both still be down there now."

"Why would he want to see my files? It's not like I ever had Internet access here." Jeremy was starting to pant now and his palms were sweating. He rubbed his hands up and down on the front of his shirt.

"He wanted to see what you knew, from St. Paul."

"But I don't know anything." The pitch of his voice crept upward.

"Of course you do! You did the research on Mark Sands for Rebecca." Abruptly she turned away and put her hand over her mouth. She was distracted by her own rebellion and their impending departure. Sometimes it was difficult to remember what she was supposed to know and what she wasn't. Especially now when things were so close to the end, everything was unraveling. At times she thought it hardly mattered. When she turned to look at Jeremy again, her face was composed, blank, the same way she made her violet eyes utterly vacant when she posed for Rafael. She thought of that look as saying, Nobody knows what I know, unless I choose to show it to you.

As Jeremy stared at her for a long moment, his features took on a dusky reddish cast she hadn't seen before. It wasn't his best look, and she knew it must have something to do with being unexpectedly overtaken by stressful news. "And how do you know about that?" he managed to say calmly after a while, but his face still had an unnaturally concentrated look.

"We talked about your work that first night in Antoine's, remember?" She said this in a light tone, giving him an encouraging smile. She wanted to look at her watch but didn't dare. Moments were ticking away.

"Yes, I remember. It was before you drugged me. But we talked only in general terms about it, I never got into the specifics of what I was doing for Rebecca or the others. I wouldn't do that."

"But maybe you did. You'd been drinking. Maybe you wanted to impress me so I'd go to bed with you. I could see that."

"I had two beers. That's nothing. And if you remember, I didn't need to impress you. You couldn't wait to take your clothes off. I didn't even have to ask you."

She ignored this. "You told me that Mark Sands was an Arenas. You were amazed at the coincidence when I said that was my name too."

He shook his head. "I never did. How do you know anything about Mark Sands? You said you'd only been in St. Paul one day when we met. He was killed on a Friday, more than a week before that. We met on Monday. That was ten days later, Luisa."

Luisa looked back at him calmly. She knew she was not going to be able to convince him, but she took one last shot. "There was an old newspaper in my room and I read about it. Listen, Jeremy, this isn't going anywhere. Don't get hung up on it. We need to leave before Rafael's plan gets started. That's the important thing, and it won't be long now."

"Maybe, but we're not going anywhere without my laptop. I've got two years of work on that hard drive, plus all my client records."

"You don't understand. You can just buy another one when we get out. You've got some money, and you must have backed it up somewhere."

"It's you that doesn't understand, Luisa. No one takes my computer." He looked at her for a long moment, his hands clenched into fists, then turned and ran from the room.

Luisa knew he was headed for Rafael's studio, where she didn't think he'd make any headway, so she finished systematically packing her things, strapped the backpack over her shoulders and after a few minutes of tidying up, went down the corridor with Jeremy's suitcase in tow. She waited a moment until Tease came out from under her nightstand and followed with a stressed look on his face. He knew what backpacks and suitcases meant—more travel, and he was hanging back. More discomfort for him. More bright lights so he'd have to find tablecloths to hide under just to take a decent nap.

The art studio was closer to the exit than her room, on the same route they'd used coming in. She'd have to figure out a way to get Jeremy away from Rafael, who'd have his hands full anyway. Then they'd be leaving through the Arenas sarcophagus.

The other exit, through the Roman saint's display, was about to be shut down for a while.

The police had gone from the cathedral, retreating to their cars at the edge of the plaza. They were careful to maintain strict vigilance; their chief was an honored guest. When the Arenas family security resumed its position, the priest emerged from the sacristy, glanced at his watch, and shrugged. It was a Méxican wedding; a few minutes wouldn't matter. He took up his position at the center of the communion rail and faced the empty cathedral. Ana looked at her own watch, a Mickey Mouse reproduction Rafael had given her to compliment her schoolboy outfit. Details were important to him. She'd synchronized it with his before she left the Aldea. It was 2:09. The guests began to come in, moving as if they had all the time in the world. Ana thought it might be more like eight or nine minutes.

Rounding a corner, Ken and Rebecca came face to face with five or six small people who looked at them with mild surprise. Before they could interact, Luisa appeared towing a battered red suitcase. A small dog behind her growled and bared his teeth. Everyone stopped. Luisa showed no surprise. Abrams stared into the calm violet eyes, his hand on his gun.

"I remember you," he said. "You were in that picture, the one with the players."

"You're Luisa Arenas, aren't you? Where are the others?" Rebecca said, making a shrewd guess, but one she knew immediately was right. She had seen it the same moment as Lester Grunge.

"They're around here somewhere," Luisa said tonelessly, as if there were more important things on her mind. "I'd avoid them if I were you. Stay away from the dog too, he's crabby." She looked back over her shoulder. "It's all right, Tease."

"I think you know who I am," said Rebecca.

"Yes, I know both of you. Hello, Detective Abrams."

Ken looked like he'd been hit by a truck.

"Where's Jeremy?" said Rebecca. "Is he down here?"

"He went to see Rafael Cantú. He needs to retrieve his laptop. Then we're leaving. I think you should do the same. You can follow us out. There's no time to explain at this point."

Abrams stepped forward, increasingly starting to connect the dots. "You were in *The Last Supper* picture too. Your hair was redder, then, and it had some curl. You were Mary Magdalene."

"Let he who is without sin cast the first stone," Luisa said, adjusting the backpack on her narrow shoulders. "I strongly suggest we move along now. These are minor things, and there's not much time left. By the way, how did you get in here?" She started to move past them as if most of this were nonsense.

Before he could answer, Abrams had an idea along the same lines. "Wait a minute." He seized her by the shoulder and she stopped. "If you were Mary Magdalene, how did you get into Mark Sands' condo?"

"A simple thing. They came out of the painting." She shrugged. "But I didn't, I stayed at the table. I was the only one who did. Maybe I was cleaning up."

He shook his head. An absurd answer, but he wanted more. "Why did they kill Mark Sands?"

"You'll have to ask Rafael. I'm not involved."

"Wait! The painting is some kind of portal?" said Rebecca. "You looked right back at me, didn't you, in my condo, and even in the gallery before that? You mean you could have come out of my painting, too?"

"At any time. In fact, one of the players did one night, while you were sleeping. He found you quite fetching, even though your mouth was open. He likes blondes, and he said you had good teeth. That's unusual here. Anyway, I'm on the way to pick up Jeremy. You'd best come along so you can meet Rafael. He knows quite a bit about you already. Maybe he'll answer your questions, if he's got time. Maybe not, it's going to be a hectic day." She sighed. "It already is, and there's more coming."

Luisa moved past a speechless Rebecca and headed into the hub. Abrams stuck his gun back in his waistband and caught up with her.

"What is this place?"

"It's the Aldea, it's our home. Rafael can tell you all about it. He's the one to ask. I shouldn't be talking to you. I'm not going to say any more. Reading me my rights won't matter down here."

A grim feeling was coming over Abrams. It wasn't only that he'd gotten sloppy, it was as if his skills, the tools that had sustained him in his job for years, now no longer applied at all. Nothing he knew seemed relevant. He grabbed Rebecca's hand and pulled her along, determined to remain calm. He thought he sometimes heard a soft shuffling noise behind them, but when he wheeled around, there was nothing. Perhaps a flash of something at a doorway, but the place was not well lit.

"How do you come out of a painting?" he said to Rebecca in a low voice, trying not to sound like an idiot for asking. "You're the one with an art degree. Help me out here."

"It was art history. I don't know much about technique."

"I have the feeling that there are parts of this we'll never solve."

They broke into a brief run to catch up with Luisa, who was not losing any time getting to the studio. They were going to interview Cantú after all. Abrams moved his gun around to the side of his waistband, wondering what use it would be. If these people came out of paintings at will, what else could they do, that he couldn't?

CHAPTER 19

The priest waited a suitable interval for stragglers. When no more came, a server opened the communion rail gate for him and he moved at a measured pace down the aisle. Heads turned to follow his graceful progress, the elaborate robes swinging with each step. *Pachelbel's Canon in D* played in the choir. When the priest reached the front doors, Ana slipped back inside the column and dropped down the steps into the side aisle.

Justo Toledano Campos, the former principal bodyguard of Enrique Arenas, soon to be his son-in-law, stood with his mother and met the priest at the cathedral door. He mopped his face and then thrust the handkerchief in his back pocket. As the three walked up the aisle, the quartet above began playing *Ave Maria* with a soloist from the México City Opera. When they were about a third of the way to the altar, eight bridesmaids appeared, dressed in simple, pale blue gowns and followed them. Below the entry steps, Enrique Arenas waited, with his youngest daughter, Bloodbath, on his arm. All eyes strained to see them.

At the saint's display, Ana took a last look around and then slid a small panel noiselessly aside and slipped into the passage. It was time to make her final report.

The steel doors to the studio yielded with surprising ease. Jeremy had expected them to be locked, possibly barred from within, and Luisa might have to be summoned to cut through them with her torch. She had kept referring to Rafael's surprise as if it were the end of days. He had no idea what the man was up to, but his feeling was of many things coming together at once, and his own anger about to reach a boiling point. Jeremy had started thinking of the painter as another Hitler, demented and sealed in his bunker under the Berlin Zoo, as the Russians advanced street by street. Hadn't Hitler started as a painter too? Maybe there were other parallels as well. Jeremy already knew that history repeated itself. The problem was always to recognize when it was happening.

Now as the door moved inward and he was about to face the man again, Jeremy had the naive hope that Cantú would not be there, that his laptop would be sitting on the table in its padded case, ready to go. He'd be able to slip away with it unseen. There would be no confrontation, no accounting. In twenty-four hours he could be back in St. Paul, back at his research. He would kick off his loafers into the corner of the tiny second bedroom he used as an office, and put his feet up while he told Rebecca about it on the other end of the line, as Luisa leaned listening against the door frame, wearing something irresistibly slinky. It would all seem funny. Santa Elena would be an ongoing joke between them, his Méxican adventure. The anecdotes would make Rebecca wish she'd come down there too. He stepped inside the studio.

Jeremy was right about the laptop. It was in its

case on the worktable ready to go, but Cantú stood next to it, wearing a long magician's robe of a fabric with a small-scale pattern. It hung in folds about him, concealing the contours of his body. On his head, cocked to one side as if he had been drinking, was another conical cap, much like a dunce cap. His arms were outstretched in welcome and a sardonic look painted his face. As Jeremy walked toward him he gestured to the computer with his head.

"Come and get it," he growled, his eyes blazing.

Jeremy avoided his gaze, but inched forward. He could hardly believe his own courage and was barely breathing as he tried to think of anything but the painter standing before him. He looked past the man at the walls. In its way the studio was like the rest of the Aldea, utilitarian and undecorated. Although the construction of the comedor studio had predated the tunneling in the lava, it was still just stone and brick, offering the eyes no stimulus, only rest and too much of it. Jeremy had never been aware of the detail of his surroundings, never sensitive to the arts or to design. Of course, he had never been called upon to research these things. But now he was struck by the inhumanity of it, the unutterable coldness. It had no heart and no soul. A colony of slaves where, as he had discovered to his dismay, none even dared imagine escape, except Luisa, but only for the two of them. Here was the place Cantú made his art and she lived with her nearly 300 cousins, but she knew better than to try to lead them out.

Jeremy's heart was now thudding like a pendulum trapped in a space too small. He could smell the paint solvent on the unfinished canvas. He felt like he couldn't speak. Jeremy was close enough to hear Cantú's coarse breathing and to see the porosity of the fabric of his robe. The printed pattern of stars and moons, brassy gold against the dull red background, had adhered only to the topmost part of the weave. Coming from a fabric store in the States, this would have been a remainder, a bolt-end sold off for a fraction of its original price. Stiff and starchy, it made a wheezing sound when the painter moved, rubbing uneasily against itself in dry friction. Soon it would start to give off sparks, a fire hazard. The entire presentation was like royalty assembled from a toy box, a cheap charade fit to fool only the most gullible or the very young. Yet few in the Aldea were young, and all were well educated. He made a mental note to ask Luisa how a fraud like Cantú could be in charge. This close, he might even have been slightly cross-eyed.

Cantú looked up into his eyes. "I see that she has released you." There was satisfaction in his tone, as if this proved his point. It removed any necessity for restraint.

Jeremy nodded without responding as he stared at the wart on the lower left corner of the man's nose, a peppercorn with a single curved black hair growing downward from it toward the corner of his mouth. It was as if by focusing only on small specific parts of Cantú's anatomy Jeremy could reduce the overall threat he posed. The pores in his nose were huge. Jeremy thought he could have stood straight pins upright in them like the numbered flagpoles on a golf green. Overlapping networks of fine lines covered Cantú's skin like a pale hair net, deepening at the corners of his eyes and mouth. His lips were colorless and thin, utterly dry, slightly open and emitting a stale, sour vapor. Behind them lurked the furry edges of the gray teeth. Without warning, Cantú raised a meaty paint-stained fist and struck Jeremy hard in the face.

Jeremy heard his jaw snap as he fell backward onto Cantú's worktable, rolled across it with his arms flailing, and flipped over the other side to the stone floor, carrying a dozen tubes of paint with him.

"Do you think you can challenge history, my dull friend? Circumvent fate? Worse yet, do you think you can defeat me? You are like water, you are colorless!" Spit flew from his lips with each word.

Jeremy turned on his back and moved partly under the table to adjust his mandible with both hands, too shocked to respond. He had no loose teeth, and his vision was starting to clear. He could see the painter only from the stomach down. The legs were planted wide apart, and below the hemline of the tent-like robe was a single forward foot encased in a soft, undefined leather slipper. It would have been much like an elf shoe except that it bore no curling tip. Blunt and shapeless at the end, in dimension and color it resembled an unattractive potato. Above it on the ankle, a red and white horizontally striped sock laddered up out of sight, spreading on the expanding hamlike calf, in almost a medieval jester effect.

A skittering sound from the tabletop above ended in a minuscule silence, and then his laptop landed upside down on his chest. For once Jeremy was grateful for the padding under his shirt. Fortunately the computer was not turned on.

"We are just moments away, now, I think," said Cantú's triumphant voice. "Go ahead, take notes if you wish. It's a unique opportunity."

From beneath the table Jeremy had a clear view of the iron-studded doors. One of them swung slowly into the room and what looked like a 10-year-old altar boy in white surplice and black cassock stepped into the studio. With a sudden shock he recognized her as the girl he'd been in bed with when he was arrested.

"Here we are then," said Cantú, brightly, "right on schedule, more or less. What is the word now, Ana?"

"They are all there, gathered and ready. When I left, Enrique and Angelina were just about to start up the aisle. The guests have all been seated. The band is playing, like on the Titanic." She held her fingers to her lips and giggled. Always in character, she made a small genuflection in Cantú's direction, but in mistakenly holding the skirts of the cassock, made it seem more like a curtsey. Her short black hair was parted in the middle and combed back behind her ears. When she glimpsed Jeremy under the table her eyes grew larger but she said nothing.

"Then you are finished, my dearest child. Come here and receive your reward."

Ana moved toward him and he placed both hands on her shoulders and bent forward to kiss her lips. "Well done," he whispered, "my sweet."

Jeremy's view of her was blocked by Cantú's bulk, which would have shadowed ten of her, but he could imagine the look on her small cherubic face.

All eighteen troops of the olive-uniformed Aldea security force moved silently down the corridor behind Abrams and Rebecca, taking advantage of each turn to move up and conceal themselves. They had seen Abrams' gun and had watched enough American television to know what it meant. They were armed only with their standard party mix and a moleskin bag full of braided garrotes. The party mix was useless except at close range, and the effect of the glitter was usually lost in the dim light. They were appropriately cautious, awaiting their moment.

Ramon Arenas, the much-decorated ninety-year-old chief of security, had personally trained the entire group. Although they served only part time, it was an elite cadre; none were more than ninety-five years old, none of them had any children, nor were any of them in long-term relationships. All wore what they called the "combat" grimace, borrowed from a spaghetti western of the sixties. Their black bat-fur berets were patterned on those of British World War II commandos. Their night vision was without equal. Tight spaces didn't spook them.

They had nothing to lose.

Rafael Cantú had been tempted to quote Churchill in his pep talk earlier that morning as he told them that today, March 27, would live in the annals of the Aldea as a day of glory equal to any in its nearly 500-year history. The usurper Arenases would be dealt a blow from which recovery would be impossible. Since it was one day after the other great anniversary of the "Forty-One," it would henceforth be a two-day fiesta.

It didn't matter that Ramon's group had no direct role to play. The heroic main task would be performed by one of the railroad employees. The commandos' job was to prevent interference of the kind already begun by Jeremy Wyman, and now continued by Ken Abrams and Rebecca Stuart. One of the security force members had sighted them at the railway and followed as the others were collected. Their idea was to track the intruders into a confined area where, before Abrams could get his gun out, they could bring the propofol party mix to bear at close range.

They had not, however, counted on Luisa showing up and leading Ken and Rebecca to Cantú's studio. Now the troops found themselves with the armed detective between them and their leader, and overtaking the invaders would only get them shot. Ramon had committed his first strategic blunder. He had never faced a real opponent before, and there had never been this many variables in their exercises, which had always worked flawlessly. For one thing, the idea that one of their own would desert and defect to the other side, as Luisa was in the process of doing at this critical time, hadn't occurred to any of them. Baron von Clausewitz had never addressed internal treachery in his writings on strategy. To him it would have been unthinkable.

To move part of his men around the hub complex and get ahead of the invaders would likely get them killed and would divide his force as well, assuming he could even get them that far ahead in the time available. His only hope now was to come into the art studio behind them and spread out. They would lose a few, of course, but some might still get through to blow the party mix into Abrams' face. Jeremy would then be garroted as well. Rebecca they would keep alive. Rafael might want her for himself. Luisa could be detained until Rafael's surprise party ended and he could also decide her fate.

Luisa parked the red suitcase upright outside the

studio doors and set her backpack beside it. She didn't look back at Abrams and Rebecca. If there was any trouble now with Rafael they could be her backup. She assumed they were there for the painter, and that they knew he was responsible even if they lacked detail on how the murders had been done. She didn't think much about how they might know this; probably it was some blunder of Rafael himself due to his arrogant carelessness.

Jeremy was a grown up and could take care of himself, with her help, of course. Women were natural leaders and nothing brought that out better than a situation like this. She found that she was repeating similar things to herself often now, making them sound authoritative and official, as if she'd heard or read them somewhere else. Had it been in Gibbon? She wasn't sure. Probably not. He really didn't think much of women. In that respect Gibbon could have been Méxican.

Placing her ear against one of the iron doors, she heard nothing, so she eased it open to see Rafael leaning his great bulk comfortably against the painting table, one elbow supporting him, looking back at her with his fingers entwined over his abdomen. He seemed to be expecting her. For several years now he had no longer been able to fold his arms across his chest, although he could still intertwine his fingers. Jeremy looked back at her from below the table but she only met the eyes of the painter. All of her anger at Cantú was now bubbling to the surface. Wearing red, with the brassy glitter of the printed gold celestial bodies, he reminded her of a Christmas tree in a cheap television movie. He didn't wait for her to speak.

"A betrayal," he said in a voice that boomed and rolled end over end through the great vault above. "Nothing less than that. How I hate the word! It brings up the recollection of our own sad history. Your action is worthy of Juan de Arenas himself. What a sad day for the Aldea, even as we have our greatest triumph. How bittersweet! To think that you are my niece."

"I am nothing to you," she said bitterly. "I am gone. None of us means anything to you except as pawns for your insane revenge. Yet you think of yourself as a creator, a maker of great art. You are delusional. To think that you studied psychology."

Luisa knew that Jeremy and the others probably understood nothing of this conversation, since it was entirely in Spanish. She looked down at him now. His eyebrows went up in an enquiring expression. She made a small gesture with her hand, out of view of Rafael behind her thigh, as if to say, Stay still and wait.

Looking back at the artist with no expression, she wondered if he were quite sane. She had spoken to be insulting, but perhaps there was something to it. Painters were different from other people. Rafael was different from other painters. At what point did these vectors of non-convergence simply slide off the map into chaos? It appeared to be imminent.

"We're leaving now," she said. "Jeremy, get up."

"He is a person, I think, of modest survival skills," Cantú said in a singsong kind of English, obviously for Jeremy's benefit. "Not what is required down here. In any case, you can't go. The party is about to begin. It's Angelina's big day and I always get excited at a family wedding." There had never been a wedding in the Aldea, which is why Ana had to do some research before Angelina's, just to understand the sequence of events.

Cantú held up a small plunger at the end of a cable, like the remote shutter release for a camera. "One squeeze of this small device and the plan is in motion. Rigoberto is in position; he will receive the signal, then he will release the brake. The train will roll. When the slack in the cable on the cars runs out, it will rip through the column. The momentum guarantees it. End of story. Nos vemos. We'll see you when we see you, if we ever do. *'Hasta la vista, baby,'* as a great politician once said."

Like the actor he had never been, Ken Abrams waited in the wings, in this case, the corridor outside, where through the slightly open doors he could hear both Luisa and the booming pronouncements of the triumphant Cantu. He understood only some of it. Rebecca was behind him, her hands gripping his right bicep, now beginning to freeze up from halted blood flow.

"Is Jeremy even in there?" she whispered.

"I think he must be, from what Luisa said. I'm going in. Stay back here."

As Abrams brought his gun up and turned toward the door, he heard a low whistle and three or four pairs of soft footsteps circled him, hands flying upwards, and a cloud of airborne pixie dust filled his vision. Instantly he stopped breathing. He felt Rebecca's grip loosen and she sagged to the floor. Circulation returned to his arm.

Abrams fired once, and two small olive-clad bodies, one behind the other, flew out of his path as he entered the studio. Nothing more came from behind except the soft receding footsteps of the others. Rebecca lay unconscious on the lava floor, but no one was left there to bother her. Once inside the studio, Abrams breathed again.

Cantú—it had to be him—faced him in a lumpy reddish nightgown that appeared to be none too clean. What a clown, Abrams thought, a grotesque. No wonder I can't stand his painting. Maybe being a painter explained this foolishness, this truncated mountain of flesh in a conjurer's outfit, holding up a camera shutter release. The man gave him a cockeyed grin, as if he'd known Abrams was coming. As he thrust the release into the air and waved it about in triumph, his pointed hat fell off, but he didn't seem to notice. Luisa melted away to Abrams' right. Beneath a worktable, he could see a normal-looking young man who had to be Jeremy start to edge away with a crablike motion, clutching his laptop to his chest. He gave Abrams a tentative, nervous smile and waved with two fingers of one hand, but said nothing.

"Don't let him press the button," shouted Luisa, now behind him. "It will bring down the cathedral."

The Arenas wedding, thought Abrams. They must be in there now, all of them. He squatted and held the pistol with both hands, focused on Cantu's forehead. There was a flash of Luisa moving quickly behind him again and the doors closed with a massive shudder, a bolt was thrown, and Luisa picked up the whimpering Tease and moved off into a corner.

As the sound of the doors closing reverberated through the barrel vault ceiling Abrams felt a great calm. Here was the tipping point, and he knew he was up to it. In his peripheral vision he saw before him now, lined up on both sides, the fifteen men and two women he had so callously executed in his dreams. From perpetrators they had become victims, and now witnesses, gathered to watch as if this were going to be number eighteen. He felt the hatred coming off Cantú like a poisonous gas.

"Drop the cable," he said, afraid that the painter wouldn't understand his English. But the painter must know his meaning, it must have been Cantú he'd overheard as he waited outside. There could be no mistake.

Yet nothing happened. The artist continued to regard him as if he were an insect that had crawled in under the door. Abrams waited for some response, some suggestion of what was coming. Then he saw it.

It was a wrinkle in Cantú's eyebrow. Perhaps nothing of significance, but to Abrams it said what was to come. It was the pivot point, the time to go or not go. You made the choice, you didn't second-guess yourself. He fired the .38 once and Cantú sagged for an instant against the worktable, then collapsed to the floor like a walrus onto concrete. He hit the point of the conical hat with his elbow as he went down and it rolled away and stopped against Jeremy's feet. Abrams stared for a moment. The seventeen witnesses were gone from his mind. All he saw was a pair of red and white striped socks protruding from Cantu's sorcerer's robe. Luisa stood off to the side with her hands over her ears. Tease cowered behind her.

Abrams whirled round, gun ready, hearing a key in the door, and then the bolt was withdrawn. Nothing else was happening but he wasn't sure that Cantú hadn't tripped the shutter release. The doors swung open and a dozen small olive clad figures were rushing toward him from the corridor. In their midst Rebecca was still down but starting to move. Two leaped over her body. He fired once into their midst and as another dropped, the rest froze, then turned and fled. Nothing sparkled in the air.

"Get up!" he yelled at Jeremy, shoving the gun into his belt. "Help me!"

Jeremy staggered to his feet and set his laptop carefully on the table.

"We've got to roll him over," Abrams finished.

Cantú lay on his broad stomach, his head in a widening pool of blood, the cord snaking away from under him. The two of them pushed mightily on his shoulder until he rolled onto his back. Abrams seized the plunger. It had not been near Cantu's hand on the floor, but he couldn't tell whether it had been pushed or not. Each second that passed with nothing happening looked more hopeful.

Rigoberto Arenas had been retired from the railway system for six years, so when he was selected by Rafael Cantú to handle the braking device on the line of hopper cars, he felt singularly honored. Of course, he had been a brakemen all his working life, so in a sense, it was only right.

It was a simple task. He was seated next to the lead car, pointed at the distant pinpoint of light at the dump. A brake shaped like a bracket was fastened to the front wheel. A steel pin through one side of it was lodged against the tie. One sharp blow from a medium hammer, like the one hanging at his side, would drive the bracket off the wheel. The string of cars would begin to roll, slowly at first, then as each connection between the cars tightened, faster and faster. About 100 meters down the line, the slack in the cable would run out, and it would violently tighten. The weight of fourteen full cars and their momentum at almost twenty kilometers per hour would cause the steel cable to slice through the soft lava column at its narrowest spot, which would then drop from the weight focused on it above.

On top of this lower column, the southeastern pier of the great cathedral dome would drop by the same amount, replicating the memorable triumph of 1656. An elegant idea, made irresistible by the fact the Arenases of the Outside had, by elaborately engraved invitation, summoned themselves to their own doom. None could decline a summons from Enrique Arenas. It now only awaited a low-pitched buzz from the battery-powered device in Rigoberto's hand. On the floor above, Rafael Cantú would choose the moment from his studio command post.

Rigoberto was so relaxed he was thinking of something else when the buzzer went off, but in a second he was on his feet, the hammer lifted above his head.

Snick.

In the studio everyone was standing motionless, straining for the sound of what? Something massy, earth shattering, like an asteroid slamming into the planet? There was nothing. Or almost nothing.

Snick.

With the echo of the gunshot in his ears Jeremy wasn't sure he really heard it. Standing next to Rafael Cantú's body, he rubbed his damp hands on his pants from touching the dead painter's arm and shoulder as they rolled him over.

Snick again. It was unmistakable this time.

Snick. . .snick. The interval was growing shorter, the speed of the cars below increasing. Jeremy knew what it meant, he had ridden the cars himself. As he was plugging in what Cantú had said about the cable and the column, Luisa was reading his face.

"It's the cars," she said, nodding with resignation, "they're moving, like Rafael said. We'd best be going now. This can't be stopped, and there's nothing more for us here. This time the Outsiders will figure it out. Don't forget your laptop."

"The cars pull down the column when the cable tightens. The line slices through it, but what's above the column?" said Abrams, almost figuring it out himself.

"It's another column, one holding up the cathedral dome, isn't it?" Still rather vague, Rebecca came unsteadily forward and gripped the edge of the door. Seeing her, Jeremy knew this was how Mark Sands felt when he went over the side of his terrace. Coughing, she stepped over a small body in the doorway and shook her head. "Live the plot," she said. "What a stupid idea. What was I thinking?"

Snick. . .snick. . .snick. The interval was shorter and shorter. Everyone heard it.

Abrams drew Rebecca against him. "Are you all right?" Not waiting for her reply, he turned to Luisa. "What happens if the dome falls? Is it right above us?"

She shook her head. "No. We should be all right. Nothing happened the last time."

"What do you mean, the last time? The last time in 1656? You people did that, too?" Ken was yelling now.

Luisa nodded, backing away. "Nothing happened down here then. That's what you asked, isn't it?"

Jeremy pulled the strap of the laptop over his head and grabbed Luisa's hand. "We'll show you the way out," he said. "The front door. Let's go!"

"Wait a minute!" Abrams grabbed Luisa's arm as they started to move. "Isn't this whole area bored through with tunnels and rooms now, much more so than in 1656? It's like a Swiss cheese, isn't it? How can you think it's going to be all right?"

Starting to see his point, a look of alarm came into Luisa's violet eyes as she nodded. Geology was one of the few subjects she hadn't taken, but this was not the same as 1656 with its population of only forty-one in the Aldea. Jeremy was already moving through the doors. Abrams pulled Rebecca and Luisa through, stepping over the bodies of the security detail. The others were gone.

Outside the studio, Jeremy seized the tow handle of his suitcase and Luisa picked up her backpack. They ran the direction of the first hub, farther under the ruins of the old cathedral. Tease sniffed at Cantú's body, growling and curling his lip, then ran after them. Running down the corridor, Abrams moved to the front with Rebecca close behind, but they hadn't gone a hundred feet when a muffled impact sounded from below, and the floor shifted discernibly beneath their feet. They all staggered when it dropped several inches. The lights flickered. They kept going, faster. Maybe it was still all right, Jeremy thought. After all, Cantú must have considered the possibility of collateral damage when he set up the collapse. In the painter's view, only the outsider Arenases deserved to die.

CHAPTER 20

The final angelic notes of the Schubert *Ave Maria* were fading into silence when a terrestrial groan, like a fault cleaving a vast iceberg, rolled through the cathedral, silencing the priest before he could begin, freezing the expressions on the faces of the wedding party and the audience. Women gripped the arms of strangers next to them. From far above, but not quite from heaven, a series of tiny, frivolous tinkles followed the groan, only audible at all because of the sudden silence. Still, the sounds went mostly unnoticed until a shower of minute fragments of glass from the splintered lantern windows at the base of the dome, much like pixie dust, rained downward in cloudy filaments over the congregation. Light flickered from an infinity of minute facets as the cosmic dust settled into the crowd's open eyes and mouths below.

At the edges of the congregation, the bodyguards covertly drew their guns, keeping their cool, but looking at each other with apprehension. Two of them rushed up behind the wedding couple, elbowing the attendants aside, turning back to face the congregation. It was a gesture of ants at a party of giants. Enrique Arenas, in the front row, dropped his face to the rail in front of him and prayed for the first time in forty years. No one heard him. On his left, his sister, Filomena, glanced at the exits, estimating which was closest. With her 240 pounds, none was close enough.

Bloodbath had endured as much as she cared to take, which was never very much, even on a good day like this. It was the first time she had ever been frightened of anything. Hoisting her wedding dress over her knees, she kicked off her four-inch heels and sprinted past the priest. She was already in motion past the altar toward the sacristy, when as an afterthought she threw her bouquet over her shoulder into the crowd. No one noticed where it fell, and the guests rose in confusion as at the same instant the first pier punched through the cathedral floor and buckled toward the interior under the dome like an overtall stack of coins. Bloodbath was already outside when two fluted segments from the pier flattened the altar. The sound drowned out the screams of the wedding guests as they scrambled over each other, elbowing their neighbors aside.

Filomena's pew, stressed beyond capacity as people sought to climb over it, collapsed. Clouds of dust rose into the vault, then darkened the dome, where, for the briefest instant, nothing more happened. The crowd's long wail died away as the dome held, balanced on the three remaining piers by the slightest difference in weight, the masonry fused together by nothing but prayer. People paused and dared to hope, at least that it would hold long enough to evacuate the cathedral. They began to run.

At the same instant the dome crumbled into an airborne mountain of rubble, exploding like an inverted volcano. The impact broke through the marble floor, causing the walls of the nave to jackknife inward, folding upon themselves like a house of cards, the roof dropping in over them.

Only the proud baroque facade held. Behind it,

an immense column of dust ascended heavenward for hundreds of feet until it dissipated into nothing. High above it, the sky was clear and lucid, as blue as the mantle of the Blessed Virgin. It was a typical day in Santa Elena in most respects, an ideal day for an important society wedding.

In the Aldea the shock threw them all to the floor. At the same instant the lights went out. Rebecca and Luisa screamed. Face down on the coarse lava, Abrams felt himself slide backward and then forward a few inches, then backward again. He felt like gravel being screened. Above and to his side the sound of huge slabs of stone breaking apart was deafening. With little hope of surviving, he put his arms over his head as fragments fell from the tunnel ceiling.

"Cover your heads!" he yelled, and his mouth filled with dust and grit.

When the grinding stopped, they began to cough painfully. Although they couldn't see it, the air was so filled with thick black dust they could have felt it between their fingers. It filled their eyes. Abrams placed his palms flat on the debris-covered floor to lift himself and found that starting about ten inches from his shoulder there was no longer any floor to his right. The corridor had split open and the other side had moved away, how far he had no idea in the darkness. He slid to his left and found the wall, then sat up with his back against it.

"Everybody sound off!" he said, setting off another round of coughing. Someone gripped his ankle.

"I'm OK, I think," said Rebecca. "Just give me a minute." There was the sound of violent spitting. "Sorry," she said.

"Jeremy! Luisa?" Abrams yelled. "Are you OK? Part of the floor has opened up. Stay where you are!"

Another gale of coughing erupted from behind him. "Christ, my suitcase is gone, I think," said Jeremy, trying to catch his breath. "But I've still got my laptop. Luisa? Luisa?"

There was no answer.

"Luisa!" Abrams' voice boomed through the fractured corridor. An echo drifted back from far below. There was no other response. Gradually the unanswering silence became unbearable.

"Luisa?" called Jeremy. His voice cracked. A fragment of stone dislodged from somewhere above and skittered downward through the ragged gap in the corridor floor, bouncing from side to side before stopping many feet below. Tease growled and then sneezed.

"My God, I think she's gone!" said Rebecca. "Jeremy, was she next to you?"

"Right behind me. Oh shit!" He began to sob, his breath coming in great gasps.

"Jeremy, Jeremy, listen," said Abrams. "Get a grip on yourself. If you have enough floor behind you, back up very carefully. Don't push her off if she's lying there injured. Put your arm out and find the edge as you go, if you can."

Abrams now wished he still smoked, although it had been nine years. He didn't want a cigarette; it was the lighter that would have been helpful. He could hear debris being swept aside as Jeremy backed up, panting hoarsely, wheezing, still sobbing. Of course the cathedral was down. There was nothing left but to save themselves if they could. There was a cry from Jeremy.

"It stopped! There's no more floor behind me and part of the wall is gone. Jesus! She's gone too." He broke down again.

"Luisa!" Abrams yelled with all his strength. "Make a sound if you can, anything! We'll come and find you! Just say something!"

In silence they all strained to hear something, but there was nothing.

"OK, does anyone hear her breathing? Anything at all?" said Abrams after a moment. No response. Another moment passed. "All right, we're going out." The last two words were twisted into a kind of choking sound. It was not the easiest thing he'd ever said, knowing she was down there somewhere, but not knowing her condition or even if she was alive. But how could she have survived if she went into the chasm? If she couldn't call out, they'd never have a chance of finding her; they'd all be killed trying. "Jeremy, I need you to focus again. How far is it to the front door you mentioned?"

Jeremy swallowed hard, struggling for composure. "There's a stairwell at the end of this corridor. I mapped all this. It might be another eighty or a hundred feet." His voice trailed off.

If it's there at all, Abrams thought, or if the corridor's not filled in with rubble from above. "I'm going to start crawling," he said. "Stay close to me. Test your support constantly." I don't know what I'm talking about, he thought, it's just a bluff. He fought back another fit of coughing.

An image of the perverse mound of Cantú's body passed through his mind. Had his gunshot caused a twitch of Cantú's finger to send the signal? Or had he already sent it when Abrams fired? And what had happened to Luisa? He would never know. He couldn't even see his own hands an inch away.

What if he had persevered and registered with the police? Maybe they would have had help by this point, but probably not. All the city resources would be focused on the cathedral, trying to save the wedding guests, all people of importance. There seemed to be so many things they would never know.

Abrams crawled along, his weight on his elbows, his hands and fingers probing before him, probing the surface ahead and to the side, listening behind for further disaster. His lungs felt like they were full of lead pellets, his nose and throat full of coal dust. In places he had to sweep aside piles of debris to get past, listening to it fall into the crevice next to him. All he could think of was water, tall icy glasses of it, hot water streaming over his body in an endless shower. Cantú couldn't have intended this. The underground must have been so riddled with passages that the structural integrity of it was compromised. The painter had probably never thought realistically of the risk he was taking with his own people. But then, realism was not his strength in painting, either.

"Everyone OK?" he yelled over his shoulder.

"OK," said Jeremy through a strangled cough. A hand closed on Abrams' ankle above his sock.

"Me too," Rebecca said.

"I think we're close to the hub," Jeremy's voice came from behind them.

As he inched forward, Abrams' hand tracked the fractured edge of the floor as it moved farther to the right. In another ten feet he was able to crawl across the intact corridor and touch the opposite wall. They had reached the farthest extremity of the fault line. He got to his feet. Of course, there could always be another.

"Jesus, we've got floor all the way across," he said, touching his hand to his face, which was dry and caked with grit. "OK, I'm going to just inch along here, feeling my way with my foot. Jeremy, how will I know we've reached the hub?"

"The walls will end in a narrow limestone casing," Jeremy said. "If you're tracking it with your hand you'll feel it raised up a bit from the lava, and it's smoother. What you want to do then is go into the first opening on the right, which is the stairwell. One flight up puts you in the short hallway that ends inside the sarcophagus. That's the only option, aside from two small rooms on the way." His voice trailed off and ended in a gasp.

"Sounds great," said Rebecca, without conviction.

"I've got the end of the corridor wall," said Abrams. "Holy shit! There's no floor, nothing at all!" He moved his foot across the irregular edge of the corridor floor. "It's broken off all across where the hub begins. Everybody stop."

Jeremy came up another step, panting. Abrams could hear the dog sniffing at the ragged edge. The last thing he wanted was to trip over it and fall into another abyss. But, of course, the dog probably only understood Spanish. There would be no telling it to back off.

"What's the distance to that next corridor over, the one on the right?"

"If I stretch out both arms," said Jeremy, his voice still shaking, "it's somewhat less than that."

"You're sure?" Abrams asked. He got to his knees and reached along the floor line in the direction of the stairwell. A jagged edge of the floor still adhered for as far as he could reach, but it was no more than three or four inches wide.

"Ken, stop, don't be a hero," said Rebecca. "We've already lost. . ."

"This is the only way out. If the cathedral's down, the other way is gone. I mapped it," said Jeremy.

"Then being heroes is all we've got left," said Abrams, thinking that the opening at the end of the rail line must be caved in too. And how could they ever find it now if they tried? It had to be a mile or more away through the invisible shattered ruins of the Aldea. "All three of us are going to be heroes," he said, trying to sound encouraging. No one replied.

As Jeremy had suggested, the edges of the corridor wall where it opened to the hub was trimmed with a band of limestone, a harder surface that would take the dings and nicks that would have crumbled the corners of the softer and more porous lava. Abrams moved his gun around to the back of his belt and gripped the stone trim in his right hand as he slid his left foot out onto the ragged edge of the hub floor, testing it to see if it would bear his weight. Although it was nowhere wider than the width of one shoe, it seemed solid.

As he moved out, flattened against the hub wall, he extended his left hand to find the next corridor opening, thinking he could feel the blank void behind and below him. He knew only that it was deeper than the length of his arm when he probed downward from the edge of it. If the hub floors had pancaked onto each other when the cathedral fell, it could be fifty feet down, or even more. Now flowing freely, his sweat was absorbed by the grit that covered his skin, forming a paste that dried and cracked in places. Like a death mask, he thought.

His left hand found the corresponding trim at the next opening and then he was across. The floor in the adjacent corridor seemed intact, at least for the few steps he took in each direction.

"I'm here," he said. "It's not that bad. Rebecca, you're next. Just don't think about anything but your footing and your grip. I'll hold my arm out to connect with yours as you come. Jeremy, support her as she starts out. Press against her back."

"Shit," she said. "How am I going to do this?" There was a quiver in her voice. She suddenly remembered again how she had felt on that sixth grade cave trip.

"We're not that far from the surface," said Jeremy. "This is probably the last real test." He was trying to sound hopeful, but all Abrams could hear was the misery in his voice.

"What would Lester Grunge do?" said Abrams, "think of it that way."

Rebecca thought of all the times she'd said that to herself, but never in such a state of terror. "All right. Here I go," she said.

"Hold on to her, Jeremy! Reach out your arm and hold her against the wall!" The scuffing sound of shoes scraping through the debris on the precipice reached Abrams. Those damn wedgy shoes she wears, he thought. Just so she can look taller! What the hell good are they now? He found his heart was pounding worse than when he'd made the trip himself. "Keep it coming, you're doing great," he said, not knowing anything of the kind. "Find my hand. It's only a few steps. Keep your feet in line, single file."

Her fingers had barely brushed his palm and his fingers curled around her cuff when her hand disappeared with a sound of fabric tearing. He'd had his hand too high! He groped blindly into the space even as she screamed and fell away into the empty hub.

"Rebecca!" yelled Jeremy, "Rebecca! I couldn't hold onto her!" His screams and wails echoed through the hollowed hub, as if all the pain from the loss of Luisa was now compounded by Rebecca's fall. Abrams tried to call out to her, but couldn't make himself heard over Jeremy's voice. She was gone. He leaned into the wall, his fingers clawing at the lava, blind, and now hopeless.

What had he done? For a man who had never fired his gun in anger until this trip, death now followed him just as in his dreams. He was overtaken by grief, swamped by an emotion for Rebecca he hadn't known he possessed. He tried to fight it back, to shelve it for later, for when they were out, for when he could think, but he was overcome.

Jeremy's voice had now declined to a pathetic incoherent whimper. Abrams was not listening. He felt his knees buckle and he slid to the floor. A voice suddenly came from below.

"Jeremy, you idiot, shut up for just a minute, will you? I'm not that far down here. I landed right on my butt."

"Oh, God!" shouted Abrams. "Are you OK?"

There was a sudden scuffle of claws at the end of the corridor and then Tease landed next to Rebecca with a grunt.

"I think he's adopted me," she said. "I'm going to have an ugly bruise right below my tattoo and my arm is kind of a mess."

"I've still got part of your sleeve," said Abrams in a more hopeful tone. "Rebecca, come toward my voice, test the floor as you come, and tell me what the wall is like ahead of you."

"OK," she said. "The floor is flat, here anyway, and the wall is open at the bottom about up to my waist, kind of in an arch, then solid above as far as I can reach."

"She's facing a corridor," said Jeremy. "I figured out that the ceiling thickness between floors is about three and a half feet."

"So she's somewhere between six and seven feet down. Rebecca, I'm going to lie on my stomach over the edge and reach down. See if you can locate my arms. Watch your footing."

A moment later they joined hands. "I've got something for you," she said. "Don't go away."

Abrams felt the squirming dog thrust into his arms. "All right. Jeremy, come on over first. I want you to kneel on my legs while I bring her up." He felt Jeremy's hand grip his and then he was in the stairwell, his laptop still in place with the strap around his neck.

"It makes it easier if you know it's only six feet down," he said.

"Is the wall smooth or rough above the arch?" Abrams asked Rebecca.

"Mostly rough," she said a moment later. "There

are some good outcroppings for footholds."

"OK. Give me your good hand and put your bad hand on my wrist with as much grip as you can. Jeremy, get on my legs. When she starts to come over get a hand on her arms and pull, but don't get off me."

There was a scrambling of feet on crumbling lava with small showers of debris falling away. She was rising as if rock climbing.

"I've got her shoulder!" yelled Jeremy.

Then she stumbled onto them, falling on Abrams' legs, landing against Jeremy. Abrams rolled over and seized her, pulling her against him, his arms pressing her tight to his chest.

"I love you," he said, surprising himself. "I'll never let you go again. She pressed her face into his filthy neck. He felt the wetness of her tears of relief, but she didn't reply.

After a moment they climbed a flight of stairs and moved cautiously down the corridor.

"It's on the right," said Jeremy, "about halfway down. I just have to grab something." There was purpose in his tone.

Abrams had the sense they were going to make it now. Jeremy retrieving something at this point was probably superfluous, but harmless. Maybe it was a memento of Luisa. He couldn't fault the guy for wanting something of hers.

"Here's the room," Jeremy said.

The others waited while he rummaged among the shelves, located what he wanted, then struggled with it panting back into the corridor.

About ten yards farther their path ended in a narrow staircase that led upward.

"As you get to the top of the stairs there'll be a sliding panel on your left," said Jeremy. "Just press on it and move it to the side. You'll be in the old crypt."

Abrams reached the top and slid the passage door open. Tease brushed past his legs into daylight.

Daylight! They stared at each other half blinded and began to laugh. Aside from rubs and smears, they were all totally black. One wall of the crypt had fallen away and several of the arches leading back under the old cathedral were collapsed. Along the edge, the wrought iron wall was down, flattened by spreading debris. With a bit of scrambling over the rubble they were able to walk out into the plaza, into the dazzling midafternoon of Santa Elena. They stopped for a moment to take in. Edged by a ragged crowd, the shattered ruin of the "new" cathedral, was now emerging in detail as the dust clouds drifted away over the city.

From her safe position in the plaza behind, Blood-bath Arenas, five months pregnant, stood barefoot in her empire-waist wedding dress. It was still hiked to her knees. Her locked hands crushed the stiff fabric against her skin as she watched to see whether anyone else had made it out. She had no idea how long she'd been standing there. It could have been days.

In the light breeze, the dust cloud began to shift beyond the far side of the ruin, and on the interior of the standing facade she could see a file of organ pipes bracketed by fragments of their shattered case, still clinging to the masonry above the vanished choir loft. Nothing within moved, other than the gently settling dust, and atop the rubble, the organ bench rocking like a cradle, back and forth, somehow perfectly balanced.

Behind her, people were still running toward the disaster, streaming across the plaza from all four sides. A small crowd had gathered around the periphery of the ruins, stopped at an invisible line a short distance away as if by a yellow crime scene tape. There were screams and wails of shock. If Bloodbath had looked at the streets around the plaza she would have seen traffic stopped, frozen in place as people emerged from their cars to stare, some leaving their doors open as they ran toward the ruin. Emergency vehicles tried to thread their way through. But Bloodbath saw none of this, heard nothing. The only sound in her head was the memory of the dome shuddering with a tectonic moan and then collapsing onto the congregation below. She had witnessed this from the same spot on the pavement where she still stood.

Bloodbath knew that everyone was dead, and she stood motionless in shock. Her husband to be, Justo, her father, her sisters, 224 guests in all. They were gone; she and her unborn child were all that remained of the Arenas family. The mayor of Santa Elena, his wife. Even the priest. Her father's best friend, the chief of police, whose salary was doubled by her family. She was stunned. She could not cry, could not even speak. Her face was as blank as her mind. She released her hem finally and closed both hands over the growing mound of her abdomen, all the family she had now.

From the old ruins behind the new ruins, Bloodbath noticed a small black dog emerge and shake itself

violently. In a kind of rebirth, she watched its color instantly change to cinnamon brown. Three human figures followed, covered with the same black dust, walking
slowly toward her out of the cloud. A small young blond
woman with short spiky hair held a single wedgy shoe in
her left hand. She had cleared much of her face and hair,
except for the sides of her nose and around her eyes. She
looked like a person wearing grotesque makeup, possibly
something for Day of the Dead. Her feet were bare and
her sweatshirt had one sleeve torn away at the shoulder.
Bloodbath could see that the woman's right arm was either badly bruised or filthy. As she approached, it was
clear there was blood dripping down her wrist, spotting
the pavement. She blinked in the clear light. They came
closer, the dog still leading the way. The injured woman
continued to advance unsteadily as the man in black next
to her paused and stared back at the cathedral rubble, his
palm shading his eyes.

As Bloodbath followed this with incomprehen-
sion, she was startled to see a gun in his belt. She had
thought nothing more could startle her. She knew all the
security detail and this man was not one of them. Looking past him into the ruins she saw in places the shining
white of the fragmented columns through the dust. The
man started to take a step toward it, but the blond woman
seized his wrist with her bloody hand and held him back,
as if to say, there's nothing you can do anymore, give it up.

The crowd at the edge of the ruins thickened.
The blonde discovered the single shoe in her other hand
and dropped it to the pavement. Other than the dust, sag-
ging in drifting sheets, and people in the crowd leaning
against each other, nothing else now stirred. Suddenly the

cinnamon dog paused, cocked his head to one side, listened for a moment, then turned and ran back toward the ruined crypt. No one else noticed him go.

Moving past the first two approaching figures was a young man with a pale forehead and a streak of matted red hair, as if he had paused on his way to the surface and dragged a forearm across his upper face and over the top of his head. A strap holding a laptop in a ripped padded case was looped around his neck. Bloodbath watched him struggle with a flat wooden box he held in both arms as if it were a treasure beyond price. What could have any value now? She couldn't have named a thing.

Tears traced irregular tracks through the black dust coating the man's cheeks. He was so close now that in the tracks Bloodbath could see freckles. The eyes themselves were like two wet holes in a mask. Even his lips were black at the corners of his mouth and he coughed as he stopped before her and set the box upright on the pavement. They looked at each other for a moment.

"The Helena Fragment," the young man said to her, pointing at the box as if that explained everything. "I'm going to call the Pope." He nodded with a firm set to his lips. Perhaps this was the solution to a problem he had worked on for a long time.

Bloodbath, who spoke no English, could only look at him, her dark eyes vacant. She nodded back once or twice without realizing it, her mouth open. What were these people doing here and why were they mostly black? Surely they hadn't been part of the wedding?

After all, her family had always made a point of not knowing any gringos.

Visit the author's web page @

www.sanmiguelallendebooks.com